W9-BTA-249

Praise for Catherine Cookson's
THE DESERT CROP

"As usual, Cookson delivered a surprising
and satisfying finish to a timeless tale."
—*Abilene Reporter-News*

"*The Desert Crop* races along,
easy to read and utterly captivating in its
characterization and events."
—*Tampa Tribune-Times*

"Her fans will not be disappointed."
—*Publishers Weekly*

"*The Desert Crop* will make a fine antidote
to a dull afternoon."
—*Orlando Sentinel*

"Told with insight, compassion, and humor,
this coming-of-age story is sure to enrapture all
the devoted fans Cookson attracted during
her long and prolific career."
—*Booklist*

Also available from MIRA Books and
CATHERINE COOKSON

THE OBSESSION
THE UPSTART

CATHERINE COOKSON

THE DESERT CROP

MIRA

If you purchased this book without a cover you should be aware that this book is stolen property. It was reported as "unsold and destroyed" to the publisher, and neither the author nor the publisher has received any payment for this "stripped book."

ISBN 1-55166-583-2

THE DESERT CROP

Copyright © 1997 by the Estate of Catherine Cookson.
This edition is reprinted by arrangement with Simon & Schuster, Inc.

All rights reserved. Except for use in any review, the reproduction or utilization of this work in whole or in part by any form by any electronic, mechanical or other means, now known or hereafter invented, including xerography, photocopying and recording, or in any information storage or retrieval system, is forbidden without the written permission of the publisher, MIRA Books, 225 Duncan Mill Road, Don Mills, Ontario, Canada M3B 3K9.

All characters in this book have no existence outside the imagination of the author and have no relation whatsoever to anyone bearing the same name or names. They are not even distantly inspired by any individual known or unknown to the author, and all incidents are pure invention.

MIRA and the Star Colophon are trademarks used under license and registered in Australia, New Zealand, Philippines, United States Patent and Trademark Office and in other countries.

Visit us at www.mirabooks.com

Printed in U.S.A.

The good die first,
And they whose hearts are dry as summer dust
Burn to the socket.

—Wordsworth

PART ONE

PART ONE

1

Daniel stared up at his father and wondered why a man so old could still retain boyish habits, for his father wasn't sitting behind but on the edge of his study desk and was swinging one leg the while he talked to Pattie. When he had anything of importance to say he always talked to Pattie, never to him, perhaps because she was four years older, being thirteen now. Yet at the same time he knew his father very often got angry with Pattie, and he was showing signs of it now because his leg was swinging more quickly than usual. She had just said to him, "Mother has only been dead for two years, and the house goes on the same way, so why…?"

"I know your mother's been dead only two years, but two years is a decent enough time to wait until one marries again. As for the house, it isn't run as it was before: Rosie is a lazy bitch; the meals get worse."

Daniel now turned his gaze on his sister, awaiting her reply, and she said, "It's a big house. She has to clean the place, besides cooking now. And there were two other maids when Mother was alive."

Daniel noticed his father's leg had become still; then he slid off the end of the desk, stood straight for a moment, before bending towards his daughter and saying, "There were lots of things different when your mother was alive; for instance, you were spoilt. If you are finding the house dirty then you should bestir yourself and get a duster in your hand, if not a pail and mop, Miss Stewart."

The plain fair-haired girl did not flinch from her father's stern gaze as she retaliated, saying, "You sent me to school, the village one, but you could send Daniel, here, to a boarding school. Why?"

"Why, miss? Because he's a boy and needs special education, whereas you, all you've got to do is to prepare yourself for marriage."

"I may not want to get married, Father. Not everybody gets married."

"Those with sense do, child, so that they are enabled to run their own household. But if you've decided already that you're not going to be married then you will have to make yourself useful in my household. Now, have you anything more to say, daughter?"

The boy watched them staring at each other; then his sister said boldly, "Yes, Father. Why are you marrying Moira Conelly? She's a relation, isn't she? Moreover, she's Irish."

Hector Stewart drew in a long breath; then turning sharply to his son, he said, "You have a sister, boy, who's going to find life very hard, for already she is proving to be a finnicky, pestering female. But I shall answer her questions and enlighten you too. I am going to marry Moira Conelly because I happen to like her. As for being related to her, her father was my father's half-cousin. Now when you're doing your mathematics, work that out. As for her nationality, you both know'—he now jerked his head towards his daughter—"that she is Irish, for she has spent two holidays here, hasn't she? That was when your mother was alive."

Daniel spoke for the first time: a slight smile on his face now, he said, "She lives in a castle, doesn't she, Father?"

Once more Hector Stewart drew in a long breath before returning his son's smile and saying, "Yes, Daniel, in a way she lives in a castle, but it isn't as we think of a castle. Nevertheless it's called a castle."

"She is old."

Hector's head jerked back towards his daughter as he demanded, "What do you mean, old?"

"She must be twenty-five."

"Yes. Yes, she is all of twenty-five years. And you consider that old?"

Pattie did not seem to be able to find an answer to this, and her father, his expression softening now and his voice too, said, "Wait till she comes: you will grow to love her; you won't be able to help yourself for she's such a happy soul. She will lighten this house."

When again Pattie seemed unable to find anything to say, or perhaps she had considered it expedient to keep her opinion to herself, her father said, "Well now, time's getting on. This young gentleman is for the road to his school tomorrow. Go and help him pack."

"I've already packed, Father," Daniel said.

"Oh, you have, have you? Ah well." He straightened his shoulders, buttoned the middle button of his collarless jacket, then looking from one to the other, his manner a little awkward now, he said, "I have work to do. I'm away to the farm. And you, Pattie, I would suggest you go to the kitchen to see what mess Rosie has concocted to present us with at supper time. As for you, boy: as it is your last night at home for a while I'll leave you to your own devices." And on this he unbuttoned the middle button of his coat again before marching out of the room.

Daniel turned to his sister. Her usually pale face was flushed, indicating she was in a temper, and his voice had a soothing note as he said, "I remember her, Pattie. She was jolly, and she made me laugh. You might get to like her. And Father said she's bringing her maid with her, and she is a working maid, so you may not have to do any work at all." He put out his hand and took hold of hers, and now her voice came strange, almost a whimper, as she said, "You won't be here, Dan. You don't know what it's been like since Mother died. He never bothers with me, and there's nobody to talk to, that's why—" she now paused and, lowering her head, shook it before going on, "when I do get the chance I keep asking him questions, just to make him talk to me."

"I shall write to you from school." Daniel's tone was tender.

She looked at him, her eyelids now blinking rapidly. "It isn't the same," she said.

"Haven't you made friends at school yet?"

"Oh, that crowd. Betty McIntosh, Theresa Holmes, they're stupid, dull, and the boys are like clodhoppers. As for Miss Brooker, she doesn't know how to teach. I could teach *her*. Mother taught me my tables when I was four. As for being able to tell the time and count up to a hundred, and reading, I can't even remember learning those things. Mother was so advanced in her knowledge. But that school! Huh!''

She now threw off his hand as if getting rid of the whole school and its occupants. And when she turned away he had the urge to pull her back and put his arms about her and hold her close, to comfort her and at the same time be comforted himself.

He now followed her out of the room, down a passage and into a stone-flagged hall from which the shallow oak stairs rose. And he watched her hesitate at the foot of the stairs, then shrug her body about and make for the kitchen door at the far end of the hall.

Daniel walked to the front door and so out on to the flagged terrace that bordered the front of the house. He walked to one of the two small stone pillars that headed the six steps which led down to the gravel drive and, laying his forearms on the flat top, he gazed away over the expanse of his father's farmland.

The house was situated on a rise and this gave a view of the patchwork of fields straight ahead and also of those stretching away to the right. To the left there was a cluster of buildings obscuring the view, behind which he knew there to be the five cottages. But away beyond the cottages the hills rose, as they did for some way behind the house, thus giving some protection against rain, sleet and the north-east winds.

Daniel did not know why, loving this house and its surrounding land as he did, that it should make him feel lonely. He had been thinking of late that if, like his sister, he had a probing mind, he would have already been given the answer. All he could tell himself was that he needed something, but he would never allow himself to go as far as to think that what he needed was to hold and be held.

He recalled the day they had buried his mother and the strange thought that had come into his head as he stood by her grave, for it was true she had never hugged him. His mother hadn't believed in hugging, and she had stopped Rosie from hugging him. His mother hadn't even believed in holding his hand.

He straightened up and sighed. He'd be glad to get back to school tomorrow. He liked Crawley House. The food wasn't very good but that didn't matter; the matron was very nice. He was very fond of her. In the spring, when he'd had a cough, she had given him linctus, and she had kept him in bed for a day and had stroked his hair. She was the first one he could remember ever stroking his hair. Rosie used to ruffle it. His father had, now and again, ruffled it, too, but no one had ever stroked it until Matron did.

In the far distance over the gardens he could see Barney Dunlop, Rosie's husband, ploughing the barley field. It had been a good harvest but the ploughing pointed out that they would soon be in autumn. He thought he would go and say goodbye to Barney. He liked Barney.

He went down the steps, turned left and walked to the end of the house and round the corner to where it opened out into the yard. There was no-one in the yard. The four horse boxes were empty, the tack room door was closed, as were the outhouse doors; but when he approached the open barn two dogs which had been lying on the straw got up lazily and sauntered towards him. They gave him no barked greeting but, one at each side, they walked just a step behind him; and he turned and looked from one to the other, saying,

"Good boy, Laddie," then, "Your ear better, Flo?" And for answer both dogs wagged their tails.

A doorway at the far end of the yard led into a walled vegetable garden. It was a large area of land, and prominent were rows of late beans and peas.

Keeping to a pathway that skirted one wall, he went through an archway and into a field that had at one time been a lawn. Walking through the long grass he was reminded of his surprise when he had returned from school last summer and realised how quickly grass grew when it was not kept cut, and also how quickly weeds spread among the flowers and obliterated them. This had been brought about, he knew, by his father's dismissal of Peter Kent and Will Brown. Peter had seen to the vegetables and the garden, and Will had helped him now and again when he wasn't attending the horses. But now the two hunters and the two carriage horses were kept down on the farm. This had all happened since his mother died.

Why? This was the question he had put to Pattie when he had first seen the long grass on the lawn, and her answer had been, "Mother's money went with her."

At the time he had thought that very odd and he had had a mental picture of the money being spread round her as she lay in her coffin on the billiard table, which had been draped in black.

Would things return to what they were before, after his father married Moira Conelly, the Irish woman? Perhaps she had money.

Everything seemed to depend on money. His father had to pay money to keep him at this school, and he had pointed out to him that he was lucky. He supposed he was.

This thought set him running and the dogs bounded away from his side and chased each other in the long grass.

The field ended where a stretch of woodland began, and he ran zig-zagging through this, the dogs at his heels now barking with excitement. Once through the wood they were into ploughed land and skirting the neat furrows. In the distance he could see Barney Dunlop unharnessing the horses from the plough. When he reached them, the old man turned and spoke as if he hadn't been made aware of his approach by the barking dogs, saying, "Why, there you are, Master Daniel. Where've you sprung from?"

"Granny Smith's Well."

The old man and the boy now smiled knowingly at each other; for a long time this had been their usual greeting and answer. It was the answer Barney's wife always gave him when he asked her where she had been: "Down Granny Smith's Well," she would say.

Granny Smith's Well was the deepest in the district and it was known never to have run dry, even in the season when no rain had fallen for weeks.

"All ready for the morrow mornin', eh?"

"Yes, all ready, Barney."

"Want to lead Princess? although she needs no leading, stone blind she could be an' still find her way. But Daisy, her daughter here"—he thumped the other horse on the rump now—"daft as a brush, she is, skittish she is, would be off to the market in Fellburn, she would, if I wasn't keepin' an eye on her."

As Daniel walked by the head of the big shire horse and listened to the old man chattering away he experienced a feeling of contentment. He wasn't sure why he felt this way, but at this end of the estate life seemed to go on in a different pattern from the other end.

The farmyard was filled with noise and movement. Arthur Beaney was driving in the cows from the pasture; Alex Towney was carrying fodder for the horses, and at the far end of the long earth yard his father was talking to Bob Shearman, the shepherd, his hand waving as if he were angry.

He had reached the stable door and let go of Princess's halter and was turning to ask Barney if he could help him water the horses, when he saw that he too was looking to where the shepherd was now coming across the yard towards them. As he passed to go into the stable Bob Shearman hissed, "You know what now, Barney? he's bloody well telling me I've got to take Falcon into the market the morrow. I asked him why not one of the carriage horses. He told me to bloody-well mind me own business. But I told him I was a horse man afore he put me on shepherding and that Falcon isn't past it; he's still got a lot of jump in him yet and would burst a blood vessel to please him. But no, it's him that'll have to go; he must keep the carriage horses for his fancy piece that's comin'. I tell you, Barney, this place is goin' to hell quickly."

"Be quiet! Be quiet!"

Bob Shearman glanced to where Barney was indicating the boy. And now he said, "What odds? he'll learn how the land lies soon enough. And when he should come into his own there'll be nowt to come in to. You mark my words."

Daniel did not ask Barney if he could help water the horses, but he said, "I'll say goodbye, Barney; I've got to go now."

"Goodbye, Master Daniel. It won't be long afore

I'll be seein' you again. Christmas isn't all that far off. What's ten weeks or so?''

Without saying goodbye to Bob Shearman Daniel turned away; but as he walked through the wood he thought of the man's words, "When he should come into his own there'll be nowt to come in to." Was this all because his mother's money had died with her, as Pattie had said? But what about the money his father got from selling the corn and the eggs and the vegetables and the milk, and of course the pigs and the sheep. That must come to a great deal, surely. What did he do with it? He couldn't ask him, so he supposed he'd never know.

Oh, well, he was glad he was going back to school tomorrow for there was so much to do there that you never had time to think about unpleasant things such as nothing to inherit when you grew up. He now called to the dogs and galloped with them through the wood.

2

Daniel didn't have to wait until the Christmas holidays to return home; he was granted three days' leave to attend his father's wedding. Over the past week he had become the centre of attraction in his House, after he had confided to Ray Melton, his friend, that his father was going to marry a lady from Ireland who lived in a castle and who was bringing her maid with her. Ray had, of course, passed this information on to the other boys in their dormitory, and consequently Daniel found himself bombarded with questions after lights out.

The lady would be his stepmother, wouldn't she?

Yes, she would.

Would he like that?

He didn't know yet.

Was she rich?

He wasn't sure.

Well, if she travelled with a maid she must be. You had to be really of the aristocracy to have a personal maid.

This last remark caused some controversy. Three of

the boys claimed that they knew of friends of their parents who had personal maids.

This was topped by someone saying that his cousin visited a manor house in Northumberland where, with the butler and the footman, there were twelve indoor servants…how many did Daniel have?

Daniel was aware that were he to be truthful and say, "One," his prestige would sink drastically. So he did not consider that he was really lying, when counting in the farmhands and their wives, he said, "Eight."

There were one or two murmurs of "Oh! Oh!" Eight seemed to be a satisfactory number on which to run a household to which an Irish lady was coming with her maid.

As Daniel settled down to sleep he told himself he must remember to explain to Ray how the eight servants were dispersed and that only one of them, Barney's wife, Rosie, worked in the house, because he had promised Ray he would invite him to tea during the coming holidays to see the farm, and, of course, the house. It was a very interesting house, one part of it being more than two hundred years old. But in the meantime that was nothing to worry about, for Ray lived miles away in a place called Corbridge.

He could feel the change in the house before he entered the door. As he jumped down from the trap, which had brought him from the station, and made for the front door, the laughter seemed to flow out of it on a wave, and it caught him up and he rode in on it to the middle of the hall, where, stepping off the stairs, he saw his future stepmother. She wasn't as he remembered her; she looked younger and prettier and more plump. And when she leant forward and held her arms out to him, crying, "Why! Daniel, you are grown up. Come here. Come here," he did not rush towards her and into her arms, but approached slowly, feeling that he should be polite and say, "How do you do?" But when her hands caught him and drew him to her breast he put his arms about her waist and looked up into her face and he laughed, and she laughed, and her laughter was almost in his ear, and it wasn't a tinkling laugh such as you would expect from a lady, but a jolly, rollicking one. And now, on loosening one arm from about him, she stretched it out and pointed to a fat, dark-haired woman now approaching from the kitchen, and said, "This is Maggie Anne, Daniel. And I'm warning you: beware of her, she practises magic and she casts spells."

The big woman laughed and seemed to swim all over him as her plump hand gripped his chin and lifted his face towards hers. "So you're Daniel, are you?" she said, "God! but you're thin, boy. You'll never brave the lions' den, not until we get some flesh on your bones." She smiled now, and he noticed that a number of her teeth were crooked and that her hair was very dark, as were her eyes.

When she let go of his chin she patted his cheek, saying, "You'll do. You'll do. You'll shape up nicely. What d'you say, me dear?" She had turned to her mistress, to whom Daniel, too, turned; and she, her head on one side, surveyed him as if she had not seen him before. "He doesn't take after his father, not in looks anyway," she said; "but he'll do splendidly for himself."

"Who doesn't take after his father?"

Hector had entered the hall from a side door, and

Moira, now turning a laughing face towards him, said, "Here's your son come home and never a greeting to him. Where have you been?"

Daniel watched his father come striding towards them and straight away put his arm around the waist of his future wife and hug her close, before turning to him and rumpling his hair, saying, "Well, here you are! and I declare you've grown another inch in the last few weeks."

"He's too thin by half." This was Maggie Ann speaking, and when Hector made to answer, it wasn't in the free and easy tone he had just used, for his voice was cold even as he smiled at the woman and said, "Well, you'll have to see that your culinary prowess in the kitchen outdoes Rosie's, won't you?"

But Maggie Ann's manner or tone didn't change as she addressed her new master: "Oh, begod!" she said on a loud laugh, "Don't expect miracles in that quarter. And look, I don't want to get up the good Rosie's back again, for it's taken me these three weeks to stroke down her ruffled feathers by each day asking her to show me the ropes, and begod! I'd like to see the ropes I couldn't untangle meself, given time of course."

Daniel watched his father stare hard at the woman before turning again to his future bride and, smiling now, saying, "I must go and change because I smell of the farmyard, and then I'll take you for that promised jaunt around the countryside and introduce you here and there." With that he hugged her to him once more, then made for the stairs, taking them two at a time, as would a man half his age.

As if they had forgotten Daniel, the two women, talking in quick exchange, now walked to the door that opened into a corridor and what had once been the servant's quarters. At the end of it a sharp turning led to the back entrance to the kitchen. It was as Daniel entered the corridor to follow the women that he heard their voices coming from this passage. His future step-mother was saying in a tone that held no laughter, "Now I warned you, Maggie Ann, what it would be like... Do you want to go home?"

The answer came: "Not without you. Do *you* want to go home?"

"Don't be silly, woman."

"He's looking down his nose at me."

"Well, to him you're a servant. I've explained it all to you."

"Begod! I was a servant across the water and neither himself nor your ma ever tripped over themselves to tell me of me position. We worked together, we talked together, we ate together, the only thing we didn't do was sleep together, except for you, for you slept with me for years. So how d'you expect me to take this new situation, I ask you?"

"Maggie Ann. You've either got to take it or you go back across the water. Now I'm only repeating what I said to you before we came."

"Aye, I know. But then, I hadn't had a taste of what it was goin' to be like. Even that Rosie, the plough-man's wife, looks at me as if I am the slush running out of the cow byre. And I have to lower meself and make believe I'm a numskull of the first water and know nothing about a kitchen or a kale pot."

"I also told you, Maggie Ann, that they don't eat as we did, neither in food, nor ways."

"Aw, you've made that evident enough an' all. It's in the kitchen I've got to sit. Look, Miss Moira, himself, your own father, was from one of the best families that ever trod Irish soil and if he could sit down with me and me like and eat his food, then who the hell in England should think themselves any better!''

There was a long pause and Daniel was making for the hall again when he heard Moira, as he was thinking of her now, say, ''It's not going to work, is it, Maggie Ann?''

This statement was followed by another silence before Maggie Ann, speaking quietly now, said, ''You know damn fine I won't leave you. You've been me life from when you were born. So there's nothing for me but to stick it and make it work. I can tell you one thing, though, Miss Moira, you'll have to make it work an' all, because that young madam looks upon you almost in the same way as her father does on me.''

''That isn't news to me, Maggie Ann—I'm well aware of that—and so it will be up to me to make her change her attitude. By tomorrow I shall be her stepmother and mistress of this house. Thanks be to God. Yes, mistress of a house. And I say again, Maggie Ann, thanks be to God. Now together we could make it work, but only if you watch your tongue and fall in with the new ways and remember that the English gentry are a different breed altogether from our lot.''

''Ah!'' Maggie Ann's voice came high now. ''What you talking about, Miss Moira, with one mouldy servant in the house—gentry? Huh! Even himself managed four, and he without a penny to his name. By the way, I'll ask you, do they know that?''

Moira's voice was low as she replied, ''They know only what I choose to tell them, and that there's money coming, which is true enough.''

''Yes; God speed the dead.''

"Go on with you, Maggie Ann. I don't wish anybody dead. But come on, give me a smile, give me a laugh. It's pulled us through so far. As Mama used to say, keep your pecker up."

"Aye, and himself used to finish, 'When the other hens are pinching your corn.'"

Keep your pecker up while the other hens are pinching your corn. What a funny saying. But then they talked funny all the time.

When Daniel heard the rustle of their skirts he quickly went back into the hall and made for the main entrance to the kitchen.

Rosie Dunlop turned from the table where she was thumping a large mound of dough with her fist and said, "Oh, hello there, Master Daniel. So you've got back."

"Yes, Rosie. You baking?"

"Bakin'? I've never stopped for the last four days. A quiet weddin', your father said, and we're having breakfast at the hotel in Fellburn, he said, only to add, there'll be a few friends dropping in for the evening: you can knock something up for that, can't you? And I've been knockin' something up, as I said, for the last four days now: he wanted hare pie, brawn, spare ribs, a leg of pork, and that was just for starters. Just push it on the table, he said, where they can help themselves. Have you met them?"

Daniel paused a moment before saying, "Yes. Yes, Rosie, I've met them. I've been talking to them in the hall."

"Well, what d'you think?"

He knew he would have to be what was called diplomatic and so he said, "I don't know, Rosie, I've only just met them."

"Well, she's been here afore. Did you like her then?"

"Yes, she appeared all right."

"But what about the other one?"

He smiled as he said, "She's very large."

"Aye, and in the head an' all, I should say, for it appears full of water, like her body. And there's a squad of them due shortly."

She now came towards him, and in a voice just above a whisper, said, "Has she money? I mean, Miss Conelly; is she bringing money in?"

"Money?" he repeated, recalling the conversation he had just overheard; "I don't know, Rosie; but I suppose she has money; perhaps when her people die."

"Live horse an' you'll get grass...that! That's what that means." Rosie flounced back to the table, and after pounding the dough for a few seconds she stopped and, motioning her head towards the bench in the corner of the long kitchen, she said, "I've made some sly cakes, a couple will never be missed. Take one to Miss Pattie."

"Pattie's in?"

"Oh, aye, she's in. Like you, she's off school for three days. Why, I don't know."

He picked up the two pieces of pastry filled with currants, saying, "Thank you, Rosie," and putting them on a plate, he added, "Where is she...Rosie?"

"Well, where she always is these days, up in her room or in the nursery."

"Yes, yes." He nodded at her before running out and across the hall and up the stairs.

On the landing he paused, undecided whether to make for Pattie's room at the far end or take the stairs that led to the nursery and schoolroom floor, and above them the attics. He decides on the latter and, without ceremony, burst into the old schoolroom to be greeted by Pattie saying, "Why didn't you call?"

"Why should I? You knew it would be me."

"How was I to know it would be you, silly? I didn't know you were back."

"Well, you should have been downstairs, then you would have seen me. Here!" and he smiled as he handed her the sly cake. "Rosie sent that for you."

She took it from him without offering any thanks and bit into it, and she'd eaten the whole square before he was halfway through his.

"You hungry?"

"Yes, I'm hungry. I didn't have any breakfast."

"Why?"

"Why? Well, because I didn't want to sit down with my laughing jackass-cum-stepmother, nor sit in the kitchen with her great sloppy maid. And Father said I had to do one or the other, so I did neither."

"You can't do anything about it, you know," Daniel said quietly, and as he watched Pattie lean against the table, the while gripping its edge, there came in him again that feeling for her that saddened him, and he didn't like it, so he looked from her to the table and the scraps of paper spread out and asked her, "What are you doing?"

She straightened up and now asked *him* a question; her voice eager, she said, "Can you recall any of Father's friends who have the nickname of Barbie?"

He thought for a moment, then said, "Barbie? Sounds like a girl's name. Short for something? No: there are the Talbots, but Mrs Talbot's called Lilian, isn't she? And then there's Frances. Mrs Farringdon, she's called Tessa, and there's Janie. But why do you ask?''

''Look''—she pointed now to the table, and he leant over and looked at the pieces of torn and charred paper, and with a stabbing finger she pointed to the signature still evident on one piece, and said, ''What does that read?'' And he, looking closer, said, ''Barbie. But this is a letter. And why all these bits?''

''Yes''—she was nodding at him—''why all these bits? Why all these letters? There were a number of them. I happened to go into the study one night this week and Father was burning papers in the grate and he asked me what I wanted. I said I wanted a book. And he said, 'Well, get it and go.' And I went. But I waited until he came out and had gone upstairs; then I went back, and there was all this charred paper, with here and there unburnt bits.'' She now stabbed her finger at the pieces of what had evidently been a letter, and went on, ''They're not all of the same letter. But look, three times there's the same name, 'Barbie'. There's only half the signature on that piece, it says, 'Bar', but look, it's the same kind of writing as this complete one, 'Barbie'. And see, on that piece of paper it says, 'You can't'. And over there—'' she now pointed to a small piece of paper about an inch long and her fingers tabbed out the words, '''Years and years'. And look at this piece.'' With her other hand now she turned over a strip of charred paper that showed an uneven white line where the tops of letters had been burnt off. And she said to him, ''What d'you make of that?''

He looked closely at the paper, and then he said, ''Oh, I think that word is 'time', but I can't make out the rest." And she said, "I can. That is 'if'." And to this he nodded: "Oh, yes, it could be."

"And the next word is, 'ever'."

"You're just guessing," he said.

"No. Look!" and now taking a pencil, she pulled a piece of clean paper towards her and wrote "ever" on it.

He nodded, saying, "Could be."

"Well," she said, "it looks as though it reads, 'if ever the time came.'"

He scrutinised the charred scrap again and said, "Perhaps you're right. But even so, what does it mean? What do you make of it?"

She turned and leant against the side of the table and, looking straight at him, she said, "Why should Father be burning those letters? Mother's name was Janice. The one downstairs, her name is Moira. Who, I ask you, is or was Barbie?"

He smiled now, saying, "Don't ask me, Pattie. It's you who have set a puzzle, but I can't see you working it out."

"I...I will some day."

His face straight now and his voice low, he said, "Why are you so bitter against Father? You said before that you talked at him because you want him to take notice of you. Well, if you do, why are you bitter?"

She shook her head twice before she said, "I suppose it's because Mother was bitter against him."

"Mother? Bitter against Father?"

"Yes"—she was bending down to him, her face now thrust into his—"Mother was bitter against Father. You know nothing, you're a fathead."

"I am not a fathead, and don't call me a fathead."

That she was surprised at his retaliation was evident, for now she almost apologised, saying to him, "Well, you know I didn't mean 'fathead' really. But, you see, Daniel, you've been away at school for more than two years now. You were just turned seven when he packed you off, and you know nothing about what's happened in the meantime. I missed you when you went to school. Do you know that?"

When he didn't answer she said, "You will be ten and I'll be fourteen in December, and you know what I'm going to do next year?"

"Leave school. You'll have to, won't you?"

"No, I'm not; and I won't. I'm...I'm going to pupil-teach, starting with the infants. Miss Brooker said I can."

"I thought you said Miss Brooker was a thickhead; that she didn't know anything."

"Well"—Pattie hunched her shoulders—"she knows I know as much as her, I suppose."

"Does Father know?"

"Not yet."

"Do you think he'll let you?"

"He'll have to."

"Oh, Pattie." He smiled sadly at her. "You know you can't make Father do anything that he doesn't want to do."

"No, perhaps not me, but his new wife will because she won't want me under her feet all day. I'll make myself felt right from the start, so she'll be glad to get rid of me. Oh, she'll back me up; I'll see to that."

He laughed, saying, "You know, Pattie, you're a terror. If you had been a man, you're the kind that would have caused riots."

"Very likely." She nodded at him. "And I wish I

had been a man, because then I wouldn't have to go and put linen on the four guest beds.''

"How many are coming?"

"Well, as far as I know, her mother and father, two brothers and their wives, and a great aunt."

"Are they staying long?"

"No, thank the Lord, only tonight; then they're taking the late train to the boat after the wedding."

"But why are they leaving it so late when Father's being married at eleven in the morning?"

"It's cheaper travelling that way, so Rosie says."

"How did she know that?"

"Well, don't you know that Rosie's half Irish? Her mother was Irish. Oh.'' She now turned to the table again and carefully gathered the pieces of charred paper together, adding, "They are spattered all over the country, the Irish. Miss Brooker said that, when I told her my father was marrying a lady from Ireland. What she actually said was, 'More of them? They're already spattered all over the country.' Come on, help me with the sheets. But mind''—she stopped abruptly on her way to the door—"don't tell Father anything about this," and she pointed to the envelope containing the remains of the letters. And his tone held indignation as he answered her, "Now why should I do that? What reason would I have?"

"Well, you never know; things slip out."

"You won't get it out of your head that I'm a dumb-bell, will you?"

She pushed him and gave one of her rare laughs in which he now joined and they went out together.

Daniel sat on the deep window-edge of the third window in the long dining-room and his eyes darted from one to the other of his future stepmother's family, and the only words he could call to mind with which to describe them were odd and different.

There was Moira's father. He was tallish and thin, very thin and very dark-haired and, like his daughter, he laughed a lot, and he never seemed to stop talking. His wife seemed about half his size but her figure was dumpy. She too was dark, and her face was lined. She looked old. She smiled a lot but she didn't laugh and she spoke only now and again. Then there was a brother named Brian. He was as tall as his father and very like him, and he, too, talked a lot, but he didn't laugh, nor did he even smile. Apparently, they called his wife Mary, because he alluded to her often, saying, Mary here said so and so. And Mary, too, talked a lot. Yet the younger son—Moira said he was younger, although he looked almost like a twin to his brother— this son was called Rory, and his wife's name was Bertha, and they stood out because they rarely spoke. And then there was the great aunt. Now she was very odd and so old that he couldn't remember having seen anyone quite as old. Yet she was what you would call spritely, for he had watched her previously walking around the room fingering the pieces of silver on the sideboard and opening the drawers of the old chest at the end of the room where the best dinner service was kept, together with the trays of cutlery. And what stood out was that everybody seemed to adhere to her wishes. They plied her with the eatables from the table and, as did all the others, she ate as if she hadn't seen food for days.

His father kept putting plates in Pattie's hands and directing her to offer their contents to the guests, but he felt he needn't have bothered because Maggie Ann, as everybody called her, was doing that all the time.

His father had seen to the drinks, too, but the company seemed to pick only two kinds, beer or whisky, and they drank a lot of each, seeming to wash the food down with it.

Although his father kept moving about the room from one guest to another, Daniel knew that he wasn't at ease.

They had been eating for more than an hour when Moira suggested they should move to the drawing-room. She did it, as he was finding out, as she seemingly did everything, on a laugh and with a funny quip; standing in the middle of the room, she called, "Would the remnants of the Conelly family of ancient lineage follow their daughter over the battlements to rest their bones in the luxury of the drawing-room."

At this and amid joined laughter she held out her hand to his father and he led her down the room, out into the hall and across it to the drawing-room door, where, relinquishing her hand, he pressed her forward into the room, then stood aside while Sean Conelly and his wife, with their aged aunt between them, passed him with a smile. Then followed the dour Brian with his wife, and lastly Rory and his wife. But when Maggie Ann came up in the rear and intent on joining the family, he put out an arm to block her way and, inclining his head towards her, he said, "Would you please see to the coffee?"

The smile slid from her face and she replied briefly, "They don't take coffee; tea's their drink when they can't get anything else."

He brought his jaws together for a moment before allowing himself to speak: then under his breath he said, "All right, it will be tea. But listen one moment: you and I must have a talk, you understand?"

She stared into his face. She understood, but she made no reply. Swinging her large body about, she made for the kitchen, pushing aside Daniel and Pattie who had been making their way towards the stairs but were stopped by their father's voice saying firmly, "Come!"

Reluctantly, it seemed, they moved towards him, and as they went to pass him he stooped and quietly but firmly he said, "Remember your manners and who you are. We have guests in the house. You understand?"

Neither of them answered nor indicated by a nod that they understood, but they went forward and into a buzz of laughter and chatter…

Daniel did not know how much later it was when the argument started, only that it was long after they had drunk tea and further glasses of whisky had been passed around. It started with the man called Brian saying, "When you used to come across to us, Hector, you gave us the impression that you lived like landed gentry, and her there, our Moira, she did the same. Well, you've got the house all right, an' the settings for it, but where's the staff? I thought we'd be greeted to a dinner tonight and be meeting all your friends."

"Shut your mouth! Shut your mouth, Brian. It always gapes wide after the hard stuff. You should keep off it. Aye, you should that, unless it's under your own roof."

"Aw, Dada, you said as much yourself."

"I said no such thing, and I warn you, behave yourself. If you soil our name with your chatter, I'll cut your throat, begod! I will. With me own hand I'll do it.''

"Huh! That'll be the day that you do anyt'ing with your own hand.''

All eyes were now turned on Brian's wife, for she too had imbibed of the hard stuff. "And why shouldn't my Brian open his mouth and tell them a t'ing or two over here? "Tisn't much opportunity we get. And as you know, neither my Brian nor me was for Moira making this match, as long in the tooth as he is.''

"How dare you! Mary Conelly.'' It was Moira bristling: no smile on her face now; no laughter in her voice.

However, immediately the attention of everyone in the room was caught by the old lady saying to Hector, "Did you meet Mr Palmerston, Hector?''

"No, Aunt Mattie.'' Good Lord, how old did she think he was?

"A great man. A great man. If anyone could have saved Ireland, he was the one. And you didn't meet him?''

"No.'' The word came sharp, definite.

"Oh, then you never heard him speak, which is a great pity. He was a great orator; he kept your men in London on their toes. Great many stupid men up there. And your Gladstone is a ditherer, a ditherer. You have nothing like the Land League here, have you?''

The answer to this came sharply: "No, thank God, else they would be out to destroy us as they are destroying Ireland.''

"Destroying Ireland? Listen to him!'' It was Brian shouting now. "Just listen to him, destroying Ireland. You can't destroy a thing twice, man. You've already killed it, or nearly. You do know, don't you, that you did away with half a million? Starved them to death. Aye, starved them to death with your bloody corn laws.''

"Nonsense! Nonsense! Even the child knows it was the potato famine.''

"Aye, but what followed the potato famine? Migration to America. And what happened when they got there? They were so depleted they died by the hundreds.''

"Look, Brian, this is not a political meeting. It is a get-together prior to a wedding. Isn't that so, dear?'' Hector had turned to Moira.

For once Moira did not make a laughing reply but she said somewhat quietly, "Yes, that was the idea, Hector, and I must apologise for my lot.''

"Begod! you'll not apologise for me, our Moira. And what's come over you, anyway? there was nobody stauncher than yourself. It was you that boycotted Jimmy Bradley first, wasn't it, following Parnell's advice to every decent Catholic.'' He now turned his gaze on Hector, saying, "The bloody landlord turned Davey Sheenan and his family out of his farm, on to the road he put them. And there was Jimmy Bradley ready to go in. But we fixed him: the cattle got no water and he couldn't buy in the market, nor sell. He's going to emigrate now an' all, God's curse on him.''

"There was a law made, I understood, that eviction had to stop. I mean—'' said Hector stiffly, only to be interrupted by the old man letting out a great, "Huh!'' of a laugh, saying, "Ah, Hector, boy, there's one law for the English and one for the Irish, that is the Irish farmers and peasants. But there's another law for the Irish Protestants; always has been. But their time's running out: the door of Home Rule is ajar and one of these days it'll be thrust open, blown open in places, oh aye, blown open, literally I mean, if you get my meaning."

"Dada! Dada! Be quiet. You know that's only talk. Been talk for a long time."

"Talk, daughter? You haven't been here in this land but days, and you're telling your Dada to be quiet, and that it's only talk. And you whose belly has gone hungry like the rest of us. You live in a castle, people say. My God! I'd change it for a good cow byre any day."

"That isn't true, Sean."

"Perhaps not, Kathleen." The old man's voice was soft now and he nodded at his wife, saying, "We're all at sixes and sevens. I never wanted to come; you know that"—he turned from her and now looked straight at Hector, who was standing stiffly before the fireplace—"because this is a kind of wedding that's never been in our family. Not in my time or my father's or our fathers' before him, but, Protestant that you are, you're still of our line. Why wouldn't you talk to the priest?"

"Oh, we've been through all this over and over. And what difference would it make, anyway?"

"None to you, seemingly, but, to her—she knows she should be married in church."

"Well, what was to stop her marrying me in a Protestant church? but you wouldn't have that, would you? So it's the registry office. Anyway—" Hector shook his head vigorously now and his voice was loud as he said, "We've been through all this. When I was with you last I told you what I had decided and I left it to her. It was up to her."

"No good'll come of it." It was Brian's wife speak-

ing again in her thin high voice. "And as I said, before
we put foot on that boat…"

Her voice was cut by the old woman now turning
on her and crying, "If you said your prayers, woman,
as often as you open your mouth, you'd be flying with
the archangels at this minute; but even then your
wings would be flapping faster than theirs."

There was a titter now from both Rory and his wife.
It was the first sound they had made since they had
come into the room. It seemed to affect Moira and,
with the exception of Brian, it was taken up by the
others until the room was now filled with laughter.
Even Pattie and Daniel, who were sitting on a small
couch in the shadow of a French screen, turned to each
other and grinned. Then Pattie, putting her mouth
close to Daniel's ear said, "I wish they were staying.
There'd be some fun, wouldn't there?"

When he didn't answer she muttered under her
breath, "Well, don't you think so?"

"Father wouldn't think so; he's mad."

After a moment she said, "Yes. Yes, he is, isn't he?
He's let himself in for something."

Daniel lowered his head now and muttered, "Did
you know anything about this business of a priest and
marrying in a Catholic church?"

"No. No. All that talk must have happened when
he was over there… Anyway, it proves one thing."

"What?"

"Well, she wanted to get married or get away from
Ireland, one or the other."

Still with bent head he said, "Did the Irish people
really starve to death?"

"Yes, I suppose so." Then with an unusual flash of
humour she moved her head closer to his and almost

spluttered as she muttered, "But this lot's going to see
that they themselves are not going to starve to death.
They've eaten enough tonight to last them for six
months. They'll be like the cows, they'll chew their
cud."

"*Daniel! Pattie!*" Their father's voice was stern.
"It's very bad manners not to share a joke. What were
you laughing about? Come on"—his voice was aiming to be merry now—"we're all dying to hear."

Daniel looked at Pattie and Pattie looked at him and
for once she hadn't a ready answer, and he realised
this. So he said, "We were talking about cows, Father,
re...regurgitating."

"Cows regurgitating?" There was silence for a moment. Then Hector, looking around his guests and on
a slight laugh, said, "They were talking about cows
chewing their cud."

"Jesus in heaven! man, you don't need to translate
the word. We might have just come over but our hair's
dry. And I was at college in Dublin until I was eighteen. Regurgitating. Regurgitating." Brian swung
round in his chair now and looked towards the children, saying in a quite pleasant voice, "And why, may
I ask, were you talking about cows regurgitating?"

Daniel rose to his feet and he looked across the
room to the man with the dark thin face and deep-set
eyes who was staring at him. And he found himself
speaking as he sometimes thought, "No reason whatever, sir, not that could be explained; it just came up
in the course of conversation about cows. Why were
we talking about cows? Well, I couldn't rightly say.
Thoughts jump, you know, from one thing to another.
It's, I suppose, what you would call a lack of...of

concentration.'' He knew he was talking like Mr Piers, who took history.

The room seemed quiet as if there were no-one in it, and then his father said, "Come along and say good-night. It's about time you were both in bed. It's going to be a busy day tomorrow."

As Daniel led the way down the room, to the women present he bowed slightly, saying, "Good-night, ma'am," and to the men he said, "Good-night, sir." And Pattie, seeming for once to follow his lead, did the same, with an added dip of the knee. Then they turned to their father and, looking up at him straight-faced and as if rehearsed, they spoke together, saying, "Good-night, Father."

They watched his Adam's apple jerk twice before he said, "Good-night, children," as he stepped aside so they could pass him.

They now walked sedately from the room, closing the door after them; they scrambled across the hall and up the stairs. And it was Pattie's room they made for, and once inside, and again as if of one mind, they threw themselves on the bed and buried their faces in the quilt in an effort to smother their laughter.

When they turned on their sides their faces were wet, and when Pattie said, "Oh, Daniel, you did sound funny. However did you manage to come out with something like that?" he replied in a measured tone, "Well, I seem to think like that, but usually I can never get it out."

"You got it out then, didn't you? It shook that big-mouthed Irishman. In fact, it shook the lot, Father most of all. Oh"—she put out her hand and caught his now— "I wish you weren't going back to school."

And he, feeling a great warmth pass over him, said, "I wish I wasn't either, Pattie."

In later years what he remembered most about that night was he and Pattie lying on the bed laughing until they cried, and that then she had held his hand.

3

The Christmas holidays were surprisingly cheerful. Daniel could not remember the house looking so bright and everybody so happy. He had been welcomed home with open arms by Moira; she had kissed him twice, the second time after exclaiming on how much he had grown. Maggie Ann too had hugged him, and she had waltzed him round the kitchen. But although Rosie had pulled a face and said Maggie Ann was mad and that she would have everybody else in the same boat as herself before long, he had noticed straight away that she, herself, was different. He couldn't put his finger on why, or how, he only knew she was different—perhaps happier would have been a better description. Yet she didn't smile a lot or laugh, like both Moira and Maggie Ann did.

And then there was his father. He had ruffled his hair as he exclaimed, "Well! well! I'll soon have to look out; you're sprouting like a bean pole. What do they feed you on in that place?"

When, later that day, he had visited the farm everyone seemed in good spirits. Only one person appeared the same as when he had left the house in September and that was Pattie.

He didn't see her until she came back from school; in fact, not until he went to meet her. He saw her from some way off and ran towards her; but she made no further move towards him. She was wearing a long coat, a scarf, and a fur bonnet and woollen mittens. She was all muffled up, except for her face which looked white and pinched. "Hello," she said. "You've got back then?"

"Hello, Pattie. By! isn't it cold?"

"Well, looking at you, one wouldn't think so: you're not wearing a topcoat."

"No, I'm not." He looked down at himself as if he were just discovering he was without an overcoat; then, turning to walk by her side, he said, "How are you?"

"How am I?" She turned towards him. "I'm sick and tired. I'm weary. And if there were any gypsies passing at this moment I'd beg to be taken away by them."

"Why?"

"Because"—her tone was vehement now—"I'm sick to death of the two merry Marthas in that house. Laughter at breakfast, dinner, and tea—and supper. But it's all put on, you know, because I've seen those two when they are by themselves and there's been no laughter on their faces then: serious they've been, nattering away. Then when I come on the scene it's 'Ha! ha! ha!' doing their turn. They're clowns, you know, both of them. And there's something behind it all; nobody can laugh all the time."

"Well, Pattie, it's likely their nature: they laugh at troubles."

"Don't be silly, laugh at troubles."

"Anyway, is Father letting you go pupil-teaching?"

"I haven't asked him yet, but Miss Brooker is coming to see him tomorrow."

"It'll be all right, you'll see." He went to take her arm, but checked himself in fear of being repulsed, because this was the old Pattie, not the girl who had lain on the bed with him and laughed until she cried. He said now, "I hear there is going to be a party; quite a do on Christmas night. The Farringdons and the Talbots are coming, and Father said I could ask Ray; you know, Ray Melton from school, and to stay the night. Are you bringing anyone?"

"Well, who would I bring? not anyone from school, would I? And if Janie Farringdon's there and Frances Talbot, what more could I want?"

Suddenly he stopped, gripped her arm and swung her round to face him while he demanded, "What is it you don't like about Moira? All right, she laughs a lot. Well, I can't see that that's a bad thing. As for Maggie Ann, she's a servant and you don't need to take any notice of her. But what is it about Moira? Is it because she's married Father?"

"No. No, it isn't because she's married to Father…I wouldn't have cared who Father married, if you want to know. Oh…!"

Whenever she couldn't find the answer to a question she would hunch her shoulders up around her chin, and they assumed this position now, and she walked on for almost a minute before she exclaimed, "I think there's something behind her. She's hiding something. I don't know what. Because why does she keep laughing all the time? People don't laugh all the time unless it's to distract you over something up."

"I like her laughing; it's a nice laugh, and she's kind. Don't you think she's kind?"

"People are not kind for nothing."

He considered this for a moment before he said, "Well, perhaps she's grateful for Father marrying her, because she's old, isn't she? twenty-five."

She turned to him now and gave him one of her rare smiles as she said, "And you, Daniel Stewart, are very young." And then he gave the lie to her words and she recognised this when, querulously, he said, "But time will take care of that, won't it?"

"Come on," she said now; "I'm freezing."

"The house is warm. There's a fire in the drawing-room, and in the dining-room, even in the study and billiard-room. And you know what? I found a hot brick in my bed to air it, likely. It was wrapped in flannel. That was nice of her, wasn't it?"

"*Oh, wonderful!*"

As they entered the hall Moira was approaching from the kitchen. She had a large bibbed white apron over her dress and her whole appearance was welcoming, as was her voice when she greeted Pattie, "Are you frozen, dear? There's some hot broth in the kitchen. Come away in and get thawed."

"I'll go and wash my hands first."

Daniel noted that Pattie's voice was quiet and civil; and when she turned away, Moira said to Daniel, "You've been out without a coat on, laddie. Do you want to catch your death?"

"I'm warm enough, Moira," he said; "but I could do with some of that broth."

"This way, sir, at your service." She bowed and swept her arm in the direction of the kitchen. And he, taking her cue, marched with head up towards the door, her laughter following him...

Later that evening, after his father had departed the house in high spirits for a meeting in Newcastle, Moira came into the study where he and Pattie were sitting reading, and addressing Pattie, she said, "Would you like to come into the kitchen, dear, and help me decorate this cake; or better still, give me an idea of what should go on the top of it. I've always been a dab hand at baking cakes but, as for titivating the tops of them, a horse could make a better job of it with his hooves."

Daniel had got up from the rug, and he looked at Pattie as she answered, "Well, you can put me in the same class as the horse," at which Moira put her head back and let out a bellow of a laugh, the while Daniel nodded quickly towards Pattie, the motion speaking clearer than his words when he said, "But you've always got bright ideas."

"She has that. Come on then." Moira turned away as if Pattie had already accepted her invitation.

When Pattie slowly rose from her chair Daniel gave her a push in the back, and although she turned her head sharply towards him she said nothing.

The kitchen was warm and full of the smells of spice, and there in the middle of the long wooden table was a large fruit loaf, and Maggie Ann, pointing to it, cried by way of greeting, "Did you ever see anything so good to look at as that? She's a dab hand, is herself, at the cakes."

"Shut up! will you?" Moira now turned to Pattie, saying, "Well, what do you think, Pattie?"

During the process of decorating the cake Daniel felt that Moira's heavy-handedness now and again was very well put on, and his liking for her grew. And when the cake was decorated with as much trimming as it could hold it was Maggie Ann who said, "Now wouldn't a cup of tea and a current bun go down nice? Sit yourselves down there around the fire. Oh, it's like home when folks are in the kitchen. I miss Rosie, you know, now she leaves at six o'clock. But as herself said, 'Ten hours is enough for anybody to work'. And she's got her own man and house to see to. We get on fine now, you know, Rosie and me. Oh aye, we do."

Daniel was pleased Pattie made no objection to sitting round the fire, because he himself wanted to stay in the kitchen with these two warm women. And when they were settled, each with a cup of tea in their hand and with a plate of buns set on a stool between them, Pattie's question, coming out of the blue, seemed to startle them for a moment, for she said, "Is it true that you lived in a castle in Ireland?"

And then there was some consternation when Maggie Ann answered, "Aye, it is," while at the same time Moira said, "Not really."

"Well, it was, it was—"

Maggie Ann's voice was cut off by Moira saying, in an unusually harsh tone, "Be quiet! Maggie Ann. For once in your life see things as they really are, or really were." And now turning to Pattie, she said, "It wasn't really a castle. It was a house, but had the name of castle. Castlemere it was called, and it could deceive people into thinking it was a castle because the man who had built it early in the century had big ideas. He was a rich Protestant. Oh my! Oh my!" She put her hand over her eyes, but she didn't laugh now. Then looking at Pattie again, she said, "Well, you know what I mean. It was such of those that had the large properties and land.''

''And still have.''

Moira cast a baneful glance at Maggie Ann before going on, ''It should happen that my grandfather was a bailiff to a Mr Jardine. But when the troubles arose in the great famine the family went hurriedly back to England, and they took most of their stuff with them, leaving just curtains here and there and a few floor coverings. But what they did was to ask my grandfather to take over the house until they came back; that is, to move his family into it so it wouldn't be rifled and the place torn to bits, especially the beautiful woodwork which would have been used for fuel. Well, years went on and, as in many parts of the country, the tenant became a sort of part owner of the land. Such was the law that in those days the tenant could even sell his leasehold without making a new contract with the owner of the place. Things were topsy-turvy, like the landlord having the rent yet not owning the place. Oh''—she shook her head—''it was a funny business. But anyway, it allowed my grandfather to bring up his family in that house. And then my father took over, by which time a lot of the land had been sold, and what is left now gives but a scratch living, if you know what I mean. As for the house, it would take a fortune to put that in order, because there's not a bit of the roof whole. Because owners have no money to spend on timber and new slates there's hardly a room in the house now that doesn't let water in.'' Now her laughter broke her flow as she ended, ''It's true what I'm telling you. Everybody that sleeps in that house has a bucket or basin or chamber pot to catch the drips; often not only one of these appliances, but two or three.''

Daniel now laughed with Moira and Maggie Ann, but Pattie's face remained impassive as she said, ''Then if it's so bad, why do the family stay there?''

''Oh, dear God in heaven! listen to her.'' Maggie Ann was flapping her hand towards Pattie now. ''Where d'you think the family would go, child? And it's a fine brick-built house. And if anybody's been turned out to the road from their cottage or shanty, himself takes them in until they pull themselves together and go off to the Americas or come to England here. But God knows why they want to come—''

''*Maggie Ann!*''

''Yes…Yes…Miss…Moira.'' The words were spaced out and the large head bobbed. Then, with her usual impulsive movement, she swivelled round on the stool, saying, ''Tell them that piece of poetry you wrote about the rain coming through the whole place. It's a funny one.'' Maggie Ann was nodding now to Daniel, and she went on, ''She makes up all these. Split your sides sometimes. Then when the mood's on her she makes up ones that have you cryin'. Oh begod! she has a funny mind, has our Miss Moira.''

''Will you shut your mouth, Maggie Ann, or you'll be left on your own for the rest of the night.''

''Do you really make up poetry, Moira?'' asked Pattie.

''Not poetry, dear, just silly rhymes.''

''Go on, Miss Moira, do that one that you did when you were but a lass, an' you called it, 'When I was Young'. Go on.''

When Moira made no response Daniel said politely, ''Do say it, Moira. I'd like to hear it, and Pattie would

too. Wouldn't you, Pattie?'' Pattie glanced at him;
then, turning to her stepmother, she paused for a moment before she said simply, ''Yes.''

At this Moira laughed, then said, ''Well, here goes!
You've asked for it;'' and at this she struck a pose
that gave her a childlike appearance, and began:

''We lived in a house at the top of
the hill:
There wasn't much roof on that old
house, but still
We all had buckets when the rain
poured through;
Mine was an old one but my father's was
new.
Mama carried hers on the top of her head,
It was very awkward when she was in bed;
The handle would keep dangling under
her chin,
Until it was fastened with a safety pin.
I always put mine on top of my chest,
To catch all the big drops, I thought
it was best;
And when it was full it overflowed
And tumbled down the stairs and into
the road.
Papa's bucket was always kept in the shed,
For it's the best place for a bucket,
he said,
Not stuck on top of your head or on
your chest;
Fancy being caught like that while in
your vest.''

Daniel laughed, Maggie Ann laughed, and even Pattie managed a smile. And now she asked, "Did it really pour through the roof in every room?"

"Yes," Moira nodded at her, "in every bedroom, that is, and into the kitchen quarters too, because that part was stuck on the end of the house and was just a single storey."

"It must have been very uncomfortable."

"It was," said Moira; "but it was a diversion and it afforded a topic of conversation." She wasn't smiling now as she spoke, and consequently had Pattie's whole attention and, apparently for the first time, her interest, for the girl asked her, "What did you do with your time? Did you work on the farm?"

"Oh, it was no farm." Moira was about to go on when Maggie Ann put in, "'Twas that. 'Twas a farm; we had a cow that gave good milk; and a litter of pigs every year, and ducks, and hens. And there was fish in the brook."

"It still wasn't a farm." Moira's voice was flat.

"Well, how did you live? How did you make money?"

"My brothers married and moved into the town where they worked. So there were only my parents and myself and Maggie Ann here. So we lived well, but plainly."

"I thought you were rich."

As Daniel exclaimed, "*Pattie!*" Moira said, "Oh, it's all right, it's all right, it was a straight question. And now, Pattie, I'll give you a straight answer. We aren't rich but we're expecting to be; at least, if not rich, then pretty warm."

"It's Aunt Mattie that has the money." It was Maggie Ann butting in again. "You saw her at the weddin'. She's himself's aunt, Mr Conelly that is, and she married a very warm man in Dublin, where she lives in a nice house, a very nice house." She nodded now. "And she has neither kith nor kin except Miss Moira's father. But Miss Moira here has always been her favourite and it has been an understood thing she'll come into her fortune. It's in a will, so I understand. Isn't that so, Miss Moira?"

"As usual you talk too much. But yes, that is the gist of how things are."

"She looked very old, the aunt," said Pattie.

Moira smiled widely now, saying, "Yes, Pattie, she *is* very old, but I would hope that she still has a number of years spared to her yet, for she is a very kind and warm person."

"If she is so wealthy, why didn't she buy you a wedding present?"

"Well"—Moira chuckled now—"she didn't *buy* me a wedding present but she gave me one; knowing what would help most, she gave me fifty pounds."

Pattie's eyebrows moved up slightly as she said, "That is a lot of money."

"Well, it isn't exactly hen corn."

"How much do you think you'll get when she dies?"

As Moira and Maggie Ann fell together laughing, Daniel exclaimed loudly, "Pattie! you shouldn't. Really!"

"Oh—" Moira was now wiping the tears of laughter away from her cheeks with her fingers as she said, "You're going to be the practical one, I can see. My dear, I couldn't give you an answer to that. I'll just have to wait and see; but as I said, I hope it isn't for a long while…"

Although Daniel did not remember how that evening finished, he only knew that the conversation in the kitchen was what remained with him as a memory of that Christmas, even more so than the party that was held on Christmas night, when Moira made everyone laugh. And he realised that all the Farringdons and some of the Talbots liked her. And also it was the first time he became aware of the plainness of Janie Farringdon and the beauty of Frances Talbot.

PART TWO

1

It seemed to Daniel that each year he came home for the Easter holidays it was to be greeted by a Moira whose belly had become prominent during the intervening months; and then at some time during the summer holidays to be horrified by her cries as she was giving birth to yet another child. He never could get used to those cries. Strangely, however, they didn't seem to affect his father, who was usually busy about the farm or, more often, away on business in Fellburn or Newcastle. Then, in 1887, matters occurred that could have predicted the pattern of his life ahead.

It was in this year that Pattie left home to be married; it was in this year too that for the first time his father struck him and he struck him back; and that Moira's seventh baby was born dead. It was also during these twelve months that Pattie, now at the age of twenty, and a more fearless young woman than ever, made a discovery that gave evidence as to why their mother had been such a cool and apparently unemotional lady. It was during this year also he discovered that he would never get to a university, and also that he loved Frances Talbot and was determined to marry her some day...

With further help from Miss Brooker, two years previously Pattie had been awarded a full teaching post, and during this period she had met a young man named John Watson, a teacher in Fellburn, and a very enlightened one, for he had found a way into her heart by being a defender of women's rights, which for the time was a very brave attitude to take. It was on this blustery day in early April that Pattie came through the front door to see Moira's six-year-old son Patrick sliding down the banister while his four-year-old sister Margaret stood screaming with glee at the foot of the stairs. But when the boy, dropping from the pillar, fell on top of her, her glee turned to tears until a quiet voice to the side of them said, "Here's Auntie Pattie."

Pattie approached the five-year-old Sean, who appeared to be the odd one out in Moira's brood, for he was as fair as the others were dark, and he was quiet while the rest of them were rowdy. His quietness was put down to his being the survivor of twins, the other having died at birth, and as Maggie Ann was wont to say, "He had been left with two brains in his head, which has made him fey. And if he had been across the water it would have been he who danced at night in the woodland with the wee folk."

"Hello, Auntie Pattie," said Patrick.

Margaret was snivelling now. "He fell on me."

"Where's your mother?"

"She's up in bed," said Patrick; "she's got a bad belly. Annie and Catherine are with her and wee Michael's in the kitchen with Maggie Ann. He's got the gripes."

Pattie nodded down at Patrick. He was certainly one

for giving you details, was Patrick. He could have been bred of Maggie Ann herself.

"Where's your father?"

"Don't know," said Patrick.

"He's out," said Margaret.

Sean now put in quietly, "He's riding his horse."

"Well, get out of the road, all of you, and go and tell Maggie Ann to make me a cup of tea."

Patrick and Margaret ran off to do her bidding but Sean remained where he was, standing looking at her, his clear grey eyes wide: "You going away, Auntie Pattie?" he asked quietly.

"Why do you ask, Sean?"

"I don't know."

"Has somebody said something to you?"

"No. No, Auntie Pattie."

"Well, yes, I *am* going away, Sean."

"I'm sorry, Auntie Pattie."

"I'm not; except, perhaps, I'll miss you."

"And I'll miss you, Auntie Pattie."

Pattie looked down into the round face with the thick fair hair tumbling about it and she wondered, as she had done many times before, how it was she could speak to this boy as if he were an adult? Perhaps it was that he talked as if he *were* an adult. There had always been something strange about Sean. He wasn't like the rest of them. He stood out, not only because he was fair, but for that something else you couldn't put a name to. She only knew that she had no time for the rest of Moira's brood; yet, even so, in a strange way she had come to like her stepmother, although perhaps pity was a more apt word than like. Yet, as her John had said in a wise way, pity was a stepping stone to love. Well, she couldn't say she loved Moira, but she had a feeling for her and it had grown with the years, as the feeling against her father had grown too.

She touched Sean gently on the cheek with her finger, then went up the stairs and, knocking on Moira's bedroom door, entered the room.

Moira was lying against a pile of pillows, cradling the ten-month-old Michael in one arm and steadying the bouncing Catherine with her other hand.

Pattie walked up to the bedside, saying, "You not feeling too good, Moira?"

"Well, Pattie, in all truth there are days when I've felt brighter."

"Is it a cold?"

"No. I think it's just laziness." She smiled.

"Yes, yes, I've no doubt about that," said Pattie. "They say it is the Irish disease, but I've thought for a long time that you didn't suffer from it. Laziness indeed! Now, if it was Maggie Ann..."

"Oh, Maggie Ann's all right. It's the weight she has to carry. You know, as I think I've told you before, Pattie, it isn't fat that's blown her out, it's water, and she'll die of it in the end. But what brings you here this morning?"

Pattie sat on the edge of the bed and, putting her hand out, she touched the baby's foot as she said, "I've come to tell my father I'm getting married."

"*Married?*" Moira jerked herself up in bed. "To that nice man, of course, the teacher?"

"Yes, to that nice man, the teacher."

"When is it to be?"

"Next week."

Moira's face stretched; the child almost slipped from her arm; then she grabbed it to her breast, repeating on a high note, "Next week? But...but how can you manage that?"

"By special license. It's all arranged."

"Eeh! my goodness." Moira lay back against the pillows shaking her head. "He won't like that."

"Like it or not, he can't do anything about it. Anyway, I think he'll be glad to be rid of me: I've always been a thorn in his flesh. But there's one thing sure, he won't give me a dowry." She smiled now.

"You're no thorn in his flesh. And I've got to say to you, Pattie, that you've been a comfort to me, although I didn't think so the first time I entered this house, nor for weeks after. But then I began to understand you: you missed your mother like I did mine. Oh yes"—she nodded her head now—"I missed my mother. To tell you the truth I missed them all across there. I missed many things." She turned her head to the side and looked down on her daughter, who was chewing on the end of the counterpane, and she said, "They say we're all human beings and much the same under the skin. But it isn't so." Turning her gaze on Pattie once more, she repeated, "It isn't so, because there's something in you that longs for the soil that bred you and that you first walked on, and the air that you breathed and the wind that fanned your face. It's the same in all countries: there's a longing in people for the place where they were born, whether it be good, bad or indifferent."

She now put her hand to her side and Pattie, quickly getting to her feet, said, "You've got a pain? You're just on six months."

"Yes, just on six months but I've been carrying this one funny. It seems to prefer the left side of me. It was kicking away yesterday as if it had clogs on."

She drew in a deep breath and smiled again. And now, putting her hand out towards Pattie, she said, "I wish I could say, my dear, what would you like for a wedding present? but you know how I'm fixed. If, for instance, I'd come into the money...mind, not that I want the old lady to go, oh no, but if I had, say, I would have bought you something good."

"Never mind about that. I don't need presents, Moira, but I'm going to say this to you." She now leant over the bed. "When you do get the money, hang on to as much of it as you can."

"Oh, now, now, that'll be difficult, for you know the saying in this country: what's yours is mine and what's mine's me own; that's referring to a man and his wife, isn't it?"

"Yes, I know that's referring to a man and his wife. But the law has now been changed. But listen, when you get your money, you make it your business to say that you want certain things for yourself. That's one of the rules men have got to stand by: they must provide wives with the necessities according to their station. And you've never had the necessities according to your station, because you've been cook, slave, butler, and mother. As for money, I know where the fifty pounds that your aunt gave you as a wedding present went. Took that, didn't he?"

"Oh, it went on the house, Pattie, as it should do. But don't worry; when the money comes, if the children are rigged out afresh and I have some new curtains, and Hector's able to engage another couple of men in place of the ones he's let go, then I'll be happy."

Pattie shook her head while she said, "It's no use talking to you." She now glanced towards the window; then going swiftly to it she looked down on to the drive, and when she saw her father riding towards the stables she said, "There he is now. I'll go down and get it over, and then I'll see you before I go."

"Oh, but Pattie, you're not just going to go out like that, are you? I mean, you're not just leaving?"

"Yes, I am, Moira. I've packed already, because I know as soon as Father and I meet there'll be a bust-up. And so I've arranged to stay with John's people until next week, and he's rented a house in Fellburn. It's only small, but that's all we need."

"*Oh, Pattie. Pattie.*"

"Now stop it, Moira. If you upset yourself that pain'll start again. Anyway, I'll see you later."

She hurried from the room and down the stairs and straight to the hall door, where she stood awaiting her father's approach.

Seeing her, Patrick and Margaret came running along the terrace. She checked their galloping into the hall and, holding them by the shoulders, she looked from one to the other and said, "Have you been up in the schoolroom this morning?"

Patrick grinned and glanced at his sister, and she giggled until Pattie shook them both, and not gently, as she said, "Well, I've told you what would happen if you missed your lessons, haven't I? I'll see to it that you are both sent to the village school, and it's a nice long tramp and you won't get away with not learning there. Do you understand?"

"We'll go up and do our sums now, Auntie Pattie, we will. We will, won't we, Margaret?"

"Yes. Yes, we will. We will, Auntie Pattie. We will."

"Well, get about it, and quick!" She now thrust

them towards the stairs, and without further ado they went. And as she looked after them she wondered what would happen to their education after she was gone. Yet the little spare time she had given to them apparently had not done much good; they were both dudheads.

She turned to the door again to see her father striding across the gravel. He always entered by the front way now, whereas at one time, when Rosie alone was there, he might have come through the kitchen; but he had made it evident from the beginning that he couldn't stand the sight of Maggie Ann nor, for that matter, could she of him, and such being her character she didn't go out of her way to hide her feelings, which certainly didn't improve matters.

As he came up the steps and saw her standing dressed for going out, he said, "Well, well! what's this? Have they thrown you out of school? Lost your job?"

She dismissed his trite remark by saying, "I want to speak to you," then walked away across the hall and down the passage and into the study.

He followed her, but slowly, and when he entered the room and saw her standing by his desk, he said, "You want to speak to me; not 'is it convenient', or 'I would like to', but 'I want to speak to you'. Well, speak!"

"I'm leaving here today. I'm going to be married next week."

That he was surprised was evident, but that he was annoyed, even angry, was more clear as he said and as if he too were Irish, "Begod! you are, are you? You're leaving here today and you're going to be married next week. No asking permission!"

"I don't have to ask your permission."

"Oh, but by God! you do, girl! You're just twenty. I can hold you until you're twenty-one, and by law—"

"Well, you're willing to try, Father, you're willing to try, and I'd already thought that you might just do that, but you haven't taken into consideration that you'll have to go before a magistrate."

"Well, as you say, madam, I might just do that. I might just do that."

"Yes, you might, Father. But were you to do that I would show you up for the man you are."

"*God Almighty!* Am I hearing aright? For the man I am? What are you talking about?"

"Do you remember a lady called Barbie?"

She watched the colour drain from his face, and now, from between his teeth, he said, "You spying little rat, you! Did you have your John follow me? By God! I could strangle you."

"No, Father, I didn't have my John follow you, and you've just given me a new slant on your character. You have just told me that Barbie is still in your life. I was referring to the time she first came into it and when Mother found out about her." She watched him now walk past her, go round his desk, then sit down; and his mouth was slightly open as he stared at her, but he didn't speak.

Looking at him, the contempt showing in her face and in her voice, she said, "You know Mother's little writing desk; the escritoire, you know? It has a secret drawer. But Mother once said to me it had two secret drawers. I didn't know whether or not she was making it up. The desk itself is of no great value, but I've always liked it, and I was going to ask you as, dear Father, you won't be giving me a dowry, if you would

give me the desk as a wedding present. It's been in
my room, you know, since Mother died. Well, it
should happen that I had lots of paper in the two side
drawers and one piece of paper happened to get
jammed in the back and so I pulled the drawer out, or
at least I tried to; and in my fingering I must have
pressed a spring. Then, the space between the two
drawers, which just looked like a broad strip of veneer,
came slowly forward and in it were three small flat
diaries. I read them, and I got a vivid picture of my
mother's life with you. How you used her legacy to
keep your harlot, and how she found out about it and
followed you and saw you saying goodbye to your
kept woman, she who wasn't really a woman but a
young girl, eighteen or so then. But for how long had
you been using her before that? And her name was
Barbie. Likely short for Barbara, but you called her
Barbie.''

She stopped here, not only because she was out of
breath but also because she thought he was about to
have a seizure, for his face was almost purple except
for the white rim around his mouth. But she felt no
pity for him as she went on, ''Moreover, you took
every penny she had, because the law said that even
the clothes she stood up in didn't belong to her. That's
what the law said, didn't it? And at one period you
told her she could go, but she wouldn't get a penny.
And her people were dead and she hadn't any friends.
She wasn't a woman who made friends, yet there was
still someone to whom she could turn and that was the
old family lawyer. It was he who arranged that when
she died, her money died with her. It was a very intricate business, she said. Yet, there wasn't all that

much left, certainly not as much as there should have been, because you had cashed her bonds, hadn't you?''

"*Get out! Out of my sight...out!*"

"Yes, Father, I'll get out, and I promise you that I'll never come back into this house again. And when I show the diaries to Daniel, well, he might have to stay here until he can earn his own living, but from the minute he reads our mother's words you will have lost him too..."

The heavy brass and glass inkwell just missed her face and hit the wall to the side of her, but the ink sprayed out on to her coat and she had to lie back against the bookcase for a moment to recover from the shock. And now she stared at her father, who was on his feet but leaning over the desk, crying, "I should have throttled you years ago. There were times when I wanted to. *Get out!*" It was a high scream.

She got out, so shaken that when she reached the hall and saw both Moira and Maggie Ann and the two elder children in a group at the foot of the stairs, she passed them without a word, and they too said nothing. But their gaze spread over her and the splashes of ink that were not only on her clothes but on her face. And they watched her walk slowly up the stairs.

In her room, Pattie did not sit down, because she knew that if she did she would start to cry. But she went to the wash-basin and wiped her face with a wet face-cloth, then took off her ink-stained coat, before picking up the loose coat that lay across the two cases at the foot of the bed and putting it on. Then, lifting the two cases and the soiled coat, she left the room without a backward glance.

There was only Maggie Ann standing in the hall, and she said, "Oh! lass. Lass. Oh, Miss Pattie; for this to happen.'' And Pattie said to her, ''Ask Patrick to run down to the stables and see if one of the men would carry these cases to the cart.''

''I'll do that, I'll do that, Miss Pattie. But oh, dear God! it's sorry to the heart of me I am to see you goin' like this. There's no luck in this house, you know, Miss Pattie. God walked out of it many years ago, and luck went with Him. He's a godless man, your father. He is. He is.''

''Please, Maggie Ann.''

''All right, all right, I'm away.'' But before she made to go she came to Pattie and, putting her huge arms about her, she drew her tightly into her embrace and kissed her.

It was too much: tears sprang from Pattie's eyes and, bending again, she lifted the cases and humped them through the front door and on to the terrace, where she stood for a good five minutes before Alex Towney came hurrying towards her.

Characteristically he said nothing, but picked up the two cases and walked down the steps and towards the path that led to the farm, and she followed him.

It wasn't until he reached the farm that he said, ''There's only the cart that'll be goin' into town, Miss Pattie, and that won't be for another half hour. I'll leave the cases here, but you come along of me, and my missis will see to you until it's time to go.''

She paused a moment before nodding to him and following him down the narrow path to the row of four cottages.

Alex Towney opened the door of the second cottage and stood aside to allow Pattie to enter the small room: then he shouted, ''You there, Alice?'' And when a woman appeared in the doorway wiping her hands on an apron and exclaimed, "Oh! Miss Pattie, Miss Pattie, what is it? What is it?" he said. "Never mind what it is, Miss Pattie would like to sit here until the cart comes back from the village, when it will take her into Fellburn. 'Tis Fellburn you want to go, miss, isn't it?"

"Yes. Yes, thank you, Alex."

Alice Towney was a motherly woman, and as such she began to fuss around, saying, "Eeh! I've never got cleaned up this mornin', miss; I've been at the poss-tub since early on. You've got to get the fine weather, and there's a bit of wind blowin' and it dries. Look, miss. Oh, do sit down, miss…that's right. Now, can I get you anything? There's a nice drop of soup in the pan there." She pointed to the open fire, and at this Pattie said, "No, thank you, Mrs Towney; I'm all right. But I wouldn't mind a glass of water."

"A glass of water it is, miss. A glass of water."

As she bustled out of the room her husband said, "It looks as if you're goin' for good, miss." And she replied, "Yes, Alex, I'm going for good."

"You'll be missed up there 'cos you were the only steady one among them. Irish folk are never steady. But speak as you find, I've always found the missis pleasant, and kindly at that. But the way things are goin', miss, between you and me, there'll be very little left to be kindly with, shortly. I've never seen a place run down so quickly. Now, if you yourself had been a man and a son…no offence meant, miss; 'cos what I'm meanin' is, you've got a head on your shoulders and you would have done something about things long afore now… Oh, here she is with the water. Now you're sure that's all you want, miss?"

"Yes. Yes, thank you, Alex."

"Well, I'll go along and see if the cart's back."...

He wasn't away five minutes before he returned, saying, "For once in his life he's back on time. Will you come along now, miss?"

Pattie thanked Mrs Towney, and when they reached the farmyard she thanked Alex too; and lastly, she said to him, "Would you make it your business, Alex, to see Daniel—she did not say Master Daniel—"and tell him I'm in Fellburn? He knows the address; he has been before."

"I'll do that, miss. He's due home the morrow, isn't he?"

"Yes, tomorrow."

His last words to her as he helped her up into the back of the cart, in which Bob Shearman, the shepherd, had laid clean sacks to cover the tramped-in sheep droppings, were, "It's a scandal you havin' to go out like this. You should have ordered the trap, miss. That's what you should have done."

What she said to him, and with a sad smile, was, "I always used to like riding in the cart. You remember, Alex?" And the man gulped in his throat before he said, "Aye, I remember, miss. Goodbye, now, and the best of luck and I hopes you'll be happy in whatever you do."

"I'll be happy, Alex. I'm getting married next week."

"*Oh! you are, miss?* Well, well; that's news, and it's glad I am to hear it. Is it the teacher man, miss?"

"It *is* the teacher man, Alex."

"Good, good. He's one of your own sort. May you live long together, miss. That's what I wish you."

"Goodbye, Alex, and thank you."

"Goodbye, miss."

As the cart trundled through the back gate and along the rutted road towards the coach road the tears started again and she screwed up her eyes and bowed her head in an effort to fight them.

2

It was late evening on the following day. The house
was quiet, the children's chatter had faded away into
sleep; and Maggie Ann was upstairs with Moira,
where she had been for the past two hours. Most of
this time Hector had spent walking from the door leading into the kitchen, across the hall, through the drawing-room to its farthest window, which gave him a
partial view of the drive, then back again into the hall
and to the front door to stare into the deepening twilight. Every now and again he would bring his teeth
together and grind them until his cheekbones tightened
against the flesh of his face.

When at last he saw his son coming from the direction of the yard he took up a position in the middle
of the hall. With his legs astride and his fists pressed
on to his hips, he waited; but he had to wait some
minutes before he came face to face with his son, because Daniel had come in by way of the kitchen and
was taking his time before entering the hall. And when
he did he paused for a moment and stared at the figure
that looked ready for battle. Then the voice came at
him, bawling, "What the hell do you mean by taking

the trap without my leave? And after I told you not to go to her, didn't I?"

Daniel walked slowly forward, to stop a couple of arm's lengths from his father, but he didn't speak. His eyes were on a level with his father's, for at sixteen he was unusually tall. As yet his body hadn't filled out, but he had broad shoulders and narrow hips and these two points promised a good figure in his manhood.

"For two pins I'd take you by that bloody scraggy neck of yours and twist it."

"Why? Because I now know the truth about you?"

"What truth? The rubbish that your neurotic mother scribbled to fill in her time? You know what your mother was? She was an unnatural woman."

As Daniel stared at the face suffused with anger, his mind was again reading the words, "I have come to such a pass that I cannot even allow myself to touch my son, for when I do I am seeing him become as his father, a ravenous beast, taking what he terms his rights without any show of tenderness or love. Animals have a love display. I recall watching the peacocks in Grandpapa's garden. This man, who was keeping a mistress on the money I provided, would also force himself on me. Only the threat that, of my own accord, I would walk out and into Fellburn and place myself in the hands of the Poor Law Guardians has restrained him, for he knows full well I would carry out this threat rather than have my body defiled again."

His father had continued talking; his voice a growl now, he was saying, "You would think I had committed a bloody murder. Tell me the man that doesn't have a mistress or someone on the side. Matthew Talbot has had a woman for years. But do you hear Lilian yarping on about it? No, she's got more sense. Even Shearman down on the farm has been carrying on with a piece in Fellburn, and to my knowledge he's fathered another hereabouts. And that narrow-minded, sanctimonious bitch throws it up in my face as if I was the only man in the land who took his pleasures on the side. And as for you, you young scut, I warned you not to listen to her.''

For the first time Daniel broke in, saying, ''No, I wasn't listening to Pattie, I was just reading Mother's diaries and discovering what she suffered under a man who doesn't know what tenderness or kindness is.''

''Oh my God! now you. Boy, you don't know what you're talking about; you've had it too easy. But let me tell you, your pleasant life has stopped from now on, for you're not going back to that school; you're staying here and learning what it is to work for your living.''

These words came as a shock to Daniel, and the prospect of being kept at home and learning farming seemed for the moment to cut off his future life, the life he had planned in his mind: he was going to stay at the High School until he was eighteen or more: Mr Pearson had indicated he had a good head on his shoulders and should then aim for an open scholarship at either Oxford or Cambridge. He fancied being a doctor because he was good at natural philosophy and chemistry.

So bleak was the prospect his father was presenting him with that, the shock over, Daniel yelled at him, ''I won't stay on the farm! I intend to go to university. You can't keep me here.''

''Well! Well! Ho! Ho!'' It was the high ironical

laugh. "Has your sister promised to pay your school fees? Huh! That churchmouse teacher of hers will hardly earn enough to feed them; she herself will have to work to keep a roof over their heads... You are my son and you'll do what you're told. You'll learn how to run this farm."

"Like hell I will! Learn how to run the farm to give you time to go whoring with...your Barbie, while Moira, year after year, becomes worn out with bearing your brood...?"

The fist caught him on the ear and sent him reeling against the pillar at the foot of the stairs. Intuitively he grabbed for support at the large wooden ball on top of the pillar.

His head was banging and through his blurred vision he could see only the outline of his father standing to the side of him, but it was enough.

It was the surprise of the spring that bore them both to the floor, and all Daniel was aware of at this moment was the great strength concentrated in his hands as they flailed at his father and of screaming words he had never before voiced.

Of a sudden he felt himself being dragged backwards across the floor, before becoming aware that Moira and Maggie Ann were standing over him and that there was a salty taste in his mouth.

The next thing he knew was they had hoisted him to his feet and were leading him away.

He heard Maggie Ann say, "It was the ring; it's split the lobe of his ear. You sit down on the chair beside him while I go and get some water;" then Moira's voice saying softly, "Where is he?" and the answer coming, "Looking after himself as usual. I shouldn't worry about him."

Through the muzziness in Daniel's head ran the thought: he's not dead then. And at this he felt a deep regret.

He opened his eyes and saw Moira's face, and his head seeming to clear, he saw that she looked tired and sad: "I'm sorry," he muttered.

"It's all right. It's all right, boy. These things happen in all families; it's part of the pattern."

"Oh, Moira; I'm not sorry that I hit him. I'm only sorry you're upset." He made to rise from the couch and she laid her hand on his shoulder, saying, "Be still now. You're bleeding."

"I'm bleeding?"

"Yes, your ear's split."

He put up his hand to the side of his face, then looked at his red fingers and, like a child repeating words, said, "Yes, I'm bleeding." Then his tone changing, he said, "That's the first time, but it'll be the last he'll hit me, because I'm leaving."

"Don't talk so."

"I am. I am, Moira. I can't stay here now."

"You mustn't leave. You can't leave. What would I do without you?"

He turned fully about and looked at her, and she nodded at him, saying, "I've lost Pattie. We became friends, you know; but you and I were friends from the very first moment. All I seem to live for now is your school holidays."

"But, Moira, I've got to go. There are things you don't understand."

She now bent over and, bringing her face towards his and her voice a mere whisper, she said, "There's nothing I don't know about him, Daniel, and that I haven't known for a long time, but I've made me bed and I've got to lie on it. And there are things in all our lives, mistakes, regrets—"

"But he doesn't regret anything. He carries on in the same way as—"

"How d'you know he doesn't regret? And you know, my dear, whatever he does with his life is between him and me, and if I can put up with it, you can put up with it. He's an unhappy man, your father. He's a failure, and all such men are unhappy, and women too. I was a failure; that's why I married him."

"What are you talking about?"

She smiled wearily now, saying, "I don't know. I just don't know. But yes, I do, and one day, when you're older, I will tell you a story and it will explain why I laugh a lot." Her voice rapid now, she whispered, "Here comes my guardian angel. We've all got one, you know."

When Maggie Ann reached the couch she exclaimed loudly, "Ah well, you've come round then; you're not going to die yet. My stars! I've never seen such a fight as that since I left God's country. You've got the strength of the devil in you, boy. D'you know you nearly throttled him? Of course he must have been half stunned with fallin' as he did on his back, else you wouldn't have got that far. But my! my! you nearly made a clean job of it."

"Be quiet! Maggie Ann, and get on with this job, or give the cloth to me."

"You sit back there, woman, and let me clean up his face, and then the mess on this good couch cover. My! I doubt if we'll get that out in the poss-tub."

After sponging his face and the hair above his ear

she pointed to the slit in the lobe, saying now to Moira, "D'you think it'll need a stitch?"

"Well, whether it does or it doesn't, you can't do it. No, I think if you just put a tight bandage round his head it might knit together overnight."

"Yes, perhaps it might. But look at that!" She pointed to his cheek and eye. "He's goin' to have a shiner there the morrow. And it's God's blessin' and the devil's luck that ring didn't meet up with his eye or else it would be out."

"I'll say this much for you, Maggie Ann, you always look on the bright side. Now go and get something that'll act as a bandage."

After Maggie Ann had again left the room Moira, taking Daniel's hand, said, "Promise me, now promise me, boy, you won't think about leaving. Oh, I know you could join the army, or the navy tomorrow, or you could go and live with Pattie and her man, and they would welcome you, I know that, but no one needs you as I do. I can't explain why, except to say that you lighten my days."

He turned his head away from her for he had become overwhelmed by the most unmanly feeling; he wanted to cry...

It was the following morning at six o'clock that he knew he couldn't leave the house, because Moira, after five hours of agony, gave birth to a dead child.

3

In one way, Hector was as good as his word: Daniel didn't return to school. The pleas put forth by Moira on his behalf received the answer, "He can go back tomorrow if you will provide the money to support him."

To this she had no answer; but for the first time in her life she wished that her Auntie Mattie were dead.

The men in the yard showed no surprise when they were presented with another assistant. Their master had addressed them when they were all together, saying, "My son is not returning to school; he's going to learn the business. I am asking each one of you to show him the ropes of your particular trade."

That was all.

Hector did not give Daniel the order when to begin work; it came through Moira. On the day Pattie was to be married, when he looked in on Moira, who was still in bed getting over the trauma of her loss, she said to him, "For my sake, Daniel, please don't go to Pattie's wedding; he has arranged that you go down to the farm this morning. The men are to show you what to do."

And it appeared that the men had arranged it among themselves how they were going to deal with the young master. First he came under the care of Barney Dunlop who, leading him into the cowshed, said, "This isn't my job, Master Daniel, but since Arthur Beaney left I've had to do me best, but''—he grinned—"I've been milking cows since the time I could toddle, so I know a little about them. Well now, we'll go and get them in and then we'll start."

So, during that first week, Daniel learned from one or the other: first, how to milk a cow; but he didn't have to learn how to dress a horse or attend a horse, because he had often done this during his holidays; he had as yet never ploughed a field or knocked staves into the ground to take the wire for fencing or turned the manure heap at the end of the yard. That job he found most distasteful, but he did it. They broke him in gently for that, by giving him the job of mucking out the stables.

During that first week he went to bed weary, yet sleep was hard to come by, because he was full of resentment against that man along the corridor with whom he wouldn't eat, taking his meals in the kitchen with Maggie Ann, much to her pleasure.

During the second week, when it rained almost continuously and the mud in the yard dragged at his feet and the steam and the smell of animal flesh in the byres seemed to choke him, he told himself more than once he wasn't going to stand it: that was all Irish blarney from Moira, him being the only bright thing in her life.

Then, during the third week, when the sun began to shine again and his body ached no longer and he found he was always hungry, Moira gave him the news that the pattern of his days was about to alter, at least somewhat.

"What d'you think, boyo?" she said as she stood before him in the field. "I've told himself for some time now the children must go to school, because there's a bill out that children must go to school and be educated: Patrick is six, and Sean five, and Margaret coming after them, and well, it would cost money, for they would have to be rigged out differently from what they are now; most of the time they are running about like scarecrows. That doesn't seem to matter when around the house, but away in school they've got to be decently put on, and if it's the village school, then better than most, if you know what I mean. But even in the village school there'd be coppers each week for their learning, and it all mounts up. So, I suggested, why not let them take advantage of *your* learning, because until she left, Pattie had taught them their letters, but now you could go on and take them practically right through their schooling. It could be done in the mornings one week and the afternoons the next. How does this appeal to you?"

It appealed to him greatly, but he wasn't inclined to show it, for the thought had come from *him*. And he said as much: "I want no favours from him. And he's out to save money."

"Oh, Daniel, Daniel; *I* suggested it to him. The thing is, he hasn't got any money to save. We're livin' from hand to mouth, as you know." She paused a moment; then turning in a half circle, she looked about her across the expanse of the fields stretching into the distance, and she said slowly, "I don't know why it doesn't pay. If this was in Ireland it would be a gold mine. Of course"—she nodded to herself—"I've got to admit, there, all the family would have a hand in it. There wouldn't just be three hired men, nor yet one woman in the kitchen. But then again''—her eyes once more roved over the land—''it's big enough and the crops are ripe enough.''

''Yes, they might be ripe enough, Moira,'' Daniel put in now, ''but there's not enough of them. There's land lying fallow, so the men say.''

''But surely three good working men would be able to manage all this?''

''Barney is an old man, Moira, and Alex Towney sees to the home gardens, doesn't he? and the drive and the lawn; and in his spare time, the vegetables. And it's those, I understand, that bring in as much money as anything when they go to the market. And they've got to be taken there and somebody's got to sell them. That's Alex's job too. And Bob Shearman, he sees to the horses, the coach, the trap, the sheep, and God knows what else. Grounds like ours, Moira, and the farm, would need six men to run them if every inch of land was to be used, and the garden kept in order.''

She looked at him, her head on one side, and she said quietly, ''Well, there's one thing sure, Daniel, you're learning fast. But what about the teaching?''

''You want me to do it?''

''Oh yes, more than anything, because Patrick is running wild; he wants pulling up, and the strap alone won't do it. And he's had that of late; too much, I think. And Sean, Sean is different. He'd soak up knowledge.'' Again she looked to the side before asking, ''Do you think Sean is different from the rest of my tribe, Daniel?''

"Yes. Yes, I do. He's the odd one out and the cleverest, at least so far."

"He's all Irish, Daniel, whereas the others aren't. What I mean by that is, there's something there in his make-up that both frightens and fascinates me. At times I see him as something out of folklore. You know what I mean?"

He didn't exactly, but he nodded to her.

With a gentle smile she turned away from him and he watched her walk across the field. She was big in the hips now and had put on weight all round and her body swayed as she picked her way over the uneven ground. For a moment he wondered why he had been so concerned about the revelation of his mother's diary, because there went all the mothers he had ever longed for rolled into one, and he knew that he loved her as if she herself had given him birth...

Later that day he was at the far end of their land where a low brick wall cut the field off from the bridle path. He had been replacing coping stones on the top of the wall in the way Bob Shearman had shown him, when along the path came two young girls, and when they were abreast of him they stopped and both smiled at him, and one after the other both said, "Hello, Daniel."

Daniel looked first at Frances Talbot; in fact, he let his eyes linger on her because, as he put it to himself, she looked all golden, dressed as she was in a light fawn coat that reached the top of her light tan boots; while her hat was not a bonnet but one of those that had an upturned brim and a high crown to her shoulders. Her eyes were blue and her full lips red, and the skin on her face he likened to the top of the cream in the dairy.

Then his eyes lifted to her companion. He had never before taken much stock of Janie Farringdon, because she was what he supposed you called homely looking; she did not draw your eye. Yes, she had nice hair; it was brown but quite straight. He had never before really looked at her face. He supposed her eyes were of a greeny-grey, and her mouth was large, too large for beauty. As for her skin, well, compared with that of Frances, you could almost say it was dull. And she was taller than Frances, tending to be lanky.

"Are you glad you've left school, Daniel?"

He shrugged his shoulders before answering Frances, saying, "Some days yes, and some days no." Then on a smile he said, "Every day I don't really know." And at this both the girls laughed and Frances said, "I'm glad I left."

"Yes, but you can stay in the house all day."

He looked at Janie. She had a nice voice. She was of the same age as Frances but she sounded older. More in order to keep his gaze away from Frances he spoke to her, saying, "You're still at school, Janie?"

"Yes, worse luck. Father says I'm there for another couple of years at least, till I'm eighteen."

"Are you going in for a career? I mean, what are you going to do?"

"Oh, I don't know." She made a small movement with her head.

"Get married, of course." This was brought out from Frances on a giggle, and when Janie replied stiffly, "Not necessarily, Frances," an awkward silence fell on the three of them, until Frances said flatly, "Well, what else is there for us?" to which Janie replied, "Don't be silly."

Frances had turned her glance from Janie on to Daniel and he, feeling the colour rising to his face, could resort only to flippancy by saying, "You could go on the stage."

Both girls laughed together now; then apropos of nothing that had been referred to in the short conversation, Frances said, "Janie's mother takes us into Fellburn every Saturday. We visit the shops, then go round the market"—she turned to Janie—"don't we?"

Janie lowered her eyes for a moment, then answered, "Yes."

"You take your stock into the market on a Saturday, don't you?" Frances remarked now.

"No, I don't; the men do."

"Oh."

"Come on. Come on; we must get home," and Janie took hold of her friend's arm and tugged her away; and as Frances tripped sideways she laughed and called out, "Bye-bye, Daniel," and he replied, "Bye-bye, Frances."

He stood watching them walking down the path and it seemed that Janie was talking rapidly, for her hat was bobbing; and he smiled to himself as he thought, she's likely admonishing Frances for being so forward... But that was an open invitation, wasn't it? And it proved one thing that made his heart thump against his ribs; she liked him...and he liked her. Oh, yes, more than liked, and had done for a long time. He couldn't remember when he hadn't liked her. She was so pretty. Oh no, not just pretty, she was beautiful. And she would grow more beautiful.

He stooped and picked up a coping stone, one of a number that had seemed very heavy a while ago but was now of no weight at all.

There was to be one advantage of having to remain

at home, which would make it worth putting up with all the stress; he'd be able to see Frances as often as possible. And yes, she had given him an idea: he could arrange it that he would go into town on a Saturday with the cart. Yes, that's what he would do.

Then, as he continued to lay one stone slantways against another, he wondered if she knew that her father had a mistress? Apparently her mother knew.

He did not get to the market with the cart on the Saturday. Bob Shearman said it was a one-man job and there was plenty for him to do on the farm, and Alex Towney endorsed this. So it was three weeks before he again met up with Frances.

It was a Sunday when he saddled up Rustler and went for a ride. He was able to do this only because his father had been housebound for the last three days with a twisted ankle.

He took a roundabout way to reach the Talbots' farm so it wouldn't be evident that he had come straight from the house.

The word farm was but a courtesy description to apply to Matthew Talbot's land, for it was more of a homestead or market garden. Not that he hadn't a large acreage, but some was hilly and fit only for sheep.

The farmhouse was situated just a stone's throw from the road, and as he neared it he saw Luke, Frances's eighteen-year-old brother, examining a bird that was perched on the strip of lawn fronting the house. And the young man stood up and called, "Hello, Daniel. Lost your way?"

Daniel dismounted, linked the horse's reins around the gatepost and walked up the narrow path, saying, "What have you there?"

"It's a mallard. Its wing is damaged, not broken. It made for the pond behind the house, but the ducks went for it... Are you coming in?"

"Yes. Yes, I might as well. I've been let out." They exchanged a glance, then both laughed.

"How are you finding it? Different from your school life, I bet."

"Yes, quite a bit; but there are good days and bad days."

"Like us all; we all have a taste of them. Ma! Are you there? Ma!"

They were now standing in the small hall, and a sleepy-eyed Mrs Talbot appeared from a room at the end of it, but on the sight of Daniel she blinked rapidly and exclaimed, "Oh! Daniel, what a surprise. Come in. Come in. You've caught me napping, really napping. Frances"—she was calling softly along a passage now—"we have a visitor. Come here."

Daniel was in the sitting-room when Frances appeared at the door, and her manner to him seemed slightly offhand as she said, "Oh, hello, Daniel. Are you lost?"

"Almost"—he smiled at her—"but I'll be all right; Rustler knows his way back home," which caused general laughter.

"How's Moira?" asked Mrs Talbot now, and he answered, "Oh, much better, stronger."

"Brave woman that, brave woman. Always a cheery word and a smile. I don't know how she does it with that crowd about her; it would drive me mad. Well, now that you're here, what about a cup of tea?"

He wasn't very fond of tea but he would have drunk anything to prolong his time with Frances, and so his answer was quite eager: "Oh, yes, yes, Mrs Talbot, that would be very nice. Thank you."

As Lilian Talbot went from the room she exclaimed to no-one in particular, "Mr Talbot is upstairs having his once-a-week nap; I won't disturb him." Then, after she had disappeared from their view, her voice came to them, calling from the hall, "Luke! that bird of yours is making for the road. You'd better come and rescue it."

"Oh." Luke laughed now as he went towards the door, echoing his mother's words, "That bird of yours; why mine?"

Left alone with Daniel, Frances now sat at one end of the couch, and when Daniel still stood she said, "You may sit down and wait until the tea comes; we don't charge for waiting."

He did not consider the remark at all frivolous, like something Maggie Ann would voice, but he smiled, and for a moment was tempted to sit on the couch beside her, but decided that would be going too fast and be out of place at the moment, and so he made for a chair opposite her. When he was seated she asked, "You never managed to get to the market?"

"No; no, I didn't. But it wasn't for want of trying."

"Oh. So why didn't you make it?"

"I was told I was needed in the yard. Apparently the yard cannot get on without my presence there."

She smiled at him quietly; then her head bowed and her voice low, she said, "I…I was silly the other day; I mean, when I was with Janie. As Janie said, I was forward."

With some gallantry he replied, "If that's what you call forward I would welcome you being forward at any time; in fact, I'd look *forward* to it."

Her head came up and she laughed a free laugh, one that almost resembled Moira's, then she said, "You talk so politely, Daniel, sometimes as if you were reading it out of a book. Oh. Oh"—she closed her eyes tightly now as she saw his colour change—"you're blushing, and it's because I've embarrassed you. It's my silly tongue. I...I don't mean it." She leant towards him now, her forearms on her knees, her hands joined. "I...I want to say the right things but they never come out. I know I sound silly and forward—"

"No, you don't; to me you could never sound silly."

They were staring at each other in silence when Luke returned, saying, "I've had to put it in a pen;" then immediately added, "Oh, by the way, I saw Ray Melton. Isn't that his name? I met him at your house one Christmas and he remembered me and he asked after you, and he did say he was going to look you up, because his family are moving to Durham and he'd be much nearer to you. His people seem well off, judging by the way he was dressed and the carriage he was in. That was later, when I saw him in it with his parents. Well, I think they were his parents."

"Yes, they are tolerably well off; they have grocery shops."

"Tolerably well off, you say;" and Luke laughed. "I wouldn't mind if we were...as tolerably well off. And it's a pity you aren't too: you were going to be a doctor, weren't you?"

"Oh,"—Daniel's chin jerked nonchalantly—"that was just a dream."

"Do you think you'll like being a farmer?"

"Yes; yes, I'm getting to like it. You have a different feel about it when you are actually doing the work.''

"I'll say. I'll say." Then, as his mother came into the room carrying a large tray of tea things, he added, "Oh, here's the drink that puts leather in your guts."

"Luke!"

"All right, Ma, all right…"

The drinking of the tea and the eating of the buttered scones took half an hour; then Daniel knew it was time to take his leave, so, rising, he said, "I'd better be on my way or Rustler will have your front gate down. He hates being tied up. But I have enjoyed the tea, Mrs Talbot, and my visit altogether."

"Well, you must do it more often. We never seem to see any of you now." Then turning to her daughter, she said, "Go on, Frances, and walk with Daniel down to the turnpike. No further, mind; don't go on to the road." Then bringing her attention to Daniel again, she said, "See that she doesn't go on to the road, will you, Daniel? And send her straight back."

Without answering, he smiled as he turned to Luke, saying, "We'll be bumping into each other in the market soon," and Luke said, "Yes; yes, we will an' all."

"Goodbye, Mrs Talbot; and thank you again for the tea."

"Well, Daniel, I can only repeat, you can have that tea whenever you have a mind to call in for it."

Again he smiled, adding, "I'll take you at your word, Mrs Talbot," as he followed Frances from the room.

After untying the reins of the horse from the gate, he walked him along the path with Frances by his side.

Within forty yards or so of the house they had to pass through an area of woodland, before emerging on to a broader stretch of road that led to what had once been a toll gate, to the side of which stood the ruins of a cottage and, beyond, the coach road.

Until now they had walked in embarrassed silence, but here they turned and looked at each other, and it was she who spoke first, saying, "Will you be riding this way every Sunday?"

"Oh no,"—he shook his head—"Not riding. I'm only riding today because Father has sprained his ankle. He doesn't usually let me near Rustler. But he hasn't been exercised for some days now."

"Couldn't you ride one of your other horses? You have more, haven't you?"

"Yes; yes, I suppose so. But I also have a pair of legs." He looked downwards, and she too looked at his legs, his long legs, and she laughed as he said, "I suppose I *could* use them to get this far; it must be all of two miles."

Suddenly she thrust out a hand to him, and he gripped it and their gaze held. Then quickly turning from him, she picked up the front of her long dress and ran back down the road. At the wood she turned and waved, and he responded, then with almost a spring he mounted the horse, jumped it on to the road over a broad ditch that was bridged by wooden planks, and galloped it all the way back to the house.

But he did not see Frances the next Sunday, nor for a number of Sundays following, because little Catherine took the croup; and what was worse, Margaret and Annie both developed whooping cough. Sean had already had whooping cough but they hadn't needed to call the doctor. However, Margaret became so ill that Moira insisted Hector send for him, and he pronounced that indeed Margaret was ill, and that they had to watch out for pneumonia because, as everybody knew, that could be fatal. Oh, yes, yes. Dr Swift had wiped the saliva from his grey moustache and repeated, Yes, that could indeed be fatal. Did they happen to have any ale in the house? The best thing to do at present would be to make it hot by sticking a poker into it, add some ginger and gentian root, then feed it by the teaspoonful to the child.

After so saying, he promised to look in the next day; if they didn't send him further word there would be no need for his visit before then.

When he had gone, Maggie Ann stood on the landing, shouting, "Beer, ginger and gentian root! I wouldn't trust him as far as I could toss him to look after a mangy bullock. I'm not putting any gentian root into that potion. It's like bitter aloes."

Nevertheless, whenever the child could swallow she was given the hot ale with ginger.

It was Sunday afternoon and Daniel was sitting by Margaret's bed holding the child, who seemed to be gasping her last after another dreadful bout of coughing, when Moira, returning to the room with another steaming mug of ale, said briefly, "Another one?"

"Yes."

Then looking up at her, he said, "It's bad, and she's in a fever. She can't go on like this, Moira."

"No, she can't go on like this: she hasn't the stamina of the others. Look, you're tired. You were up all night; go and lie down."

"What about you?"

"Oh, I'm used to it. Now, if you won't lie down, why not take a run out? It's a nice day. It's a while since you went over to the Talbots. Oh, it's all right;

I've not been spying on you.'' She laughed. "Lilian called in yesterday for a minute. She said you had dropped in to tea.'' She bent over her child now and wiped the sputum from her lips as she added, "She's a bonny girl, that Frances. And Janie Farringdon is a nice girl, too.''

Another time he would have laughed and said, "What are you trying to do?'' but he made no response, not even to question why she had mentioned Janie Farringdon. He did say, though, "I'll go and get a breath of fresh air, but I'm not taking any strolls.''

On opening the bedroom door he was confronted by his father, but they passed each other without speaking. They had not said a direct word to each other for weeks now. It was always, Would you tell Father so and so? Or Moira would say, Your Father wants so and so done.

Further along the landing stood Sean, and the boy asked, "How is Margaret?''

"Much the same, Sean.''

"She's very ill, isn't she?''

"Yes, she's ill, Sean. Very ill.'' He turned the boy about and they walked together down the stairs and out on to the terrace.

The day was warm, the sky a deep blue. It was a day for walking, for walking the two miles to see Frances.

"You expect her to die, don't you?''

Daniel looked sharply down on the boy, saying, "No,'' and stammered, "No...no; no, I don't expect her to die. Well, I mean, she's very ill but—''

"People who get pneumonia nearly always die.''

Daniel continued to stare at this half-brother of his and, as before, he could not believe that he was but

five years old, because there was the oddity of age
already on him: he didn't think like a five-year-old, he
didn't talk like a five-year-old, he didn't look at you
like a child of only five years. And now he was really
startled when the boy said, "When Mama had the
baby that was dead, Maggie Ann said it was one less
to feed and that God had a way of evening things out.
D'you think that's what He means to do with Margaret?"

Daniel was unable to answer for a moment, then
dropping on to his hunkers he placed his hands on the
boy's shoulders and looked into his eyes as he said,
"Why do you say such things, Sean? What puts them
into your head? You know, you're only a little boy.
Don't you know you're only a little boy?"

"No. No! I just know I'm me an' that there's some
folks I like, some folks I love, and some I hate."

Slowly Daniel drew himself upwards, then turned
his face to the view before him. This child of five was
saying there were people he liked, and some he loved
and some he hated. Even he, coming up seventeen,
couldn't have expressed his feelings more plainly
about love and hate. He turned now and looked down
on his half-brother, but the child was gazing into the
distance. He thought, There's something uncanny
about him. He seems to be imbued with all the weird-
ness of the Irish, which was very noticeable in Maggie
Ann, and yes, in Moira too.

Of a sudden he shivered, and when he turned
abruptly to go indoors the boy followed him. And in
the hall he said, "May I sit up with her along of you
tonight, Daniel?" And Daniel, as if it were he who
was responsible for the boy's doings, said, "Yes. Yes,
you may sit up, but you'll likely fall asleep."

"I won't."

Again Daniel looked down on this fair-haired boy, and thought, No; if he says he won't, he won't.

The bedroom was like an oven heated by steam. Maggie Ann was sitting beside Margaret's bed. The child was breathing heavily as if she were asleep, but it was Maggie Ann who was asleep, whereas Sean, sitting near her, was wide awake, as were his mother, sitting opposite near the head of the bed, and Daniel towards the foot.

The sound of Margaret's breathing was such that each tearing breath seemed to cut into Daniel and he wished, for her own sake, that the end would come quickly.

When Moira sat back for a moment in her chair he put out his hand and caught hers; then, with his other hand, he hitched his chair nearer until now they were sitting side by side, both gazing at the child.

And that was the last thing he remembered until somewhere around dawn, when he awoke to see the light streaking through the curtains and the lamp about to gut itself out. Blinking through his bleared lids he looked to where Moira was fast asleep in the basket chair, then to the bed where, side by side, lay Margaret and Sean. They were hand in hand and both breathing deeply and regularly.

He sat transfixed by the amazing scene, a sight that made him shiver. And such was the effect on him that he did not move until Moira let out a long low sigh; and when she opened her eyes, he was quick to grip her hand as he motioned with his head towards the bed. "Dear God in heaven! 'Tis, Sean," she breathed; and to himself he repeated, "'Tis Sean," and he shivered again.

4

It was on Daniel's seventeenth birthday that he and his father again almost came to blows.

It had been a happy day: Moira and Maggie Ann had made him a birthday tea. The long dining-table had been piled high with an extraordinary amount of fancy things to eat. The family always ate well, but plainly; however, today there were jellies and iced buns, and coconut cones in various colours. And as well as the birthday cake there was a cold chocolate pudding.

Seated at the table had been Patrick, Sean, Margaret, Annabella and Annie. Catherine was placed in a high chair, while Michael bounced in his cot set to the side of the fireplace.

But also seated at the table were Frances Talbot, Janie Farringdon and Ray Melton. Frances and Janie had been invited by Moira, but Ray's visit had been unexpected. Being on his Christmas vacation and now living quite near in Durham, he had looked up his old school-friend and to his surprise had found that the sixteen-year-old schoolboy he remembered was no more, for he had been confronted by a seventeen-year-old young man. But they had both been pleased with the meeting and it was a natural thing for Daniel to invite him to stay to tea; and, surprisingly, Ray turned out to be the life and soul of the party. Then, after tea, he had brought squeals of delight from the children with his very real imitations of animals and birds, the squeals turning to screams when, imitating the cry of a monkey, he jumped up on the back of the padded couch and leapt along it on his hands and feet.

But no amount of coaxing from either Daniel or the children could get Moira to recite one of her funny poems. They were kitchen chatter, she said, and had no place in a birthday party.

When at six o'clock Mr Farringdon's carriage arrived to take his daughter and her friend home, Ray Melton also took his departure in his trap, and as Daniel stood in the drive watching the departure of his three friends, as he thought of them now, he told himself that he could not remember enjoying a day so much. He was so glad that Ray had looked him up again, and also that Janie Farringdon had come to his party, because Moira seemed to like her a lot. It was as if Janie were filling the place of Pattie in her life.

And then there had been Frances, his Frances, as he thought of her. She was so beautiful that at times there would pass over him a wave of feeling that bordered on ecstasy; but one which, at the same time, left him empty because it lacked fulfilment.

Maggie Ann's voice came bellowing at him from the door, "Come in out of that! You'll freeze to death…you haven't got a coat on."

Once he was in the hall she closed the door quickly behind him, then tugged at his arm, whispering, "Himself has just come in. He…he came in the side way a minute ago and has gone into the study. It looks as if he's got a bottle or two with him again. Strange, isn't it, lad, he hasn't been out to his meetings these last two weeks, have you noticed? He's brooding over something, so look out for squalls.'' Then, releasing her hold on his arm and her tone changing, she said aloud, ''Wasn't that a pip of a party! Oh, I've never enjoyed myself so much since I came across the water. And isn't that young fella a card, with his imitations? I've never seen anything like it. From a chicken to an elephant, he did, and that monkey business! Why! me stays nearly went with me laughing.''

He laughed now, saying, ''He used to do that at school and frighten the maids to death, especially when he roared like a lion on the attic stairs above which they slept.''

''And isn't that Janie a nice girl? No swank about her; and them rotten with money. You'd expect the likes of her to pump swank, wouldn't you?''

''Oh, Maggie Ann,''—he laughed outright—''one of these days you'll shock even me.''

''Now what have I said that is shocking? 'Tis just another name for wind.''

He was still laughing when he left her to put on his topcoat, cap and muffler so as to make the late round of the farm—it was his turn for the duty.

It was almost two hours later when he returned. Maggie Ann was in the kitchen, the children would be in bed. Moira, she said, was somewhere about. Did he want a cup of tea or anything? No; not till later, he said; after he'd been up to see the children.

On the landing, he could hear their voices calling to each other from their rooms in the guest corridor.

He opened the first door and poked his head round

it, saying, "Get to sleep, you two!" And Patrick called back to him, "'Twas a lovely party, Daniel. Could we have another one at Christmas like that?"

"Maybe," he said; "maybe. Good-night, Sean."

"Good-night, Daniel."

He pulled the door closed; then crossed the corridor and pushed open the door to the girls' room; and in the dim light he could just make out Margaret and Annie sitting up in bed close together, their faces beaming with smiles, and Margaret called, "Did you really like your birthday present, Daniel? We all had a hand in it."

"I did indeed, Margaret. It was just the very thing, because I'm going to start to smoke. I'm buying a pipe the next time I go into town."

"But the pipe rack holds four."

"Well, then, on my next birthday you can buy me another pipe to go in it, then another and another."

"I painted the back of it, Daniel."

"Did you, Annie? Well, it's a lovely colour. Now go to sleep. God bless."

"Good-night, Daniel. God bless."

"God bless, Daniel. Good-night."

He now went to his own room and there he lit his lamp, pulled the patchwork quilt from the bed and, putting it round him, sat in a deep easy chair to the side of his writing desk and, picking up a book, began to read.

He had got used to sitting like this. The only time he read by the fire in the drawing-room was when he was sure his father had gone out to his meetings, and it was impossible to read in the kitchen with Maggie Ann chattering all the time. He could, he knew, have brought wood and coal upstairs and lit a fire in the grate, but he didn't consider it worth the bother, because in a short while he'd go down and have some supper in the kitchen, then come back upstairs and read in bed...

And this was the procedure he followed on the evening of his seventeenth birthday. He'd had a good supper in the kitchen, seated at the table with both Moira and Maggie Ann. Then he had said good-night to them and they both had almost simultaneously answered, "Good-night, Daniel and a happy year ahead."

When, some time later, he'd undressed, got into his nightshirt and jumped between the cold sheets, he told himself again it had been a happy day, except for the fact that there had been no word exchanged between himself and his father. But what did it matter? Yet he knew that the situation could not continue as it was: at some time or other they would have to speak.

He was reading *Rural Rides* by William Cobbett and was amazed that this man who had started out as a farm labourer could have risen to such literary heights. It made him think how little he was doing with his own life, and at this stage he could see no sign of further accomplishment.

When the book almost fell out of his hands he wet the pads of his thumb and first finger and nipped out the flame of the candle.

The next moment he was wide awake, his shoulders off the pillow, his head turned to one side and listening to his father's yelling.

Getting quickly out of bed he groped for and pulled on a dressing-gown he had long since outgrown; then felt his way towards the door and out into the dark corridor.

Still groping, he made for the sound of the bawling

voice coming from the room at the end of the corridor, and he became still when his father's voice, reaching top pitch, yelled the words: "*What did you say?*"

Now Moira's voice came as loud, crying, "You heard what I said. I told you in the beginning, and I say it again now, you can have me at any time of the night or day when you're sober, but I'll not have you on my body when you are filthy drunk. I saw too much of it over there."

"You'll have me, woman, on your body whenever I think fit. Drunk or sober, d'you hear?"

"Yes, I hear. But you hear me now, Hector Stewart; you're working something off through your drink and I've a good idea what it is: your fancy woman has got tired of you. It must be that, because your twice-weekly meetings have ceased, haven't they? I'm not the thick, laughing Irish fool you've taken me for over the years: you married me because there was the promise of money in the offing. Well, I had my own reasons for marrying you, and one day I'll tell you what they were. In the meantime you're not going to take it out on me because you've lost your whore..."

When there came to him the sound of a blow as loud as a hard hand slapping a bullock's rump, he jumped forward and thrust open the door, an action which startled them both.

For a moment he stopped and gazed at them: at his father in his nightshirt, and Moira, one hand held to her face, the other now trying to cover her naked breasts with her torn nightgown.

"You hit her, you dirty cowardly scut, you!"

"Get out before I kill you. And I will. I will!" his father screamed. And almost with a leap Moira was in front of Daniel, forcing him back through the door, crying at him now, "Get away! For God's sake! Get away! Don't interfere. It's got nothing to do with you. Get away!"

Her manner and her voice seemed to sweep the hatred and anger from him, and for a moment he felt like a small boy who had crept into his parents' bedroom and witnessed something unusual. She gave him one hard push, then, turning quickly, she thrust her arms out and endeavoured to push her enraged husband back into the room; but so drunk was he that he staggered and fell on to the floor, and this enabled her to slam shut the bedroom door.

As Daniel stood leaning against the wall he became aware of a faint light penetrating the darkness, and he turned his head and looked towards the end of the corridor. There he could just make out the bulky figure of Maggie Ann, the candle lantern in her hand.

When he made his way towards her she said, "They've been at it?"

"He hit her. She'll be black and blue. It was like a thump; I heard it."

"He'll pay for it, never fear. I wish to God the devil would take him. But, lad, you shouldn't have interfered. You should never interfere in matters like that."

"But he was yelling the place down; and the things he said to her!"

"Well, again I say, you shouldn't be listenin'; like that, you hear more than what's good for you. Now get yourself to bed. It's a pity your day had to end like that, because it was champion: the nice lasses there and the lad and the bairns enjoying themselves." She had turned away and her voice faded as she mounted the attic stairs; but he remained standing where he was in the dark.

You hear more than what's good for you, she had said. Yes, perhaps he had. She…she, like his mother, was having to put up with the ignominy of knowing that she had to take a back seat; in fact, that she was there just to be used for breeding. And of the two he was more sorry for Moira, for she'd had to bear him six children, eight with the one that died and the one born dead. The thought made him close his eyes tightly and stare into a blackness darker still.

When he got into bed he stretched out his arms and gripped the brass rails of the bedhead, and he saw a picture of Frances; although it was overlaid by another of Moira and her large bare breasts. It wasn't the first time he had seen her breasts. He had watched her feeding the babies as they had come each year; at least, the first four. But the last two, he recalled, she had seemed to feed when he was out of the room. And of course he had only seen the operation during a comparatively short period while he was home for the holidays. But tonight he had seen her stripped bare almost to the waist. Then, his father in a nightshirt…he had looked ridiculous. Did all men look ridiculous in nightshirts? Did he look ridiculous in a nightshirt?

When he married Frances he wouldn't wear such a stupid garment; he wouldn't wear anything. His hands swung down from the rails and he turned on to his side and buried his face in the pillow.

The day before Christmas Eve he went into Fellburn in answer to Pattie's letter. She had asked him to call; she had a little present for him. She also said she was missing him. They had met a few times since she had left home, once in her in-laws' house, other times in the town; but this was the first time he had been to her house. And it came as a shock to him.

It was a small house, one of a long terrace. It had a blue-painted front door, two rooms downstairs and two rooms up. The stairs to the upper rooms led out of the living-room. The second room downstairs was a kitchen, with an open black range; and it held a white-topped table, four kitchen chairs and a dresser. There were two other doors, one leading to a scullery, the other into a back yard, where there was a coal-house and an outdoor dry lavatory, so called.

On opening the door to him her face lit up and she held out both hands, saying, "Welcome to our humble abode. Oh, come in, come in, Dan. It's so good to see you. How are you? John won't be long; it's nearly dinner time. Come in here."

He squeezed past her in the narrow passage so she could close the door; then she led him into what was their sitting-room. A fire was burning brightly in the grate. There was a chintz-covered couch and two easy chairs, a very ordinary looking sideboard, and a glass cabinet holding what he took to be, at first glance, cups and trophies of some kind.

"Oh, I am glad to see you. How are you?"

"Oh, all right."

"Just all right?"

"That's it, just all right. But you look blooming."

"I feel blooming, Dan. This"—she spread her hands wide—"must be past a surprise and a kind of shock to you. But I can tell you something: I've never been so happy in my life, and I want it to go on."

"I'm so glad for you, Pattie. I...I thought you might miss the house, and space, if nothing else."

"You know something, Dan? I grew to hate that

house as much as I did him. How is he faring, by the way?"

"I wouldn't really know, Pattie: we don't speak."

"*No?*" Her eyebrows were raised. "How d'you get on…I mean…well—?"

"Oh, Moira's the go-between."

"How long has this been going on?"

"Months; in fact, since the night you showed me the diaries. I made up my mind I wasn't going to say anything but he went for me because I had used the trap, and it all boiled out, and I nearly throttled him. I would have, too, I think, if Moira and Maggie Ann hadn't pulled me off him."

At that moment they heard the back door being opened, and she said, "Here's John now."

And when Daniel heard his stiff-necked, as he had always imagined, plain and unattractive sister call, "We're in here, dear," the look on her face almost made him envious.

John Watson was a man of middle height. He was fifteen years older than Pattie, but had an almost boyish youthfulness about him, and his handshake was firm. "It's good to see you again, Daniel," he said. "How are you?"

"All right, thank you. How are you?"

"Never better, Daniel." Then bending towards Daniel the while putting his arm about Pattie's waist and pulling her against his side, he added, "As I can't thank her father, I can thank you for having such a splendid sister."

Daniel noted that Pattie did not exclaim, as many another young woman would have done, Oh, go on with you! She just looked at her husband and smiled;

in fact, they smiled at each other. Then John said, "Well, now, I have an hour and fifteen minutes: I propose we eat for fifteen minutes and talk for the rest."

"Well, I don't mind eating for fifteen minutes, and I am quite willing to listen for an hour..."

John Watson did take up most of the hour in talking, his topics ranging from prime ministers and their politics to women's rights, and when Pattie said, "Your pudding's getting cold, dear," he paused for a while before starting again and saying, "Women have been treated abominably over the years, Daniel. They haven't been able to call their soul their own: even the clothes on their back belonged to the husband. But that's all changed now because the new law means that, in the future, a married woman owns what is hers by right."

Again Pattie interrupted John's flow. "Would you like tea or coffee, Dan?"

"Coffee, if you don't mind, Pattie."

"How's the farm going?" John asked, having interpreted the cue from Pattie that he had monopolised the conversation long enough.

"Not as well as farms should go, John."

"Are you going to stay on there?"

"I can't see me doing anything else in the near future. Quite candidly, Father's not the only one who's waiting for Moira to come into her money, because I am, too. Then I may be able to make a change and start a life of my own."

They drank the coffee in the sitting-room, the conversation being general until it was time for John to leave.

He shook Daniel's hand warmly, saying, "You

must be in town every now and again, so pop in, and if this door's shut come round to my people's; that one's always open. They take in stray dogs, cats, beggars, so they wouldn't mind a young strapping farmer.''

"Go on with you," Pattie pushed her husband towards the door, and Daniel noted that they stood for some time in the narrow passage before she returned to the room, saying, "That's John? So you can understand how I'm enjoying my new life.''

"Yes, he's a very interesting man, a highly intelligent one and a modest one into the bargain. Such men are rare.''

"That's the word, Daniel, rare. He doesn't know his own value.''

"Well, he knows *your* value.''

"I'm very lucky. I get fearful at nights at how lucky I've been, when I think that I might have been stuck in that house for the rest of my life because I had no assets except my mind.''

"Oh, Pattie, don't be silly. You are attractive; always have been.''

She smiled softly at him and as he looked at her he marvelled at the change in her, the all-round change. After a moment he said, "I too will have to be going because I have some shopping to do; little bits of things for the children.'' Then bowing his head, he said, "I'm sorry, Pattie, I haven't got a present for you. Quite candidly I haven't any money at all. He never gives me a penny. I've got to rely on Moira slipping me something. Whether he gives money to her with the intention that she should give me some kind of allowance, I don't know. Of course, I'm only doing half time on the farm; the rest is with the children. But still, during those three days I'm working hour for hour with the men. We'll have to have a showdown soon, or else I'll feel bound to make a move, in spite of Moira's pleadings. I wouldn't be there now if it wasn't for her."

"You want to face up to him and tell him you're going to walk out unless he gives you a wage of some kind."

"If I face up to him it'll mean another row and we'll likely come to more blows."

He picked up his overcoat from a chair, and as he did so she opened a drawer and took out a parcel. "It's nothing really," she said as she gave it to him, "and you'll find it full of mistakes. Believe it or not, I knitted it. It's what Moira would call a gansey."

"Oh, thank you, my dear. Thank you." And Daniel felt a great tenderness for her when, standing in front of him, she buttoned his overcoat from the neck downwards, then handed him his hat and, standing back from him, said, "Nobody would believe you're just seventeen. You could pass for twenty any day."

"I feel twenty; even older at times."

As she led the way to the door she said, "Are you seeing Frances Talbot these days?" And after a pause he answered, "Yes. Yes, I see her when I can."

They were standing in the passage, she with the outer door in her hand, when she looked at him and said, "Is it serious? I mean—"

"I know what you mean, Pattie. Yes, with me it is, and I think it is with her, too. Oh, yes, with her, too."

"You never thought about Janie Farringdon?"

He gave an embarrassed laugh now as he said, "You said that to me once before. No, I've never thought about Janie. She's a nice enough girl, but not for me. I think I've always loved Frances, and I can't imagine myself ever wanting anyone else.''

She leant forward now and kissed him on the cheek; then he went out, saying, "Happy Christmas, Pattie. And to John, too; I forgot to wish him it.''

"And the same to you, Daniel. And if I don't see you before the new year, let's hope it's a happy one for you.''

He turned his head away and pursed his lips but didn't confirm her words.

She watched him walk down the street. He was a fine-looking boy who looked like a man, but when he grew to manhood he would be striking. As she closed the door she said to herself, I wish it had been Janie he had fallen for. Frances is too beautiful to be good for him, or anyone else, for that matter; in fact, I think she's a flibbertigibbet.

5

It was 1888 and the second Sunday in June. Frances was walking with Daniel to the turnpike, and as they made their way through the wood, she said, "Oh, Ray is funny. You know, when he met us in the town yesterday and took Mother and me into that café for coffee, he did one of his animal imitations. It was of a hen cackling, and although he did it quietly and had Mother nearly choking, the people at the next table brought the three of us into fits, as the woman looked on the floor expecting, I'm sure, to see a hen. Oh, he is funny."

Stopping suddenly and pulling her round to face him he did what, for weeks past, he had told himself he would do on the following Sunday; he leant forward and kissed her on the lips.

Standing apart once more she looked first up the road then along the wood path before saying, "Oh, Daniel, you...you really shouldn't. Anyone could... could have come along."

"Have we ever before met a soul on this walk? Anyway, you wanted me to kiss you, didn't you? You wanted it as much as I did. That's why you kept on about Ray—"

"No. No, it wasn't." For a moment she was indignant; then, her head drooping, she said, "Yes, Daniel, yes, I did. I...I've been longing for you to kiss me."

"Oh, Frances." He put his arms around her now and, holding her close, he said, "I don't know why I haven't had the nerve to do it before. I've thought about you every night and what it would be like and... Oh! Frances." Again his mouth was on hers and now she was responding enthusiastically.

When the kiss was finished and their agitated breaths were fanning each other's face, he said firmly, "Will you marry me, Frances?" But when, in response, she went all coy again, saying, "Oh, my! my goodness! We've only... Well, I mean—" he almost barked at her, "Stop that! One minute you talk sensibly and the next like some silly village girl, with 'We've only...well' and 'Well, I mean...'"

When, with surprising strength, she pushed him violently away, his back came up against a tree, and there he remained staring at her as in a voice as strident as his, she cried, "I'll thank you not to link me up with silly village girls. One minute you ask me to marry you, and then you tell me what you think of me. Well, as my father says, there's more fish in the sea than has ever been caught. And you're not the only one who has been wanting to kiss me, let me tell you; and *his* people are loaded with money and not breaking their necks to make ends meet." And on this she bounced her head at him before flouncing away.

He made no move to follow her, nor did he make any call to her to stay, but gazed after her in amazement. She had given him a big taste of her sensible side and he didn't like it. He knew she was referring to Ray, but he felt positive she was jumping to conclusions there, because Ray was jolly with everyone. His aim in life seemed to be to make others laugh; in a way he was akin to Moira and Maggie Ann. Moreover, Ray was his friend, the only real friend he had.

His head drooped, and walking slowly and thoughtfully he made his way towards home. He was already apologising to her in his mind and what was more, next Sunday he would speak to her father and ask him if he was agreeable to his courting her. And if that was made public, well, then they would be engaged...then they would get married. When? This he didn't know; he could put no date to it, because he'd have to earn a living now.

His step quickened: he must speak to his father straight out and tell him he'd have to have some kind of a permanent wage, or go into the town and find work. One thing—there would be no need to worry about accommodation: Pattie and John would welcome him.

He had it all cut and dried; it just needed carrying out.

It was the following morning at about nine thirty when Maggie Ann's voice calling stridently, "Daniel! Daniel!" brought him and the children from the schoolroom on to the landing, and there, looking down on the excited face of Maggie Ann, he asked, "What is it?"

"Come down here a minute. I have news for you...no, not you lot! Get back into your lessons, every one of you."

"I want a wee-wee, Maggie Ann."

"You're havin' no wee-wee at this minute, Annie. 'Tisn't five minutes ago since you emptied your bladder, so get back with the rest of them there. See to her, Patrick; and you'd better put her on the pot in case she wets the floor."

By the time Maggie Ann's tirade had ended Daniel had reached the foot of the stairs, and now she drew him by the arm along the short passage and into the corridor. There she stopped and, her hands now clasped between her great breasts, she said, "It's come at last: God's taken her. A letter's just arrived. She died on Thursday, and likely they're putting her into the ground at this minute, God rest her soul." She looked up towards the ceiling. "The letter's from Brian. He says he'll be over, once the will's been read, to see herself. Oh, I can't believe it." She stretched her arms wide. "After all these years of waiting she'll have a bit of money of her own, and a big bit at that, from what I understand. And I've warned her to see that he doesn't get his hands on it, but to put it straight into the English bank. And put your name on it, I said. But she's got it all planned out. We'll go right into the heart of Newcastle and first she'll rig out the bairns and then see to herself, because she's never had a new thing for God knows how long."

"Does my father know?"

"Oh yes, he knows. He's in the study with her now. And you know something? He spoke civil to me. For the first time in his life he's spoken civil to me. You know, Daniel, that man represents all Englishmen, 'cos when he wants anything he'll kiss you on the mouth, an' when he's got it he'll put his toe in your arse. So I've warned her, 'Don't listen to his palaver,' I said, for it'll be another horse he wants, a hunter.

Oh aye, not a plough horse, an' the carriage mended and his debts paid. Anyway, lad, God send Brian quickly. But while I'm on about what she'll do with the money, one of the first things will be too see to you, lad, and put you on your feet, perhaps send you back to your learnin', if that's what you want.''

As she hurried away all smiles, he climbed the attic stairs again, a smile on his face, for the prospects were bright. She would set him up; yes, he was sure of that. Whatever he wanted to do she would set him up. But he would have to go back to school to get to university. Oh no! not that now because, in that case, it would be years before he could think of marrying Frances. No, he would start some business, a shop of some kind. The Meltons started in a small way, so he understood, with a house window shop over the water in Howdon. Well, he could start in a small way too.

As he re-entered the schoolroom Patrick demanded, ''What is it, Daniel? What's Maggie Ann so excited about? Is it good news?''

''Yes, it's good news, Patrick.'' He patted the boy's dark head, then sat down at the table and, looking from one to the other, he said, ''How would you like to go into Newcastle to the shops and have new clothes bought you?''

''A real suit, with knickerbockers?''

''Yes, Patrick, a real suit, with knickerbockers.''

''I want a pretty dress.''

''Well, you'll have a pretty dress, Margaret.'' Now Daniel looked at Sean. ''What would you like, Sean?'' he asked him.

The boy lowered his head to one side for a moment, then said, ''I'll have a big cap, one that comes over me ears and covers me nose, shuts me mouth up and reaches me toes.''

As they all laughed, Daniel put his hand across the table and gently slapped the hand that was holding the slate, and Patrick cried, "He's like Mama, he's got a silly head."

"Your mother hasn't got a silly head," Daniel reprimanded the boy now. And Patrick said, "I didn't mean silly, but always making up rhymes."

"Come on, all of you, back to work. We were counting the sheep that were left in the field after the farmer had lost four and bought six."

Just as Daniel was about to ask, Well, how many are in the field now? seeing that there were twenty-nine in the beginning, Moira's voice was heard calling, "Daniel! Daniel!" Once again he sprang up, and this time the children came with him and followed him on to the attic landing where, from the foot of the stairs, she cried, "Come down a minute. Yes. Yes, and let them come too. All of you! All of you!"

When once more he was standing in the corridor, with the children bouncing round them, he looked at Moira and said quietly, "I'm so glad, Moira."

She now linked her arm in his, and as they walked towards the stairhead she said, "If you are glad, boyo, just imagine how I feel at this moment. From a child, I have known that my Auntie Mattie loved me. She hadn't any children of her own and she would have taken me, only my ma wouldn't let me go. But she always said that whatever she had was mine. That was before she married O'Leary, and he was a man of property, and although she was my father's aunt there was no love lost between them. And really, she couldn't stand my ma or the rest of the family, but she

would come and she would stay for weeks on end."
She started to laugh now, so much so that her body
shook as she said, "She would eat us out of house
and home and not bring a victual in nor leave a penny
when she went. She did it on purpose; she had a funny
sense of humour. At times we used to laugh together
about nothing, laugh until the tears ran down our faces.
That seemed to be her motto, laugh it off. But I can
tell you, me ma and da didn't laugh after she had gone,
yet they would welcome her again with open arms as
soon as she put her nose in the door." Moira's laughter faded and as she went down the main staircase she
muttered, "But she stood by me; she always stood by
me, and for that alone I wish her a long and happy
rest in heaven."

For the next three days everyone in the house was
on tenterhooks. They didn't know when Brian would
arrive. When eventually he did, surprisingly early on
the Thursday morning, it was at exactly a quarter to
nine. Apparently he had got a lift on a carrier's cart
that passed the boundary of the farm on its way to
Durham.

"Oh, Brian, Brian, am I glad to see you." Before
she had taken in his expression Moira had thrown her
arms around her brother. And when Maggie Ann appeared in the hall she too embraced him, greeting him
the while, and when she finished with, "You're like
the sight of God's holy angel," he answered, "I hope
you'll go on thinking that, but I doubt it."

It was at this point that they both looked closely at
him. And now Moira, the wide smile having left her
face, said, "Come on in, come on in to the drawing-
room. Have you had your breakfast?"

"Yes, I had a good meal in the town. I slept there overnight, 'cos it was late when I got in."

"Oh, you slept in the town, in an hotel?" This was from Maggie Ann, because an hotel spelt money.

"No, not in an hotel, in a lodging house; a boarding house, as they call them. It was clean and decent and the breakfast was good. I think you had better sit down, both of you."

Neither of the women said another word but did as he said, and as Brian took another seat and began with the words, "Prepare yourself," the drawing-room door was thrust open and Hector entered, a broad smile on his face as he exclaimed, "Hello! there, Brian." His hand was outstretched as Brian rose from the chair to take it, saying solemnly, "Hello to yourself."

"You're early. Did you travel overnight?"

"No, I've just been telling them, I spent it in the town."

"Oh, oh. Have you eaten?"

"Yes, yes. I would sit down."

"Sit down? Why should I?" Hector's voice had changed.

"Well, stand if you like. It's up to every man to greet disaster in his own way."

"What d'you mean, disaster?" The words seemed to have been dragged through Moira's lips. She was sitting now, her hands clasped tightly in her lap, her eyes unblinking; then she said, "Get on with it. What is it?"

"She potched you. The old girl potched you, Moira. She diddled you as she diddled everybody all her life. She is where she is now, laughing. I hope she frizzles in hell because what I'm goin' to say isn't only hurtin' you, it's hurtin' us, an' all; because you always said we'd have a share in it, didn't you?''

''But the will?'' It was a small voice coming from the large frame of Maggie Ann. ''She always said her will was made out.''

''Oh, aye, Maggie Ann, it was made out and right from the beginning.''

''How much have I got?''

Brian looked at Moira now, saying quietly, ''One hundred pounds.''

As Moira lay back in the chair and closed her eyes the door opened and Daniel came in. He was smiling but the smile slid from his face when he observed the group in the middle of the room, three seated and one standing and not one of them taking the slightest notice of his entry. He stayed where he was just within the doorway and listened to Maggie Ann now yelling, ''A hundred pounds! You can't mean it, Brian, you can't mean it. Where's the rest gone?''

''Well, where d'you think?'' Brian glowered at her. ''To the bastard. All eleven thousand, nine hundred pounds of it, and all tied up nicely and nobody can touch it. Da was goin' to make a claim because he was her nearest surviving relative but he soon found out that was useless. He might have stood some chance, so it was said, if it had been a few years earlier, but there are new laws now about women inheriting. Anyway, there it is.''

''Who is this...this bastard you talk about?'' Hector's voice came menacingly from low in his throat.

Brian looked at him, then glanced at Moira before looking back at the man again and saying, ''She hasn't told you?''

''Told me what?''

"Oh," Brian got to his feet, "well, that's up to her. Why d'you think that, us bein' Catholics, didn't kick up hell's shindies about her marryin' in a God-forsaken registry office? If she had been without taint you would have never got near her unless it was through a priest and the Mass."

It was Maggie Ann who rose to her feet now and, putting her hand out towards Brian, she said, "Come away, come away into the kitchen." And after he had cast one look between his sister and her husband, he allowed Maggie Ann to lead him from the room; and Maggie Ann left the door open, expecting Daniel to follow her, which he did, as far as to step into the hall, but there he turned and looked to see Moira, on her feet now. Facing his father, she cried bitterly, "He's right for once. D'you think they would have let you marry me, you a Protestant and, as he said, in a registry office, if it wasn't that they wanted to get rid of me because I had sinned? *Oh, yes, I had sinned*: but if it had been with one of the clan it wouldn't have mattered, they would have had me married off. But he happened to be an English soldier. And so, while still fifteen, I gave birth to a daughter and I've never seen her since. She was adopted, and I was left on their hands and no decent man would have me. But you came along and—" She was gabbling now.

Hector made no move; nor did he speak for a moment until, as if the substance of her words had just penetrated his mind, he yelled, "You! you bitch, you! You came to me supposedly as pure as a virgin. You acted like one that night. God!" He put both hands to his head now and seemed to tear at his hair, while he went on, "And you've had the audacity, you, you filthy scut, to deny me my rights. And now the bait you held out has turned into rotten fish. Not a penny! God in heaven! I'll throttle you, woman.''

As he made to spring, so did Daniel, only to find himself gripped from behind and hearing Maggie Ann's voice yelling over his shoulder, ''I wouldn't lay hands on her if I was you. Her brother's in the kitchen and he's not only good with his fists, he's a champion knife-thrower, won prizes at the fair for it.'' Her voice was almost a screech now: ''Don't! if you value your neck, lay hands on her.''

When Hector turned and dashed up the room towards Maggie Ann, she pulled Daniel to the side, and as Hector brought his quivering fists in front of her face, he cried, ''One day, before you leave this house, I'll drive that between your eyes.''

And she answered him grimly, but quietly, ''It'll be with your dying breath, then.''

Again he had his hands to his head; and now he was rushing across the hall and to the front door, while Maggie Ann, pushing Daniel into the room, said to him, ''Comfort her. I must go to Brian and get him out of this house as quick as possible, or God alone knows what'll happen next.''

Quietly, Daniel closed the drawing-room door behind him and just as quietly walked up the room to where Moira was sitting, her elbows on a sofa table, her head resting in her hands. And he hesitated before he touched her because through his mind there was running the thought: She had a child before she came to Father. And she'd had to sleep with him all these years and bear his children likely without ever loving him. And then there was the fact that she, having had a child, seemed to drive his father mad, even though he himself had had mistresses for years. But would the fact of her having had a child have mattered if she had been left the money? Maybe, but perhaps not so much; no, not so much. The world was topsy-turvy and, in a way, dirty.

Moira raised her head now. Her face was dry: she hadn't been crying, but there was a depth of sorrow in her eyes as she looked at him and said, "You are shocked?"

"No, Moira, no."

She looked away from him and down the long room and her voice was barely a mutter now as she said, "You've no idea, boy, what it was like living in that house knowing that I was condemned to it for years; and not really because I'd had a child, for if it had been to an Irishman, somebody they knew, it might have even been laughed off—many of the children round about didn't know who their fathers were, anyway. But, you see, he was an Englishman, a soldier, and I loved him and he loved me. Although we were both very young we knew we loved each other, really loved." She turned now and, her head back, she looked up into his face, saying, "That is why I have loved you, because, in a way, you are so like him. He was tall and slim with that same look on his face that you have at times, and he was kind; but he was English, and a soldier, and so to them he was the devil incarnate. And what did they do? He was killed. The man they had picked out for me to marry, he shot him, supposedly because I had been brought to shame; but no, the killer was a member of a Fenian movement and out to destroy anything that was English. You have no idea of the feeling of hate that surrounds them; no, not surrounds, but threads through them all for anything English. They are all carrying on a fight

that started hundreds of years ago. True, they had suffered at the hands of the landlords, and were still suffering, but they couldn't see that there are ordinary
English people the same as there are ordinary Irish
folk.''

"Your daughter, you have never seen her?"

"No; from the time they took her from the bed
where Maggie Ann had laid her by my side, I only
know she was passed over to Auntie Mattie, and from
there she was passed on to a family. But I could never
get Auntie Mattie to tell me who or where these people
were. But now"—she gave a small hard laugh—
"she's a rich woman, and Auntie Mattie had the last
laugh. I should hate her, but I can't, because she knew
me and she knew that had she left me all that money
I would have halved it with them at home. I don't
think she would have minded so much the money being spent here, but she would have if any of the family
had laid hands on it, particularly her nephew, and
Brian himself. She was the only one who knew that I
was seeing Paul. That was his name, Paul Brownlow,
from the county of Essex in England. He would have
married me, oh, yes, he would have married me. He
didn't even know that I was carrying his child when
they shot him. It was dear, dear patriotic Brian himself
that saw me meeting him; then they practically tied
me up in the house so that I wouldn't see him again.
But when the child began to show then the sparks flew
and the Fenian boys demanded justice.''

He heard himself say, "Didn't you care for Father
at all when you married him?"

"I liked him. Anyway, I wouldn't have cared who
I married at that time. My only desire was to get out
of that house and away from the stigma that was like

a red cross on my back, and on my front. It could have been painted there. I even heard women in the market say that Paddy Mulcahy had to flee the country because of me; not that Paddy Mulcahy had killed an innocent man, not in battle or skirmish, but in the back of the head as he was walking along a street, and''— she turned to Daniel again—''the life here appeared like heaven. Can you understand that? But strangely, you know, Maggie Ann never has thought that way, and she would go back again into that house if it wasn't for me. But then, of course, to them she is clean, untouched, pure as the Virgin Mary herself.'' Her voice rose now almost to a cry as she exclaimed, ''Those men! They can drink until they are senseless, they can whore until they're worn out; they can practise cruelty, both mental and physical, on humans and animal alike, yet let one of their own clan, the female of course, just have one lick of the apple that they can chew to the core and they are damned. I've sometimes known families who have sent their daughters over to this hated England rather than suffer the shame of them giving birth to a bastard there.

''Why did God make us so unequal''—she was now stabbing the question at Daniel—''eh? You're on the verge of manhood: there are needs stirring in you, and you'll give vent to them sooner or later. But should that girl, that Frances you're so gone on, should her needs cause her to let them be eased by another young fellow or whatever, what would you say? You, the kind understanding Daniel, the man in you, what would he say? I know what he would say, Daniel, I know what he would do: he would make you throw her off as if she was a leech stuck on your skin, because the manhood in you would have been affronted.

But, of course, had she eased herself with you it would have been different; and you may have married her, but once you owned her, the fact that she had been easy pickings would have stuck in your craw... Oh, don't look like that, boy; I know what I'm talking about.'' She turned from him now, her hand going up to her brow as she exclaimed, ''And oh dear God! this day's just beginning; there'll be an end to it.'' And she left the room leaving him standing, stunned by her knowledge, not only of those men among whom she had been brought up, but of himself.

As Moira said, the day wasn't over, and it really didn't end until eleven o'clock that night.

Before Daniel went up to bed she said to him, ''Now, Daniel, when he comes in he'll likely be the worse for drink... What am I saying? He *will* be the worse for drink; he'll be roaring mad. Now, whatever you hear, whatever happens, keep out of it. It isn't your business, and believe me, Daniel, I can take care of myself. I can handle this, and I'll do so in my own way. Now go on up an' stay in your room no matter what happens. I'll be all right; I've made my own arrangements.''...

He was first made aware that his father had returned when he heard the distant shouting, then the sound of banging and thuds as if the furniture in the study were being thrown around, the effect of which was heightened because that room was situated partly under his bedroom.

When the banging and thudding ceased there was a period of quiet for about ten minutes, and then his father's voice came to him as if it were outside his door, yelling, "Come back into the room, you bitch! I haven't finished with you; I haven't even started."

There was the sound of a door being opened and banged closed, followed by a noise indicating that a door apparently wouldn't open, for now his father was thudding on it with his fists as he yelled, "Open this bloody door or I'll kick it in. D'you hear me, you dirty Irish slut, you! All these years hoodwinking me: the innocent laughing girl, the sweet pure Irish rose! God in heaven! it's as that ignorant Paddy said, you made no fuss about where you would be married, and they would have let you be married in a brothel to get rid of you!"

When there followed the sound of kicking, Daniel got out of bed and stood near his door; but he didn't open it. And now he bit on his lip as he heard his father use mouthful after mouthful of cursing and filth to describe what he thought of Moira. When at last the tirade ceased, there came the sound of the children crying and he knew that she must have the two youngest in the room with her.

"All right! All right!" his father was now yelling, "there'll come tomorrow, when you'll have to face me, and begod! you won't see out of your eyes for a week, I promise you, I promise you. And I promise you more than that, for there's going to be changes here. Oh yes, that fat hulk downstairs is going back across the water quicker than she ever moved before. And as for my eldest son...are you listening? your stepmother's favourite boy. Well, pin your ears back, because from now on your soft job of tutoring is finished. It's a six to six day for you in future and day in and day out, and see how you like that. And you'll do it, won't you? because she's got you tied to her

apron strings. Her blarney has got to you an' all, and
from the beginning you've supped from her like a new
born lamb! As the saying goes among that dumb-
headed, treacherous lot of Irish, hell's cure to you!''

PART THREE

PART THREE

1

"One pound, five shillings, Mr Stewart."

"One pound, ten shillings, Mr Baxter."

"Oh, come on, come on, Mr Stewart, have a heart, the place is swamped with carrots."

"It may be, but these are clean and all of a size. One pound, ten shillings, *Mr Baxter*."

Daniel smiled as he stressed the man's name and the wholesaler shook his head, saying, "I can't do it. I can't do it. If I let you push me up on this, it'll be the same for the beans and the peas an' the whole lot."

"Well, there's always McIntyre's."

"You wouldn't have the nerve to go to him after that do a few years back, would you?"

"Oh, yes, I would, Mr Baxter; we're on speaking terms again. He just bid me good-day coming through the market. And anyway, you were in that do yourself. Now weren't you?"

"No, no. I...I never bought things on the side, nor gave backhanders, never, not from any of the carriers. And from your men, never. I might have given them the price of a pint now and again—"

"Oh, yes, yes, the price of a pint. Well, we won't rake it all up. One pound, seven and six."

The wholesaler shook his head, saying, "I never used to have this trouble, you know, when your men brought the stuff in. Well, all right, all right, let's get it all reckoned up. What have we here? A hundredweight of onions, four hundredweight of taties. Oh, by the way——" he stopped in his reckoning, saying, "you know the fellow you sacked, Fairbrother, over the backhanding business? well he's on his uppers. He called in here yesterday and said if I saw you, would I put a word in for him, because he understood that things were bucking up on the farm, and you were thinking about taking on another man because his place has never been filled. You would have no trouble with him if you did."

"Oh," Daniel jerked up his chin, "that doesn't really lie with me; it will depend on what my father says."

"Will it, Mr Stewart?" The wholesaler was grinning now. "I hear that for all that matters you're practically running that place now."

"You should never believe all you hear, you know that, Mr Baxter. Anyway, what d'you make it?"

"Ten pounds and fourpence to the penny."

The wholesaler counted out the money and laid it on top of a barrel, and Daniel, picking it up, said, "Well, I guess you'll make twice as much out of that lot."

"Oh, listen to you. Listen to you. You don't take into account the overheads and the stuff they bring back from the stalls that'll be rotten in a couple of days. Double the amount? I'll be lucky."

"You always have been, Mr Baxter, you always have been. Good-day to you."

"Good-day to you, Mr Stewart." And now the wholesaler watched the tall young fellow in the tweed jacket and the brown leggings stalk out of the warehouse, and he shook his head as he said to himself, "You wouldn't believe it, would you? the difference in that lad, or the lad that was two or three years ago. Then, he hardly knew a bull from a bullock, and look at him now, running that place, and the house gardens, too, with only three hands, it is said. Of course, there was his father, but everybody knew what his father was like, hardly ever sober, all since that trouble with his wife, he understood, the Irish woman, when her fortune didn't transpire. He had been banking on that for years, apparently. And it was rumoured too that he used to have a woman in the town, but she went off to America with some bloke, and he had a drinking bout then an' all. At one time that farm and house were classy, but that was when the young fellow's mother was alive. Quite a lady she was, but very reserved, not like the present Mrs Stewart, a full-blown woman, but bonny and pleasant, Oh aye, as pleasant as they come."

He turned now and examined the produce that Daniel had brought in and he nodded to himself, saying, "That was a good guess; perhaps not double, but near enough. Good quality stuff. Yes, good quality stuff..."

Daniel drove the cart round the outskirts of the market, across the main thoroughfare and into a side lane that was bordered by a field, and it was into this that he turned and brought the horse to a stop facing the way he had come, and sat waiting.

Leaning back against the iron rail that supported the high seat, he let himself indulge in a moment of satisfaction. He reckoned that on the whole deal he had raised Mr Baxter four and sixpence. Then his body stiffened as he thought, And *he's* not getting that, or even half of it. I'll pay the men first, then take my own wage, and give Moira her due, and a pound extra for shoes for Patrick, Sean, and Annie: then he'll be lucky to get what's left.

In his mind now, he began to wonder as to how this present situation had come about. He had hated his father before the night when he had aimed to kick Moira's door in, but since then he had despised him as he watched him slowly disintegrate into a drunken sot.

There had been a period of bawling and shouting and threatening which Moira seemed to sail through unperturbed. This had been replaced with a sullenness, when he would hardly speak for days until he had taken on another load of drink, after which it would be maudlin talk of his ruined life and the no-good family he had reared.

But when the real cause of his father's trouble had been made known to Daniel he found it hard to believe. One day Moira had said to him, ''You've got to be sorry for your father, Daniel, and I mean that. He's lost something, the only thing…person he ever loved in his life. The woman, or the girl as she was then, became as much of a torment to him as she was to your own mother. Well, she hasn't been a torment to me, for I understood his need. He never loved me, nor I him. As I told you, I loved one man and unfortunately for your father, he loved only one woman. And one night he threw her at me: he told me all about her. At the time he wasn't fully drunk, just talkative. Apparently he had known her since she was fifteen...known her in all ways. And then he had tried to give her up when he married me, because at that time there was still a sense of fairness in him. However, it was no good; he found he couldn't live without her. Well, his little girl grew up and he must have tried to hang on to her by spending the money on her that should have been spent on the farm and the children, if not on me. But it obviously wasn't enough, for she left him for another man and he's been lost ever since.''

Staring along the road towards where he knew Frances would appear at any minute, he asked himself if he were to lose her, would he feel the same as his father had done about that girl: would he go to pieces? For a moment he received no answer, but when it came he was surprised, because it said, No; you would fight to keep your pride. But then he actually shook his head: what was he thinking about? That would never happen to him.

He now sat bolt upright on the seat: there was his girl, his lovely Frances. The sight of her in the distance, even the way she walked, the way she held her head, everything about her enchanted him. They were to be engaged at Christmas. It would have been at this time last year, except that her father put a stop to it, saying she was too young, which was a stupid reason, because only a few weeks previously she had been bridesmaid at her cousin's wedding, and the bride had been eighteen years old. No; her father wanted to see how he made out. He had even asked him if he was thinking of taking a farm of his own when he eventually got married, not saying openly that he wasn't going to allow his daughter to start her married life in her father-in-law's house, with two Irish women and the madcap squad of children that roamed wild around the place. And, of course, her father was right, because he, Daniel, could never bring Frances back to the house as a bride; he'd have to have some place of his own. How it was to come about, though, God only knew. He would just have to follow Moira's advice: take things as they come and it would all work out in the end. He had done so before.

He jumped down from the cart and ran towards her, and there being no-one in the lane, he put his arms around her and kissed her; and she kissed him back, saying on a gasp, "Oh! Daniel; it's like escaping from prison trying to get away on my own. I wouldn't have managed it this morning but we met up with Janie and her mother. So Father left us to go into the market, and Mother, good soul that she is, said, 'Off you go! Ten minutes, no more.' Oh, Daniel.'' She lay back in the circle of his arms and moved her head slowly as she said, "Why weren't you born a rich man?"

And he smiled at her, saying, "I was, comparatively; well, what you would call warm; but things have cooled down a lot since then."

She laughed gently as she stroked his cheek: "You have a wonderful way of looking at things. You never seem to be without hope."

"Oh; oh, don't you believe it: I'm devoid of hope every night when I lie in bed awake yet dreaming and hoping for the day when—'' his jaws tightened now and he pulled her roughly towards him, and again he was kissing her.

After a moment and slightly breathless she said, "I was over having tea with Janie yesterday, and who do

you think called in? Your dear friend, Ray. You know
something? He's sweet on her. I used to think it was
me.'' She pulled a face at him. ''But no; there they
were talking twenty to the dozen. To tell you the truth
I felt out of it; their conversation went over my head.
They were talking about Wilkie Collins. I don't know
whether he's just died, but they were chattering away
about him and Matthew Arnold. Apparently *he* died
last year. I asked them if they had been left anything
in his will, and of course our Luke had to butt in,
saying, 'Don't show your ignorance.' But I told them,
the three of them, I knew as much about books as they
did and, I bet, more about Mrs Henry Wood's stories.
Anyway, there it is; you're not the only one that's
going a-courting, Mr Stewart; your dear friend, I'm
sure, has his eye on our Janie. Of course—'' she drew
herself from his arms and they walked up the path
towards the horse and cart as she went on, ''they'll be
well-matched because she's brainy. I've always envied
her. You know, Daniel, nature is not a good divider:
it often gives you a pretty face, but not much on
top—''

''Don't talk such rot. You've got a mind that can
match Janie's any day.''

She stopped and looked at him and said tenderly,
''You think so, Daniel? You really think I'm as clever
as Janie?''

''It isn't a matter of being clever; you've got everything that Janie hasn't: you've got beauty and personality. Oh, my dear...'' His arms were around her
again, and he pressed her close as she replied, ''I'd
like to believe you, oh, I would, but I know you're
just being kind as usual. Compared with Janie I'm a
numskull.''

"Don't you say that ever. To me you're beautiful and bright. Oh, my dear, my own Frances, you're like a star, one single star shining in a dark sky. And you know, sometimes that's what my life is like on the farm: a dark sky, and I can't see a way out. Yet you keep me going with hope that some day…some day… Must you go now?"

"Yes, darling, I must." She had pressed herself from him, "Look"—she now thrust her hand into the pocket of her dust-coat—"I picked up this bent penny from the road this morning. Carriage wheels must have gone over it. Look." She held it up before his face. "You know what they say about a bent penny; it's lucky. Take it and prove it right, because…oh—" she bit on her lip for a moment before whispering, "I want us married, and soon. Oh, Daniel," and in an impetuous movement she now flung herself on him and her mouth covered his; then quickly thrusting him away again, she sped down the lane, leaving him trembling.

When she had passed from his view he looked down at the black bent penny and his hand closed around it, and he gripped it until his nails dug into his palm. Then he turned and went back to the cart and drove home: and there the bent penny was to demonstrate its luck.

In the farmyard he handed the horse and cart over to Barney, who asked him straight away, "Well, how did it go? Did you get your price?"

"Not quite, but near enough. Of course, I didn't expect the top, but I'm satisfied."

As Barney went to unharness the horse he muttered, "Your father's been through. Took the small cart and some sheep. Bob followed him to the road. He wasn't making for the market, but upwards, likely to Ted

Brownlow's; he butchers in his spare time, and butchers the price an' all. Like goin' to a moneylender, goin' to him. Thought you'd better know.''

Daniel drew in a sharp breath between his clenched teeth before he said, ''Yes, I'd better know. Thanks, Barney.'' Then he turned and hurried back through the yard and towards the house.

As he neared the drive he stopped, for drawn up at the steps was a private carriage. A groom was standing by it, and when Daniel came abreast of him the man touched his hat and said, ''Sir.'' Daniel inclined his head towards him but did not speak.

In the hall he heard voices coming from the drawing-room, and with cautious steps he made his way towards it.

Quietly he opened the door, then became still. Two women were sitting facing each other; one was Moira, but his eyes became riveted on the other, for she too was Moira as she might have been twenty years ago.

Moira rose to her feet and held out her hand towards Daniel as he came hesitantly up the room. And when she brought him to a halt opposite the seated young woman and, with evident pride in her voice, said, ''This, Daniel, is my daughter,'' the young woman inclined her head, responding, ''How d'you do?'' And the tone of her voice and her manner put her immediately in the same class as the carriage outside, and his surprise left his mouth agape until, seeming to come to his senses, he said, ''Pardon me. I must appear stupid; the likeness staggered me, you are so like Moira. But''—he gave an embarrassed laugh—''of course you would be, wouldn't you?''

''Sit yourself down, Daniel, and listen to this. 'Tis strange what she tells me. Her name is Melissa''—she smiled as she nodded from one to the other—"and she's been living all these years in Carlisle. Now can you believe that? She tells me she knew nothing about me. Isn't that so?"

The young woman nodded, saying, "Yes, that is so, and...and I might never have been told if I wasn't about to be married and leave the country. I'm off to France very soon: my husband-to-be is French, and my mama"—one shoulder gave the slightest of shrugs now—"well, I must now say my *adoptive* mama, is half-French, and as my adoptive father died last year she's going back to her people and my marriage is to be to a friend of that family—"

"But...but weren't you told anything when you inherited the money from"—he indicated Moira with his hand, then added—"her Aunt Mattie?"

"No. No. When I received that money I imagined it was because Mrs Harding was a friend of my mama's and she had no other relatives to whom to leave her money. If I had known of the circumstances then I would have surely, well, if not refused it, have shared it with you." She was looking at Moira now, and Moira said, "Yes, I'm sure you would, my dear, I'm sure you would. But never mind about the money; you didn't tell me how you managed to find me."

"Oh, my mama did that. She got an agent in Ireland to find out discreetly if you were still living there and she was informed that you had married a English gentleman, a farmer, and that the farm was somewhere in the county of Durham. Well, it was quite easy from then." The young woman smiled, then said sadly, "I'm sorry our meeting has been so long in coming."

"You...you don't hold it against me, my dear?"

"Oh, no, no. And I've been so fortunate to have

been brought up by the Cunninghams and to have received such an education—''

"They are a wealthy family, then?''

"Yes, they are wealthy people.''

Daniel looked at this girl, this young and beautiful young woman, this cultured young woman, this daughter of Moira, who had lady stamped all over her. It was in her voice, in her manner, in her bearing. She had a certain dignity about her; there was none of the open-armed embracing that characterised her mother. He watched her reach out for a large soft doeskin bag that lay on the table to her side and, opening it, take out an oblong piece of paper and hand it to Moira, saying, "I have a number of faults, but the main one is extravagance. I always want to spend money; I can see no reason in keeping it.'' Her smile was broad now. "I've always had a generous allowance, but when that legacy came to me from out of the blue I...I bought a lot of unnecessary presents for people who didn't need them, I'm afraid, and that is all that is left of my personal account. My mama agreed with me that it should go to you. Of course, it should have been much more and, as I said, had I known—''

Her words were cut off by Moira who, one hand to her throat, was saying brokenly, "Oh, my dear. My dear. Oh no! Two thousand, four hundred pounds. Dear God in heaven! It is too much. If this is the last of your money, won't you need it to help with your wedding?''

The young woman now got to her feet, saying, "I don't think I'll need to worry about money ever in my life. I never have had to. I only wish it was double or treble that amount; in fact, all that was left to me. I'm—'' she wetted her lips now and there was a break in her voice as she said, "I'm sorry our meeting has to be so short this time, but I shall doubtless be visiting England from time to time—my future husband has businesses in London—and I would love to call on you, if I may?"

"Oh, lass. Lass."

It was such a common term to apply to this beautiful, stylishly dressed young woman, and when Daniel saw them clasping each other he turned quickly and went from the room.

It was almost ten minutes later that they came into the hall, and Daniel, having opened the door, said to the girl, "Have you driven all the way from Carlisle?" and she replied, "Oh no! We are staying with friends at Tipton Hall, just beyond Newcastle. This is their carriage."

"By! The children would have loved to see it."

"You have children?" Melissa said, "They will be my half-brothers and sisters. Where are they?"

"Oh, my dear," Moira said, "scattered about the wood. They run wild most of the time. The two younger ones are up in the nursery. Next time you are coming, let me know in advance and I'll have them all spruced up for you."

They did not embrace again, but just held hands for a moment; then Moira stood at the top of the steps, both hands now clutching her throat, and she did not release them until her daughter, after stepping into the carriage, turned and waved to her, and she waved back. It wasn't an enthusiastic wave, but slow, its very movement indicating sadness.

The carriage had disappeared for some minutes but she still remained on the steps, gazing down the drive. When eventually she turned and faced Daniel, he saw that she was too full for words and so, taking her arm, he led her back into the drawing-room.

After seating her, he picked up the cheque from the table and, putting it into her hand, he said, "Push that down your bodice. Don't let on to anyone about it. No-one, not even Maggie Ann."

"Oh, I must tell Maggie Ann."

"*No!* nobody. D'you hear me? *Nobody*. And by the way, where is Maggie Ann?"

"Well, she scattered with the bairns when she saw the fine carriage coming up the drive. She must have thought I was having a special visitor, as indeed I had, didn't I, Daniel?"

"Indeed, you had. Indeed, you had; a beautiful young lady that you can be proud of."

"Oh yes, a young lady indeed. It's as well things happened as they did. I never thought I would thank God for bearing a child, and me not married. But just think, if she had been brought up over the water among my crowd, just think. And look at her: no swank about her and willing to accept me, Daniel, willing to accept me."

"And why not? You can hold your own with anybody in the land. You don't need fine clothes to make you out. And she's all you. Oh yes, she's all you: without you inside her, her clothes and fine education would be as nothing."

"You're always a comfort, Daniel. What would I do without you?"

"Never mind that. On Monday you're going to get yourself titivated up and you're going to Newcastle...not Fellburn but Newcastle, and to a bank there, and you're putting that money in, in your own name. And then you're going to a solicitor."

"Oh, be quiet. Be quiet."

"I'll not be quiet. Now I mean it, you're going to a solicitor. You can think about what you're going to say tonight, and tomorrow. Write it out in ordinary words what you want doing with the money should anything happen to you. But in the meantime, you can take out bits and pieces to keep you going, and the rest will accumulate interest. So there you are."

"You've got it all cut and dried, haven't you?"

"Yes, for once I've got it all cut and dried. And you'll do this, won't you? Just to please me, you'll do this?"

She looked at him for a long moment, then she said, "Yes, Daniel, I'll do it. I'll put two thousand, four hundred pounds into the bank under the name of Mrs Moira Stewart. It should be just plain Moira Conelly, but if I put it under that name and anything should happen to me before me time—although if I'm to believe Maggie Ann, nothing happens to anybody before their time—the squad across the water would be on to it."

"The squad across the water can't do anything if there's a statement made by you through a solicitor that the money should go to the children. Now, say nothing to anyone, but on Monday you take the train into Newcastle and you go to a bank. We'll talk about which one and also about a solicitor. We could go to the one that deals with this property but that wouldn't be wise. I think there's an old firm near Bridge Street, up one of the cuttings. I've passed it at times; it has a curved brass plate on the wall. Look, I'll tell you what I'll do. Tomorrow afternoon I'll take a ride out in the trap and do a bit of looking around. Being a

Sunday it'll be quiet in the city, and nobody will know where I've been.''

He had forgotten for the moment where he spent his Sunday afternoons, or at least some part of them, but when he recalled it he told himself he'd look in on her as he came back.

There was the sound of scampering feet across the hall and Maggie Ann's strident voice yelling, ''Stop your gallop, you lot!'' And when the drawing-room door opened and Margaret cried, ''Ma! our Patrick keeps nipping me, and Sean and him have been fightin','' Moira said, ''Don't tell tales, Margaret. And look at the sight of you. Where've you been? You're mud up to the eyes.''

The little girl cried, ''Patrick chased me into the wet bed at the bottom of the field.''

''Come here, Patrick.'' Daniel beckoned the boy towards him, and taking him by the shoulders, he shook him as he said, ''Now, from next week on and all during your holidays you're going to work; you'll start mucking out. You're nine years old; you should have been put to it before now.''

''Aw! Daniel, man. Will I get paid?''

Daniel puffed out his cheeks before he said, ''Yes, you'll get paid. You'll work at least six hours a day and you'll get a ha'penny an hour. Now how much is that for six days?''

While the boy was reckoning in his head, Sean said quietly, ''One and sixpence.''

''Shut up! you. I knew what it was, clever clouts!''

''Well, why didn't you say so?'' Sean's tone was level; then he, looking at Daniel, asked, ''Can I work an' all?''

''Yes, you may work an' all, until you have to go back to school, but when you come home at night, and all day Saturday, you can both earn a ha'penny an hour doing odd jobs. That understood?'' He looked at Patrick and the boy screwed up his face for a moment, before saying, ''All depends what jobs.''

''You'll see soon enough.''

''More mucking out?''

''Yes, me boy, more mucking out. Anyway, you can have your choice. It'll be either the stables or the schoolroom. 'Tis up to you. Seeing there's no time like the present, go and change into your clogs and your old pants straight away. I'm changing my clothes too, and we'll go down and I'll start you on.''

He now turned to Sean and said, ''What about it, Sean?''

And Sean answered with a grin, ''All right, but I don't mind being upstairs.''...

During Daniel's bargaining with the children Moira had taken Maggie Ann to the end of the long room and told her what had transpired with her visitor, leaving out the matter of the cheque. And when Margaret seemed intent on joining them, Daniel said, ''Go on! you, and get into the kitchen and under the tap. Go on with you.''

It was significant of where Daniel stood in the house when the child obeyed him without further demur. And now he made his way down the room, there to see Maggie Ann with her head bowed and her arms hugging her huge waist, and her body swaying backwards and forwards in a rocking movement as she muttered, ''And I didn't see her! I didn't see her! You could have called me.''

''How could I? And the children, the sight they are. And look at you. I'm bad enough, but you look as though you, too, have been in the wet beds at the bottom of the field. And your hair like rats' tails hanging around your face; and two buttons off the front of your blouse.''

"If she was as nice as you say, she wouldn't have minded that. Did you tell her of me, an' my staying with you all these years?"

Daniel watched Moira draw in her bottom lip between her teeth before replying, "Of course I did. Of course I did. Who else would I talk about? You were the first one who held her, and, as you've so often said, you were also the last one to hold her before they took her away."

Maggie Ann's great body began to shake; her head drooped further, and she turned away and went slowly up the room and out into the hall. And as Daniel watched her, her sadness seeped into him; and then it was pressed deeper still with pity when Moira's voice came to him on an agonised mutter, "God forgive me; I never mentioned her."

2

''What actually makes the wind, Daniel?''

''Well, it's the air, Sean.''

''I know it's the air, but what actually makes the
air make the wind?''

Daniel paused for a moment; then on a laugh he
said, ''It's the atmosphere. It's like the clashing of the
cold air meeting the warm air.''

''But what...I mean, but what makes the atmosphere? Where does it come from?''

''Nobody knows that. Well, look up there into that
blackness and what do you see? You see a few hundred stars, but there are a few thousand stars, a few
million stars. They go on and on into infinity, space.''

''In...finity?''

''Yes, for ever and ever.''

''Well, which part does God take up? I mean in the
in...finity?''

Daniel bowed his head and closed his eyes the while
smiling, then peered down on the fair face turned up
to him and said, ''That question has been asked, I'm
sure, billions of times since man crawled the earth,
and there's nobody been able to answer it.''

"But the prayer says God in heaven."

"That's just symbolic."

"Sym...bolic?"

"Yes, that's what I said, symbolic. It's just a description, a sort of simplified description to give people a picture—" he paused here, wanting to get his words right, then repeated, "to give people a picture, something which they can hold in their minds of the Creator of the world, so to speak. I don't know the real answer to that, but if I was to say what I actually think I would describe heaven or hell as how we live our lives."

"But...but if God made us, Daniel, why did he make some of us bad an' some of us good?"

"Oh, I don't think God made some of us bad and some of us good; I think that depends upon ourselves; we can be either bad or good, we have our choice. Anyway, what started all this?"

"It's the sky. I'm...I'm always thinkin' about the sky an' the wind an' the rain. Then, in that history book you showed me last night, there was a mountain that spewed up fire, real ashes and brimstone. Is that hell?"

"No. No, it isn't hell, it's a volcano. I told you."

"Yes, I know you said it's a vol...cano, but it's like the description of hell, that...that priest from Ireland who came to see Mama the other week...he said to her, I heard him, that if she didn't learn us the faith we'd be damned in hell with fire and brimstone."

"Oh, him. Now, I told you before to take no notice of him...your mama didn't. And Maggie Ann told him where he could go to, didn't she? As she said—" He now bent and brought his head down to the boy's level and whispered on a laugh, "She sent him off with sparks in his backside, for he'd got at her, too, hadn't he?'' He was straightening himself up when the boy suddenly said, ''Why is Dada wicked?''

''*Sean!*'' Daniel's voice was stern now. ''Your father isn't wicked. Who put that into your head?''

''He doesn't love Mama.''

''How do you know he doesn't love your mama?''

The boy said, ''I hear them. I've got good ears, and Maggie Ann talks.''

''Maggie Ann talks too much, and you shouldn't listen to grown-ups. They talk a language you don't understand yet.''

''Why do you stick up for your father, Daniel, when *you* don't like him?''

Daniel found his mouth going into a gape, and he could find no words at the moment to answer this boy, this seven-year-old boy who thought in the same way as he himself had done when he was seventeen; in fact, who probed and reasoned more than he himself had ever done at that age. There had always been something strange about Sean, and, of late, he had wondered more than once what was to become of him or, what was more to the point, what would he become? When thinking of careers for both Patrick and him he could find a number of niches in which Patrick could be placed, in which there would be no call on the little brain and intelligence he possessed. But he had never been able to find a niche in which to place Sean.

When the boy's voice came to him, saying, ''Oh, it doesn't matter,'' and he turned from the terrace and went indoors, Daniel felt utterly nonplussed, for it was as if he had been rebuked by an elder for being unable to answer a simple question.

After a moment, he was about to follow the boy when he made out the form of his father striding across the drive, so he stayed where he was in case he should think he was going indoors so as to avoid him.

But when his father came up the steps and saw him standing in the shadow of the doorway, he paused and said, "Oh, I want to have a word with you," and straight away passed him, went across the hall and down the passage and into the study. And after a moment Daniel followed him.

When he saw his father had taken his seat behind the desk he knew there was something unpleasant about to be said; and he wasn't wrong, because Hector started with, "Why did you tell Dunlop to leave the dyke field fallow?"

"Because I thought it was time; it's had two crops of potatoes in it."

"I don't care if it's had ten: it's my business what crops are sown and where and when. You go too far."

Daniel said nothing. He knew this wasn't the real issue of the conversation, for it was nearly a week ago now when, talking to Barney, he had said, "It's wise, isn't it, to move the potato crop now and again?" And Barney had said, "That's what they're sayin' now. There's all new-fangled ideas comin' in. But look at the stints round about; some of them hold nothin' but taties year after year. Still, I think it would be a wise thing to do." And so he had said, "Well, we'll leave it at that."

He now watched his father pull open a drawer and bring out a file, leaf through it, then stop at a page as if he were reading part of it, before he said, "Six of the herd will go to the market next week."

"*What?*"

"You heard what I said. I said, six of the herd will go to market next week."

"You mean the milkers?"

"What else? What other herd have we? Dromedaries? Elephants? Yes, six of the milkers."

"*You can't do that.*" Daniel had taken a step towards the desk. "I've…we've just got…I mean it's just been built up. The main money comes from the milk."

"Who's running this farm, you or me? I let you take over the market produce and since then you've got big ideas, but—"

"You didn't let me take over the market produce; you were hardly sober for three weeks; you didn't know what you were doing. And I had told you that Bob Shearman was cashing in on the side. But what did you say to that? You hadn't the guts to tackle him; you said, they always got a rake-off, that it was a sort of understood thing among the market men. But Shearman was raking off as much as you were paying him. And when I took the stuff into market myself and blew his little game, you could do nothing but sack him. But you didn't put me in charge of anything. I've had to take on jobs that you were too drunk or too damned lazy to see to."

As he watched his father's hand go out and his fingers stretch over the glass inkwell, the same one that had found its way almost to Pattie's head, he said quickly, "You try that on with me, Father, and you'll get it straight back; and my aim will be steadier than yours, far steadier. And let me tell you something right now: you send that bunch to market and I walk out. There's nothing to keep me here. And anyway, I'll tell you something else: I want to get married soon; and I can pick up a job in the town tomorrow, Pattie'll see to that.''

"Oh, yes, my God! Pattie'll see to everything, that bitch will. Yes; oh yes, that bitch will, even to fix up you marrying Miss Frances Talbot. Well, let me tell you something, Mr Smarty, from what I hear, her dear father doesn't favour your advances towards his daughter, because he has another young dog in his eye for her.''

For a moment Daniel was silent, because his father's words had brought a slight worry to the forefront of his mind. He knew that her father wanted the best for her, but not that he already had someone in his eye. Anyway, that was village inn talk. If there had been anyone else after her, Frances herself would have teased him with the fact. So what he said now was, "Well, let me tell you that, marriage or no marriage, I can still walk out of here tomorrow; and where would you be then? On your backside, because you're no more fit to run this place now than one of the old codgers you slurp your beer with in the inn, men you'd turn up your nose at when in your right senses.''

His father banged the file closed, dragged open the desk drawer and threw it in; then said, "Well, I'll give you a choice, Mr Big Head: it's either the cattle or one of the men, and if the latter's the case then Patrick stays off that school and works for his keep. And don't say, 'Oh no, you don't', because you started my sons on labouring, didn't you? So now he can do it in earnest, and next year the other one will be ready as well. Take your choice and I'll leave it to you which of the three in the yard has to go.''

Glaring at the man now glaring back at him, Daniel

growled, "You think you've got me, don't you, because you know we can't run this place even now on the few men we have. There used to be six in that yard. Anyway, if you're so badly in need of money, why not sell Rustler? He'd bring a good price. You could always ride Tracer or Pru when they weren't in the carts."

Hector Stewart rose slowly from the chair, and with his hands flat on the desk he leant over it and the words came from deep in his throat as he said, "One of these days I swear I'll do for you."

So venomous was the threat that Daniel shuddered under it for a moment, but then, squaring his shoulders he said, "Well, until then, Father, I'll forfeit my wage in order to keep a man on, and whatever you wanted ready money for will have to wait, won't it?"

He was about to turn away when his father said sarcastically, "Well, I'll leave you, son, to tell that to the bank when they want to foreclose because I cannot pay the interest on the mortgage."

Daniel had nothing to say in reply to this: candidly he hadn't thought about it: his father and he had never talked about the house. Whatever they'd had to say to each other had been about the farm, and then in fighting terms. There should have been good money from the corn crops, with hardly a poppy among them. And then there was the milk. Except for what they used in the house and that allotted to the workers, the rest all went to the market; there was no cheese or butter made, for unfortunately, from the beginning, Moira had shown no interest in that side of the farm. Arthur Beaney's wife had at one time been dairymaid, but she now had rheumatics in her hands; in fact, in her whole body.

From time to time it had occurred to him that much more money could have been made out of the sidelines of the produce of the farm, and it would not have needed all that much extra labour; say a girl and a young fellow. Besides making cream and butter, the number of poultry could have been doubled and fattened for Christmas. With a little more help at lambing time more could be safely reared, instead of being left to die on the hills. Last spring, six had been lost. And what he had to admit to himself was that even good hands took advantage when there was no-one really holding the reins; things which such hands could see needed to be done were neglected. And really he, himself, was in no position to pull up the men. Nevertheless, he did speak out now and again.

As he made for the door his father yelled at him, "One day I'll wipe that look off your face, if it's the last thing I do. You've played the man too soon, because at bottom you're still green behind the ears and your nappy's still wet."

In the corridor, his jaw clenched, Daniel was brought to a halt by the sight of Sean hurrying towards the hall, and when he reached him he bent over him, saying under his breath, "One of these days you'll listen too closely and you won't like what you hear. You've got to stop this sneaking round doors."

"I wasn't sneaking round doors. I don't need to sneak around doors; I told you, I've got good ears. Mama heard you and she went upstairs, an' she says to tell you she wants a word."

He gave the boy a slight push before going upstairs. He did not knock on Moira's bedroom door, nor on the one opposite, to which room she sometimes adjourned, but went to the small room that was next to the girls' bedroom, and which Moira called her sewing-room. This was where she now spent a great deal of her time turning and patching for them all.

He tapped on the door, then opened it to see her sitting, her hands idle; and in the shadow of the lamp she looked like a picture he had seen hanging on the staircase of Crawley House School. He couldn't remember the name of the painter, but it was entitled "The Mother".

She did not move as she said, "What is it this time?" And when he told her she said, "Look, Daniel. Let me break into that money, for he could still sell the beasts and you could do nothing to stop him. And, what is more, you are not going to go without a wage in order to keep a man on; if you don't use some of that money for him, use it for yourself."

"That money will be used neither for him nor for me, Moira. You know as well as I do where most of the money he takes in goes. Let him keep dry for a while, and then he'll be able to meet the interest."

"Sit down, Daniel." She swept some clothes from a wooden chair, and he sat down. And now she said quietly, "You know me: I don't take much interest in the farm, never have; my interest has been with the children and the house. But one thing I'm aware of is that the price of corn seems to go down every year. Oh, I know"—she moved her hand with a halting movement—"the fields have been good. Anyway, we'll put that on one side for the moment. I have something to tell you."

He waited, and when he saw her lips move one over the other as if preventing the words from coming out of her mouth, he said, "You're not ill, are you?"

She paused a moment before she answered, "Not

ill, not in that way, but I have something in my belly that is growing.''

"*Oh, no! Moira, no!*" He almost added, How could you?

"Don't look so shocked, lad, for no matter what I think or what I might like to do I'm still your father's wife, and from time to time I'm made to recognise it. So there it is."

"Does...does he know?"

"Not yet, but I don't suppose it'll be of that much interest when the great news is broken to him." She stressed the word "great", then looked down on her hands where they lay one on top of the other on her lap before adding, "And now enough of me; I want to talk about you. You'll soon be twenty. I was going to add, 'and a fully fledged man,' but I think you were knocked into a man from the day you left that school. Now listen. Last Tuesday, when I was in Fellburn, I happened to run into Pattie."

"You never told me."

"No. No, I didn't. I know you drop in there from time to time and I thought, well, I would leave it to her to put it to you. But it's just this, in a nutshell. She can get you a post; at least, after you've taken a short course. And, as she put it, if you want to get married soon, you'll do it quicker from her end than you will from this. Now, now"—she held up her hand—"wait a moment, wait a moment. I know what you're going to say: the farm would fall to pieces without you. Well, very likely, but this is how I see it at the moment. If you weren't here he would just have to pull his socks up or we'd all find ourselves out on the road, and not much better than we would have been if it had happened across the water; in fact, worse, because it'd be hard to find another country to take us in, wouldn't it?'' She smiled broadly now. ''And I really think, I do, although I'd be making one of the biggest sacrifices of me own life, that if you went, it would bring him to his senses. Now, don't say you're not going to leave me and the children, and there's no way he will alter, not for the good. I know it all, Daniel, before you say it. But I also know this: you've got a life of your own ahead of you, and that girl is ready for marriage, as you are yourself, ripe for it.''

He found he could not prevent the red flush rising to his hair nor his mind endorsing every word she said: at least about marriage; he was ripe for it. But what he said was, ''You're asking me to leave you and the children in the hope that things will improve with my absence or that they will remain stable, and you are going to have another child, and he as much interested as if you were a calving cow, for let's face it, he pays no attention to the children, to none of them, not even to Bridget, and she's still in your arms. Do you know I've never seen that man romp with one of his own, not once. But then he never romped with Pattie or me; a pat on the head was as far as it went. Look, Moira, as you say, I'm ripe for marriage and I don't deny it, but I've thought out something recently that'll serve all purposes. I could get married and we could live here but apart; I could do up the old wing. What is it used for? Only storing. Well, there's barns and sheds outside. But in there are four rooms; in fact, the hall is all of twenty-five feet long. That could be turned into what it once was, a living-room and a staircase could be built to replace the old ladder. Oh, it isn't the day or yesterday that I've thought of what could be done in that old wing. And the stonework's splendid. The walls are all of two foot depth. And the arched windows are a picture. So you can tell Pattie, or I'll tell her myself, that I can make my own arrangements for my future. Not that I don't appreciate her efforts to help me; I do. I'm very fond of Pattie and John, and I wish I could see them more often, because they seem to be living in a different world, and in touch with the doings of the day; but there—" He rose to his feet and, going round the small table and bending over her, he said, "There you are, Mother Moira, you're not getting rid of me. Those are my plans. And come Sunday I will put them to…the other party, and I know she'll see eye to eye with me."

"Do you think so?"

"Think so?" He straightened up. "I'm sure of it. Now come on out of this room; to me, it always smells of wet clothing; I'm sure you patch the lads' pants before they are dry."

She laughed softly as she took his hand and they went out together, high hopes in one, the reality of life in the other.

3

Altogether, it had been a wet summer. They had been very fortunate in getting in the corn during the only dry couple of weeks. For the past week it seemed to have rained all day and most of the night and the land was like a quagmire. So Daniel's horse was almost up to its forelocks when it stepped into a hole in the road that was camouflaged by the running water.

When he reached the Talbots' yard, Luke shouted to him from the barn, "You must be out of your mind attempting that road the day. Bring it in here."

Daniel dismounted in the barn and, taking off his hat and cape, he shook them, saying, "It never ceases. How are your fields?"

"Same as yours, I should say, with stuff ruined; but then it's a good job we managed to get the main crop up before it started in earnest again. Still, there's a lot of damage done. How about you?"

"Much the same. Is your father in?"

"Yes. Yes, why do you ask?"

"Well—" Daniel grinned, pursued his lips, then said, "I want a word with him."

"Oh. Oh"—Luke arched his eyebrows—"that kind

of a word? Well, between you and me, Daniel, don't expect to be greeted with open arms.'' Luke's voice was serious. ''I'm telling you, forewarned is forearmed. Now if it was me I would say, go ahead, but…but then I'm a soft-headed youth, so he tells me.''

''Has he been discussing us…I mean, Frances and me?''

''Oh, you'd be surprised. He never seems to talk about anything else to her.''

''It's as bad as that, is it?''

When Luke didn't answer, only made a movement with his shoulder, Daniel said, ''Well, thanks, anyway, for telling me what I'm to expect. But it makes no difference, you know, not to me or her. By the way, where is he?''

''Well, if he hasn't gone upstairs to bed yet, he should be in his den. Here''—he lifted up Daniel's cape from where it lay over an empty barrel—''I'd put that over you again before you make a run for it; and I'll dry him down for you.'' He patted the horse's rump.

''Thanks, Luke.''

Daniel ran from the barn to the house, where, after ringing the bell, he had to wait a moment or so before the door was opened by Frances, surprise showing on her face as she said, ''Oh, you must have had a job to get through in this.'' She glanced quickly to either side of her, then reached up and kissed him, saying now, ''Mother's in the sitting-room,'' and in a whisper, ''Father's in his room. He'll soon be going upstairs, then we can have it to ourselves.'' She smiled a secret smile, which he did not return. What he said now was, ''I want to have a word with your father.''

"A word? What about?" Her voice was still a whisper.

"About us, of course." His voice too was a whisper now, but harsh: "I want to tell him we're to be officially engaged at Christmas."

As though she had been slighted, she said, "Without asking my permission?"

"Yes, miss, without asking your permission. Don't you think it's about time? Anyway, we've talked it out, haven't we?"

Her whole attitude changing now, she said, "He's...he's not for it, Daniel, so be prepared."

This, however, did not prompt him to say anything further, but he squeezed her hand, and she pointed towards the passage and in a low voice she said, "The second door down."

He knocked on the door, but wasn't bidden to come in. Instead, the door was pulled open and there stood Mr Talbot, saying, "Oh! it's you. Nobody knocks on doors in this house. What's brought you here on a day like this? It would drown a duck. But then, need I ask? Come in."

The room was small and its space was taken up with a table that served as a desk, on which were scattered various papers; a bookcase on one wall was devoid of books, although each shelf held what looked like newspapers and slim magazines. There was only one chair and that was behind the table. Mr Talbot seated his stocky form in it and, looking up at Daniel, he said, "Well, I don't suppose you've come to ask after my health, have you?"

"No, not quite."

"Well, get on with it."

"Well, sir...Mr Talbot, I would like to become officially engaged to Frances, say at Christmas?"

"Oh"—the blunt head wagged—"you would, would you? Well, now, that's a straight question, but I won't give it a straight answer; instead, I'll ask you another question. What have you to offer my daughter? If she became engaged to you at Christmas, which would mean the promise of marriage later on, what can you offer her, I say?"

Yes, what could he offer her? Not much, so far as he could see at the moment. But in the future? Yes, the future. The renovated block at the end of the house.

Thinking about it now the prospect didn't seem bright even to himself, but he said, "I'm thinking about renovating the old part of the house. It would make a good habitation and...and the farm will prosper."

"*That's enough.*" Mr Talbot was on his feet now, his arm thrust out, his wagging finger almost touching Daniel's chest. "You've got a nerve, I'll say that. You come here and ask to be engaged to my daughter and tell me you're going to stick her in a byre at the end of your house."

"*It's no byre.*"

"Don't you shout at me in my own house, young man; I know what it is, it's the original part of that place, and it's mouldy and has been used as a store for years; ever since your grandfather's time, in fact. He stuck stuff in there when I was a lad. And you propose putting my daughter into that? And you talk about a prosperous farm? Who owns the farm? Your father does, and by the time he's finished with his drinking there'll be nothing left of it. It's been galloping downhill for years. Then there's his fat Irish wife with her brood running wild. Prosperous farm, indeed! when his two little sons are put to work on it. Now you get yourself away; and you may come back and ask to become engaged to my daughter when you have some prospects. You told her a while back that your sister could get you a decent job in the town; well, if I were you, I'd think on that, because as long as that father of yours is alive I can see no prospect there for you and definitely *not for her*."

Just as he'd had the urge to hit his father, so now the same feeling almost overwhelmed him, urging him to take his fist and land it in the square face; if not that, to lash him with his tongue and tell him that he was a little ignorant nobody, a smallholder who had come into the district little more than a squatter, riding on a flat cart with his mother and father, their belongings around them, and for the following ten years of his life had lived in Willow Cottage down by the river, a place that had since dropped to bits with mould and rot.

He took neither of these paths; instead, he turned and marched from the room, to be met by Frances and her mother in the hallway. And as he grabbed up his cape from the chair, Mrs Talbot said under her breath, "Don't worry, Daniel, don't worry." Then turning to her daughter, she muttered quickly, "Put your coat over your head and go with Daniel to the barn."

As Frances ran by his side across the yard to the barn, she cried, "What happened? He was yelling. What happened?"

Daniel could not answer her, for he was too burnt up inside.

Luke wasn't in the barn, and Daniel went straight

to his horse and for a moment he leant against the saddle, his hands gripping it.

Frances now demanded, "Look! Tell me what happened. What did he say?"

He turned to her, his voice bitter. "Too much," he said; "far too much. He forgets himself, your father. Do you know that? He forgets what he once was. Speaking to me as if I was dirt beneath his feet. I nearly reminded him of his beginnings. Yes, I did."

"What do you mean, by his beginnings?" Frances was on her dignity now.

"Just that he's got nothing to brag about, that's all."

"Well, you have nothing to brag about either, I mean, not the way the farm is now."

"The farm hasn't always been like it is, nor has my father, nor his father. They were the big names around here. But if I'd been some dumbhead from the village asking for your hand I couldn't have had a worse reception. He asked what I had to offer you and I told him I...I meant to get the old house put right for us."

"*You told him that!* That old storehouse at the end?...oh!"

"It wasn't always an old storehouse. In fact, it never was a storehouse, and it could be made into a fine house, as it once was."

She stepped back now from him, saying, "Well, I can understand how he reacted to that. If you had told me of *your* plans for our future, I could have saved you the trouble of putting that proposition to him, because you wouldn't get me living in that place while that woman and her horde live in your grand house."

"That woman, by the way, is my stepmother, and she is Mrs Stewart."

"I don't care what she is called, she's still just an Irish woman, and a very ordinary Irish woman."

"She is no ordinary Irish woman. She's an Irish lady who was brought up in a castle…"

Why was he saying these things? What was happening between them? He turned once again to the saddle and, as if addressing it, he said, "Oh, Frances, Frances, what's come over us? I'm sorry. I'm sorry."

However, she wasn't to be placated and in a still voice she said, "You look down on my father, don't you?"

He swung round towards her. "I look down on no-one, Frances; but it was the way he went for me, how he made me feel as if I was someone who had come crawling, as if I were nobody—"

"He could stop me seeing you. Do you know that?"

"He won't. I would see you somehow. And anyway, when you're twenty-one he can do nothing about it."

She was almost shouting now when she said, "But I'm not twenty-one, and won't be for another year or more. And you're not twenty-one either."

"No." He hung his head. "You're right, I'm not twenty-one; but I feel thirty-one, forty-one, especially when I think of you."

His head was raised now and he took two steps towards her. But he didn't touch her and his voice was thick as he muttered, "I love you, Frances. I love you so much it's eating me up. And if I could only know that some time in the future we would come to-gether… Oh God!" He swung away from her and, moving quickly to the half-open barn door, he dragged it closed. Then swinging her about, he took her into his arms and so fierce was his kissing that she fell back against the door, and he held her tightly until her kissing and her body responded to his.

When on a gasp his hold slackened on her and he muttered, "I love you. I love you, and I need you," she too muttered, "I do too, Daniel. Oh yes, I do too. If only...if only we could be married."

"Frances! Frances! Are you there?" The voice came from the yard and they sprang apart, and he walked quickly to his horse as she, straightening her hair and grabbing up the coat from where it had fallen, pulled open the barn door and shouted hoarsely, "I'm...I'm here, Father."

"Come out of there!"

She gave a swift glance behind her, then ran across the yard to where her father was standing outside the house door in an oilskin and broad-brimmed cap.

Daniel did not immediately mount the horse but waited until he heard the end of the distant exchange between them, followed by the banging of a door; not until then did he mount and ride out of the yard.

As the animal ploughed through the mud he had a very down-to-earth thought: feeling as they both did, should he take her and she became pregnant, her father would be only too pleased to see her married to him and for her to live anywhere. Anywhere. *Anywhere*.

4

It was the first Saturday after his twentieth birthday in December, 1889. On this morning, as he usually managed to do when in Fellburn, he looked in on Pattie, knowing that she often managed to be at home around eleven o'clock.

Having heard laughter as he entered the house by the back door, he paused a moment; and then Pattie appeared at the kitchen door, saying, "Oh! you look frozen. Get your coat off and come in; the tea's still hot. I've got company."

When he entered the little sitting-room and saw Janie Farringdon he said, "Oh, hello, Janie."

"Hello, Daniel," she replied.

As he took his seat before the small bright fire he said, "I haven't seen you for weeks; in fact, a few months."

"Well, you wouldn't," put in Pattie, now handing him a cup of tea; "she's been in Holland."

"Holland?" He looked at Janie again, enquiring, "On holiday?"

"Some and some. Father was after stones." She

cast a glance towards Pattie now, saying, "I get told off for calling them stones and yet that's all they are."

"Stones for the jeweller's shop?" Daniel nodded at her. "Were they diamonds?"

"Yes, in the main. They seem to be the most popular, especially for engagement rings. By the way"—Janie again turned her head towards Pattie—"Jessie Bannister asked me to be bridesmaid. I politely refused," and she laughed as she added, "I've got to draw the line somewhere, or sometime, I'm becoming the standard bridesmaid."

"Well, you shouldn't give such good presents; they know they're on to a good thing."

Again Janie laughed, the while pulling a face as she admitted, "Yes, I suppose you're right."

"What excuse did you give? because she's very dominant, is Jessie."

"Oh, I said I was getting much too tall to be a bridesmaid. Well, imagine, she's having two four-year-olds, and there would be me standing between them like a lamp-post."

Daniel sat looking from one to the other, amused by their conversation, yet thinking the while how close they seemed. But then, Pattie had always liked Janie. Although his sister was quite a bit older, they both seemed to be on the same mental level.

Pattie startled him now by exclaiming, "What am I thinking about! Happy birthday, dear." She was leaning over him and kissing him. "Twenty. I can't believe it. Yet you know something?" She was now wagging her finger at him. "You'll grow old quickly because you could pass for twenty-five this minute, couldn't he, Janie?"

"Oh, don't expect me to add insult to injury. Anyway, a happy birthday, Daniel. Birthdays are odd, don't you think? I've only got six months to go to my twenty-first and Papa said the other day that I wouldn't feel liberated until then. But as I told him, I've felt liberated for years. I take after Mother, for she didn't turn a hair when I said I was going to take night classes with those creatures called 'men' present.''

"You are going to teach?'' There was a note of surprise in Daniel's voice. "Do you get many, I mean, turning up for classes?''

"You'd be surprised,'' said Pattie, nodding at him now. "I wish we in the schools could rely on getting as many children. It's you farmers, you know''—the nodding was emphatic now—"cheap labour. They don't seem to recognise that it's an offence to keep a child from full schooling, and has been these last ten years. It hasn't got through to them yet; and they should be fined. If it touched their pockets that would bring them to their senses. And it's the same wherever there's a factory. Of course, at rock bottom it's the parents.''

"I suppose they need the money, even if it is so little—''

"Oh, now you, *Miss Farringdon*, don't you start and go soft on them.''

"Who's going soft?'' said Janie. "You're the one to talk, and John is worse: he should have his head seen to, the things he does. I don't know why he married you, because as far as I can gather he's never in the house.''

Daniel was smiling now. They were, he supposed, what some of these newspapers called the new generation, and which many more said should be suppressed, for women were wanting not only to take up positions in the cities, but become doctors and even advocates of the law. And then there were women who said they should have votes, when it had taken years for the ordinary man to claim the power to vote.

He was amazed as he realised how mentally close they were: their interests were along the same lines. And physically, too, they weren't unalike, except that Janie was bigger made than Pattie, bigger boned, and, if anything, plainer. But her face, topped by that mass of brown hair, was pleasant.. And she had lovely hands. He hadn't noticed this before, but then, of course, he had never looked at her hands. There had been no need to; but he did so now because he noticed that she used them as she was speaking. She had a way of spreading out her fingers and her hand in a curving motion as if the gesture itself would strengthen or help to express what she was saying.

They drank more tea and they chatted on. Pattie asked how things were...back there, and he told her as much as he considered to be wise, especially in front of Janie.

It was when he stood up, saying, "Well, I'd better be off; I didn't unharness the horse because I must be back soon; I left him and the cart in Baxter's yard," that Janie rose too, saying, "Father will be stamping like your horse, Daniel; I'd better be off as well." She looked at her watch. "I said I would meet them in the market at half past eleven and it's a quarter to twelve now."

So, together, they said goodbye to Pattie and walked side by side during the ten minutes it took them to reach the market. And he found himself laughing most of the way—she had a keen wit—and as they reached the market place he realised it was the first time he had really talked to her, or she to him. Previously, whenever he had met her, it had always been in the company of someone else, usually Frances.

She was asking him a question now, and with regard to Frances: "When are you going to be married, Daniel?" she said.

"Oh. Oh, that's a question I'd like to be able to give a straight answer to. If I had my way I'd say, next week, because you know, we've been courting, as the term goes, since we were sixteen. Of course"— he laughed now—"Tommy Jobling, down in the village, has been courting Chrissie McFarlane for nine years because she's got her father to look after and he's got his mother to see to, and these two adults must be playing them one against the other. The parents are supposed to hate each other like poison, so it's no good the couple expecting to go and live with either of them. They've become the village joke."

They were laughing as they crossed the market place to where, outside the Lion Hotel, stood a carriage with her father standing by the door.

"Ah, that's what's kept you, meeting up with young men. It doesn't matter about your father and mother standing here freezing."

"Oh, hello, Daniel," Mrs Farringdon leant forward out of the carriage. "How are you? It's such a long time since I saw you. You promised to call last time. Do you remember?"

"Yes. Yes, I did, Mrs Farringdon. But it's the weather, you know. If I could arrange that we have rain in one field and sunshine in the other I would know what to do with my time."

Mrs Farringdon laughed and said, "Oh, you farmers!"

"Can we give you a lift, Daniel?"

"Thank you, Mr Farringdon; but I've left the horse and cart in the market yard over there"—he pointed—"and I have some shopping to do."

"But you'll look in on us, won't you?" It was Mrs Farringdon speaking again. "Make him promise. Make him promise, Tom."

"Oh, woman! be quiet. He's just told you he hasn't got control of the weather... Are you going to get in or not, daughter?" Then in a lower voice he said, "Roger's up on the box there swearing into his muffler. Go and get yourself in."

Janie now turned to Daniel, saying, "Goodbye, Daniel," and he answered, "Goodbye, Janie." Then he added, "I've enjoyed the morning...I mean, our crack."

She stared at him for a moment, then smiled, but she said nothing more before turning and stepping up into the carriage.

As Mr Farringdon was about to follow his daughter he paused a moment; then, looking at Daniel he said under his breath, "Everything all right at home?"

"Yes. Yes, thanks, Mr Farringdon."

The older man now exclaimed, "Good! Good! Perhaps we'll see you soon, then?"

Daniel stood on the kerb and watched the carriage draw away before he turned to make his way back across the market place. And it was as he led the horse and cart from the yard that a voice called to him, "Hello! Daniel. Stop a minute."

When he turned about and saw Ray Melton hurrying towards him, he said, "Oh, hello. You got back, then. I heard you were abroad."

"Oh, I've been back for some time. Like to come for a drink?"

"No, thank you. I have to make my way home."

"Well, you can give me a lift. I came in by train, but I was coming your way in any case; I was going to look you up this afternoon."

"You were?"

"Yes."

"Looking for a job?"

Ray put his head back and laughed loudly as Daniel cried, "Gee up! there. What happened at Oxford?"

"Oh, you heard about that?"

"Don't be silly!" Daniel cast a quick glance at his laughing companion, saying, "It set our part of the country on fire. Did your father really throw you out after you were sent down?"

"Well, as Dr Gibson, who was the means of seeing to my disposal, would say, metaphorically speaking, yes. Yet, on the other hand, I was given a choice. I could come into the business, and he would even open another store for me, a different kind of store, one that sold everything, in an upper class way, of course; not paraffin oil, fire lighters, and broken biscuits; or I could take myself into the wide world and see what it was all about."

"So you took yourself away into the wide world?"

"Yes and no. I went to France. Father has a cousin there who, I might add, is made from a different mould from himself. If I hadn't known about life before I met him, he would certainly have become my tutor. My French isn't all that bright, and the ladies to whom I was introduced knew no English. But, as my dear father's cousin said, love speaks all languages." He laughed loudly now and punched Daniel on the arm, saying, "Dan! boy, you wouldn't believe. Nobody around this quarter has lived."

"No, perhaps not," said Daniel in a noncommittal tone; "but still, we're all managing to crawl up out of the slime."

"Oh, don't be so stuffy. You know, Dan, and I've said this to you before, I just don't know how you stick it, because since you left Crawley House, I bet you've never been out of this neck of the woods... Still seeing Frances?"

"You could say that. Yes, you could say that."

"Well, that must be some consolation, anyway, because she's a spanker, isn't she? Dress her the way some of those French misses do and oh! Oh! la-la!"

Ray jerked in his seat as Daniel turned on him, shouting now, "She doesn't need fancy clothes to make her out. And I'll thank you not to class her in the same breath as those particular *ladies* you met on your travels."

The horse had trotted about twenty yards before Ray said, "Look here, Dan, there's no need to jump down my throat. What's the matter with you, anyway? You never used to be like this. If you ask me, what I think you need is a break. And of course it's understandable with—"

Daniel kept his gaze ahead as he enquired, "Go on. What is understandable?"

"Oh, for God's sake! Come off it, Dan. We've been pals for years. We know everything there is to know about each other, and our families. Well, all right, I'll say it, your attitude is understandable with your father hardly ever sober and the whole responsibility for that tribe resting on you."

Again Daniel had the urge to strike out and knock

his longtime friend off the cart. Yet, at the same time, he was made to wonder why he was feeling like this against him. Was it because of the opportunities privilege had given him and he had wasted? Was it because it was the way he had referred to Frances? Or was it because he knew, as everyone in the district did, that his father had turned into a sot, and that the responsibility of the farm and the family had fallen on him? He supposed it was a combination of all those things; but mainly the fact that Ray had wasted his privileges. What would he have given to have been in his place, to go to university, Durham say, or any university; but to be given the chance to go to Oxford and then to be sent down because you disgraced yourself created in him not only envy but also anger at the waste of such an opportunity.

They drove on in silence for some way.

It was when they were passing the old turnpike gate and the ruined cottage that Ray said sharply, "You can drop me here!" After alighting from the cart and without giving Daniel a backward glance, he mounted the bank, jumped over the wooden bar, then hurried along the path that led to the wood.

Daniel did not immediately move the horse on, but sat staring at the tall striding figure. That path led to only one house, the Talbots' and Frances. Of course, further on, but another two miles or so, was Janie's place, and he had been friendly with Janie too.

"Get up there." He allowed the horse to walk the rest of the journey, and in the farmyard he handed it over to Alex Towney, who asked him, "Had a good morning, Mr Daniel?"

And he answered, "Not up to usual, Alex. I didn't expect to really, for there wasn't much to go in, was there?'' And he looked hard at Alex who, looking back at him, said, ''No, you're right there. You're right there.''

As Daniel entered the kitchen, Maggie Ann came shambling out of the larder, and he remarked to himself that it must be his imagination that her body seemed to be getting larger every day. Her feet and ankles looked almost as big as his own thighs. And as she dropped a tin tray of cooking ingredients on to the table, she nodded towards the mat to where Michael was sitting and smiling towards Daniel, and she said, ''He got on to his pins and walked three steps. You did, didn't you, boy?''

She leant across the table and the small boy grinned up at her.

''Did he now? Well! Well! That is something.''

Daniel hoisted the boy up and after he had planted him steady on his feet, he moved back from him, saying, ''Come on! then;' and watched as, stumbling, the child made an erratic run towards him, and then lay against him laughing and saying, ''Dan...el, Dan...el.''

The child was backward both in his speech and in his walking, but he was a loving, happy-natured boy. And now Daniel held him shoulder high, crying as he did so, ''Clever fellow! Clever fellow!''

When he returned him to the floor, the boy immediately sat down. And now Maggie Ann said, ''Good news all round this morning,'' and jerked her head upwards: ''She's had a letter.'' And her voice now dropping to a hoarse whisper, she enlightened him: ''It was from France.''

''From France, eh? Her daughter?''

''Aye, her daughter.''

He hurried now from the room, calling, "I could do with a bite, Maggie Ann. Perhaps a drop of broth before I get changed."

"It'll be on the table when you come back."

He ran up the stairs and along the corridor and into the sewing-room.

Moira was busily stitching at a small dress but she immediately laid it aside, saying, "Hello! Daniel. How did it go; a good morning?"

"Not bad for the little I took in. But what's this I hear? You've had a letter from France?"

"Yes, indeed; indeed I've had a letter from France." She nodded at him, her face abeam now. "And not only a letter, but look! take a look for yourself." She now put her hand down her bodice and took out a long thin envelope, and as he opened it there fell out a piece of paper which he was quick to retrieve from the floor. And when he looked at it and read out, "Fifty pounds! A cheque for...!" Moira interrupted him, saying, "Read the letter. Read the letter."

And so he read:

My dear Mother,
I had hoped to be in England this month, but my mama is coming to spend some time with us, as the weather is more clement here...at least for some part of the day. But my husband must be in England at the end of February and remain there for March. So I would like to call on you again, and my husband has expressed a wish to meet you too. I know you will be pleased to learn that I am very happy, so very happy. I hope this

short letter will find you in good health. I send you my love and deep respect.

Your daughter,
Melissa.

Slowly he folded up the letter and, putting the cheque inside it, he replaced it in the envelope and handed it back to her. As she took it from him her eyes were moist and her lips trembling, and when he said softly, "You've got a wonderful daughter, Moira," she was unable to answer him for a moment. Then, picking up the end of her white apron she rubbed it round her face, saying, "I look upon it as a kind of miracle, you know, Daniel, a kind of miracle. And…and to send me more money; fifty pounds! What am I going to do with it?"

"You're going to put it where the other is, that's what you're going to do with it."

"Oh, I could buy so much for the house and for Christmas."

"And have Father ask where you got it from?"

When she nodded he went on, "Take my advice, Moira, put it into the bank. It'll come in for the children sometime, if not for yourself."

Her hands now moved over her apron as if smoothing the creases out of it and she said, "But they all need warmer clothes, Daniel. And Maggie Ann hasn't had a new rag to her back for years."

"Well," he said, bending down towards her, "just imagine what the result would be if he saw them all running round in new coats and Maggie Ann sporting a new shawl or some such. As for the children not being warmly clad, they are clad all right. They've got decent things for school, your fingers have seen to that. And what do they need while running round here like wild Indians? Do you ever see them unless they are up to the eyes in mud, except in weather like this? But then the backsides of the lads' pants are worn through with sliding down the banks.''

She smiled now, saying, ''I know you're right. Yes, I know you're right, Daniel, but it goes against the grain to stick money in that bank when I could be spending it.'' She laughed.

''Oh, you'll spend it one of these days, never you fear.''

''I'll be happier if you would take it and spend it. You know what I mean?''

''We won't go into that again. But just think: you've got something to look forward to now; February, she said, and she'll bring her husband. She's all you, Moira, inside. No matter who has brought her up and made her into this fine lady, she's still all you.''

''Oh! Daniel. God forbid, all me!''

''God wouldn't forbid. Anyway, I'm going to get changed and have a bite now; and afterwards you'll know where to find me if you want me.''

In the kitchen, a pan of broth was bubbling on the hob, and the table was set for him, but Maggie Ann wasn't there. The four-year-old Catherine was sitting on the mat. She looked up at him and when he asked, ''Where's Maggie Ann?'' she answered, ''She's gone over to the slide. Annie fell over an' hurt her foot an' she's yellin' blue murder, an' she wouldn't get up for Margaret or Sean. She's always yellin' blue murder, Annie, isn't she?''

It was as he went out of the kitchen door that he heard the terrible scream. It seemed to lift him from the ground and to carry him towards the curve of the drive where the gutter was frozen over and which the children used as a slide.

The first sight that met his eye was his father seated on Rustler, with the horse prancing almost in a circle; and, lying to the side of the road, a contorted heap that was Maggie Ann, surrounded by the screaming children.

As Daniel reached the group his father dismounted and yelled at him, "She came straight under his hooves." Then he bawled at the children, "Shut up! Shut up! will you?"

But they didn't obey him. Annie was standing hopping on one foot now while clinging to Margaret and they were both screaming; Patrick too was yelling; only Sean was quiet, and he was kneeling by Maggie Ann's head. From the mound of flesh there was no movement at all.

Daniel, too, was now on his knees. He had pushed the boy aside and his hands were cradling Maggie Ann's face as he cried," Maggie Ann! Maggie Ann!"

When there was no response he put a hand on her chest; then tore at the tasselled loop of the shawl that had caught around a button. And now thrusting his hand into her blouse, he pressed his fingers on to a garment that covered her soft flesh, and waited, then let out an audible sigh. Looking up at his father, he said, "She's…she's breathing. She's breathing…just; but she must be badly hurt somewhere."

He now turned to the children, crying, "Stop that noise, Margaret!" And looking at his father again he said, "She'll have to be carried in; she can't be left here until she comes round."

"We'll never be able to carry her."

No; he was right. He now turned to Patrick, crying, "Run to the farm and tell them to bring a door. Get Alex and Arthur if possible… Maggie Ann! Maggie

Ann! Come on! Come on!'' Daniel was now gently
patting her puffed cheeks, and when there was no response, he cried to Margaret, "Run into the house. Get
your mother, and bring a bed quilt."

The horse, now standing at the verge of the drive,
let out a number of long and frightened neighs, and
Daniel raised his head and watched his father go to it,
bring it on to the drive, then hand the reins to Sean,
saying, "Take him to the stable." The boy did not
move, but just stared at his father, who then yelled at
the boy, "You heard me! Take him to the stable, *now!
now!*"

When the boy still did not move, a blow across his
ear sent him stumbling almost to the ground, and Daniel cried, "Stop that! Father. I'd have thought you'd
done enough damage already."

"Damage? What the hell d'you mean! I tell you she
walked straight in front of the beast." He now turned
and looked to where his small son was again kneeling
alongside the twisted form of "the Irish bitch" as he
thought of her, and with his teeth audibly grinding he
yelled at him, "I'll deal with you later;" then grabbed
the slack rein and dragged the frightened animal to the
yard and stables.

Meanwhile, Daniel had pulled the scattered shawl
around Maggie Ann and, when she slowly raised her
lids and looked up at him, he said softly, "You'll be
all right, dear. You'll be all right. You've just had a
fall. Can you sit up?"

She said nothing, only remained still. But when
Sean put a hand on her cheek in an effort to turn her
head towards him, she muttered the word, "Cold".
And at this Daniel immediately stood up, took off his

coat and put it around her shoulders, then said, "Can...can you straighten your leg, dear?"

She did not seem to understand his words for she just stared at him, and he said, "Your leg's twisted underneath you, Maggie Ann. Can you straighten it?"

Slowly she muttered, "I...I can't feel it, Daniel."

"Are you in pain?"

Her head moved just the slightest in denial. Then Moira was standing over them, her words emerging on an anguished breath: "Oh! Maggie Ann, Maggie Ann! What is it?"

Maggie Ann looked at her beloved friend...her mistress, but made no answer; and Daniel said, "She must have fallen heavily and hit her head. She's likely got concussion. I've sent for a door."

"What happened?"

It was Sean who looked up at his mother as if he could give her the answer, and again she said, "What happened?" but the boy did not speak. "Father said she stepped in front of the horse," Daniel said.

"Oh God in heaven! Where is he?"

"In the stables."

She knelt down on the frozen ground by Maggie Ann's side and, raising her head, she said, "My dear, my dear. Are you hurt? Are you paining?"

Maggie Ann looked at her and again she made a very small motion with her head before muttering, "No. No, Miss Moira...dear, no pain."

They all now looked up the drive to where Arthur Beaney and Alex Towney were carrying a door between them, followed by their master.

"Is she hurt bad?" asked Alex.

"We don't know," Daniel answered; "but let us get her inside, then we'll see."

It took the two farm-hands and Daniel, assisted by Moira, to lift Maggie Ann on to the door. It was noticeable that Hector didn't touch her, although he did take hold of the hook at the back end of the accident door, as they called it, and so helped to carry the woman whom, for years, he had wanted out of his household and whom he considered one of the larger banes of his life, up the drive to the house and into her room.

Once they had laid Maggie Ann on the bed Moira said to Daniel, "I can manage myself now, if you'll send Margaret to me."

After the men had left the room, taking the door with them, Daniel stood by the bed and, looking at Moira, he said, "Margaret's no good. She won't be any use in turning her. Let me help."

Moira looked at him for a moment, then said, "As you say. As you say. Well now, we've got to get her things off. Can you raise her up for a little until I can pull the blouse out of her skirt?"

Daniel put his arms about Maggie Ann and lifted her up, without her showing any sign of hurt, although she seemed inclined to lay her head against his shoulder.

When the removal of her blouse, petticoat and bodyshirt exposed the fleshy breasts he turned towards the wall and Moira said, "Lay her back and hold the quilt up so I can strip her skirt and underthings off."

This done, Moira grabbed a clean shift from the top drawer of a chest, and again he had to hold up the swollen body.

When his hands touched the soft flesh he shivered visibly, and Moira, pulling the shift over Maggie Ann's head, pulled it down her back as far as it would

go, then said, "Lay her back now." And as Moira
fastened the top button of the shift and pulled it down
over Maggie Ann's breasts there swept over Daniel a
surge of pity that made him want to drop down by the
bedside and to lay his head on the shoulder of this
dear creature and cry as a child might.

"I think we'd better get the doctor."

"Yes. Yes." He was glad to turn away. "I'll go for
him myself."

"Do that. And now you can send Margaret in to
me."

As Daniel made for the door Moira moved quickly
towards him and whispered, "Let's hope it hasn't been
a blow on her head, because if anything was to happen
to that woman more than half me life would go with
her. She's my stay, always has been. So be quick now.
Be quick."

Not until three hours later did the doctor come.
Moira stood at one side of the bed while he made his
examination. Then when he had finished he washed
his hands in the bowl of water standing on the little
wash-hand stand that had at one time been used by
the housekeeper of the establishment, this having been
her bedroom. He said nothing as he dried his hands
on the towel that Moira had offered him; but back at
the bedside he put his hand on Maggie Ann's brow,
saying, "I will send you some medicine; it will ease
your headache." Maggie Ann had smiled slightly, and
her voice was faint as she said, "Thank you, Doctor.
Thank you, indeed."

It was Daniel, who had been standing further back
in the room, that he motioned to the door. Then, still
without speaking, he led Daniel along the corridor to

where, at the end, one door led into the kitchen and the other into the hall. He said, "I'm lost. Which door?"

Daniel opened the door into the hall and the doctor went straight to the chair where he had left his overcoat, his gloves and his tall hat. He stood looking down at them for a moment before turning to Daniel, when he said simply, "I don't know where she is injured, other than that she was kicked in the back, probably in the kidneys."

"Oh God, no! No!" Only Daniel himself heard his words, although they were yelling through his brain. "Oh no! no! Poor, dear Maggie Ann. *Oh no!*"

"If she has care and attention," the doctor went on, "she could live for some time, although it's not that she'll die from the blow. It's the dropsy that'll take her, and that could be in a week, a month or a year. Much will depend on how she reacts to the enforced rest she must take. I will prescribe something to relieve the excess water. She should have seen a doctor years ago, before she got into her present condition. I don't know how she's managed to get about. Didn't any of you realise she must have been in pain?"

"She...she never complained." The words were sticking in Daniel's throat and he had to swallow before he could add, "She was always so cheerful; in fact, she kept everyone else cheerful. That's the Irish in her, I suppose."

"Well, her excess water would hardly have made her cheerful, I can tell you. But, as I said, the tablets should help to relieve the pressure, although they won't cure her completely, and it will be a painful process, especially after that kick from the horse. If she was a younger woman and otherwise healthy, I

would have arranged for her to see a specialist, who
might have suggested some alternative treatment. But
as things are, it would be a waste of time at her age
and in her condition. The pain she would suffer would
be much worse than anything she has hitherto experienced. Well, good-day to you.''

As Daniel opened the door to let him out the doctor
sniffed at the air, saying, ''We're going to have snow
and I hate the damned stuff.''

Daniel watched him mount his trap and drive away
before he slowly closed the door, then stood with his
back to it, his hand over his eyes.

When, from the far end of the hall, Moira's voice
called, ''Well?'' he started, then moved towards her.

''She was kicked in the kidneys.''

Instead of coming out with an Irish exclamation,
such as Mother of God! or Dear Jesus!, Moira dropped
her heavy body on to a hall chair and, crossing her
arms, her hands pressed under her oxters, she rocked
herself back and forth. Had she let out a wail, the
picture would have been complete, but she uttered no
sound; nor did Daniel say anything; and when, after a
time, the rocking stopped and she rose from the chair,
and without a word turned and made her way back to
Maggie Ann's room, Daniel went slowly into the
kitchen, there to see six of the children grouped around
the hearth, and all silent. It was an odd scene, because
there had never seemed a moment when Margaret, or
Annie, or Catherine would not be jumping, skipping,
or scampering here or there, outside or inside. As for
Patrick, he seemed to spend his time looking for trouble and always found it. Sean was the only quiet one
among them, yet it was an observing quietness, nothing seeming to escape his notice: he would recall and

refer to things that the others had passed over or forgotten weeks before. And there, too, sitting on the mat, was the youngest, Michael.

When no one spoke he addressed Margaret, saying, "Where's Bridget?"

"Up in her cot. Mama had her in the sewing-room."

"Well, you'd better go and see her."

Margaret didn't move from where she was sitting, but turned to Patrick, and when Patrick did not speak either she said, "What's wrong with Maggie Ann? What did the doctor say? Is she going to die?"

"No." His voice was loud. "No, she's not going to die. She's…she's hurt her back."

"Will she be able to walk again?" This was from Patrick, and Daniel looked at the boy before answering slowly, "Not for some time. And well, now you're all here, this is the best time to have a word with you. Maggie Ann's going to need nursing. So you'll all have to pig in and do what you're told. You, Patrick and Margaret…well, in your own ways you'll have to take charge of the others. Patrick, you'll see to the fires, because Maggie Ann won't be able to do it any more, and your mother will be looking after her most of the time. And Margaret, you'll set the table and clear the things away and wash up the crocks, and Annie will help you, and Catherine too."

It was Annie who now piped in, saying, "I've hurt my foot on the slide, Daniel."

"Well, I noticed it didn't stop you from walking. And the more you use it the sooner it will be better."

"But who'll make our dinners, Daniel?" This was from Catherine, and the question stumped him for a moment; but then he said, "I'll go and see if Rosie can manage a few hours a day. But you know that she's also in a bad way, so it will be only the main meal she can do. And anyway, most of you will be able to see to the rest, won't you?'' He looked from one to the other but no one answered him; and so he barked, ''Won't you?''

''Yes. Yes, Daniel.'' The answer came in a jumble of voices which, he noticed, did not include one from Sean. But he let this pass.

Quietly now, he enlarged on his proposals. ''It'll soon be the Christmas holidays,'' he said; ''but before then I shall go and see the teacher and ask that you all be excused, at least for the next week or so, until we can arrange a new way of working. So, come on: get started! all of you.''

As he made for the door Patrick said, ''Father was here and he says he's going to shoot the horse.''

These words only brought Daniel to a temporary halt: he couldn't see his father shooting the only means of transport he had to get him to the village or beyond. However, should he shoot the horse, he, Daniel would shoot him. Yes, begod! he would shoot him.

It did not seem strange to him that he was thinking in the manner of the two women in the house because, after all, they had both in a way, between them, brought him up; they had both been his mother.

Word soon got around that Hector Stewart's horse had kicked his Irish servant up in the air and that she had landed on her back like a burst balloon. Broken it was and, some said, in a number of places. She wasn't expected to survive, not for all that long, anyway. And the big fellow had threatened to shoot his horse; although somebody must have stopped him, that is if

ever he tried, because he was still astride it every day.
It was a good job he had a son like Daniel, one so
very capable. But then, on the other hand, it was also
said that Daniel was near with money, and would give
you a snappy answer if you stepped out of place. Oh,
they were a funny lot up there on that farm. One thing
was sure, it was galloping down hill and it wouldn't
be long before it reached the bottom.

Since the difficult meeting Daniel had had with Mr
Talbot, he and Frances had not been able to meet on
a Sunday; in fact, her father had forbidden her to see
him. But it should happen that every Wednesday Mr
Talbot journeyed into Newcastle to a wholesaler's
there, sometimes taking stock in, sometimes bringing
fresh stock back. And it was on these afternoons that
Frances, with her mother's knowledge, escaped to the
wood and there met Daniel for a long or short period
depending on the weather and Luke's warning whistle.

But on this particular Wednesday, when Daniel had
not put in an appearance, she walked to the turnpike,
dropped down on to the road, then made her way to
the house.

She had of course heard about the accident but her
visit was not due to concern for the victim but really
to find out why Daniel hadn't put in an appearance
when, on the previous Wednesday, his love-making
had been so ardent he had almost eaten her alive.

Now she knocked at the front door, her excuse
ready: her mother had sent her to enquire how Miss
McTaggart was faring.

It was Margaret who opened the door and she said,
"Oh, hello, come in." And with the innocent percep-
tiveness of a child she added, "Daniel isn't here; he's
down at the farm. Will I tell Mama?"

"Yes, please."

While waiting in the hall, Frances looked about her. It was a fine hall, one she had always liked. It was a fine house altogether. She wouldn't have minded in the least being the mistress; that is, the sole mistress. It was a magnificent staircase too, with banisters so wide. Daniel had once told her, laughingly, that they got that way with the children sliding down them.

She turned and looked about her. There was also some good furniture here. That was a beautiful old clock in the corner. And that splendid open fireplace with the stonework leading up to the high ceiling; it would be wonderful with a big wood fire blazing there. But although it was freezing outside there was no sign that a fire had been lit in it for some time, and the hall was deadly cold.

She turned swiftly when she heard Moira's voice, saying, "Oh! there, my dear."

"Hello, Mrs Stewart. My mother asked me to call and find out how your—" she was about to say "servant", but changed it to —"Miss McTaggart is?"

"Oh, pretty much the same, I'm afraid. But come in a moment." Moira led the way into the drawing-room. "Do sit down. The fire's dropped low, I'm afraid; our routine's gone all to pot these days." She took a log out of the oak chest standing to the side of the fireplace and pressed it into the dying embers, then lifted up the bellows from the side and blew on the ashes until a flame sprang up. Dusting her hands one against the other she took a seat on the couch opposite Frances and said, "It's kind of your mother to enquire. How is she keeping?"

"Oh, very well, thank you. What is really wrong with Miss McTaggart?"

"Oh,"—Moira let out a long sigh—"as you've already heard, I'm sure, she hurt her back and that has aggravated her original trouble. She has excess water, you know. But it's amazing how cheerful she is, much more cheerful than any of us, I may say. But then she was born that way; some people are, you know." She now nodded towards Frances. "Would...would you like to have a word with her?"

"Oh no, no; I won't trouble her."

The last thing she would be able to bear, she knew, would be to look on a woman with excess water, especially that particular one—the size of her!—and to hear the voice that had always grated on her. She didn't like the Irish brogue. This woman's accent was more bearable, for there was a lilt to it and it wasn't as coarse-sounding as her servant's. After all, that's all the woman was, a servant; yet at times Daniel talked of her as if she were a close relative, and one that he particularly cared for, too.

As if she had read her thoughts, Moira said, "Daniel's been very upset this week. He's so fond of Maggie Ann. By the way, I know he wouldn't want you to leave without his seeing you, so I sent one of the children down for him. He should be here at any moment."

"Oh, you shouldn't have done that. That wasn't my intention in coming," she lied. "It was because mother wondered how that poor woman is, and then again wondered how you yourself was faring." As she finished speaking she looked more closely at the plump woman, who was wearing a slack dress. It had no waistline; indeed it was shaped more like a night-dress with lace-edged collar and cuffs.

As it dawned on her, almost with horror, that this

woman was again pregnant, she saw it as another great stumbling block, pushing her marriage to Daniel still further off. Moreover, it was disgusting; she had seven children already. And the last time they met, Daniel had suggested that if the worst came to the worst—and what did he mean by that? she had wondered—she could always come and live here until he got the house at the end put in order. Was he mad? or he must think she was, even to suggest that she might come into the house with this Irish woman over her, together with her squad of children, and another one pending. It was as her father said, there were more fish in the sea. But, oh dear, she did love Daniel. She wanted him as she had wanted nothing in life before and, she thought, in the future. She rose abruptly to her feet, saying, "I...I mustn't keep you."

"Aren't you going to wait for Daniel?"

"I...I might meet him outside; in fact, I can take a walk to the farm. I know the way quite well."

Moira's face was unsmiling as she said, "Yes, do that, do that, my dear." She led the way out of the drawing-room and to the front door, and as Frances emerged it seemed that she had hardly touched the top step before the door closed behind her.

But there, striding on to the drive from the yard, came Daniel, and she hurried towards him and he to her, and he held out his hand, saying, "I'm...I'm sorry I couldn't make it. You've heard about the trouble?"

"Yes. Yes, Mother thought that...well, I should come and enquire."

"That was nice of her. Oh"—he looked about him—"shall we go back in the house? It's so cold out here for you."

"No, no. I said goodbye to your stepmother."

He now looked towards the end of the house, saying, "I know where we'll go. Come," and he led her almost at a run along the front of the house to where the whole façade suddenly changed, for here the plain stone front was interlaced with cross timbers. Pushing open a battered-looking but still heavy oak door, he closed it behind them; then, standing in the dimness amid the odd mixture of smells, he took her in his arms and kissed her hard before releasing her and saying, almost lightly, "That's better." Then, turning her around, he said, "Look! Look at the length of this room. Imagine it all cleared of hams, carcasses, casks, the lot, and a roaring fire in that open fireplace." He pointed through the dimness. "And look at that window at the end; it's really beautiful stained glass. It's broken in one or two parts, but that can easily be seen to. And look, this is where we could have a staircase built." He pointed to the ladder that led upwards. "And through here—" He was again tugging her, but hard now because she was reluctant to follow him, through a door at the end of the room, and there he said, "These were the kitchen and eating quarters all of two hundred years ago." He pushed aside a bale of hay. "It's as dry as a bone, this room; which is why we keep the hay in here. That door leads outside." He pointed. "Look at the size of the bolts on it; it would keep out a regiment."

"Daniel"—she spoke his name not loudly but very precisely and clearly—"look, get it into your head, please: I couldn't, I just couldn't live here."

"Darling, darling Frances, nobody's asking you to live here as it is. I...I could make this into a better place than the house itself, more interesting. And that loft upstairs would make a magnificent bedroom from which you could see for miles, right over the treetops into Fellburn itself. We're on high ground here, you know.''

She snapped her hand from his. ''Daniel!'' Her tone was gritty now. ''I won't! I can't live in a place like this, and next door to…well, your stepmother and all those children.''

''You wouldn't hear the children, not through these walls.'' His voice was quiet now. ''You wouldn't see my stepmother, not unless you wanted to; although you couldn't see a better person, not in a day's walk, I tell you.''

''Daniel''—her tone was an appeal now—''I wish…I wish I could see it your way because… Oh, my dear''—her head was moving in a desperate fashion now—''I do, I really do, and I would do anything for you, anything. Do you hear? Anything you want, that you really want at this moment. Do you understand me?'' Her arms were about him now, as she went on, ''Yes, Daniel; anything but live in this end of the house. In the house proper, if it was ours…yes, oh yes; but not in this place, this old and smelly… Oh, I'm sorry. I'm sorry.''

Her body was pressing close to his now and for a moment his arms had been hanging slackly by his side, but now they were around her, pulling her tightly to him, and she was whispering, ''Can…can anyone come in here?''

The answer came thickly from his throat, ''No. No.'' But even saying this he pulled her back towards the door and, taking one arm from around her, he slid in the rusty bolt; then glancing about him in the dimness, he drew her to where there were a number of single bales of hay forming a narrow platform, and together they fell onto them.

He kissed her; he kissed her repeatedly; he unbuttoned the front of her coat and buried his lips in the nape of her neck; yet his hands did not stray down her body, because there was a voice shouting at him, penetrating the passion, demanding to be heard; If she has a baby, what then? and she wouldn't come and live here; and with Moira nearly on her time and Maggie Ann perhaps on her deathbed, and the children, too. All these were his responsibility. Frances wasn't that yet; but if he gave her a child she would be and he'd have to leave. And what would become of them next door, not to mention the house? Oh, to hell! with the house and everybody in it. He wanted this girl, this beloved girl. His body and mind had been crying out for her for years; in fact, all his life, for he couldn't recall a time when he hadn't loved her. What was the matter with him?

"Oh, Daniel. Daniel." Her nails were digging into him.

When his body rolled off her and he lay on his back, his teeth clenched, she was hanging on to his neck, crying, "Daniel. Daniel. What is it? Please, please, Daniel, please...please take me."

He turned to face her, muttering, "God knows, Frances, I want to, with every pore of me I want to, but...but the result...the result. If—"

"It doesn't matter, it doesn't matter about the result, I tell you." Her mouth was on his, covering it as never before, and her hands were going over him like those of a practised whore. And he had already learned the ways of a practised whore, twice, to his humiliation.

When, after almost tossing her aside, he sprang up

and turned his back on her, she flung round, face down, and seemed to bury herself in the hay while thrashing it with her fists. Then, after a long interval, she too was on her feet and straightening her clothes, dusting herself down, buttoning up her coat, picking her hat up from where it had fallen to the side of the bales and dragging it on to her head. And her body now half bent towards him, she cried, "I'll never forgive you for this, Daniel Stewart, as long as I live. You...you've humiliated me for the last time. You've driven me to the point of madness over these past months, egging me on...every time egging me on—"

"Frances! please!" His voice had a low deep plea in it. "Please! please! Try to understand. There's nothing on God's earth I want more than to take you at this moment, to love you, oh, to love you, but what if you were to have a child and you wouldn't come here to live? You say you wouldn't, that nothing would induce you. Then I would have to leave, wouldn't I? And I can't. I'm bound here, at least for a time."

"Yes. Yes,"—her lips were in a snarl now—"but not for a time, for eternity! And with the two great Irish hulks. Your father should never have married dear Moira; you should have married her, shouldn't you? *Shouldn't you?*...One last word; as my father says, there's more fish in the sea than has ever been caught, and there happens to be one big fish after me. He has been for some time, and he's known to both of us. So, put that in your pipe and smoke it, Mr Daniel Stewart!"

When she went to the door and wrenched the bolt back, he made no move either to halt her or to follow her: the last word he would have associated with her was common. Yet, over the past few minutes she had spoken like Maggie Ann or Rosie would have done and in the same manner.

He turned now and sank down on to the baled hay. There are more fish in the sea—and he's known to both of us. Well, there was only one man known to both of them whom she was likely to look upon with favour, or at least, her father would, and that was Ray. However, Ray was interested in Janie. Or was he?...But she wouldn't go to Ray; it was all talk; she was his. Yet that last tirade sounded final: she had been humiliated. Oh, dear God, that was the last thing he wanted, to make her suffer humiliation, because he was feeling the same emotion himself. He had, in a way, humiliated himself by repulsing her when his whole being was crying out for her.

After rising from the hay he had to dust himself down before leaving the storehouse, and when he moved out of the clammy stuffiness into the biting fresh air it was, for a moment, as if he had taken a long draught of ale, for he felt slightly giddy, as if he were drunk.

He made his way to the kitchen. There was no one there, so he brewed a pot of tea, making it almost black; and, sitting at the table, he drank two cups. He was still sitting there when Moira came in. She showed surprise by saying, "Oh, I...I thought you'd be away walking. I mean...did you see—?" only to stop when she saw the expression on his face. "Trouble?" she asked.

"Yes, Moira, you could say trouble."

"She wants you to leave here?"

He had been looking down to where his hands were joined tightly on the edge of the table, and then he fumbled, saying, "No…well, not quite. It wasn't really that, it was—"

"But what is the mainspring of it all? And it's natural. This house…well, not the house, but us, the children, the conditions…she couldn't see herself living here. And your idea of doing up the old place…well, you know, Daniel, that in itself would take a great deal of money; and a bride such as she would want to furnish it in her own way, not with bits and pieces from here. I understand. I understand her."

"Well, it's more than I do." Daniel got to his feet now. "Anyway, it's finished."

"Finished? You mean that?"

"Yes, as far as she's concerned, anyway. One person will be over the moon; and that'll be her dear papa, because he has been against me from the beginning. Not her mother, or Luke…they would be for me, but when it comes to decisions they don't count."

She went to him and put her hands on his shoulders and looked into his face as she said, "You're young; twenty years old. There are other girls or, better still, other women. I know how you feel: there's nobody in the world but her; and you'll go on feeling that for a long time. But then it'll pass."

"Well, Moira, I wish time would pass quickly, but I'm afraid there'll only ever be her for me."

Moira sighed and nodded at him, saying, "I still feel the same way about Paul, Melissa's father, yet I know now I could have loved again, and *your* father too, if he had turned out to be a different kind of man. It's very odd, Daniel, the little things that stop you from loving a person. If he hadn't scorned Maggie Ann from the first and treated her like dirt; if he had even given her the slightest respect due to an ordinary servant. But then I can't blame him in that case, can I? because"—she smiled now—"Maggie Ann could never act like an ordinary servant. And she had been with me from the day I was born and she brought Melissa into the world. There are strong, strong ties between her and me, stronger, much stronger than those that exist between my own mother and myself. I carry no feelings for my own mother as I do for Maggie Ann. They say blood is thicker than water, and so one should remember you are carrying the same mixture in your veins, but that has never held with me. I've never felt any close ties with my family, yet I have with Ireland, my country. You know, I still long for Ireland, even after all these years here. How many now? Nearly ten years, but at times it seems I've been away a lifetime, and in this house a lifetime. Yet at others I feel that I left Ireland yesterday. But there, I've learned a lot in the last ten years that I never would have learned in the old country. I met you, and that makes up for so much. Well now—" she stepped back from him and more briskly now, she said, "you'll be having me singing *Ireland Forever* and *Up the Fenians*, if I don't look out. Are you going back to the farm?"

"Yes. Yes, I'm going back now."

"Well, go and look in and say a word to Maggie Ann before you go. I know it's only a couple of hours since you saw her but she loves to have a little crack with you."

He said nothing more but went out and along the corridor. He stopped before he reached Maggie Ann's room and Frances's words came back to him: "You are bound to the two great Irish hulks for eternity. You should have married dear Moira."

* * *

The doctor had called twice during the week, and Moira was helping him on with his coat once again when she said, "How are you finding her?"

"Oh, well, much the same. She was concussed for a time but that seems to be improved and she's cheerful enough; oh! yes. Anyway, I gather she's of a very cheerful nature."

"Yes. Yes, she is, Doctor."

"Well then, the only trouble you're going to have with her, as far as I can see, is keeping her clean."

"That won't be any trouble."

"Those tablets I gave her on Monday haven't as yet started to have much effect: she'll know about it when they do. Oh! dear me. I've often got to wonder if the cure isn't worse than the disease in some cases. And now, what about yourself? You're looking a bit peaky. When do you expect it?"

"Not until the beginning of March."

"Oh, you've got some way to go yet, then."

When she opened the door she cried in a surprised tone, "Well! well! Hello, Janie." And Janie answered, "I was just about to ring the bell. I've been to the back door and couldn't get an answer. Good-morning, Dr Swift."

"Good-morning, Miss Farringdon. You're out of your way, aren't you?"

"One is never out of one's way visiting friends, Doctor."

"Oh, I stand reprimanded. You're right, one is never out of one's way visiting friends. Well, good-day to you, Mrs Stewart. I may not be in till Monday, but should you need me you know where I am."

"I do, Doctor, I do, and thank you very much."

"You're welcome. You're welcome."

Watching the doctor making his way down to his trap, Moira said to Janie, "How did you get here?"

"The same way as the doctor: in a trap; but I took the liberty of putting both it and the horse into the shelter over there under the open barn."

"Oh, that was sensible. Come in, my dear. Come in."

"I've called to see how Miss McTaggart is, not only on my own account but on Pattie's. We were at a lecture last night in Newcastle and I told her of what I had heard about Miss McTaggart being hurt and she asked me to call and tell you how sorry she was and that she would be writing today."

"That's nice of her. "Tis a pity she can't bring herself to come. But there, you know all about it, don't you, Janie? Now would you like a hot drink?"

"I wouldn't say no, but I don't want to put you to any bother. I tell you what I would like, though, and that's a word with your Maggie Ann, as everybody calls her, that's if she is allowed visitors."

"Oh, she'd be delighted. Look, I'll take you to her, then I'll bring a drink in. Oh, that would please her. Come along, my dear. You'll find her cheery, but I must tell you, her...her days are numbered."...

When Janie entered the room she went straight to the bed and, taking the hand outstretched towards her, she said, "Oh, I am sorry to hear of your accident. How are you feeling?"

"Never better, my dear, never better. I've wanted to do this all me life, lie in bed and be waited on. Sit yourself down. To tell you the truth I did this on purpose; 'twas the only way I could stretch me legs."

As Moira went out of the room Janie bit on her lip for a moment before she made herself say, "At times,

I too long to stay in bed, but I've got a martinet of a father. He always wants to be up and about and take me with him. Now Mother is different. She stays in bed whenever she gets the chance, but that's only when Father's away on business.''

There was silence between them for a moment while they looked at each other; then Maggie Ann said, ''Tis some time since I saw you. You're looking bonny.''

Janie cast her eyes downwards for a moment, then smiled and said, ''May I call you Maggie Ann?''

''What else is me name? When the doctor said Miss McTaggart, I looked round the room for her.''

''Well, Maggie Ann, like all those of your nationality, you'd sin your soul to pay a compliment and to put someone at their ease, now wouldn't you?''

Maggie Ann did not answer for a moment, but she looked at this young woman and said, ''From the first time I saw you, when you were a schoolgirl, I think it was when you came to a party here, I thought, she'll make a nice body, that one, and I'm never mistaken about character. Now this is not Irish blarney, and I repeat, you are bonny, because your nature shines through. And that's what pays in the long run, just as with Moira. It always used to be 'Miss Moira', because after all we were mistress and maid, but of latter years the 'miss' has been dropped, because we're sisters under the skin. She is another one with a bonny nature. And people with bonny natures often get the dirty end of the stick, yet somehow I don't think you will, because you've got a level head on your shoulders, and Daniel said that some time ago. 'Janie's got a level head on her shoulders, and quite a lot in her head,' he said.''

"Did he?"

"Yes, he did, and that's the English truth, not the Irish blarney."

They were both laughing when Margaret arrived, carrying a tray holding three cups of tea and a bowl of sugar. And on the sight of her, Maggie Ann said, "Did you know I had a private nurse?"

"No. No, I wasn't aware of it."

"Oh yes; yes I have, and her name is Miss Margaret Stewart, and she looks after me as no-one else in this house does. And I've got two manservants an' all."

"You haven't!"

"Oh aye, I have that: Mr Patrick and Mr Sean. But then of course, I forget me place; you don't give manservants 'mister': Patrick, being the butler, will be called Stewart, just Stewart, and Sean being the footman...well, he'll be called Stewart, an' all." But using a different tone of voice, she added, "You know what I mean?"

Janie couldn't say, "Yes, I know what you mean," to this badinage from a woman who was obviously so ill.

"How many have you, Janie...I mean, servants?"

"Oh, not many, as servants go: four inside with the cook, and three outside."

"Seven? Oh, well I have the same. Seven here, right down to Bridget, though I must say she's not much use at the present time because all she does is squawk... Oh, thank you, Margaret. That looks lovely. Where's your mama?"

"Oh, she had to go and see to the squawker. But you know something, Maggie Ann, Michael's walked almost the full length of the hall this morning."

"You don't say?"

"I do. Yes, all on his own. And he tried to say 'porridge' at breakfast."

"Well! Well! That *is* news." Maggie Ann now turned her head towards Janie, saying, "Michael has been slow on the walking and the talking, and him three years old. It is wonderful news, isn't it?"

"Yes, indeed. I have a cousin in Bradford whose little girl didn't talk until she was five, and she's never stopped since."

"Not till she was five?"

"No, not a word. Then one day, at the table, she said a complete sentence, and her mother almost choked with surprise, and had to be attended to. It appears, so her doctor said, that she was one of these people who just like to listen, so she took everything in and said nothing."

"Well, that could be Michael all over again, because his face is as bright as a button, isn't it, Margaret?"

"Yes. Yes, it is, Maggie Ann."

When Moira came back into the room Janie saw straightaway that there was moisture in her eyes, and so, likely, the baby's needs had been a very tactful excuse made by this little girl here. She said to her now, "Have you broken up for the holiday?" and Margaret answered, "No; the others will next week, though, but *we* all got leave because Mama needed us. Annie could have gone, but it would have meant one of us taking her, then bringing her home again, because it's a long walk."

Moira now said, "They've all been splendid. I don't know what Maggie Ann and I would have done without them."

The tea drunk, Janie thanked Moira for it; then rising, she looked down on Maggie Ann and said, "I must away. I always overstay my welcome wherever I go. It's a fault I have."

"Oh, my dear, dear young woman, you could never overstay your welcome here, could she, Moira?"

"No. No, she couldn't. You're welcome at any time. I think I've told you that before, Janie."

"Yes, you have, Mrs Stewart, and I thank you for it. Moreover, I'll take advantage of it in the future."

"You're not just being polite there, are you? But do look in again on me, because I really would like to see you."

"Yes, I certainly shall, Maggie Ann. But goodbye for now."

"Goodbye, my dear. Goodbye."

In the hall Janie said quietly, "It's so sad, and more so, I think, because she's so cheerful. Her whole aim seems to be...well, to lighten the atmosphere, is the only way I can put it; or perhaps it would be simpler to say, to turn any pity away from herself. She's a brave heart."

"She is indeed, my dear, she's a brave heart. And God alone knows what I'll do without her. But that is to come. Will you do me a favour?"

"Anything. Anything, I'd be only too pleased."

"Well, it's a present I would like bought. You see, I won't be able to get into town; the village'll be as far as I make; but I won't find the quality in the village. I want to buy a very good briar pipe and a pouch and some good quality tobacco. You see, it's for Daniel. Once or twice I've seen him drawing on a pipe late at night. It's a wooden one but it looks an old smelly thing to me and I think he would enjoy a briar. And I'm sure you would know exactly what to buy him; at least, your father would. Now there's a sovereign. Will that be enough?''

''More than enough. Now is there anything else you would like; say, presents for the children?''

''Oh, I make their presents as I do their clothes and they enjoy those as much as anything. I knit and sew for them through the winter months. No; if you would just get me the pipe for Daniel; it'll be a pleasant surprise to him because he's very low at the moment...''

Whether it was intentionally or not Moira added, ''As far as I can gather he's broken with Frances.''

''He's broken with...? You mean, they are no longer en...engaged?''

''Well, if they ever were, dear; I mean, officially, that is. Anyway, I should imagine it's finished. I don't know what caused it.'' She now jerked her head to the side as if chastising herself as she went on, ''Yes, I do; or at least in part. I think he wanted them to get married, but in no way would she consider living in this house, and that was natural enough, and still less did she agree with what he thought was a brilliant idea. Yet I could understand her refusal of this plan, which was to renovate the old part at the end, now used as a store. It was the original house and he had it in his mind to reconstruct it as a private dwelling. Apparently she would have none of it. And again I say I can understand it, because it would take a lot of time and money to make that habitable.''

''It...it might only be a tiff. He cares for her deeply. I...I know that, and I think she does for him too. So, as I said, it could just be something slight and they could be reconciled within a few days.''

''Oh, they've had tiffs before, and I've seen the results of them, but nothing like this one. And another

thing, my dear: if you see Pattie, tell her that Maggie
Ann would be delighted to receive a letter from her,
although''—she smiled now—''she could neither read
nor write, dear soul. But what she would like much
better would be to see her face. Tell her that himself
is out most mornings, sometimes all day. He may be
on the farm or round about. I know she hasn't any
transport, but perhaps you wouldn't mind bringing her.
If only she would come.''

''I'll ask her. I'll do my best. In any case, I'll be
back before Christmas.''

'''Tis good of you.''

''Oh, not at all, not at all. It's a pleasure for me just
to be able to come. Goodbye now.''

''Goodbye, my dear. Goodbye.''

''Don't stand at the door, it's too cold, and I've got
to get the trap out, but before I do I'll have to talk to
Nelson''—she laughed now—''the pony you know; I
have to make my excuses for leaving him for so
long.''

Moira gave an unusually clear laugh, such as she
hadn't done for many a long day; and as she closed
the door she said to no-one in particular, ''There goes
a fine young woman. But what really made me ask
her to get him a pipe and pouch? The one he has is
not bad at all and he's used to it,'' to which she gave
herself no answer, but crossed the hall and was about
to open the door into the passage when it almost thrust
her back, and there appeared Sean, who had managed
to open it by pressing his side against it the while
bumping a large scuttle of coal in front of him.

''Oh, my dear, you've filled that much too full. You
should have got one of them to give you a hand. Never

attempt to carry that on your own again. Here, let me have it.''

"Leave it alone, Mama."

She looked down on her fair-haired son and, bending over him, she asked, "What is it, Sean? You're very quiet these days." She did not go on to explain her question by adding, You have hardly spoken a dozen words since they brought Maggie Ann into the house. Instead she asked him, "Is something troubling you?"

He looked into her face for some seconds before he said, "Maggie Ann is going to die, isn't she?"

She pulled herself up straight. "We're all going to die, Sean, at some time or other. But a young boy like you has no need to worry about it yet."

"I'm not worrying about me dying, Mama, but about Maggie Ann dying."

"She won't die for a long time."

"What do you mean by a long time? A week? A month? A year?"

"I don't know. That is a question only God can answer, because even the doctor didn't know. Now look here! Give me one side of that handle and you take the other and no arguing."

So, lopsidedly, they carried the bucket between them and when they reached the other side of the hall and she went to turn up the passage towards the study, he stopped her by letting go of the handle and saying, "No; 'tis for the drawing-room."

She was about to say, Your father likes a fire in the study. You know what happens if it isn't ablaze, but something in the boy's face checked her. And as if she were obeying someone older she picked up the handle of the bucket again and after motioning to him to do likewise, they carried it into the drawing-room, she thinking, He's a strange child, and closing her mind on the answer she might have given to the question: Why wouldn't he take it into the study?

5

During the week preceding Christmas the weather had offered a sample of everything it could provide: with rain, sleet, high winds, then rain again, the latter causing the most havoc because it came down steadily for three days and the roads became quagmires, with many impassable. But on the Sunday morning the sun dared to show its weak face for a time, and, from her bed, Maggie Ann moved her head to the side and looked towards the window, saying, "There now! Isn't that a sight for sore eyes?" She now looked from Moira to Daniel for an answer, and when neither of them spoke she demanded on a laugh, "Well, isn't it?"

"It'll take more than that weak ray to dry up the roads," said Daniel. "The cows haven't been got out in the yards for days now. And, you know, this morning Betsy asked me to teach her to swim out of the byre, for the mooing of the others is getting her down. She's aging fast and so I suppose the chatter of the young ones gets on her nerves."

Both Moira and Maggie Ann laughed; then Moira

said, "Go on now and get your breakfast. You must be starving."

After Daniel had left the room Maggie Ann, in a low mutter, said, "'Tisn't fair. Five in the mornin' till all hours at night; he should have help." She didn't go on to say, as she had done many times before, that his father should be down there with him instead of snoring his drink off; and then coming down and demanding his breakfast at eight o'clock in the mornin' as if he were landed gentry.

But Moira knew what she was thinking and she said, "Don't you worry your head about him. He's as strong as a bull; what you've got to concern yourself with is following doctor's orders and taking these tablets."

"What's the use, Moira? I ask you plainly, what's the use? Can you see any difference? I'm still a balloon. Before, if I wasn't quite a painless balloon, I wasn't troubled in all me veins as if the devil was already in me and scooting boiling water through them. No; no more, Moira. You and me know what we know; and for the time that is left, let me be at ease and happy among you all."

"For...God's...sake! Maggie Ann, will you stop talking like that or you'll break me up?"

"Well, I'll just have to break you up, won't I? because as I've got to face it, so you've got to face it an' all. And we've got to do some talkin', you an' me, about the future. Not that I'm sure where mine's goin' to be. God himself knows I've never done any harm to anybody except through me tongue, which runs away with me at times and shows which way me feelin's are blowin'. When we meet up I suppose He'll decide. But then there's you and the children: if you're spared the comin' one, that'll be eight on your heels; so, what are you goin' to do with yourself and them?''

Now leaning her hands on the edge of the bed, Moira brought her face down to Maggie Ann's, saying softly and firmly, ''I don't know what I'm going to do, my dear, only that, like you, I'll have to leave it in God's hands.''

''Yes. Yes. I suppose you're right. He'll be the one to deal with it. One thing I wish He could do for me, but I see little hope of it, and that's bury me in Ireland. I can't see meself restin' easy in English soil, because as you know yourself, I've never taken to it. It hasn't the quality about it, and it doesn't give off the colour in the grass like it does over there. Now does it?''

Moira straightened her back, gave one long hopeless look down on the bloated face, then hurried from the room, along the passage and into the kitchen.

There she leant against the door, and Daniel, rising from the table, said, ''What is it? She's worse?''

''No. No.'' She shook her head, then rubbed her hand round her face, saying as she went towards the fire, ''It's the way she talks. She talks about death as if she was going on a holiday...well, on a sort of journey, as I suppose it is, but she's not a bit afraid of it. For me, all me life I've been scared of dying; but there she lies, not able to move much and aiming to keep everyone else cheerful.''

''Well, wouldn't you rather have her that way than being afraid of...what she knows is to come?''

''I suppose so, but she's just said she's sorry only for one thing, and that is she can't be buried across the water, because the ground is different there, or some such. ''Oh—'' She took the kettle off the hob and filled up the brown teapot standing on the edge of the table, and then she muttered, "I don't know how I'm going to stand this, one life coming and one life going. And I've got to say it, I'd give the one I'm carrying and a dozen like it just to keep her here."

Whatever answer Daniel would have given to this was checked by the door opening and his father appearing; and what made them both look at him was that he wasn't dressed for riding but was in his ordinary working-day apparel. Moira put in quickly, "I didn't know you were up. I'll get your breakfast in a minute."

Both she and Daniel were then surprised at his tone when he said, "That doesn't matter; it can wait," as he walked towards the long kitchen table where, his hands gripping the back of a wooden chair, he looked from one to the other as he said, "I'd better tell you because it concerns us all;" and turning to Daniel, he addressed him pointedly, saying, "It's no use you getting on your high horse and telling me what can be done, and what should be done, and what hasn't been done; the fact is we're up against it and I'm having to sell Westfields."

"*What!*" The expression on Daniel's face could have been described as comical, so twisted was it; then he stammered, "W...W...Westfields? It's the most fertile part of the land, and runs the complete length of Barton's!"

"Tell me something new, something I've never heard before, not something I was brought up with, and my father before me. That's why it's being sold: because *it is fertile.*"

"But...but I understood Barton is finished, that he's having to sell up." Daniel's voice had risen almost to a shout.

"Yes, and you understand right. But the man who's buying Barton's hasn't got enough land for his various purposes: he doesn't only want to farm, he wants to build, and on Barton's land."

"Well then, if that's the case"—Daniel's head was bobbing now like a puppet's—"if that's the case then get this man to buy us out an' all, because with that land gone we, too, could be sunk."

"*Then, young man,* Mr Manager, Mr Know-all, can you tell me what else I can do to save *this house* and the remains of the farm from going into the hands of the bank?"

"I can't tell you what you can do now, but I can tell you what you shouldn't have done over the past years: you shouldn't have spent so much on *your drink* and *your whores.*"

"Daniel! Daniel!" Moira was standing in front of him, forcibly pushing him back towards the outer door, the while he still attempted to thrust her aside as he went on yelling, "I can't say it too often: that you lived on my mother for years and you've never been man enough to earn a living for your family."

One arm stretched out, Moira opened the back door and pushed him outside, and he in turn almost knocked one of the children backwards.

After the door was clashed closed he stood in the yard staring at it, then looked to the side to see Sean leaning against the wall rubbing an elbow. And he turned on him, still shouting, "Serves you damn well right! Listening at doors again."

"Daniel...I want to talk to you."

"Well, I don't want to talk to you, not now. You've kept your mouth closed for days, so keep it that way." And with this, he marched across the yard and into

the stable block, and there, leaning over the half door
of an empty stall, he lifted his fist and banged it
against the stanchion.

After a moment or so he turned and leant against
the stanchion and from there he looked towards the
barn door to where Sean was standing, and he bowed
his head as he said, "I'm sorry. I'm sorry."

"'Tis all right."

When the boy came towards him Daniel said,
"What did you want to say?"

"Doesn't matter, not now."

"Go on, go on, whatever it is."

"No, not now. But...but can I ask you something
else?"

"Yes, anything." Daniel looked wearily down on
the boy, and Sean, looking up at him, said, "Do you
think Maggie Ann will die before the year is out?"

At this Daniel lifted his head, took a deep breath
and stopped the sharp retort he was about to give.
Instead, he said, "I don't know that, Sean; nor does
anyone else. She'll go in God's good time, as she herself would say. But...but don't worry about her, because she's happy. In a strange way, she's happy,
and—" he now took hold of the boy's hand and
walked him towards the door, saying, "you've got to
believe that; it would make her sad if she saw that you
were sorry for her. She likes you to sit with her,
doesn't she? Well, go on now, because I've got to do
some work, or at least some thinking. You understand?"

"Yes. Yes, Daniel, I understand."

At this, the boy withdrew his hand from Daniel's,
then walked slowly across the yard and into the house
again. Daniel turned back into the stables and, lifting

an old jacket from a peg, he put it on, because he couldn't trust himself to go back into the house to get his coat.

He now walked, not towards the farm proper, but through the tangled gardens that eventually led to the Westfields, which area was a good third of their complete acreage.

Almost two hours later Daniel returned to the house and, when he saw the pony and trap standing under cover of the open barn, for a split second his mind cried, It's Frances. But then his reason told him Frances would never be allowed to use their trap to come here. And anyway, this was a very smart outfit.

He went quietly into the kitchen thinking that whoever the visitor was, Moira would have taken them into the drawing-room; but immediately he was brought to a halt by the sound of the gabble of voices and laughter coming from along the corridor. Whoever the visitors were, they were in Maggie Ann's room.

He racked his brain for a moment as to who would Moira take into Maggie Ann's room. And the answer came: Pattie. But Pattie wouldn't come in a trap. Why not? Some friend could have brought her. But then she wouldn't risk meeting Father. Well, he would have to see who was causing this unusual joyful chatter.

However, before he reached the end of the corridor he knew who the visitor was, because he remembered Moira telling him Janie had called earlier in the week.

He opened the door into a crowded room, for the whole family was present, even Bridget, propped up at the end of the bed. And on a table to the side of the window was stacked a pile of coloured parcels, some small, some large; and Moira was crying to Margaret, "Now leave them be! Leave them be!"

"Look, Daniel, presents!"—Catherine was jumping up and down—"in pretty boxes for Christmas; and look at Maggie Ann's shawl!" She was clinging on to his hand now.

He didn't look towards the bed and Maggie Ann, but at Janie, who was standing close to the bed-head, and he said, "Hello, Janie. By! you've started something, haven't you? We'll be expected to keep this up, you know."

"And a very good thing, I should say," and she nodded at him.

"Daniel!" said Moira. "Will you cast your attention this way for a minute and see what this dear girl has brought Maggie Ann?"

Daniel was now standing by the bedside looking down on Maggie Ann's pallid but smiling face, for about her shoulders and across the top of the quilt was draped a blue shawl. That it was of fine wool he could see, and of its kind and quality he was informed the next moment by Maggie Ann herself saying, "Did you ever see anything so beautiful? It's as blue as the sky on a summer's day. And it's cashmere, real cashmere. Feel it."

He leant forward and rubbed his fingers over the long silken fringe, and said, "It's indeed beautiful, and as soft as down." He now looked up towards Janie and paused for a moment before he said, "This is very kind of you, Janie…altogether, it's very kind of you."

"Janie said we should have a Christmas tree. You could cut the top off one of the firs and stick it in a butter barrel. She said that's what they used to do at her house. And then you hang coloured papers and baubles on it and the presents. You get them on Christmas mornin'. That's what they do at your house, isn't it, Janie?"

"Yes. Yes, it is, Margaret."

She turned to explain to Daniel, saying, "It's very easy to do; but perhaps you've made one before?"

"No, no. But I read that Prince Albert thought up the idea; or perhaps it was something that he had been brought up with."

"Yes, it was." Then Janie turned to Moira, saying, "Father picked up the idea when I was little. But with the first attempt he nearly set the house on fire, for while he and Mother were decorating it with streamers and holly his cigar came in contact with the paper and away it all went up...up!" She demonstrated by lifting her hands. And now, turning to the children who were laughing, she said, "The funniest part was, that they didn't know whether to throw it out of the window or run with it through the hall. But anyway, it would have been very heavy to lift, being in a tub. And to make matters worse one of the maids brought a bucket of water and another a dish of salt, and between them they quenched the flaming tree, but not without a lot of mess. My mother said she would never have another one."

"Did you have another, miss?"

"Yes, Patrick, the next year; but she never let my father go near it."

There was more laughter until Margaret said, "Can we take our presents and keep them till Christmas, Mama?"

"No, you can't! I've already told you they are not to be opened until Christmas morning; and that's in ten days' time."

"We wouldn't open them, Mama," piped Catherine.

"Of course you wouldn't," said Moira, "until you got outside the door. And that's where you're all going, for Maggie Ann has had enough of you."

"Oh, Maggie Ann never has enough of them," said Maggie Ann now. "And I'll tell you what, my dears, you'll have your Christmas tree and you'll have it in here. So off you go now, as your mama bids you."

When the children went out, all exclaiming on the wonders of a Christmas tree and the presents to be hung on it, and itself in Maggie Ann's room, Moira picked up the child from the bed, saying, "I'm going to make a drink, and you"—she inclined her head towards Daniel—"sit yourself down for a minute and act like a normal human being does on a Sunday."

"Yes, do, Daniel," said Maggie Ann. "Both of you sit down beside me and let's have a crack for, you know, I've never liked Sundays. Never in me life have I liked Sundays. A day of rest, they called it, it was always the heaviest in the week for me, for I had to be up afore my clothes were on, and there I would be cookin', not only for the family but for the tribes that seemed to drop in. Most people seemed to take it into their head that they would like to go and see old so and so on a Sunday. And they always timed their coming, at least they did over there, just around dinner time, and they would always say they didn't want to put you out. But there, you had to squeeze in another two or four, sometimes more, an' that would be besides relations." An' money was tight at times in Moira's family, oh aye, it was that, and I had to do a lot of stretching with the food." She smiled widely now. "I used to give them their suet puddin' first, generous helpings I would give them of that, so when it came to the meat they hadn't much room for it, although some would eat until they had stomachs on them like poisoned pups.''

When Janie's laugh rang out, Daniel was forced to join in with it, although at the moment he felt in no mood for laughter: Janie's very presence and the gifts she had brought were, in a way, adding to the irritation seething in him, which was the residue of the flaming temper that had filled him earlier as he had stalked the fields his father proposed to sell.

He stared at her now. She looked so relaxed, so at ease...at home, as it were. Her home life must be the antithesis of what she saw taking place in this house.

She was saying to him now, ''I saw Pattie last night...and John. We were at a lecture in Newcastle. It was on modern literature, and very interesting. Do you manage to read much? Oh, that's a silly question, isn't it? I'm sure, when you finish at night, all you want to do is to drop into bed.''

Before he could answer, Maggie Ann put in, ''Yes, you're right there, girl. Working from five in the mornin' till nine at night doesn't leave much time for readin'. But still, I think he's done his share. You used to keep us alive, didn't you? with your chatter about books when you were at that school. You used to quote from Mr Dickens and men like Collins and a Mrs Gaskell. See! aren't I clever? You didn't think I could remember names, but there you are, I do.'' She moved her head slowly as she went on, ''I've never been able to write me own name or read a word from a page, but me memory now...I have a memory like, say, the elephant has.''

''Well,'' said Janie, kindly, ''you learn as much by

listening, and if you have a good memory into the bargain, then you very often can take more in than those who can read and write." Then turning to Daniel, she said, "I've just finished a book by Mrs Gaskell. She's an excellent writer; like Dickens, in a way, but in a different style. I've always thought Dickens's characters are more like caricatures. What d'you think?"

"Oh, I haven't read him since my schooldays; but yes, I think you're right."

"Whereas Mrs Gaskell's characters seem to step out of the pages; they're believable, and she shows up the conditions of the workers to such an extent that, on the other hand, you are saying to yourself, *it's unbelievable* that people can live in such conditions and be expected to work such long, long hours."

More to make conversation than anything else, he said, "Quite candidly, I can't recall reading Mrs Gaskell. Dickens, yes; but not her. She sounds very interesting."

"Oh, she is, she is. I have two of her books at home. I'll bring them for you if you would like them."

"Yes. Yes, thank you." He tried to sound enthusiastic; then, getting to his feet, he said, "If you'll excuse me I'll go and see what Moira's doing with that coffee, and then I feel I need a change of"—he swept his hand down his rough coat—"and it being Sunday. What d'you say, Maggie Ann?"

"I say you look good in anything to me. But I've never seen you in that old coat before. The last time I saw it, it was hanging in the stables."

"You're right there; but I happened to go out without a coat and I was in a hurry and I didn't want to come back in, so I made use of it.'' Then aiming to be jocular, he said, ''But, madam, if you don't like my attire, you know what you can do.'' And on this he went out on a forced laugh.

With the room to themselves they were quiet for a moment, until Maggie Ann, stroking the soft shawl lying over her chest, said, ''Apart from Moira, you are the kindest person I've had the good fortune to meet in me life. And I thank you, me dear young woman, for this gift, and I will wear it every day as long as I live and perhaps after. But that apart—'' Now looking at the shawl and her fingers still moving over it, she went on, ''I'm goin' to ask you two very personal questions and because I'm a sick woman, you'll feel you must humour me. From what I know of you I think you're a very honest person, so you mustn't humour me; but you can say either yes, or...well, I know you won't say, 'You should mind your own business', but you can say politely, 'I'll not answer your question, Miss McTaggart.' Now me first question is: Do you like our Daniel?''

There was a long pause before Janie answered, ''Yes, I like Daniel.''

Maggie Ann had stopped stroking the shawl and now she turned her head as much as it was possible and looked at the tall figure sitting by her bedside, who was wearing a green velvet coat. It was open and showing a brown dress with a belted waist; and on her head she had a green velour hat. It had a high crown, but was not, like those now in the height of fashion, covered with flowers and feathers. The face beneath was a good face, and to Maggie Ann at this moment the flush on it was making it beautiful. And quietly she asked her second question, "Do you, or could you, more than like him?"

Janie stared down into the wide face. The round dark eyes were bright, and she said, "Before I answer your question, Maggie Ann, I would like a promise."

"Fair enough. Fair enough."

"Whichever way I answer it, and I *will* answer it, I want you to promise that you will not repeat what I have said, or suggest what I think, to the person concerned or those near him."

After a moment Maggie Ann said, "You have me promise as if it was God's word: I'll never repeat what you're about to say."

It was a long moment before Janie said, "Yes, I more than like Daniel, and I have done for a long, long time. I cannot remember when I knew how I felt about him, but I do know now that whatever happens in my life, I shall retain this feeling for him. Yet I also know that I don't exist for him. There is only one person in his life and that is Frances. They are apart now but whether they come together or not I cannot imagine there will come a time when he will not love her, for such is my feeling for him, so his has been for Frances. I will say one last thing. It may sound spiteful, but it is how I feel; she is not worthy of him."

Again there was silence between them until Maggie Ann's hand went out and Janie put hers into it. And now Maggie Ann said, "You never spoke a truer word than with your last utterance, for I've always known that if he gets her she'll do him no good, because she's an upstart and she'd drive him to do things against his whole nature. But thank you, lass, for your confidence. No-one could have spoken more plainly or honestly. I liked you afore, I've always liked you, but now I admire you. And I'll tell you this; there won't be an hour until I leave this world that I won't think of you and pray that one day you'll find great happiness. Whether it's with him or whoever, it'll come." Then, on the sound of voices in the corridor she exclaimed, "Enough. Enough. Here they come. God bless you, lass."

When the door opened Maggie Ann was laughing. "Coffee!" she was saying; "I could have made a six-course dinner in the time it takes them to fetch a cup of coffee."

6

The black coat of depression that hung over Daniel was lifted momentarily three days before Christmas Day when he received a note. Consisting of only two lines, the contents set his heart thumping against his ribs. "Can you be in the wood at three o'clock on Friday? I have something to say to you, if not to tell you."

The last five words puzzled him; yet clearly she wanted to see him.

Up in his bedroom he again read the note: I have something to say to you, if not to tell you. Well, he would have something to say to her, too. He would again tell her how much he loved her, and he would tell her that he would always love her, always and always.

Friday. That was today. What was he thinking about? Of course, it was today.

He stood up and caught a glimpse of himself in the cheval mirror standing crosswise in the corner of the room. What did he look like! A scarecrow—he just needed some straw in his hair. He also needed new working breeches, new leggings, new boots. He had two good suits, although one no longer fitted him. He'd have to ask Moira to let it out, and he'd use it for work. But anyway, today, as it was freezing, he could hide his shabbiness with his topcoat, which was of quite good quality.

He now stared at his reflection in the mirror and thought how ludicrous it was that this big house, so well appointed, even if, these days, run down with dust and untidiness, and the farm that was once one of the most prosperous in the district, if not in the country, even if not as large as some, had been reduced to a shadow of their former glory. According to Barney, a lavish ball had been held here at least twice a year, when the yard and front of the house had been packed with carriages, with the horses unhitched and led down to the farm. Well, that would never happen again. And yet, not only this house but all the farms for miles around were in similar straits. Farming in general was in a very bad way, with the prices of corn and wheat dropping each year. As for the vegetables, most of the crops had been washed out of the ground before they'd had a chance to mature. It was the weather. But then it was always the weather, wasn't it, that controlled the fortunes of a farmer? Nevertheless, the weather couldn't take all the blame for what had happened to this farm and house.

As he swung round from the mirror he cried within himself, No, it isn't always the weather, it's drink and neglect and the satisfying of one man's lust. And the thought brought him to a standstill: lust. No, no. The feeling that he had for Frances wasn't lust. Need...oh yes, a great, great need; but it was prompted by love, because he could never see that need being fulfilled by anybody but her...

At ten minutes to three he was standing in the wood, and although he had an overcoat coat on, a muffler, and a tweed cap pulled well down on his head, he had to stamp his feet and keep moving, so severe was the cold. The roads were hard now, the trees stiff, the branches like artificial arms stuck on the trunks.

When he spotted her in the distance he became still; then he hurried towards her.

Although neither of them put out hands towards the other, their gazes linked and held. Her face was framed in a fur bonnet, and she was wearing a thick grey Melton cloth coat that reached down to the top of her boots. The collar of the coat was turned up, forming a frame around the bonnet and the lower part of her face.

As if they were meeting formally he said, "How are you?"

"I'm very well, but I must get back soon, so we'd better not waste words. As I said in my letter, I've come to ask you something."

"Well"—his voice was quiet—"go on, ask me."

She lowered her lids for a moment, nipped at her lip, then turned and looked towards the gnarled roots spreading from a tree on to the path.

Then, her head snapping upwards, she said, "I'm going to give you one more chance and meet you half-way. I'll wait six months, longer if you'll promise me you will then leave here and we could be married." Her voice softening now, she went on, "I don't care where we go, Daniel, but one thing I won't do is live in any part of that house; at least, not as it stands now with the crop in it. And what's more, Father wouldn't allow it. I'm under age, and he would put his foot down. Anyway, he has other ideas for me...Well?"

His face was stiff. He was about to speak, but found he couldn't for the moment—his Adam's apple was jerking in his throat—but when the words did come out they weren't on a yell, nor even harsh, but quiet and firm: "We've been over this already, Frances; this is the crux of all the trouble and nothing has altered, not a jot. But that isn't quite true, for the situation has worsened, if anything, because I suppose your father has already heard—he too has an ear to the inn chatter—that Father is going to sell the Westfield strip. So what, in your heart of hearts, would you think of me if I walked out on that family, with Maggie Ann dying and Moira about to have another child? And then there are the children, the crop, as you call them; as far as I can see, looking at things plainly, I'm their only stay. But it can't go on forever. I...I feel things will clear up some time."

"Oh, yes, yes," Frances retorted, "wait until the one she's carrying is married, eh? Another twenty years and then you'd be free, wouldn't you? Well, you've answered my question and you'll be sorry for it because, as I put in my letter, I have something to tell you, but I thought I'd give you one more chance to see things my way; just for once, to see things my way. Well now, since you don't want me, somebody else does: your dear friend Ray Melton. He'll see I won't have to live like a pig in a sty, or be a kind of servant to a crop of half-Irish peasants... Oh, you can grit your teeth, Daniel Stewart, but that's what they are, and I can tell you now, Ray has already been to my father to ask if the road is clear, and Father said that in his opinion the road had always been clear, because he would never have countenanced my marrying you anyway. And he told him to go ahead. I'm seeing him tonight, and when he asks me, I shall say yes. Well, I've asked you my question and I've said what I had to tell you. How d'you like it?''

He stared into the face of this beautiful girl, screwed up as it was with a mixture of what he could only describe as disdain and hate. He had never seen her like this, nor had he heard her talk like this. That she didn't like Moira and the children, he understood, and she had never said anything to their credit, but the venom that had been in her tone shocked him.

The thought crept in from the back of his mind that she had a mean soul. At bottom, he thought, she's got a mean soul. But he rejected the thought. It was her love for him that was driving her to say such things, and her need. Oh yes, her need. He knew all about her need as he did about his own. He had scorned her need, at least so she had thought, but now he had the urge to grab her, drag her into the thicket to the side of the road and there put a child into her.

And what then? Would he then take her away and marry her? Or if she was obliged to come and live with him, what kind of a life would that be for all concerned? As it was, only he was suffering at the moment. No, no; he must be fair; she was suffering too, but mostly because of her need, and that would soon be satisfied. Ray would see to that...but what then?

Ray. Hatred flared up in him for his long-time friend. He had always liked Ray, perhaps because his was such a different character from his own. A bit wild, but always amusing. And in some respects Ray had been kind. But then, he had always had plenty of money to be kind with. When he had first heard he was going to university it seemed to him that Ray could wish for nothing more. But he *had* wished for something more, and he would get it because he had money; or his people had, with their line of shops. But would they welcome Miss Frances Talbot as the wife of their only son, and her father and mother who, after all, were homely folk and just one step above farm labourers? He wondered. But why was he wondering? Why was he standing there just staring at her, unable to say a word?

Her voice seemed to come from a long distance to him as she cried, "It's no use looking at me like that. And if you've got nothing to say, I'm going. But I'll say one last thing: you love me and you're throwing me over for a lot of no-good individuals, and that means from your father downwards, and you'll be sorry for it. As long as you live you'll be sorry for it. You mark my words, Daniel Stewart. Yes, indeed, you mark my words."

He watched her stepping away from him. When she stumbled on a rut and almost overbalanced he made no movement towards her, not even putting out his hand, but just watched her pause for a moment as she stared fixedly at him, then flounce around and hurry away at between a run and a walk.

Instead of standing there until she had disappeared from view, he too turned away, although not towards home. He pushed his way through the dead bracken and into the woodland, and there, with his arm outstretched, he supported himself against a tree. It was over, quite over, finally over. He knew this for a certainty now. But she had said, "As long as you live you'll be sorry for it."...

He remained in the wood until he began to shiver, when he turned and made his way home.

He entered the house through the front door and went straight up the stairs and into his bedroom. There, he took off his overcoat and hung it in the wardrobe. And again he looked at his reflection in the cheval mirror; but this time his thoughts prompted no voice inside him to retaliate in any way against his life, for they were being choked by an emotion that now caused him to swing about and push the door bolt home. Then, because he was blinded by this weakness that seemed to be sweeping away his manhood, he made for the head of the bed and there he twisted his body until his face lay buried in the pillow, and it became wet with the agony of rejection.

Christmas came and went. The tree had been put up in Maggie Ann's room and the children had never known such excitement as they experienced when opening the coloured parcels, from which the girls were careful to keep the fancy paper and bows.

The presents ranged from school bags to pretty dresses, and each parcel contained a book of one kind or another. But the excitement reached its height when Moira opened hers to find a grey silk blouse with a pink bow at the collar and matching buttons at the front. And when Daniel opened his and found two books, one *Mary Barton* by Mrs Gaskell, the other *Conditions Of The Working Class* by Engels, he had stared at them, then given a wry smile as he said, "She's aiming to get me into politics."

Moira said, "But isn't that nice of her? Isn't she the kindest body in the world?" And when he opened the parcel from Moira and saw the pipe, the pouch and the tobacco, at first he made no remark on it, but went straight to her and kissed her, then said, "You forgot something."

"What is that, Daniel?" She seemed concerned.

"The smoking cap and the velvet jacket."

There was laughter all round, because even the younger children couldn't see their wonderful Daniel sitting smoking in a cap and velvet jacket.

One person was missing from the celebrations; but then he had never once stepped into Maggie Ann's room. And on this, no-one remarked, not to Maggie Ann nor to each other.

When, earlier that morning, Moira had handed her husband an unwrapped scarf, saying quietly, "With Christmas wishes to you, Hector," she had not added the word "happy". He had looked at the scarf for some seconds, before he said, "Thank you. It's...it's what's needed in this weather... Thank you." Then he had looked at her and for the first time in their acquaintance he admitted his failure, for now he said, "I've made a hash of things, haven't I?"

She had come back with no apology for him. Perhaps if he had said, I'm sorry, Moira; but no; he had simply made a statement which was true, and she hadn't been aware of any deep regret in it, and she knew that if the conversation had gone on he would have blamed circumstances, fate and the weather. Oh yes, the weather. He had said, "I've made a hash of things," at the same time almost adding, But it wasn't my fault. Oh, she knew this man. Ten years spent in his bed and out of it, there was nothing about him she didn't know. She had said, "If you would join us in the drawing-room this night and have a game with the children t'would make them happy," and to this he had answered, "I'll see. I'll see how things go," which meant that if he wasn't in the inn, or if he was sober enough; and she had left it at that.

So Christmas had passed and in the days before the New Year it appeared that Maggie Ann seemed to be fading. She still smiled, she still talked, but not so often. What was noticeable to the whole family, however, was that Sean would sit by her side for hours, his hand in hers and with neither of them uttering a word.

This morning they were sitting like this when Maggie Ann said, "What is it like outside, Sean?"

"'Tis very cold, Maggie Ann. The ground is like iron; it's been freezing for days. But I think snow is near. I saw a flake come down early on."

"Just one?"

"Yes, Maggie Ann, just one. I waited for others but none came."

"'Tis a sign, that, the same as a falling star. The falling star means another soul has just gone into heaven, and one single flake of snow means a soul is waiting to be born."

"Is that a fact, Maggie Ann?"

"'Tis, Sean, 'tis."

Moira, coming into the room at that moment, said, "You, Sean, sitting there like a stook and the fire low, what d'you mean by it? You'll have Maggie Ann freezing. Look, her nose is red."

"My nose has always been red," Maggie Ann responded, "And the room's like an oven. But go on, boy, get some more coal in; your mama wants to roast us alive."

Sean rose from his seat and looked at his mother. There was a half-smile on the women's faces as he picked up the scuttle and left the room, with Moira following him as far as the kitchen.

He was lifting the latch of the coalhouse when he saw his father coming out of the stable. As usual, he was riding Rustler and the horse neighed loudly when his nostrils met the cold air. Sean stood stiffly, looking up at his father as he passed, and although his father knew he was there, he did not turn his head and look down on his son, but put his horse into a trot and went from the yard.

The boy left the scuttle in the coalhouse, then ran back to the kitchen door, and pushing it open, said, "I think I'll chop some wood first, Mama."

"Good. But come in and wrap up well. Where's Patrick?"

"He's down at the farm. They didn't need me; there's nothing much that can be done."

"And there'll be less if it snows."

"Yes, Mama."

Sean went out and into the corridor, and from there into a room on the left that had at one time been the butler's pantry and was now used as a cloakroom for the children's clothes. And there, taking an old coat from a peg, he put it on, then pulled a flap-eared cap on to his head. Lastly, he wound a muffler around his neck; but he took no gloves.

When outside, instead of making for the chopping block behind the stables, he followed the path his father had taken on the horse, which was a short cut to the village. This route bordered the gardens, crossed over the wooden bridge spanning the little stream, went on past the copse, along by the bog field, and from there went through the gate and on to the main road.

Sean reached the wooden bridge, where he stood for a moment looking ahead to where the copse bordered one side of the narrow path, the other side of which gave way to a steep bank leading down to the frozen stream. In the spring the stream would rush and tumble between the banks it had carved out for itself over the years and squeeze its spume-tipped waters under the wooden bridge. Then it spread out and meandered by the side of the bog fields and through the adjoining estate until it reached the river, by which time it had broadened considerably. But here it was only a strip of ice about ten feet wide, although the drop to it from the path was all of twenty feet.

Sean walked from the bridge until he was standing opposite the copse and looking down to where the bank dropped sheer to the frozen stream. Presently, he turned and looked back to the copse, where the bracken lay in mounds of frozen fronds; and he stepped in among it, his feet breaking the undergrowth as if it were glass. So far in, he turned and saw that he had cleared a path of sorts through the shoulder-high tangle. He retraced his steps, then repeated the process, walking into the bracken and out again.

At last, seeming satisfied, he returned to the bridge, crossed it, and walked back to the chopping block and wood pile. This was made up of lengths of cut branches, some as thick as a man's forearm. These were from a tree that had fallen in a recent storm. It had been a big tree and had provided wood for the fires for some time. Now, although the pile was still long it was low, and he walked along it until he found a piece measuring two feet or so and of a thickness that he could grip in his hand.

He now looked about for a similar piece, and after

finding it he laid it to one side; then with the first piece in his hand, he went and stood some ten feet from the high wall that backed the stables, and for the next fifteen minutes he practised throwing the wood at the wall.

At first, his aim was too low and he had to raise his arm higher, and when he was satisfied as to the position his arm should be in for the wood to hit a certain point on the wall, he continued to practise the throw, until a voice startled him, saying, "What d'you think you're doing?"

He actually jumped round to see Daniel, then gasped and stammered, "Pl...pl...playing."

"Playing? Pelting wood at the wall? I heard the thuds in the yard. You don't usually play with the wood." Daniel bent over him now, saying, "What's the matter: come on, tell me what's the matter."

"Nothing, Daniel, I just...just felt like it."

"Well, when you're feeling like bashing something there's a reason for it. Come on." Daniel put his arm around Sean's shoulder, guessing the reason: the boy was so fond of Maggie Ann, and she of him. And he was such a sensitive youngster: aloof, in a way, and different. And of late, he had noticed that when the others were playing, generally Sean would stand aside or take a stroll, that is when he wasn't sitting with Maggie Ann.

When he now said to him, "Come on back to the farm with me," Sean answered, "I'm going to take wood in for Maggie Ann's fire."

"Oh well, do that. But"—again Daniel bent over the boy—"whatever's got into your head, don't take it out on the wall." And he smiled at Sean now, adding, "You could knock it over; the pointing's gone in places, you know." He now gently cuffed his brother's ear, then walked away.

Left alone again, Sean picked up the two pieces of wood. The one that was now frayed at the ends through contact with the wall he threw on top of the pile. But the other he examined closely. One end came to a rough point, the other bore the straight cut of the saw. He now weighed it in his hand. It was heavy, but not too heavy, no heavier than the piece he had been wielding. Walking to the edge of the pile he laid it to the side before chopping up a few lengths from the pile, which he then carried indoors to Maggie Ann's room.

The fire had already been built up, so he laid the logs neatly one on top of the other to the side of the hearth; then he sat down on the chair that was permanently placed by the bed. And when Maggie Ann turned her face slowly towards him and smiled, he smiled gently back at her, then took her white puffed hand in his and held it.

After a moment she said, "What's worryin' you, me dear?"

"You are."

"Oh, that's no news to me. I've worried everybody all me life. But here I am now lyin' and not sayin' a wrong word to anybody, not gettin' in anybody's way, and you tell me I'm worryin' you."

She stopped talking, and he made no remark, and so they sat staring at each other, until at last she said quietly, "Now, we've had all this out: there's nothin' to worry about. You've got a very wise head on your shoulders. You're too old for your years, I would say, but it'll carry you far. Oh, yes, it'll carry you far; and I'll be with you. I've told you that, haven't I? I'll be

with you all the way. As I said, there are things you
know that I don't know, but there are things I know
that you don't know, feelings that don't come from
my head, because that has never been very bright, but
from my heart. They are like yours. So, what d'you
say? Let's sit quiet, eh? for a time and enjoy our feelings.''

She turned her face wearily away from him and, her
breath coming in hard gasps, she closed her eyes; but
he did not close his; nor was he worried for her at this
moment, for he knew that her time to go had not yet
come.

How long he had sat on the frozen bracken he did
not know, but Sean knew that his father would eventually return from the village this way: when the main
road was covered in slush or ice, as it was now, he
always used the back way, because the path was sheltered. His time for returning from the village was usually around two o'clock, but it was well past that time
now. However, he reasoned that if his father had gone
into Fellburn then he must get back before dark, and
the twilight was already beginning, which meant it had
turned three o'clock.

He had kept flapping his arms and shuffling his feet
to stop them going stiff, and up till now he had resisted
getting up and stamping, because then he would
crackle the bracken and that could be heard. But he
had also reasoned that a man on a horse wouldn't have
heard him anyway. No, he wasn't worried about the
man on the horse hearing him stamping his feet, but
Patrick or Margaret or Annie might take it into their
heads to come this way when they couldn't find him
about the house.

When he actually heard the horse's hooves he made to spring to his feet, but his legs were so stiff that he almost fell over and he had to grip the ice-bound fronds to steady himself.

Grabbing up the piece of wood by his side, he peered over the bracken and through the bare branches of the trees and saw the horse and rider approaching. And now, taking four steps forward, he waited.

When the sound of the horse neighing came to him he crouched a little, his arm now raised, his hand shaking as it gripped his weapon near the broad, clean-cut edge.

Just before the horse's head came into full view he let fly the piece of wood, and with his eyes almost staring out of his head, he followed its arc. But it failed to hit the target, which was the rider. Instead, it struck the horse on the side of the neck, causing the animal to rear up, its forelegs pawing the air. His father, too, reared up from the saddle before turning a somersault in the air, and, with a smothered cry, dropped out of view.

Sean now watched the horse prance in a complete circle before galloping off.

Time passed before Sean raised himself from his knees and crept slowly on to the path, to look down on the contorted figure lying on the ice; and then he sat on the top of the bank and let himself slide down the icy slope to land within feet of his father.

When he rose from his hands and knees he made no movement towards the still figure lying there; he noted that there was one leg twisted right up behind the other, and that the two arms were wide spread. But there was no sign of blood coming from his now bare head or face. His father's hat lay some distance away against what would have been the bank of the little stream.

When Sean started to shiver, even though he didn't actually feel cold, he turned and tried to make his way up to the path again. But when with every step he took he slid backwards, he stood for a moment, considering what he should do. He looked to where the bank rose steeply and right to the beams of the bridge itself, and it was to this he made his way, although not without slithering and falling several times.

The cross trusses of the bridge he used as a ladder by pulling himself from one to the other. And when at last he could stand upright, he set off at a shambling run, and started to look for the horse.

Within minutes he found Rustler standing pawing the frozen ground, for the slack reins had caught on the jagged broken branch of a tree and so had brought it to a standstill.

On the sight of him, the horse neighed loudly. Sean stroked its nose and spoke quietly to it, then he looked at the shoulder where the piece of wood had struck it. The skin was grazed and blood was oozing from it.

He now brought the horse back on to the path; then leading it by a roundabout way, he eventually came to the wood pile. There, he drew it to a standstill and stood listening; and after a moment, hearing no sound of activity coming either from the yard or from the house, he hurriedly led the horse round the corner and into a stable. He unharnessed it, fed and watered it, patted it, then left it, saying, "Easy now. Easy now. Rest; you're all right."

Outside again, he quickly retraced his steps to the wooden bridge, and there, letting himself down on to the ice, he moved cautiously towards where his father

lay motionless. But as he neared him in the fading
light, he noticed one arm move, and then the head.
And his immediate instinct was to turn and flee. But
when the weak voice came to him, calling, "Sean!
Sean!" he forced himself to walk forward until he was
standing within a few feet of the leg that was sticking
straight out.

He watched his father now try to raise his shoulders,
the effort making him close his eyes and grit his teeth;
then he said, "Boy, I'm...I'm hurt. Go...go—" and
he gasped before ending, "go...and get...help."

Sean did not move, nor did he speak, until his father, seemingly making a great effort, brought his arm
above his head, the fist doubled, and he cried, "Do
you hear me, boy? I've...I think I've broken my leg.
I...I can't move. Go and get help!"

Still Sean did not move or speak; at least, not for a
moment; then he said, "You drove your horse straight
at her."

"Wh...at?"

"You drove your horse straight at Maggie Ann.
You were in the middle of the drive, she was at the
edge. You turned Rustler head on. You...you meant
to kill her. 'Twas...'twas on your face."

There was no movement from the arm now and the
face was still, the eyes closed, but when the voice
came it wasn't in the form of a command; the tone
was soft, pleading. "Sean. Sean, please go and get
help. I...I didn't kill Maggie Ann; she's alive."

"She is dying and can hardly move."

"Sean, please do as I ask. Go and get help or else
I'll die here. Don't you realise that?" The eyes were
open now, staring at him. "And you will have killed
me. Do...do you realize that? If you don't go and get

me help quickly, I shall freeze and...and *you* will be to blame.'' Again he was gasping. Then he said, ''Do you understand what I'm saying?''

''Yes, Dada; I understand what you're saying; you'll die if you don't get help.'' And on this he slowly turned away, his father's voice following him, angrily yelling, although not with its full force.

When Sean reached the bridge and looked back along the frozen stream he could just make out his father's arm waving frantically in the air.

It was as he crossed the bridge and made his way towards the front of the house that the first flakes of snow began to fall, and on the sight of them there arose in him a sickness that caused him to run towards the back of the house and make for the outdoor closet, only to be stopped half-way across the yard by Moira, a shawl over her head, crying at him, ''Where d'you think you've been? The others have been looking for you. Come in, boy.''

He did not go to her but he stopped dead, bent over, and vomited.

They were all in Maggie Ann's room, and amid the talk and the chatter of the children, Moira stooped over Maggie Ann and asked her: ''It's too much for you?''

''Did I ever have too much of the children? No, me dear. And I meself feel as light as a feather tonight; at least, I would do if it wasn't for this fella's face.'' She thumbed slowly towards Sean, who was sitting by the head of the bed. ''Did you ever see him look so peaky? And with a face on him as long as a broken fiddle. Sick, you said, he's been. Well, it's the way he eats. I've told him he doesn't take enough time over his food, and he doesn't think about what he's eatin'.''

"Well, there's one thing I do know," Moira said, "you're chatterin' too much and you'll pay for it with a wakeful night."

"I'll do nothing of the sort"—the words now came out between gasps—"I'm...I'm goin' to keep awake until New Year's mornin'."

Margaret put in, "But, Maggie Ann, it's New Year's Eve tomorrow; you couldn't keep awake all that time."

"I'll do me best, dear. I'll do me best. And I tell you what you can do for me. Sing me a song together with your mama. We haven't had a sing-song for many a long night."

Moira was about to exclaim and not quietly, Oh, no! No! No sing-song tonight. With one thing and another she'd had a heavy day, and here it was seven o'clock at night and Hector hadn't shown his face. He'd had money on him when he went out, but she'd like to bet he wouldn't have any when he came home. She shook her head. Did that man think of anybody but himself? Not one present had he bought for the children, at Christmas, not even an orange. Perhaps he really did think, as he'd said to her the last time they'd had words, "They're your family, every damn one of 'em, and you've taken the one that was mine." And she recalled she had answered him by saying, "I couldn't take what you never had."

But where had he got to tonight, with no sign of him and it snowing hard? Of course, there was always the probability that he had picked up with another woman. But no, that would mean more money than he had to spare: what money he had these days went on drink, and his pleasures he took free as his right as a husband.

She gave a little shudder, then turned her attention to Daniel who, she was glad to see, looked a little less strained than he had done lately. He was addressing her, saying quietly, "Maggie Ann wants a song. What's it going to be, Margaret?" He had turned to the six-year-old girl, who had the features of her mother and who would likely grow to resemble her altogether, for she had a pleasant nature, and Margaret said, "*The Dear Little Shamrock.*"

"*The Dear Little Shamrock* it is," put in Maggie Ann from the bed, her head nodding slightly.

And so Moira, seated in the midst of her children, her arm round her daughter's waist, sang:

There's a dear little plant that
grows in our isle,
'Twas Saint Patrick himself sure that
set it.
And the sun on his labour with pleasure
did smile,
And the dew from his eye often wet it.
It shines thro' the bog, thro' the
brake, thro' the mireland,
And he call'd it the dear little
shamrock of Ireland.

Then with Moira beating time, they all sang the chorus:

The dear little shamrock,
The sweet little shamrock,
The dear little, sweet little shamrock
of Ireland.

And so it went on for another two verses and chorus.

"Sing a funny one, Ma, sing a funny one," said Patrick.

"Oh, no, not tonight, Patrick; I'm not in the mood for funny ones. Wait till New Year comes in."

Now Maggie Ann asked quietly, "Would you sing me, *Oh! Erin Dear*?"

Moira hesitated, then closed her eyes for a moment. Of all the Irish songs that would promote tears, *Oh! Erin Dear* was the one: it was indeed an exile's lament, and the tune was one called *The Londonderry Air*, one that even non-singers could manage. But Maggie Ann had asked for it and the children knew it, for it had been Maggie Ann's lullaby to get them to sleep through their pains of toothache or tummy ache. She glanced at Daniel, and the look on his face expressed her own thoughts. But there it was; Maggie Ann had asked for it. Without more ado she started:

"Oh! Erin Dear, my thoughts are with you ever;
No other land can stir my heart like thee.
Why did I from my friends and dear ones sever;
To make my home so far across the sea?
I miss my jovial sons and winsome daughters;
The songs of children on the village green.
I yearn to hear the sound of rushing waters;
And more than all I miss my faithful sweet Eileen."

The children were all singing with her, but softly, and she went on,

The strangers here are kind and noble hearted
And sure, I blush to think of all their care;
But thoughts will rise of thee, from whom I'm
parted,
That wake the sigh and haste the fallen tear.
I dream at night of sunset on the shingle,
Of jaunting cars, and nestling shamrocks green;
Och! then I wake and all my senses tingle
With memories of my home and you, my sweet
colleen.

Maggie Ann lay quiet, the tears streaming down her
face, and by gesture Daniel ushered the children from
the room. And when in the hall Patrick said, "'Twas
a good night, wasn't it, Daniel? Maggie Ann enjoyed
it, didn't she?" he answered, "Yes, yes, it was a good
night, and she enjoyed it. Now, go on, all of you, and
make your way to bed. And Margaret, see that Michael's washed, will you?"

"Wash…my…self!"

At this response the children all laughed, for Michael was now both walking and talking, although not
brilliantly in either direction.

Daniel was making his way to the study when
Moira's voice, calling his name softly, checked him,
and he turned towards her. Straight away she said,
"Do you think anything could have happened to
him?"

"No. He's been as drunk as a noodle before this
and Rustler's always brought him home. That horse
could find its way in the dark through any part of the
grounds. I think he's gone into Fellburn and likely it's
coming down heavier there than here, which it often

does, and he's staying somewhere for the night. It would be the sensible thing to do.''

"Yes. Yes, I suppose so." She nodded at him. "But...but we'll leave the front door unbolted, just in case he lands.''

"Yes. Yes, we could do that; we're not likely to get any tramps around in this weather.''

"What are you going to do?''

"Well, there's one thing I *would* like to do, Moira, but I can't, because he's got all the bills and papers locked up, and that is to go through the accounts and see how we really do stand. But we'll have to have a showdown shortly, because if a third of the land's got to go, one of the men will have to go with it, and there'll have to be changes all round. So, instead, I was going into the study to read a book. It's one of those that Janie bought me for Christmas, and I know the next time we meet she'll ask how I liked it and I won't have the face to say I haven't read it yet.''

"Janie's a good girl, none better, and she's got a head on her shoulders. And yes, that is what she's likely to do the first time she claps eyes on you, ask you what you think of the book. So go on. See you bank up the fire. I'll go and see the children settled and then I'll sit with Maggie Ann. If he doesn't put in an appearance soon I'll make up the basket chair and sleep there.''

He nodded to her and turned away, and she climbed the stairs, thinking, He'll read her book, but he cannot see her; he can see nothing but that other one.

At six o'clock the next morning Daniel quietly opened Maggie Ann's door and tiptoed across to where Moira was asleep in the basket chair; and when he shook her gently and she started, he held up a warning finger, then turned from her and made to leave the room again, beckoning her to follow him.

Drawing her old dressing-gown around her and blinking the sleep from her eyes, Moira went into the passage where Daniel was turning up the wick of the oil lamp, and in a whisper, she said, "What is it? What is it?"

"He...he must have come in some time ago, as Rustler's in one of the stables; not the usual one when he isn't on the farm, and he was kicking up a racket. He must have sensed I was about, although I don't know how, because the snow's a good four inches thick. Anyway, he was agitated, and when I smoothed him down and took him along to his own box I noticed that his shoulder was skinned and had been bleeding as if something had fallen on it, or he'd had a blow."

"Hector would never hit that horse."

"No, no, he wouldn't, I know that. If he cares about nothing else, or no-one, he cares for Rustler. I must go to the farm and get ointment; that shoulder looks sore. Anyway"—he jerked his head upwards—"he must be in bed sleeping it off. But I was up till long after eleven and he wasn't in then."

"Four inches of snow, you say?"

"Yes, and more to come by the looks of it, *and* it's drifting."

"Did you make yourself a drink?"

"No, I didn't bother. I am late as it is."

"Don't be silly. They'll be on the job down there, even in this, because they'll be expecting you, and there isn't much that can be done. So look, hang on a minute till I get into my clothes and we'll have a drink. Go and blow up the fire and put the kettle on.''

He did as she said, and by the time Moira came into the room he was mashing the tea.

Sitting down by the corner of the table, she remarked, as she always did to someone who was making the tea, "Let it draw." Then she added, "Sit yourself down. You're on your legs enough all day."

"What kind of a night has she had?" Daniel asked.

"Restless. That song nearly broke her up, and me too. I'll never sing it again as long as I live."

It was when she handed him the cup of tea that he asked, "Would you like to go back to Ireland, Moira?"

"What a question to ask me, and at this time of the morning. You might as well have asked me if I'd like to go to heaven."

He smiled at her now, then said, "Well, if I'd asked you that you'd straight away have said yes. So am I to take it that you *would* like to go back?"

She looked at him for a moment before she said, "I still can't answer you in truth, because I would have to say yes and no. Sometimes I long for it, at others I know if I hadn't come over here because the prospects seemed good, and they had turned out that way, things might have been different. But then again, he wasn't to blame for all that, because at the time he brought me I was so desperate to escape from that so-called castle, I would have gone off with a Chinaman or anyone who would have had me."

"Oh, Moira." He did not laugh at her remark but said, "For someone like you to be hit by circumstances that made you hold yourself so cheap was a sin before God. And it was perpetrated by your family, that's the worst of it.''

She smiled a sad smile now, saying, ''No; not only them, it was more because of the cause, because of politics, because he was a soldier, an English soldier. Oh, you've no idea of the hate that pervaded that countryside. No, no''—she sighed now—''I'll never go back, and I mustn't forget I was thankful to God to be brought here in the first place. And as I've said before, He's given me great compensation, not only in my own children, but also in you... And now, do you want another cup of tea?''

''Yes. Yes, I'll have another.''

As she poured it out she said, ''Look, I'll just slip upstairs and see where he's landed himself. It's a wonder he didn't rouse the children. I can't understand it. And I had left young Bridget up there in her cot alongside Margaret's bed, because if I'd had her down here and she started squawking in the night she would have woken Maggie Ann.''

She left him now, walking quickly, and in the hall she picked up a small lamp from the hallstand before going upstairs. On the landing she went on tiptoe to her bedroom door and, gently turning the handle, she pushed it open. Then she raised the lamp head high and looked in amazement at her bed, with the covers still drawn up over the pillows. Turning quickly away she opened an adjacent door that had at one time opened into a dressing-room. There stood a couch in it, but no-one lay on it. Surely he would not have gone into any of the children's rooms? She opened the doors of the three rooms that were still unoccupied and didn't bother to close the door of the third before, running, she made for the stairs.

When she burst into the kitchen it was to see Daniel, who had donned his cap and muffler and was ready to go out again. "He's not in! not in any of the rooms," she cried.

"*Not in?* Have you looked everywhere?"

"Yes, yes. Oh…oh, no. No;"—she shook her head—"not downstairs."

Again she was running, and he followed her now.

Minutes later, when they were again standing in the hall, they stared at each other until Daniel said, "He must be somewhere about; he's stabled the horse."

"Well, he'll likely be outside, possibly lying in the snow for God knows how long."

He was making quickly for the hall door when he turned to her and said, "Get the boys up! They can come and help look. But we won't go to the farm yet. We don't want to give them more to talk about than they have already."

Moira hurried up the stairs again, only to stop on the landing and hug her waist for a moment whilst drawing in deep breaths.

When she reached the boys' room she had to shake Patrick, but Sean was already awake. And she whispered now, "Get up and get into your clothes, both of you. Wrap up well. We're going looking for your dada. His horse is in the stable but he hasn't come into the house. He must have fallen outside."

Patrick did not openly protest but he grunted, "He'll be lying in one of the stables."

"He's not lying in the stables. Daniel found Rustler there, but it wasn't his own place, so he moved him along to it. And he would have seen your dada if he had been there. Come on now, hurry up."…

The two boys and Daniel, carrying candle lanterns,

went their different ways for the search. The boys had been told that should they come across their father they were to whistle. And it was hardly ten minutes later that both Daniel and Patrick heard the thin whistle and knew that Sean had found their father. They both came hurrying from different directions, guided by the intermittent whistle and eventually reached the wooden bridge, where Daniel and Patrick stood looking at Sean, his lantern hanging from his limp hand and pointing with his other into the darkness. "Down the bank opposite the copse," he muttered.

Daniel was running ahead now, Patrick on his heels. Then they were both standing at the top of the bank, looking down at the form, the snow-covered arms outstretched against the upward slope of the bank as if he was attempting to crawl to the top.

"Oh my God!" Daniel's words were a soft cry, and passing his lantern to Patrick, he said, "Hold it high, I must go down." He sat on the top of the bank and in much the same manner as Sean had done the day before, he slid down. His, however, was a slower descent, for the snow gathered by his boots acted as a brake.

At the bottom, he stumbled towards his father, and he had no need to turn him over to find if there was any life left in him, for the rigidity of the body told him that his father had been dead for some time.

In the dim light reaching him from the lantern Patrick was holding, Daniel called to him. "We've... we've got to get help...the men," and he tried to climb the bank, but with the same result as apparently had met his father's efforts earlier. So he now called quietly, "Sean. Sean," and when the boy appeared within the radiance of the lantern, he said, "Go for

the men; I can't get up the bank. Tell them to bring
ropes and a door.''

"You can get up if you walk along to the bridge."

"What?"

"I said, you can come up if you walk along to the
bridge.''

Daniel saw the boy's lantern swinging backwards
and forwards as he moved away along the bank, and
as one following a leader he groped his way through
the snow in the direction that the light led him. And
when he came to the struts of the bridge Sean called
down huskily to him, "You can climb up by the side."

Within a couple of minutes he was standing on the
bridge staring down at his father's dead white face,
but before he had time to speak he heard Patrick's
voice crying, "I...I can't stay there, Daniel, not by
myself, I can't.''

When the frightened boy appeared, Daniel put his
arm around his shoulder, saying, "'Tis all right, all
right. Anyway we can't do any good by ourselves; we
must go and get the men. Come along, both of you."

When they reached the house he pressed the two
boys before him into the kitchen, there to see Moira
muffled up in a cloak and hood ready to go outside.
She stopped at the sight of them and, looking from
the two white-faced boys to Daniel, she said, "You've
found him then?"

"Yes. Yes, we've found him. Sit down."

Obediently she sat down and, pushing the hood
back from her hair, she said simply, "Where?"

"In the stream where the bank is steep. He must
have fallen. He was hurt in some way and couldn't
get out.''

"But...but the horse? He had stabled his horse."

"Yes, he had stabled his horse," Daniel's voice was quiet and flat.

"Well, he wouldn't stable his horse in the dark and go back there. What is all this?"

Their attention was immediately directed to Sean, who said, "I...I stabled the horse. Well, it was in the horsebox and it hadn't been seen to and...and"—his head drooped now—"I thought he...Dada, was too drunk to see to it, and...and had gone to bed."

"God in heaven! God in heaven!"

Daniel now said, "I must away and get the men. You'd better decide where he's to lie, upstairs or down. It'll take us some time, all of an hour or more. We'll need a couple of the big lanterns. Come, Patrick." On this he turned and left the kitchen without further words. He had said nothing to comfort Moira, because he knew she wouldn't need comfort over the loss of his father. Yet, in himself, he was still seeing the outstretched arms, the hands gripping the snow as if in appeal, and he was filled with pity for this man who had sired him. However, at the same time, the feeling of pity was being almost swamped by one of fear, but of what he did not know. That is, not until the men laid his father on the makeshift stretcher and covered him with a blanket, leaving the stiffened arms still stretched beyond his head. And it was as Daniel stooped to take his end of the stretcher that his foot slipped on a piece of wood. It had been covered with snow but the tramping around had exposed part of it. And as his foot touched it, it rolled to the side, so suggesting that it hadn't been frozen to the ice or to the ground like everything else round about, and in the flickering light of the lanterns he seemed to recognise it. It was about two feet long, and he could see it flying through the air and hitting the wall…

Moira had the bedroom ready, and dawn was just breaking by the time she had her husband washed and dressed in his last nightshirt and lying in his bed as if fast asleep but having a bad dream, for his features were contorted.

Before dinner time everyone in the village knew Farmer Stewart was dead. Fallen off his horse, he had, and into an icy gulley. Well, it was to be expected, for he had never been really sober for months. However, the landlord of the inn soon made plain he hadn't been drinking there yesterday, 'cos he hadn't seen hilt nor hair of him; he must have taken the load on in Fellburn. But why his horse had thrown him, only God alone knew, because that particular animal would stand outside the inn for hours. Even when children would untether it, it would still wait for him, and as steady as a rock it was, and could jump a gate or a ditch as good as a three-year-old. Well, what would now happen to the farm? Everybody knew what would happen to the farm; it would go on sinking as it had been doing for years, because it wasn't to be expected that that young fellow could carry the load that his father must have left on him.

7

It was Daniel who broke the news to Maggie Ann, and when she made no comment but only stared at him, he said, "I know you didn't get on, not from the start, and neither did he and I; we were in the same boat; but he's gone now."

When she did speak she not only surprised him but she lifted the cover of that corner of fear in his mind and exposed it again when she said, "Where's Sean?"

"He's helping to clear the snow from the drive."

"Would you like to send him in?"

"Yes. Yes, Maggie Ann, I'll do that."

When a few minutes later he stood by Sean and said, "Maggie Ann wants to see you," the boy, after glancing at him, laid his shovel down and walked into the house.

When he reached Maggie Ann's bedside he did not sit down immediately as he usually did, but stood halfway up the bedside, his eyes on the heaving bedclothes.

"Sit down, Sean."

When the boy was seated, she said, "Take your hands from between your knees and tell me what happened!'' Then looking in the direction of the door, she said, "Where's your mama?"

"With the doctor. He's just come."

"Well, in that case there'll be no-one in for a time, so just start from the beginning."

It was some time before the boy spoke, and then, looking at her, and his voice trembling, he said, "He ran you down on purpose; he ran you down."

"Yes, we know that, we've known that from the beginning, haven't we? But the vengeance wasn't yours, boy. You should have left it to God, or someone who could deal with it. But go on, tell me how it came about."

His head lowered and the words coming slowly, Sean described what he had done. When he had finished, she released his hand, and again he pressed them both between his knees. And there was silence in the room, until at last she said, "You know what you've done, don't you? You've saddled yourself with a sin for the rest of your life and you'll have to pay dearly for it, because it'll never go away. You've always known that you're not like the others, haven't you? I've always had the idea that God made you for something special, but not that, not that. Yet, at the same time I'm glad he's gone, because a man who'd ride down a defenceless woman, as I was, and me handicapped by me bulk… Oh, he knew that. He knew that I couldn't jump aside. Well, he was bound to come to a bad end. But I wish to God it hadn't been through you."

The boy had his head bowed deeply now and began to mutter, and Maggie Ann said, "What is that you say, child?" And Sean whimpered, "He was goin' to sell the land an' all, and Barney said he knew he'd be the one that would have to go, 'cos he's gettin' on in years. And there would be no pension and he didn't known whether he'd be left in his cottage or not, as he'd heard tell that the others were going to be let for rent. And...and then there was Daniel. He'd leave; I knew he would if the place got smaller.''

After he had finished his muttering, Maggie Ann did not say anything for some time. Her breath was coming in sharp gasps, evidence of her agitation. And when she did speak her voice was low and her words came slowly: ''You cannot hope to save the world...from its troubles, Sean. God puts burdens on our backs the day we're born. An' if folks are wise they'll learn to carry them, because no-one else can carry them for them. And anyway, Sean, your back'll have to broaden to bear yours. So stop your worritin' about other people. What I think you should do now is to ask your mama if you can go to a Mass an' see a priest. And anyway, now I know she'll have one to see me: it was more than her life was worth to have one set foot in the house before, but now the road's clear I can pick up my faith and die a happy death. Ah! me dear, don't cry, don't cry. But there is one thing I would ask of you, and it is this: that you lie your soul away rather than let your mama know the ins and outs of how he met his end. You'll do that?''

He was unable to speak but he bobbed his head, and she said again, ''Now, come on, come on, 'tis done, 'tis somethin' that can't be undone. Lift up your head an' face life, for it's goin' to be a long one. An' you can take comfort from knowing that, by your act, you've given freedom to two people in this house. And it's New Year's Eve today and from tomorrow they can start a new life. They don't even have to wait until he's buried.''

8

The funeral took place on the third of January. The thaw had set in and the roads were a quagmire of slush, which perhaps accounted for the sparse attendance of mourners. It was impossible for anyone to follow the carriages on foot and so the three farmhands arrived at the cemetery in the farm waggon behind the three carriages. The first held Daniel and Patrick— Sean was in bed with a stomach upset—the other occupant being Daniel's brother-in-law, John. The second cab held Mr Farringdon and his eldest son Robert, and Hector Stewart's solicitor. The third cab held four farmers whose presence was guided by the look of things more than any liking for the deceased man, whom they considered had always been too big for his boots and had acted like a gentleman farmer without having the wherewithal to live up to one. And it was noticeable to the four men that Stewart's nearest neighbour, Matthew Talbot, was not present in the cortège.

Back in the house the gloom of the day was deepened by the half-drawn curtains. In the kitchen, at one end of the table, Moira was slicing the ham, while at the other Pattie chopped carrots and leeks prior to putting them into the big kale pot on the hob, where the stock for the soup was bubbling. It was as if she had never left the house. She had arrived yesterday and she and John had slept upstairs, that is after they had sat talking into the early hours with Moira and Daniel.

Moira was now saying to Pattie, "It was good of Janie to come with her father and brother. He's a very nice gentleman, her father."

"Yes; they are a nice family."

"She's got a way with the children an' all, for she's got them all up there now, sitting round Sean's bed and telling them stories as if she had been doing it all her life."

"How long has Sean been like this, Moira? He's changed."

"Well, it's a long time since you saw him, dear."

"Oh, I don't mean in that way. Yes, he's grown, I know, but I think there's something worrying him. He used to chat to me, but I couldn't get a word out of him yesterday."

"Well, to tell you the truth he's not been the same since Maggie Ann met with her accident. He was very fond of her, you know, and she of him, and he hardly ever leaves her side."

"It isn't right that he should be like this. He's too old for a child; he's not nine yet."

"He's always been old, Pattie, from the day he was born. He's not like the others, you know; he was one of twins."

"Yes, so you've said."

"They're always strange, the one that's left. Something missing in them, I think. Or on the other hand, as Maggie Ann said, something seems to be added to them; like two lives being spent in one.''

"And Daniel. You know, I hoped he would make a break and come into the town, but there's little chance of that now. Is there?''

"I shouldn't think so. If I'm truthful, Pattie, I should hope not.''

"Is it really all over between him and Frances?''

"Again, I should say I hope so, but he mopes when he's not worrying about the farm, and the work, and the frustration of it all. I doubt if he'll ever get her out of his system.''

"He's a fool. She's a skittish piece. You know, I've seen her in the town with Ray Melton.''

"Well, I hope he takes her on and soon.''

"He will if her father has anything to do with it, because the Meltons are pretty warm, with all their shops.''

After Pattie had scooped the vegetables into the pot she turned to Moira, saying, "Look, sit down; you look beat. By the way, when is it due?''

"Oh, some time to go yet, early March, nearly eight weeks, I should say.'' Then suddenly bending over, Moira exclaimed, "Oh! Oh!'' and Pattie moved quickly to her, saying, "What is it? Sit down. Have you got a pain?''

Moira could not speak for a moment, and she had to lower herself slowly down on to the chair, and as she gritted her teeth together the sound was audible to Pattie, who almost whimpered, "Oh, don't say something's going to happen, Moira. As you said, you're weeks away.''

"Don't worry, don't worry; it's just stitch. I often

get it. Look, will you heat me a drop of milk, dear, and put some ginger in it?''

As Pattie busied herself with the pan of milk, thrusting it into the brightest part of the fire, the door opened and Janie came in, and she paused a moment before hurrying forward towards Moira and saying, ''You're feeling ill?''

''No, no, dear; it's just a stitch. Anyway, it's gone now. Where are the children?''

''Oh, they've gone up to the nursery. I've shown them a new game; at least, it's as old as the hills. But it's very competitive and it'll keep them going. And by the way, Sean got up and dressed; he's gone with them.''

''He has? Oh, that's good, that's good. He must be feeling better.''

''Yes.'' Janie nodded. ''Of a sudden, he sat up and said just that; 'I'm feeling better; I'm going to get my clothes on.'''

Pattie now poured the milk into a cup, added the ginger, stirred it, then handed it to Moira before turning to Janie and saying, ''If you want to make yourself useful, you could carry those plates from the table over there into the dining-room.''

When Janie had left the room carrying a tray of plates Moira said, ''You're on good terms, you two.''

''Yes, we are, because she's my type of person. She's teaching now, you know.''

''Is she indeed? I would have thought there was no need for her to do that, with them being so moneyed.''

''Oh, Moira''—Pattie laughed gently—''there's needs in all of us that money can't fill.''

''Yes, yes, that's true. It was a silly thing for me to

say. Yet, at the same time, I would say that money can go a long way towards soothing the wants. It's a good salve, is money, and I hope that that lawyer man, when he gets going later on in the day, will be able to say that we're due for a good bit of salve. But as yet, we don't know whom Hector has left the farm to; and whether it's Daniel or me, there's three thousand pounds to be found for the bank. Well, if it's me, I can almost clear it, Pattie, for it may surprise you to know that I have two thousand, five hundred pounds to me name in the bank.''

''What?''

"Yes, yes. You can open your mouth that wide, but it's money sent to me from me daughter, and Daniel wouldn't touch a penny of it. It was he who made me put it away in me own name in case Hector got his hands on it. And I know now that if the place has been solely left to him, I'll have to fight to hand that money over to the bank.''

"I think that whoever it's left to, Moira, the other can claim a share. In law I think the wife is due for a third of the husband's property and if it's left to the wife the eldest son can claim some, so John was saying. But two thousand, five hundred pounds! That's a small fortune. And it's been lying there all this time and you needing things. Why didn't you spend some of it on yourself and the children?''

"And where could I explain I had got the money from? Eh?''

"Yes. Yes, of course, there is that. But that amount would put the place back on its feet.''

"No, no it wouldn't, Pattie. It will ease the debt. But this place will have to work for itself before it's back on its feet. And Daniel has pointed this out all along. But now that he'll have a free hand we'll just have to wait and see how things go. One thing I do know, there'll be changes here, whether for the good or the bad, I don't know.''

"By the way," said Pattie now, "did Father never press you to ask for help from your daughter's people?"

"No, because although he knew about her, he never met her. He was in a deep drinking bout at the time. Yet, I thought it strange, for her private carriage and liveried driver couldn't have passed through the village without comment. Of course, they may not have known where it was headed for, but because little escapes any one of them, I waited for Hector to put the question to me. He never did, and I was peeved in a way, 'cos I wanted to brag about her." She looked down the length of the kitchen now as if gazing into the past, and she repeated softly to herself, "She's the only thing I have to be proud of."

It was as if she had never borne another child.

9

The voice of the village said there certainly were changes being made on old Stewart's place since the young one took over. Going around like a terrier after a rat, he was, stirring up everybody. The only thing he couldn't stir up or alter was the weather and, according to Arthur Beaney, that seemed to be frustrating him. And then there was the fact that he wasn't selling the Westfields, which surely indicated that things weren't as bad as had been made out. Farmer Preston had confided in Davey Rington, who owned the inn, that to his knowledge old Stewart had been up to his neck in debt to the bank and they were just waiting to foreclose. Well, apparently something had stopped them from foreclosing, and that could only be money. But where had it come from?

This was explained, at least to the villagers, at the end of February, when a fine carriage stopped at the inn before making its way to the farm. It had leaked out earlier through Rosie Dunlop that Mrs Stewart, the Irish one, had had a daughter before she married Stewart, and the said daughter had been brought up as a lady and had married a rich Frenchman. And they had stopped at the inn, and the man himself, the Frenchman, who spoke English as good as the next, bought two bottles of whisky, a bottle of port and several bottles of wine, and had his driver carry it out to the carriage. Now would you believe that?

This last piece of gossip from the inn was fresh, because it had happened only that morning. And now Monsieur Jacques Fonière and his wife Melissa were seated at the dining table with Moira, Daniel, and a lady who had been introduced as a family friend, Janie. And Janie and Monsieur Jacques were getting along splendidly, for as Janie said, she hadn't had the chance to practise her French on anyone for a long time. She admitted that her father could speak the language, but he had asked why he should do so when he could get all he wanted in English. As for her mother, she said, her French was limited to what she had learned in the schoolroom.

Daniel had to admit that his knowledge of the language was on the schoolroom level, too, and Moira noticed he seemed to be looking with new eyes at Janie, an animated creature now as she conversed fluently with the attractive Frenchman.

The wine that had accompanied the dinner had relaxed them all, for earlier in the day there had been a very emotional meeting when Moira had taken her daughter in to see Maggie Ann. Moira had prepared her for what she would find, but nevertheless the sight of the woman entrapped in her mound of flesh, her face already carrying the death pallor on it, had shocked her to the extent that she was unable to speak for a time. And when the two soft, bloated hands held hers the tears had sprung from her eyes, until Maggie Ann, her own eyes wet, had said, ''Oh, my dear, my

dear, don't cry over me. This is one of the happiest
moments of me life for, you know, I was the first one
that held you. Yes, I took you from her womb''—she
had turned her eyes on to Moira—"and laughed as I
held you, for you yelled into my face. But my laughter
turned to tears, even to wails, when later they took
you away. But thanks be to God they did. Oh, yes,
thanks be to God they did, for you're somethin' to be
proud of, me dear. And your mama is that proud of
you! Sit down, sit down, and tell me all about your
life.''

And Melissa had sat down; and she had talked to
this old woman, who had apparently been on the point
of death for weeks, but was still clinging to life. And
she understood how her mother loved this woman and
what a loss she would be when she went.

At one point Maggie Ann had said, "Have you ever
been to Ireland; I mean, have you been back since you
were taken away from it all those years ago?" And
Melissa had said, "No, I haven't; but it is strange that
you ask, because my husband was talking about us
going there for a holiday later on in the year.''

"Oh, you'll love Ireland,'' Maggie had said. "And
you must go and see the house.'' And then she had
stopped and closed her eyes for a moment before she
had added, "No, don't go near the house where you
were born, because you'd meet up with the lot of them
there, an' they're like leeches; they'd suck you dry an'
you won't know they're doin' it. Am I right, Moira?"
She had turned and looked at Moira now and Moira
had answered, "Yes, in a way you're right, Maggie
Ann, as always.''...

It was later that night that Melissa said to Moira,

"Have you ever longed to go back to your own people?"

After a pause, Moira said, "No, not so much to my own people but to the land itself, yes. But then, I ask you, who doesn't long for the place of their birth, the land of their birth? But here I am, and here I must stay. It seems to be God's will. The only thing that's worrying me at the moment is that the one inside me"—she patted her belly—"will not come before Maggie Ann goes. Or if that is not to be, it will wait until she's put to rest."

"You're having a hard life, Mother."

"No, no," said Moira, now shaking her head, "life is much easier than it's been for years." She didn't say, since my husband died. "And if the weather turns good, the farm should look up this year, and things will be easier all round. And I pray for them to be easier for Daniel."

They were sitting alone during this conversation and now Melissa leant forward and in a low voice she said, "You hinted that Daniel has had a bad love affair. Has it ended?"

"Completely, I hope. Oh, yes, I pray to God, completely. But he still pines for her."

"Miss Farringdon...Janie; she is such a nice person. Do you think he might turn to her?"

"That is another thing I pray for, but I know it is useless, because he treats her just as a friend, as if she were another man friend. I've always thought that a man could never make a real friend of a woman, but he seems to have done so, and she likewise. The way they talk at times, you should hear them, about books and the state of the country and who should be up there in Parliament and who shouldn't. Oh, it goes on from one thing to another.'' As Moira smiled widely and shook her head, Melissa said, "It's a pity, but perhaps she is already affianced.''

"No. No, nothing like that, and that's because men are stone blind.'' And now she asked her daughter, "Are you happy, dear? Really happy?''

And to this Melissa said, "I haven't words to answer that question correctly. At times I feel guilty at being so happy, and other people so sad. He is wonderful, don't you think, my Jacques? Mama wasn't happy at first about the association because he is almost twice my age, but now she too thinks him perfect. And he is so kind; kind to everyone. But as he says himself, it is no effort to be kind when you've got the wherewithal with which to be kind. But as I see it, many people have money and they are not kind. What do you say, Mother?''

"I say the same as you, my dear. The more money some men get the more they want and stick to.'' Then she leant forward and gripped her daughter's hand, saying, "I'm so glad you're going to stay the night here and will meet Pattie tomorrow. You'll like Pattie. She is another Janie, although not a bit like her brother Daniel. Chalk and cheese they are, yet they get on like a house on fire.''

When the door was opened quickly and Daniel entered the room, Moira immediately asked him, "What is it?'' And for answer he replied, "Maggie Ann has had a turn. She's breathing heavily, finding it an effort to speak. Janie is with her and Jacques too. I sent the children upstairs. We were all in the room together. She was laughing one minute and then the change came.''

Moira rose heavily from her chair, saying, "I think you'd better fetch the priest."

"But...but she had the Last Rites some time ago."

"Yes, I know, I know. But it would be a comfort to her to see him again."

"I'll have to use the trap and it will take all of two hours to get him here."

"Well, will you do it?"

"Of course I'll do it." His voice was harsh. "I'll be on me way now."

"Wrap up well, and be careful driving, for the roads are slushy."

Daniel now turned quickly away, thinking, And anyway, the only one she'll want near her at the end is Moira...or Sean...

Maggie Ann died at midnight. She seemed to be conscious to the end and her last glance was on Moira and she smiled at her.

10

It should happen that the weather for the past few days had been almost spring-like. The five older children, Patrick included, had been sent to school, leaving only Michael and the baby Bridget in the house with Moira when suddenly she collapsed at the foot of the stairs and she heard Michael crying, "Mama! Mama! Get...up! Get...up!"

She struggled to her feet and sat on the bottom step, one arm clinging to the stout post of the banister, trying to get the words out to her small and backward son, to tell him to run to the farm and get help, when the pain seized her again.

Then, as if in answer to her plea, there came a knock on the door, and she managed to gesticulate towards it. The boy, understanding, shambled to the door, and there stood on tiptoe and reached up to the sneck, then almost tumbled backwards as the door opened and Janie stepped into the hall.

In an instant she was at Moira's side, crying, "Oh, dear! it's coming."

In answer, Moira could only groan; and Janie, pulling off her coat and hat, looked about her wildly for a moment before crouching down to the boy and saying slowly, "Michael, can you run to the farm and get Daniel?"

He stared back at her, then bounced his head; and his walk quickened to a shambling run as he made for the open door.

"Can you...can you manage to walk into the drawing-room? You...you can lie on the couch."

After a moment and with an effort, Moira got to her feet and Janie put her arm about her and helped her into the drawing-room; and she had just lifted her legs up on to the couch when she heard a commotion in the hall.

She rushed to the open door to see Alex Towney with Michael struggling in his arms, and Alex said, "I...I was coming to the tack room to get some gear and there he was running towards the farm path. I thought I'd better bring him." He stopped when he heard a deep groan, and Janie explained quickly, "I was sending him to the farm to get Daniel; Mrs Stewart is on her time. We need the doctor."

"Oh. Oh, I see. Oh, I'll get back and tell him. Better still, I'll go for the doctor meself an' tell the boss he'll be more use here. Are you on your own, miss?"

"Yes. Yes."

"Well, as I said, he'll be more use here. Sorry, laddie." He lowered the struggling child on to the hall floor; then, nodding as he made to go out, he said, "He was havin' a try, anyway. He's comin' on; he must be right enough in the head."

Oh. Janie's jaw tightened for a moment. These people and the things they said: He may be right enough in the head. Of course the boy was right enough in the head. "Come here, dear. Come here." She held out her arms towards Michael, and when he had toddled towards her, she wiped his tear-stained face and said, "You're a clever boy, a very clever boy." Then she asked him, "Where is Bridget?"

"Kitchen."

"Oh, well now, will you go and stay with her? That's a good boy."

When the child made for the kitchen she hurried back into the drawing-room.

Moira's legs were stretched out now but she was breathing in gasps and, haltingly, she said, "'Tis early, yet...not surprised...'tis been troubling me for some time."

"Mr Towney has gone for the doctor and Daniel should be here any minute now."

"The children...Rosie...Rosie was to come and try and...and give a hand but...but her rheumatics. Margaret's good, quite sensible. Off school...must keep her off school."

"Listen, Moira, dear, don't worry about the children. They'll be perfectly all right. And there's me; I've got nothing to do but sit filing my nails all day." She smiled reassuringly down on the sweating face.

"Teaching, thought you were."

"Not till next month."

"Oh! Oh!" Moira was now grappling with another spasm. Her knees were up, her arms were gripping her belly, and Janie's arms were about her holding her whilst she soothed her, saying, "There, there, it won't be long. The doctor will be here soon."

When at last the spasm subsided and Moira sank back into the cushions, Janie, her own body trembling now, said, "Look, I think I'd better unloosen your skirt and underthings. Are you wearing corsets?"

"No."

"Well, let me undo your things and take your skirt off. But wait, I'll run upstairs and get a bed cover to put over you."

Taking the stairs two at a time she pushed open the door of the first room on the landing, to see a single bed. She whipped the quilt from it and also grabbed up a couple of pillows and a towel that was hanging from the rail on the wash-hand stand. And as she flew downstairs again she knew she had been in Daniel's room, for there on the bedside table were the books she had loaned him, and also the pipe she had purchased for Moira to give him as a Christmas present.

Having unloosened Moira's skirt and the tapes of the two petticoats, she said, "Do you think you can ease your skirt off?"

"Oh, Janie, I...I should be up...upstairs and...and in bed."

"Well, you're in no fit state to make the stairs now, at least without help. Look, let me ease your skirt off. I have this cover to put over you."

But before Janie could attempt to take Moira's skirt off, Moira's body was once again contorted; and now she was crying out aloud, "Oh God! Oh God!" Then as the spasm eased she muttered, "It's...it's coming. I'm sure, Janie, it's coming."

"*Oh, no! No!*" For a moment Janie sounded horrified and she stood with one hand gripping her throat; but then swiftly she bent down and without more ado she dragged the skirt down over Moira's legs and threw it aside. Tentatively now, she lifted the petticoats and saw what looked like a black blob emerging from between Moira's legs.

Wildly, she looked about her for a moment. Then

when Moira gave another cry she thrust back the petticoats and, forcing herself to fix her gaze on the emerging head, she cried, "It's all right. It's all right. You'll be all right, Moira."

Janie had never in her life seen a baby being born or even imagined the process. In fact, she had never looked upon any bare body but her own.

"Oh...oh...oh... Oh God!"

The groan and the heave brought the head out, then the shoulders followed. Automatically Janie's hands went down and held the child as it seemed to flow in one swift movement from Moira's body.

Janie was kneeling by the side of the couch, her elbows on the end of it, her hands holding the wet slimy child with the cord attached to it. Moira was quiet now. For a moment it seemed as if she had gone to sleep. And then she muttered, "Cut...cut the cord."

"Oh, Moira, I...I haven't anything, I mean, I..."

With a great effort Moira heaved herself up and, seeing Janie holding the child in an awkward fashion as she knelt on the floor, she said briefly, "Scissors, in the work-basket." She pointed to the side of the fireplace.

Janie let the child slip from her hands on to the couch and rushed to the work basket, found the scissors, then stood hesitating with them in her hand until Moira, pointing, said between gasps, "Cut half-way." Janie almost had to close her eyes as she obeyed this order and when Moira said, "Knot it," she did so with shaking fingers. Then Moira exclaimed, "Quickly now! It isn't crying. Lift it up. What is it?"

"A...a boy."

"Then lift it up, by the legs."

"*What!*"

"Janie, lift him by the legs, turn him upside down and shake him."

Janie's own body was shaking as she followed this procedure, but when there was still no cry from the small body Moira said quietly, "Give him to me."

Janie now laid the baby in Moira's arms and she, looking down on it, whimpered, "No, no. Ah no; 'twould have been my last. I wanted it because it would have been my last. And a boy, I wanted a boy." Suddenly she lay back and the child almost rolled from her arms and would have done so if Janie hadn't caught it in hers.

And now Janie held the little limp body to her breast and looked down into its blue face. There was black hair on its head and its limbs were perfectly formed.

The tears were rolling fast from her eyes and dropped on to the small body just as Daniel rushed into the room, only to come to a halt as he took in the situation. Slowly, he walked up to Janie and, after looking down at the baby in her arms, he turned to Moira and kneeling by her side, he took her hand in his and said, "Oh, my dear, I'm sorry." Yet even as his voice expressed compassion he knew that he was glad the child was stillborn, for surely seven was enough for any woman to see to and, because of the circumstances in this house and the future that lay before them, another infant would have been one too many.

Moira turned and looked at him, saying, "I...I wanted him."

"Yes, I know, dear, I know."

She turned her head away from him now, muttering, "Nothing but death in this house."

She was right; there seemed nothing but death in this house. His father, Maggie Ann, and now the child. But he did not match his thoughts to his words, as he said to her, "But you have seven lovely children, Moira, and they'll all be scrambling in shortly wanting their mother. So, rest now. I'll make you a drink."

He rose from his knees and turned to where Janie had placed the baby on a chair and was looking down on it. Going to her side, he too looked down on it, then said, "You brought it along, Janie. That was fine."

Her voice was flat as she said, "I didn't bring it; it just came. But why did it have to be dead?"

To this he could give her no answer, but picking up the child, he said, "I'll lay it in the study; the afterbirth is yet to come."

"*What?*" The word was sharp. Janie had turned herself towards him and again she said, "What?" and he realised she didn't know what he was referring to, only that this messy business wasn't yet over. She was the same age as himself and had likely never before witnessed a birth of any kind, having been brought up in a very sheltered home. He doubted that she had had any dealings with children other than those in this house, for her two brothers were unmarried. But she had been obliged, during the last few minutes, to help bring a child into the world. He said, "It's all right, I'll...I'll do it."

"No, no. Whatever it is, I'll...I'll see to it," Janie said hastily.

When she suddenly swayed, he gripped her arm and turned her from the couch and pushed her down into a chair, saying, "Stay there." Then he himself did what had to be done, although not without a trembling in his stomach. Although he had brought lambs into the world and had thrust his arm into a cow to bring out a live calf, and last year had witnessed with delight Daisy giving birth to a foal, this was different.

But at last it was done, and all the while Moira had lain silent. As he left the room with the dish and the towel, Janie was still sitting in the chair, but when, some minutes later, he returned from the kitchen it was to see her standing in the hall leaning against the banister post. Going quickly to her he turned her about, saying, "Come on. Come on. You did splendidly."

"Oh Daniel, I'm…I'm ashamed."

"Don't be silly." He had her by the shoulders now, shaking her. "That was your first experience, wasn't it?" Then he added jovially, "I don't suppose you've seen a cut finger before today. Now if you had been brought up on a farm it would have been different. But you haven't, and I repeat, you did splendidly, as well as Pattie would have done…or better."

"I'm sorry. I…I always thought I was a strong individual and would be able to face up to any situation, and especially with someone that one likes. And I've never fainted in my life."

"You didn't faint."

"I had a damned good try."

The phrase coming from her started him chuckling and he said, "You know what you can do now? You can go into the kitchen and brew a pot of tea and fill the sugar basin. She will need sugar. And then the horde will be in shortly. And if you want to do another brave thing, you can stay with them for a while and calm them down. See they have something to eat. Eh?"

She smiled weakly at him. "Yes. I'll do that. It will be a form of compensation."

He lifted his hand and touched her cheek, saying softly as he did so, "You're a fine girl, Janie."

She just managed to reach the kitchen before the tears again swam down her face and this time she turned her face to the door and, lowering her head into the crook of her arm, she sobbed as she had never done before.

PART FOUR

1

It was late September of 1891 and it was clear that Daniel was fighting a losing battle to make the farm profitable. This wasn't due to a slackening of his labour, or that of the three men he still had working, but to the parched ground of two seasons. It would seem that during all the winter months it had rained or snowed and that the sun had shone solely in late spring and summer. Now, with autumn here, there hadn't been a drop of rain for five weeks. The streams were dry and the rivers were running low and the buckets lay empty at the bottom of the wells. Even the famous Granny Smith Well had but a dribble flowing into it. The water carts were visiting some districts and an order had gone out from the town that anyone found using valuable water on flower gardens and such would be liable to prosecution.

The natural outcome of this was that some farmers had given up the struggle. Because the sparse grass on the hills was burnt dry, there was no feed for the sheep, while here and there cattle had died. Daniel's vegetables, too, were a write-off.

The drought had not only affected the land but had

definitely impregnated the tempers of all who worked on it and even those who didn't, because now Pattie and John were in an argument that had started as a discussion with Daniel and Janie. The divided opinions had brought sharp rejoinders, such as when Daniel said with weary cynicism, "Well, I don't know why we're bothering about the land. Why don't we just let the coal owners and the shipyard magnates take it over as they're doing here, there and everywhere. I'd like to bet *their* gardens are not going short of water and their horses are still pulling *their* four-in-hands."

"Well, as you're talking about that, Daniel, the four-in-hands and the gardens and the mansions all give employment to one section of society, and the places where they've made their money keep hundreds, if not thousands, alive."

"Yes, but where, John? Down in the depths of the earth; and they are working for starvation wages in shipyards."

"That's nonsense!" said Pattie. "Look at Palmers in Jarrow; the workers there are able to buy their own properties."

"Oh, Jarrow!" said Daniel, tossing his head, "You'd think Palmers was the only shipyard on God's earth. What about the docks? Have you read about London dockers living like rats, and eating like rats an' all?"

"We're not talking about London, we're talking about this end of the country."

"Oh, as long as they're all right at this end, damn London! damn everybody else!"

"Daniel, and you, Pattie—" Moira looked from one to the other now, and her voice was quiet and rather weary sounding as she said, "I think this discussion should come to an end." Then smiling, she added, "If we were in Ireland you, Daniel and John, would both have your coats off and the blood would be flowing by now. And there would be you, Pattie, standing with a shillelagh and ready to hit your brother on the head should he be the winner."

They were all forced to grin sheepishly now and Moira, looking towards Janie, said, "There's one who hasn't opened her mouth for five minutes. And, you know, you started this, Janie, didn't you? talking about the residents of the historic houses of this country not having the respect that was once considered their due, and all because of the doings of the Prince of Wales and his associations with certain ladies…one in particular."

"Yes…but I wasn't condemning them—I mean the populace—nor the Prince, because I've always considered the old Queen much too rigid in her ideas."

"What does your father think?" put in John.

"Oh, along the same lines. I think I've imbibed my ideas from him; he's a very liberal man."

"And your mother?"

"Ah!" Janie smiled now. "No matter what Mother thinks she goes along with Father."

"Well, there you are—" it was Pattie now waving her hand at Janie as she said, "it dies hard. Papa says stand, we all stand; Papa says sit, we all sit."

"It isn't like that at all, Pattie," replied Janie quickly. "Father is a very moderate man. He has travelled a great deal in his business; he's seen the rights and wrongs in many countries, but he always comes back and says we are the most liberal country in the world."

"Then God help the rest of them, that's all I say, Janie."

"All right, Pattie; you say what you think, and I'll say what I think. And when John and Daniel have taken their coats off and bloodied their noses, you and I will pull out each other's hair."

There was real laughter at this, and when it died down Moira said, "Oh, I could be back in the old country; except for the blood and the cursing, I could be right there."

"Oh, we'll provide the cursing," said John. "Where would you like to start? I can go through the alphabet."

"I've no doubt about that, John," said Moira; "but if you ask my opinion, we all need a cup of strong tea with plenty of sugar in it, and perhaps just a drop of Saint Patrick's potion, or the Devil's temptation. "No, no"—she put up her hand to check Janie rising—"I want to escape from the battle zone, so just leave it to me."

After Moira had left the room there was an embarrassed silence for a moment until Pattie, addressing Daniel, said, "Does she talk about Ireland very much?"

"No, not at all."

"Well, I'd like to bet that she thinks about it all the more. She's not the same, is she? The life seems to have gone out of her. It was the loss of Maggie Ann, and then the baby on top of it."

"We all miss Maggie Ann," Daniel said quietly.

"And what about Sean? That boy hardly ever opens his mouth. At one time he used to jabber away to me. The last time I came, that priest was here talking to him. Do you think he's a good influence?"

Daniel looked to the side for a moment, which appeared as though he were trying to recollect something, but what he was aiming to do was to push the thought of Sean and his silence into the back of his mind yet again. He knew what he should have done from the moment he found that piece of wood; but how could he have confronted that child and said, "You have deliberately killed your father...my father?" No. It was something that had to be buried, in case Moira should have the slightest suspicion. One thing he hadn't been able to do was let himself be alone with the boy; although he was not really a boy but some fey creature, one that only Moira's land could produce.

"I don't know. Moira's showing no objection, and after all she's a Catholic, and it is her business, so I don't interfere."

Changing the subject, John now said, "It's amazing how Michael's come on, isn't it? He chatters like a little parrot now. It's often the way, you know, with children who start late: once they've got the feel of their tongue they wag it incessantly. And he walks steadily, now, doesn't he?"

"When is her daughter coming again?" Pattie asked Janie. "You saw her when she was last here; you said you had a long talk with her. Did she say where she was going?"

"Presumably back to her home in France."

"Is that all she said?"

"Look, dear sister," Daniel put in, "stop pestering Janie. How could she remember all that was said? And anyway, it's none of your business. You're a proper Nosey Parker, always were. That husband of yours"—he glanced at John—"should keep you in order. God protect me from free-thinking women.'' Then, as he was passing Janie's chair, he bent over her and said, ''Don't follow her lead, I'm telling you, because I don't want to have to fight with you an' all.''

After he had left the room Pattie looked at Janie, who was leaning back in her chair, her eyes half closed, and her hand gently wafting the collar of her white silk open-necked blouse, and she said, ''You know something? He is the most stupid individual of a man that ever stepped into trousers!''

''Pattie!'' John's tone held a slight reprimand, and she turned on him, saying, ''Well, he is. Something should be done with him.''...

That night, when she got home, Pattie took up her pen and wrote a letter, and it was concerned with what she considered should be done with her brother.

2

It was a Saturday morning and Daniel was in Fellburn talking to the wholesaler. Mr Baxter was bemoaning his fate. "I tell you, Mr Stewart," he was saying, "this drought is going to kill more businesses off than the cholera killed people. There's hardly a thing coming in from round about, and as for the prices in the market, why, you could buy a gold watch for what they're wantin' for a pound of vegetables these days. And there's no let-up, for when it does decide to rain there'll be floods, you'll see. The topsoil's just like dust now, blown clean off in many places; but come the rain the rest will go in floods. I tell you it's ruination. It's all over the country, but not so bad as up here, because the wheat lands down there are surviving whereas the corn crops here have just perished. How are you faring? But need I ask?"

"No, you needn't ask, Mr Baxter: as things are now, they can't last much longer. It's the cattle I'm worried about."

"Well, you're surviving, an' that's something, because Rington's gone bust. Did you know that?"

"I heard he was in a bad way."

"Aye; we're all in a bad way. Just look round you here: empty crates. And how the poor buggers in Bog's End are surviving, God alone knows. But I'll tell you something." His voice lowered and he took a step nearer to Daniel as he said, "You were connected with the Talbots, weren't you, at one time? Well, *he's* still bringing stuff in. Now I ask you, how's he managing that? Not a lot, I'll grant you, but more than anybody else round here, and you can't grow vegetables by spitting on them. I think the water company want to take a walk around there. What d'you say?"

Daniel said nothing to this, but shrugging his shoulders he turned away, saying, "Well, I'll be seeing you one of these days with full skips, I hope."

"So do I, Mr Stewart. So do I."

Daniel did not go into the market because he couldn't bear to see the sparsely dressed stalls, nor the prices they were asking for inferior quality produce. Instead, he made for the main street and a draper's shop, because Moira had asked him to get her some silks and some thread.

He was within some yards of the shop when there emerged from it a well-dressed young woman. She turned in his direction, then stopped, and he could not pass her on the narrow pavement as there were cabs, carts, traps and drays filling the road. So he stood, and she stood, and they looked at each other. He noted that she was dressed as he'd never seen her before, well-dressed although in a flaunting fashion. Her light straw hat had a stream of ribbons hanging from it and she was wearing a lilac dress with a square neck which showed her creamy skin to advantage, and on top of the dress was a cream silk dust coat.

"Well! Well!" she said.

He gave no answer to this but looked at her closely. She was still beautiful; in fact, more so than when he had last seen her, which was well over a year ago. And she seemed to have matured in that time. The girl was gone: the figure had developed, particularly her bust, and the woman was very much to the fore. But it was her face that held his attention.

"Wonderful weather we're having, don't you think?"

Still he made no answer.

"I hear your land is like a desert and nearly all your crops have failed. It must be worrying for you."

"Just a bit"—his voice sounded quite level—"but if I knew where to steal water, which is against the law, I would, like your father, be able to carry on my business."

She stared at him and he watched the stiff smile slide from her face and her lips become compressed, while the light in her eyes darkened, before she said, "I'm going to be married soon. Think of that when you're sweating your life out in that desert of yours among the crop of Irish idiots."

There flared up inside him the desire to lift his hand and send her flying. He saw her for the first time as a cheap creature, a spiteful creature, and he couldn't prevent himself from hitting back, if only verbally, by saying, "I do hope that your rush to the altar is not being occasioned by your seduction of poor Ray."

He watched her breasts rise until they pressed the slack coat apart; her face aflame, she hissed at him, "I hate you, Daniel Stewart, and I'll hate you till I die;" then she turned about; but a voice calling, "Fran!" turned her once more towards Daniel, and she looked beyond him, then tossed her head in the air. He, too, turned and saw Ray Melton standing beside a horse and trap that was tethered outside the post office. At this Daniel strode into the draper's shop.

He bought two bobbins of thread and was given half a paper strip of pins to make up for the farthing change. Having thanked the assistant, who said, "It's been a pleasure serving you, sir. Please call again," he emerged from the shop. To his surprise he was confronted by his one-time friend.

Ray was the first to speak: he said, "What did you say to her? You've upset her. What did you say?"

"What did I say to her? Oh"—Daniel's voice was airy—"I forget; it was of no importance."

Ray Melton now cast his glance downwards for a moment, then nipped on his bottom lip before he said, "I knew we would meet up sometime and…and to tell you the truth I've been dreading it, because we were friends, weren't we?" He was now looking fully at Daniel as he went on, "And it must have seemed a dirty trick; but there you are, you know what effect she had on you, and I might as well tell you, Daniel, that I fell for her from the first—I just couldn't help myself—but as long as you were in the running I kept on the sideline. However, once I understood it was broken up…well, I ask you, what would you have done?"

Daniel drew in a long breath and let it out slowly before he said, "Likely much the same."

Ray Melton half-smiled now as he said, "You're not sore at me? Well, I thought you'd be mad."

"One grows up."

This reply seemed to puzzle Ray Melton, but he nodded and said, "I…I suppose so. Well, anyway, I'm glad I've spoken to you, because I can tell you I felt pretty awful at the time.''

"You had no need. I wish you luck." Daniel pulled out his watch. "I have an appointment; I must be off."

"Oh. Oh well, goodbye, Daniel. As I said, I'm glad I spoke to you and...and that you're all right."

"Never better. Goodbye, Ray."

He turned about, knowing that his desire to strike Frances had been nothing to what he had wanted to do to Ray. How he had stopped himself from lashing out at his one-time friend he didn't know and yet it wasn't Ray he was really mad at; it wasn't him he wanted to hurt, it was her. As he had looked at her he had thought, She's a slut, and a mean one into the bargain. Yes, that's what he had thought as he looked at her; and she had had the nerve to call Moira's family a crop of Irish idiots!

Well, it was over, and when he came to think about it, Ray had played the game honestly from the beginning, for he himself had had no inkling of how Ray felt about her.

Of a sudden he experienced a sense of relief, for he knew he had been dreading meeting her face to face; he had been afraid of his own reactions. Although for months now he had slept without going through the torment of his loss, he still knew he was haunted by the beauty of her. And on first sight of her this morning he realised that the woman had grown more beautiful than the girl; that is until her face had darkened with her venom and obliterated the appeal of those melting eyes, the soft lips, and the skin which he had but to touch to make his blood race and his feelings heat up as if under a brazier.

But now what? Was he free of her? Yes...and no.

Free of her as she was now, and as he knew her character to be, but not free of the girl who had aroused his love when he was but a boy and fostered it into his manhood.

Now there was the future; it was stretching ahead, his to do what he liked with... Oh God in heaven—he sounded to himself like Maggie Ann—did you ever hear such damned nonsense? Free to do what he liked with, and seven children there to bring up. Was that going to be his future?

But were they *his* responsibility?

Yes. Yes, they were; they were his half-brothers and sisters. To all intents and purposes, Moira was his mother. And there was one thing Frances had been right about: should he ever come across any one he could marry, how could he ask her to share that house and that ready-made family, the eldest but ten and the youngest not yet three? Surely, any right-thinking girl would want a family of her own, as he himself would. And what would the place be like then? A menagerie.

"You would pass a friend without saying, 'Top o' the mornin' to you'? Now would you?"

"Oh, hello, Mr Farringdon. I'm sorry, I was miles away."

"Yes, you looked it. How did you think me Irish sounded?"

"Dreadful."

"Oh! and I myself thought it was perfect. Where are you off to?"

"I was making for the stables to pick up the cart."

"Well, I'm at a loose end. My wife and daughter just said to me, 'Get on with it. Pass the time any way you like, only leave us alone.' They've gone shopping, so I was making for The Crown." He pointed to the hotel. "Come and keep me company for five minutes."

"Be glad to, sir. Be glad to."

A few minutes later, seated in a corner of the saloon, Tom Farringdon said, "Well, how are things going? But need I ask? It's a bad time all round."

"Yes, it is, sir, it is."

"The only good thing is that rain's bound to come soon. Taking the law of averages and past years into account, it should start early in October. But then, what do we get? Floods. It's an awful country for weather... What're you drinking?"

"I'll have a light ale."

"I think I'll have the same; it'll be cool; at least, I hope so."

After they had been served with the beer and Daniel had drunk half of his, Mr Farringdon pushed his emptied glass to one side and, leaning towards Daniel, he said, "I've been wanting to say this to you for some time, Daniel, but I never seem to see you. Of course, you never have time to come across, I understand that. I get all my news of you from Janie, and she doesn't see you so often now that she's teaching. It's a damn silly thing to do. She's got no need to bother teaching. That's your sister's influence. Did you know that?"

"Yes, I suppose so; but I think Janie wanted an occupation; she's got a very strong mind of her own."

"You don't have to tell me that, Daniel. Oh dear me! she worries me, that girl."

"Worries you? Why?"

"Well...I mean, what's going to become of her?"

"Oh, I think she'll work out her own destiny; she'll never do anything she doesn't want to do. She won't be influenced."

"Again, I must say you're right in your summing up of her character. Anyway, it wasn't her I wanted to talk about, but you. Now, I don't want you to be offended but, and I've meant to say this to you for some time, is there any way I can be of use? You can have a loan of as much as you need, interest free, at any time."

Daniel looked down into his glass, nipped his bottom lip tightly then drew the air sharply up into his nostrils before he said, "Thank you. Thank you very much, Mr Farringdon." He had not raised his head, but was still looking down into the beer as he went on, "You're the first one to offer me a helping hand. Moira saved the farm when my father died. She had some money from her daughter and I had made her put it into the bank because I felt she would need it herself some day. But, as she said, it was in the family." He now raised his head and looked into the round, intelligent eyes set in the clean-shaven face that was topped by thick, greying hair, and he said, "I can manage for a time. If I can get over the winter without any more mishaps and hang on to the cattle and the land, I'll pull through. If I feel I can't, I'll come to you, sir. But whether I do or not I'll always remember your offer. It means a lot to me at this moment, for to tell you the truth I'm feeling at a low ebb in all ways."

Tom Farringdon did not comment on this confidence, but he sat back in his chair, called the waiter and asked him to refill the glasses, and not until this was done did he say, "There'll come a time, likely early next year, when I'll be away...well, when we'll all be away. I'm trying to persuade Janie to come with us. I'm going to do some business in Italy and then go on to Spain, which will cover two or three months.

But should you need help during that period, then just go to my solicitor and he'll have my instructions to let you have what you want.''

Daniel put his hand to his brow, then ran it through his hair and his voice was a little above a murmur when at last he spoke: ''It's odd, you know, sir; one minute you feel there's nothing but blackness staring you in the face, and you can't see what's to become of your life. Mine appeared to be working on that farm, and for years ahead dragging out a living for Moira and the children. And you stop me in the street and invite me in for a drink, then you sit there and you hold out a lifeline, even arrange for it to be there for me to clutch at when you're abroad. I...I can't believe it. But I'll say this, I feel it's started to rain.''

At this Tom Farringdon gave a bellow of a laugh saying, ''Well, I only hope that by this time next year you find yourself wet through. Now, I must finish this beer and go and look for those women.''

As they rose from the table Daniel said, ''When do you expect to go, sir?''

''Oh, it hasn't been fixed yet. It could be in February; somewhere around that time. My main job will be to get Janie to give up the teaching. But''—he turned his head to the side—''I want to get her away to see the world. Although she's travelled quite a bit, I want her to meet people and to stop her moping.''

''Janie moping? I could never imagine Janie moping; she's always so lively. She bucks up everyone in the house when she comes. I have few friends, you know, Mr Farringdon, but I consider her my best friend. She has been that to me; if she had been a man she couldn't have been a better friend.''

Tom Farringdon turned and looked at Daniel; not

only looked at him but stared hard into his face, then he nodded and said, "Yes. Yes, it's good to have a friend…man or woman. Well, now, I must be off. But look, you'd always be very welcome at home, you know."

"Thank you, sir, I'll try to visit. And…and thank you for everything."

"No need. No need."

Once outside the hotel they went their separate ways, with Daniel now feeling not a little puzzled. Janie's father wanted to take her away so she could meet other people, and all because she moped. That wasn't Janie, not the Janie he knew, not the Janie Pattie and John knew. And she'd be away for months.

He was still thinking about this when he climbed on to the farm cart and said, "Gee up! there"; but before he reached home he was thinking he had found the reason for Mr Farringdon's wanting to take his daughter abroad and for her to mix with other people: he was hoping that she would meet someone and be married. Yes, that was it, that was the reason.

He couldn't imagine what it would be like to know that Janie was married. But she was worth a good man, and in her father's set it would likely be a rich man too, or somebody comfortably off. And then it would be goodbye to his one friend, the friend who popped in now and again and who always brought a lightness with her; a friend he could talk to as he couldn't talk to Moira; because Moira didn't trouble herself with books or with the doings of the day. Moira found all the interest she needed to fill her life in her family.

He was back to where he was when he was walking along the street in Fellburn prior to meeting Mr Farringdon: the future was Moira and the children, and the striving for daily bread.

Daniel's striving for daily bread did not lessen all through the weeks of autumn, and before long it was Christmas week again. The dry summer, as he had prophesied, finally gave way to flooding rain. Where, before, the land had been parched, the wells dry, the cattle dying, now the flooded rivers flowed over the land, and many of the cattle drowned.

The sky this morning was low and seemed to leave little space between the heavens and the earth, and Moira remarked she had smelt snow in the wind.

He himself had smelt the snow in the wind as he came back from the farm. He had been down there since six this morning. He had found the men already there and in a cheery mood, which irritated him, and he had asked himself if they would be so cheery in the New Year when he had to stand one of them off.

It would have to be Barney, and he would have to give him a pension, which couldn't be less than three shillings a week. But, this being Christmas week, they were all looking forward to the extra shilling in their pay packets, together with a piglet either to kill or to add to the one or two they would have in their own stints. And then there were the wives. Last year Moira had revived a custom that had died with his mother, that of giving some little present to the wives. His mother had always made up parcels of tea and sugar and some sweetmeats, especially if there were children. So he had asked Moira if she would knit them some little thing, such as a tea cosy or mittens or, better still, give them a present of one of her fruit loaves. And this she had done. So altogether there was an air of expectancy at the farm.

But there was no expectancy for him as he sat in the study going through his ledger. He had just closed it with an impatient bang and was about to rise from the chair when he heard a commotion in the passage outside, then Moira's voice calling, "Daniel! Daniel!"

He stood up as she came into the room. She was clutching a large envelope to her breast and her face looked brighter than he had seen it for a long time.

"What news! What news! I...I must sit down."

"A letter from Melissa?"

"Who else? Who else, Daniel? Who else? And what a message." She now opened the envelope, and extracted first what looked like a photograph, next a letter, and then an oblong piece of paper, before she said, "Look at that!"

He took the photograph from her. It showed a long low house, part of it covered with creeper, a pathway edged with flower-beds leading to a front door, and to the left what appeared to be a wooden summerhouse.

"Isn't it beautiful?"

"Yes, it's a bonny place, but, why—?"

"They've bought it; at least, Melissa's husband has."

"Where is it?"

"In Ireland, of course."

"Oh, in Ireland. But why? Are they going to live there?"

"Just for the holidays, she says in this letter." She now handed him the letter and he read:

My dear Mother,

You will no doubt be surprised to learn that we have bought a holiday home in your old country. Jacques fell in love with the place as soon as he saw it. It is a lovely old house with ten rooms and a maze of outbuildings.

There is not much land attached—only twenty acres. The people who sold it to us would not let it go unless we also took their stock. It is a very small stock, consisting of only two cows, a dozen sheep, hens, ducks and geese. It is in the care of a Mr Rafferty, who worked for the previous owners. Now what I want to suggest is that you and the children come for a holiday. You may make it as soon as you like. I'm sure you will love it and it will do you so much good. As for the children, I think it will be a delight for them, as there is a stream running through the land.

I'm sure, too, that Daniel will wish you to take advantage of a holiday. Do write and tell me that you will come soon, for it seems a shame to leave the place empty for long. The enclosed cheque is for you to spend on the children for Christmas presents and on yourself, of course. Please believe me when I send you my affection.

Your daughter,
Melissa.

P.S. All arrangements will be made for your travel. Just write to the above address and tell me when you would like to come.

He folded up the letter and handed it back to Moira, who said, "Well, what have you got to say?"

He gave a little "Huh!" of a laugh before he said, "It's wonderful. And just think how the squad will enjoy themselves. As for that stream, I can see them in it now; they'll be swimming like ducks."

Moira's face was unsmiling as she said, "You're not really happy about it."

"Of course I am, my dear, of course I am, but I can't deny that I'm going to miss you all. What would you think if I told you to get yourself away now. Oh, Moira"—he leaned forward and caught her hands—"I'm delighted for you, and that she is so kind to you, because, you know, under the circumstances it could have been very different. But of course, she's all you under the skin."

"Yes, under the skin, but very polished on top of it. But oh, I am so proud of her! And look at that." She held out the cheque. "Another fifty pounds. Her husband's money must grow on trees. But I'll say one thing for him, he plucks it off and gives it to others. And that is a rare thing, especially with them that have money. Anyway"—she smiled broadly—"we're going to have a real fine Christmas. And the coming New Year augurs good all round. What d'you think?"

His mind jumped for the moment back to the ledger in the study, but he smiled back at her, saying, "You know what, Moira, you know what I have a good mind to do during this holiday time?"

"No; what, Daniel? What have you a good mind to do?"

"Get stinking drunk, really mortallious, so much so that I'd have to be helped upstairs and put to bed."

"Do that, do that, Daniel, but don't expect to be helped upstairs and put to bed, at least not by me, because if I saw you the worse for drink, you know what I would do?"

"No; what would you do?"

"Throw a bucket of cold water over you; not one but two, or as many as I could lay my hands on quickly."

"I believe you would."

"Yes. Yes, I would, Daniel." Her voice and expression were serious. "I've seen enough drink in my time and I can't laugh at it any more. No, Daniel; do anything to ease your mind…and your body, but don't do it through drink."

"I was only joking, Moira." His voice was low and apologetic. And she nodded at him, saying, "Yes. Yes, I suppose you were. But as they say, there's many a true word spoken in jest and I would hate to see you take the same road as your father."

"Oh, Moira, Moira," His voice was no longer low. And hers wasn't either as she said, "Oh, you can say 'Moira, Moira', like that but everything has a beginning. You've got to start somewhere and the way your mind has been of late, my dear, I wouldn't have been surprised if you had taken to drink; but at the same time, had it happened, I know I wouldn't be able to live with you. Oh, but what are we talking about? Why be so serious? Come on, I'm sorry I've made you look so glum. Let's go and tell the children the good news."

Daniel followed Moira into the hall, where she stood calling, "You, Margaret! Sean! Patrick!" He didn't wait for the children to come at her bidding, but went ahead of her to the kitchen, picked up his working coat and cap and went out. Prominent in his mind at that moment were her words, "Do anything to ease your mind or body, except drink." What exactly did she mean by "anything"? Was she suggesting she would rather have him go to a brothel in Fellburn or Newcastle? Her words had been plain enough.

And this letter from her daughter. He was glad she was going to get the chance of a holiday; indeed, that they were all going to get the chance of a holiday. And where would that leave him? Alone in that house for the first time in his life, that's where, because even Rosie was now finding it impossible to stand for hours in the kitchen, for her legs were almost as bloated as had been Maggie Ann's; besides which she was an old woman. Well, what was he worrying about? He would be able to fend for himself. But it was the thought of the house with no-one in it. Anyway, it would only be for a few weeks and he'd appreciate them more when they returned, and their absence would give him a breathing space to think of what he was going to do with his life.

Oh, dear God! He kicked viciously at a stone in the path and saw it rise and whirl into the distance. Didn't he know what he was going to do with his life? It was all mapped out every inch of the way as far as he could see, with one innovation: the brothels in the town.

Janie had brought Christmas presents and had stayed most of the day helping the children to decorate the hall and the drawing-room, as well as the top of a fir tree that Daniel had stuck in a tub, but which had caused much laughter and some concern when it tended to lean first one way and then the other.

Moira had asked her to visit one Christmas Day for tea, but Janie said she would have to refuse as her parents had already invited guests. But she promised to come on New Year's Eve and even spend the night, as her father, mother, and elder brother Hal, were going to London for two or three days. She had declined to accompany them because she had already promised Pattie to spend New Year's Day with her and John; and because her younger brother would be spending the holidays with his fiancée's family, as she put it to Moira, she'd be only too pleased to see the New Year in with them all…

So it should happen that Janie came early on New Year's Eve and she helped Moira to make pastries for the high tea that was to be set for the children as a treat. And later in the evening she saw them all to bed amid laughter and screeches as they chased each other from room to room, when she was surprised to see that even Sean joined in the game. And when they were at last tucked up it was he who took her hand and held it against his cheek, an action she felt to be so tender as to bring a lump to her throat.

When she bent and kissed him, Patrick, in the other bed, let out a bellow of a laugh and hid himself under the bedclothes; but Janie didn't attempt to kiss him, she lightly smacked his bottom, at which he squealed.

At the bedroom door she turned to look at Sean, who was lying still, his eyes large and bright and shadowless, even though the bedside lamp was turned down low.

Later, when Moira was upstairs changing her dress,

Janie, sitting by the roaring fire with Daniel, said to him, "They're all very excited, as if they had been to a party."

"Well, to them, today has been as good as any party; but I think a lot of the excitement is the prospect of the trip ahead. You know, they've never been away from here in their lives. Patrick and Sean have been on the cart as far as Newcastle, but that's about the limit of their travelling."

She was silent for the moment, then said amusingly, "Sean is different from the others, don't you think?"

He too hesitated before he answered, "Yes. Yes, indeed, he's different from the rest." His voice sounded flat and this caused her to make a statement. "You don't like that. Perhaps you wish he wasn't?"

"Oh, it's no use wishing about another's character; we are all as we are made. You can't change what's inside."

"I don't agree with you."

He turned his head sharply towards her, a smile on his face, as he said, "No?"

"No. You take Patrick, for instance. He's the roughest of all the children, but were you to send him to a good school, in two or three years time you wouldn't recognise him."

"You're right in part. Oh, you're right in part. His veneer would be thick in two or three years time—he was nodding at her now, a smile still on his face— "but underneath he would still be Patrick. His instincts will keep him 'Patrick' all his life, and at one time or other his natural nature will break through his façade and there you'll have the real Patrick."

"You're very cynical, aren't you?"

"Me? No. I'm not cynical. I'm just making a statement about nature. Animals are the same. You could take a fox cub from the set and bring it up in the house, but it will still grow up as a fox inside, and when it first sees a rabbit or a young deer it would make for it.''

"And you deny that you're cynical; you're like Pattie, you know.''

"Well, I don't mind being compared with my sister. By the way, she tells me that you've stopped teaching. That was a short career.''

"Yes, it was.''

"Why? Why did you stop?''

"Oh, for various reasons. I thought it was no use starting a new term, because I think, as I told you, Father wants me to go travelling with them.''

"And you're going?''

"I don't know. I haven't quite made up my mind yet.''

"But what will you do if you don't go? Will you be left at home alone?''

"Oh no; there'll still be Hal and Robert, and Robert's not getting married until the summer; then it's Hal's turn. I think that's why Father wants to get Mother away for a time, before, as he put it, the wedding fever hits everybody.'' Janie had turned her head somewhat at the mention of weddings: she wondered if he knew that Frances was going to be married in March. But would it make any difference to him? Would the fact that she was married get her out of his system? She doubted it.

When Moira came into the room she turned to her and exclaimed, "Oh! you do look nice, Moira. I've never seen you in that dress. Is it new?''

"Yes; newly turned for the third time. It's really

inside out now. And the lining itself made three summer smocks for the girls."

"Well, it looks lovely. Mauve suits you."

"Funny—" Moira laughed; then bending down, she turned up the hem of the dress, saying, "Look! Look! it's really brown on the right side and shot mauve on the inside. I like the inside best, don't you?" She was laughing as she took her seat to the side of the fireplace, saying, "But why do we bother to get dressed up? I mean, I needn't have got dressed up for you, need I, Janie? And as for you, Daniel, you've seen me going round like a tramp for so many years, one more night wouldn't make any difference. So why did I bother tonight?"

"Vanity."

"Vanity? Me! I never look in the mirror from one week's end to the other. As Maggie Ann used to say, you don't want to give yourself a shock every day, do you?" She now drooped her head and looked towards the fire as she said softly, "How I miss that woman. I never really felt alone when she was here, but when she went, part of me went with her. She was full of blarney and she never stopped talking. But practically everything she said had a meaning at the root of it: folklore, fantasy, or just superstition."

Daniel rose to his feet now, saying, "I think I'll have a drink;" then to Moira he said, "I'm allowed one before twelve o'clock, aren't I?" And she thrust her hand out to him as she countered him with, "You can have as many as you know you can carry; but the point is, will you know how many you can carry?"

"I think so; I'll stop at fifteen."

As he went to pass her she slapped his arm, saying,

"You didn't ask us what we would like, did he, Janie? Never asked us if we've got a mouth on us."

"Well, what would you like, Janie? There's beer, and whisky, and there's port."

"I think I'll plump for the port," said Janie, and Moira added, "I too will plump for the port."

It was as they sat with their drinks that Moira raised her glass, first towards Janie and then Daniel, saying, "Here's to the year that's passing and may nothing in it ever be repeated; and to the year that's coming, may it bring us health and what each of us wants most."

Neither Daniel nor Janie said, I'll drink to that, but just raised their glasses to Moira's before they drank.

It was Janie who brought up the holiday, saying, "Have you decided when you're going to Ireland, Moira?"

"Well, yes," said Moira. "Daniel and I talked it over, and we think we'll go towards the end of January, because it's no use waiting for the Irish Sea to be calm—it's never calm; it doesn't know the meaning of it. There'll be seven seasick children and one seasick woman, that's for sure."

"How long do you intend staying?" asked Janie.

"A month. Oh, that'll be long enough; a month. Imagine the state of this house and him in it alone." She thumbed towards Daniel. "I've offered to see if I can get anyone in from the village but he'll have none of that. The big fellow says he can surely look after himself for a month. And 'tis a pity you'll be away about that time, too, Janie, else you could have come and popped in now and again and seen if he was alive."

"Yes, I suppose we'll be off then too; at least, Father will be transporting Mother across to Holland.

I've asked him why he doesn't go and live there, he's so fond of it. But his excuse for his frequent visits is that they are business trips.''

"What time is it?" Moira glanced at the clock. "Ten to twelve. My! how time flies when you're enjoying a crack. I think we'd better get ourselves muffled up and to the door. I love to hear the ships' sirens, and the fog horns, and the hooters from the factories, and the church bells all mingled together. It's only once a year you hear them and they always do something for me. I don't know"—she moved her head slowly—"the combined sound seems to speak of hope, somehow, hope that might never come to anything, but for the moment it's there.''

It was five minutes to twelve when they opened the front door, and Daniel stood between them looking out into the darkness. There were stars in the sky and there was a frost that caught at the breath. "There'll be snow by tomorrow," he said. Then they stood quiet, waiting until the first sound came to them: it was the distant peal of church bells in Fellburn, and immediately it was joined by a chorus of hooters and ships' sirens and the long boom of the fog horns. And Moira, with tears in her eyes now and a sob in her voice, said, "Death and birth, death and birth. We're into another." Then turning to Daniel, she said, "A happy New Year, Daniel, my dear," to which he quickly responded, "And to you, Moira, dear," and put his arms about her and kissed her. Then he turned to Janie, and his hands went out to her and caught hers and he said, "A happy New Year, Janie. A happy New Year." And she answered with a break in her voice, "And to you, Daniel, to you, a happy New Year."

Why he did it he didn't know; perhaps it was because she looked lost and lonely like himself, but he put his arms about her and kissed her on the lips. And as Moira closed the door on the New Year, Janie closed her eyes. She had got what she had come for. She had hoped for it as a natural gesture to bring in the New Year, but she had been doubtful it would happen; and even then, not warmly and fully on her lips.

4

It was on the second Saturday in January that Pattie appeared unexpectedly at the house. She came in the back way, startling Moira, who was at the table chopping up vegetables.

"Oh, my goodness! Where've you come from? You did give me a start. How on earth did you get here through all the slush and muck?"

"I swam; or very nearly!"

"Is anything the matter?"

"No, not really; I just wanted to have a talk with you."

"And you've come out all this way in this weather to have a talk with me? Well, it must be important. Sit yourself down. Let me have your coat. Margaret, pull that chair up for Auntie Pattie."

"Hello, Auntie Pattie."

"Hello, Margaret...where are the others?"

"Oh, up in the schoolroom or thereabouts where they've been all the week," Moira answered. "They couldn't get to school, you know. Even when the thaw set in they would have been up to their knees in slush, for who would have expected rain on top of all that snow? Anyway, what would you like? There's hot broth, or a cup of tea."

"I'll have the broth; I'm frozen inside."

While Pattie drank the bowl of broth, Moira resisted pressing the reason for her visit on such a morning; but as soon as the bowl was empty she said, "There's a good fire in the drawing-room, so would you like to go in there?"

"Yes. Yes, I would."

When Margaret made to follow them, her mother admonished her: "Bide where you are. Finish chopping those vegetables."

Once seated in the drawing-room, Moira glanced at Pattie as she leaned forward and held out her hands to the blaze; then she said, "Well now, tell me; I'm dying to know. Nothing wrong with John, is there?"

"No, nothing wrong with John. I wouldn't be here if there was anything wrong with John, now would I?"

"No, looking at it like that, you wouldn't. Well, why are you here? Not that I don't welcome you every time you come in the door; but in this weather, and it promising worse."

"Well, that's why I'm here this morning, *because* it's promising worse and I wanted to have a talk with you; a serious talk."

Moira stared at this young woman who wasn't in the habit of wasting words—those that came from her razor-like mind were never spoken idly.

"It's about your holiday, and Ireland."

"Yes? Well, what about it? It's all set. Melissa sent me the tickets—I got them only yesterday—and more than enough money to get us across— Oh, yes, more than enough—and a note to say that we'd be met at the boat because, I understand, it's a good distance to the house.''

What Pattie said next brought Moira upright in her chair and bristling not a little. ''Do you want to see Daniel live his life as he is now, going on until he is middle-aged and your children grown up, or do you want to see him happily settled and with his own family?''

''Pattie…Pattie, what are you saying to me? Are you accusing me of something?''

''No. I'm simply asking you a straight question. Do you want to see him happy, because as long as you and the children are here, he'll stay here. And he won't bring a wife of any kind into this house. Have you thought of that? any kind. Frances Talbot wouldn't have any of it, and I doubt if anybody else would either. But of that, I'm not quite sure.''

''Would you mind telling me, Pattie,'' said Moira, rather stiffly now, ''what you're getting at?''

''Yes. Yes, I'll tell you, Moira. It's this. When you go to Ireland, if you care anything for Daniel, you'll stay there with the children, because the house you're going to is not your daughter's, it's yours… She's already put it in your name, and it's because she knows that you would love to return to your own country and have your children brought up there that she's done this. But in the ordinary way, if you went there on holiday, you would come back here and life would go on as usual; and as for Daniel, well, Frances Talbot is being married in March, that's sure, because her father will see that she marries where the money is. But there's someone else standing, as it were, waiting, and who has been patient for years, because she loved him long before that silly, conceited piece he went mad about even thought of him. And you know whom I'm talking about…Janie. But as long as you're here he won't turn to Janie: like most blind men he's got to be in a corner before he gropes his way out and sees things and people as they really are.''

It was some time before Moira spoke, then she said quietly, ''How have you come to know all this? Not about Janie, because I've known for a long time how she felt about Daniel, but Daniel's heart seemed set on the other one and still is, I think. But how did you come to know about the house and what my daughter intended to do?''

Pattie looked away, then held her hands out again towards the blaze. She knew that if she spoke the truth she'd put a damper on the whole scheme, if not kill it forever, because she dare not tell her that she wrote to Melissa and suggested that if it were possible she should set Moira up in Ireland because she had never really been happy here; and moreover that Daniel would never marry as long as she remained in this house and had the children to bring up. And that Melissa wrote back and thanked her and said she had put it to her husband and he was all for it, but that it would have to be done tactfully, when she was already in Ireland and settled in the house. So instead she said to Moira, ''It was your daughter's idea. She got in touch with me and asked me what I thought. And I told her what I thought. But knowing that you wouldn't like to be too near your own people—'' she glanced now at Moira, saying, ''I thought I was right in saying that— I suggested that they should find a place some way off, say fifty miles away. And this is what they did; close to Dungannon. But I must confess, Moira, I didn't tell her that I aimed to come to you and ask

you to free Daniel, because that's what I'm now doing."

Moira got to her feet and walked across the room
to one of the tall windows and stood gazing out on to
the bleak day. She was upset; in fact, she felt humiliated. In as many words she had been accused of keeping Daniel from living his own life. Yet, she knew
that, later on when she came to think about it, the
accusation was correct, because the thought of living
in this house without Daniel would have been unbearable to her; and also to his bringing a wife into it,
which Pattie had said he would never do. But even if
he had, that too would have been unbearable because
she would no longer be the mistress of the house, but
merely a stepmother-in-law who was relegated to the
kitchen. And after all, would she mind not coming
back here? and would she object to living in that beautiful house in Ireland with the two cows, and the hens,
and the ducks, and the geese, and the stream at the
bottom of the garden? No, she would love to be back
in her own country among her own folk. Well, not
really her own folk. No, she didn't want to be in the
midst of them again; just to see them now and then,
perhaps, but to have no real truck with them. She'd
had twenty-five years of that, which had been hell. No,
it wasn't the idea she minded, it had been the way
Pattie had shot it at her. That razor-like mind of hers
had no blunt edges. She turned towards the fire again
and, taking her seat, she said, "You're nothing if not
straightforward, Pattie."

"Well, I couldn't see any other way of putting it.
It's been worrying me to death since I first knew of
your daughter's intentions. And I thought it was a
wonderful idea. In the ordinary way you would have

only taken it as a place to go for a holiday, because in your mind there would always have been the thought that you must return and look after Daniel. Now, isn't that so?''

Moira's head bobbed two or three times before she replied, "Yes, I suppose you're right. That is so." Then she added, "What am I to do? How am I to explain it to him?"

"Oh, you'll just go as if you were off on holiday. Then, I suggest that you write to him and put it to him, saying that you would like to stay there and would he be able to manage on his own? But he mustn't have any inkling of what's going to happen before you go. It must be done from that end, a sort of *fait accompli*. Well, what I mean is, when the deed's already done, there's nothing much he can do about it."

"Oh, yes, I see, I see. *Fait accompli*. Yes, yes, of course. But...but how in the name of God am I going to keep this up and say goodbye to him, knowing that I'm going for good? and the children too?"

"Oh, it isn't as if you'll never see him again. He would love to go over to Ireland and visit you. He's never been there; in fact, he's never been anywhere. Do you understand that, Moira? He's a man, for all his young years; he's a man and he's never been anywhere, really, except around the extent of this farm-land. Of course, he had his schooldays, but then again, you won't know that my father didn't pay a penny for his fees. My mother had arranged that there was a certain amount of money given to the school to see him through till he was eighteen; and once he was eighteen, that was that. But, you remember, Father kept him back when he was sixteen. He talked as if he wasn't paying any more school fees for him, but *he* had never paid a penny in the first place, and Daniel would never have had a decent education if it hadn't been that my mother had foreseen how things would turn out.''

"Dear God! The things you learn. I thought I knew everything about Hector. But that was mean. I understood he had paid for him for eight years or more, but then couldn't afford to go on. I recall he said as much to me when I asked him if he would send the boy back to his school. Well, well, he's where the good Lord pleases, or the devil, and how he came to his end will never be really known. And I must be honest, I felt no sorrow at his going, and the more I learn of him the less guilt I feel about that. But about my future, Pattie: what if he takes it badly and thinks the worst of me for not coming back?''

"He won't, not if you put it to him as a question or a statement that you would like to stay there. But you could add that if he wants you back and is missing you all very much, you'd return. And in that case, well, it would be up to him what answer he would send to you... Where is he now?''

"Oh, at the market. He took some sheep in. And by the way, how did you get here?''

"I hired a cab from the station to the crossroads and tramped the rest. I came through the farm. It wasn't too bad.''

"But how are you going to get back?''

"Well, I'll wait until he comes back and he can turn the trap or the farm cart around and lumber me to the station.'' She rose now and came and knelt by Moira's side and, taking her hand, she said, "You're not mad at me, are you? You don't think me awful?''

"Oh, Pattie, dear, think you awful? I think you are the most caring individual a body could meet in a day's walk. I...I admit I was a little upset at first, because it came as a shock. You talk about a blind man, well, I've been a blind woman, a selfish one, I think, too, because you know, Daniel's been like a son to me and I know I've been like a mother to him, and I'll miss him. There's no doubt about that, I'll miss him. But oh, if I'm honest, I'll be glad to be back across the water. And I know one thing: Maggie Ann's spirit will go with me, because if she was here she'd be doing a jig from one end of the house to the other at the very thought of seeing our land again. It's odd, isn't it? the pull the ground on which you were born has on you."

"Yes, nationality is a very odd thing. As you say, it's a pull, a very strong pull. And you know something, Moira? Daniel won't be the only one who'll miss you. I'll miss you, and I feel this is the moment to come clean and apologise for my manner to you when you first came into this house. You laughed a lot then. You and Maggie Ann were always laughing. But I had to learn a lot about human nature before I understood why you laughed such a lot." She reached up and kissed Moira on the cheek, and Moira's arm went about her and held her close.

They drew apart as the door opened and Sean came into the room and Moira greeted him with, "Well, what are you after?"

"Nothing, Mama. I just want to get warm." And he glanced from one to the other before moving to the fire and holding out his hands towards the flame.

5

It was the evening before they were due to leave. The hall was littered with bass hampers and boxes. Moira emphasised that no-one was to carry a bundle: Melissa had planned and arranged the intricate journey to Belfast. Here they would be met for the final stage to the house. Melissa had even arranged for cabins to be provided for them on the boat should the weather be inclement, so she had stated in her last letter. And Moira had laughed about the word "inclement" being attached to the Irish Sea.

For the last two or three days it had been impossible to keep the children under any kind of control, and today they had scampered here and there repeating their goodbyes to the men and their wives on the farm and saying goodbye to their special play places in the wood. They even stormed the village shop, buying a quantity of barley sugar sticks because this, Barney had told them, was a sure prevention for seasickness.

Mrs Mulcaster, who kept the shop, was very interested in all they had to say; and the customers who were present listened enthralled to their chatter as they described the beautiful house and grounds that belonged to their new sister Melissa. This information came from Margaret. And when there was surprise at the mention of a new sister, it was Patrick who boldly said that their mother had been married before she came to England, and that their half-sister's dada had died.

Well, this was only what Moira had told the children. And Patrick's words, of course, were borne out by the fact of the spanking outfit that had stopped at the inn last year.

Well, well! had said the villagers; at last things must be looking up for them up there on the hill; and not before time, some said, for that young fellow had worked like ten men since he had left school, and it had piled the years on him and made him near with money, so near he was likely to count the turnips.

So now the children were ready for bed for the last time in this house, had they but known it, the house in which they had been born. And this night, Daniel did not go upstairs, as he sometimes did, rampaging from one room to the other, threatening dire events if they didn't stop their squealing and settle down, which threats usually produced more chasing, and more squealing. Instead, he sat in the study behind his desk, his hands idle, his feelings so mixed he couldn't have explained how he felt if he had tried. He only knew he would miss them all, Moira in particular. And it was no use saying, what was a month? Anyway, it would soon pass; the house was going to be like an island and himself the only one on it. Of course, Janie had promised to call in and Pattie and John were coming over each Sunday, weather permitting. But there were the meal times, and the evenings, and the scampering of feet, and the checking of this one or that.

When a tap came on the door, he called, "Yes? Come in," and in a way he wasn't surprised to see it was Sean.

Sean and he had hardly exchanged a word for some time now, and they each knew why. He saw no light around the boy now; it was more as though he were in a dark shadow. And when he came and stood by his side, saying, "Can I talk to you, Daniel?" Daniel said, "You've never before had to ask if you could talk to me."

"I haven't talked to you for a long time."

"I know that, Sean, I know that."

"We're going away tomorrow."

"Well," Daniel gave a little laugh, "I'd be a very dim individual indeed, wouldn't I, if I didn't know that, too."

"Yes, you would. But what you don't know is, I'm not coming back."

"What? What did you say?"

"I'm not coming back."

"Oh, that's news. Does your mama know that?"

"No, not yet."

"Well, that will certainly be news to her. And what do you intend to do in Ireland, may I ask?"

The boy looked down towards the floor, then to the side before he said, "Father Lowe said I could be sent to a school in a sem...seminary, then"—he now lifted his head and looked straight at Daniel as he finished— "train to be a priest."

Daniel remained silent as he looked into the round clear eyes and the pale face. He wanted to make a joke of it, but he knew he mustn't, so what he said was, "A priest? That's a tall order, isn't it? Do you *want* to be a priest?"

"Yes. Yes, I must become one, because, as Father Lowe said, it will take a lifetime to wipe out my sin."

Again there was silence before Daniel said one word: "Sin?"

"Yes. The sin of killing my father."

As if he had taken a blow in the stomach, Daniel's bowels jerked. He had the desire to push the boy away from him, or to rise quickly and put distance between them, a lot of distance. And when Sean said, "You picked up the branch, didn't you, and put it back on the pile?" he made no reply, and the boy went on, "He was a bad man. He killed Maggie Ann."

"What? What are you saying?"

"I'm saying my dada killed Maggie Ann. He rode her down, straight at her."

"*He what?* He rode her...? He didn't!"

"Yes, he did. He was in the middle of the drive and she was near the verge. He turned Rustler and went straight for her. She was so big, she couldn't jump clear."

Daniel's voice was small as he said, "Surely Rustler would have shied?"

"It didn't shy. Rustler is a steady horse; but it did its best not to trample right on her; the animal seemed to know it was wrong. But death was in my dada's face. He hated Maggie Ann. He meant to kill her."

Daniel turned from the boy and stared at the desk. Then he put both hands on his ledger as he said, "Have...have you mentioned this to anyone else?"

"Only Maggie Ann. She knew."

He leaned towards the boy and Sean nodded at him, saying, "We talked about it and I promised her never to tell Mama. Besides, he hit Mama more than once, and he hit you an' all. He was bad."

Daniel now made himself look at the ledger as he asked, "Did you plan what you were going to do?"

The answer was brief. "Yes."

"You planned it?" There was astonishment in Daniel's voice now.

"Well, I stood waiting in the copse and I threw the wood. I didn't mean to hit Rustler, but he reared and Dad fell off and down to the stream."

"But...but that's what you intended to happen if the branch had hit him?"

The boy remained silent; then Daniel said, "Did...did he die straight away?"

"No...well, he seemed as though he had at first, but I couldn't get up the bank and I had to go along the stream and pull myself up by the bridge." He explained it as a child might have, to suggest how astute he had been to work that out. Then he went on, "I caught Rustler and put him in the stable and dabbed some of Maggie Ann's cream on his shoulder. He was still trembling; he was frightened."

"You say the horse was frightened, Sean." He paused. "Were you frightened?"

The clear eyes looked into his and again the answer was brief: "No."

And once more Daniel felt the blow to his stomach.

"What did you do next?" Daniel asked quietly.

"I...I went back and Dada was awake and he ordered me to go and get the men."

"Why didn't you?"

Sean did not answer this, but he went on, "I told him that he had killed Maggie Ann and he said Maggie Ann was still alive. And I said, yes, but that she was dying and she didn't want to die. And...and then I went away."

Again Daniel had the urge to move back from this child, this boy who was not yet ten years old. He stared at him now as he said, "You did a very terrible thing, do you know that?"

"That's what the priest said. Just what you've said, Daniel, that I did a very terrible thing."

"Are you sorry for it now?"

The boy again looked down to the side and then to the floor before he said in a low mutter, "No, not really. He was a bad man and Maggie Ann was a lovely woman. We all loved Maggie Ann."

Daniel put in quickly now, "You didn't tell her exactly what you had done, Sean?"

The boy's eyelids flickered and he said, "Well, she knew anyway."

"And what did she say?" Daniel's voice was a whisper now.

"Just that it was between her and me and God. And God understood why I had done it and He would forgive me so long as I didn't let on to Mama..." Of a sudden the boy's voice rose, and there was a plea in it as he cried, "I'm not like the others, Daniel. I wish I was, but I'm not. I'm affected, I mean, by things. And I'm always listening and...and I hear things. And at times I'm frightened; not...not always, not always. I wasn't frightened when I left Dada lying there, not till after, and then I was very frightened. And I know things that I know I shouldn't."

There was a break in the boy's voice now and tears in his eyes and when he flung himself against Daniel's knees he hesitated for just one second before his arms went about the boy and he hugged him, then hoisted him up to his knees and held him close. And when the whimper came, "Do you hate me, Daniel?" Daniel replied immediately, "Hate you? No. No; I love you. That's why I'm sad for you. But promise me one thing." He lifted the boy's head from his chest and, holding it now between his hands he said, "Promise me, Sean, you'll never do another bad thing. No matter how you are provoked and no matter what you think, you'll never hurt anyone or wish them ill again. Promise me?"

"Yes, Daniel, yes, I've already promised that. I've promised God."

Once more Daniel pulled the boy close to him. Here was this child saying that he had promised God never to do a bad thing again, and he had his life to get through. The weight he was carrying on his little shoulders was already enormous. He had killed a man as surely as if he had taken a gun and shot him, and the man was his own father. The weight of that sin wouldn't diminish with the years; it would grow heavier. And he muttered to himself, "God help him," for he would need help, and he wished earnestly at this moment that the boy would return from Ireland and be under his care, because now he understood him. As he said, he wasn't like the others: he was of a dual nature and he would have to fight it all his life. He also had something else, that strange something that wasn't really a part of ordinary human nature but from a dimension that was unknown. The Catholic priest would likely tell him it was of the spirit, but in his own mind there were no words with which to name it; except, perhaps, that it was unnatural. Whatever it was he had, it made him shiver.

"Oh, there you are. All the rest are in bed." Moira came into the room, but Sean did not immediately slip from Daniel's hold. And when he did and Moira saw his tear-stained face she put her hand on his head, saying, "Go on to bed now, dear. I'll be up in a minute. The others are tucked in."

And when the boy walked past her without speaking, she turned to Daniel, saying, "I feel that myself. I'm trying to keep it back. And I'm not going to talk to you, because I know if I do you'll have me on your knee too." She aimed to smile.

He rose from the chair, saying lightly, "Good gracious! you would think you were going to the ends of the earth and forever. What's a month? I'll just be getting used to the peace and quiet when you come storming back with the horde."

He was surprised when she turned quickly from him and left the room. He stood thinking for a moment. She had been behaving oddly these last couple of weeks, busying herself here and there, putting the house to rights, scouring, cleaning. She had taken down all the bedroom curtains and washed them. She would have done the same with those downstairs only they were too big and heavy. And, as she said herself, if she moved them off the rails the faded brocade would drop to bits.

He had an uneasy feeling on him. He wanted to go to her and say, Look, are you really happy about this holiday? You were at the beginning, but something's changed you. For days now, we haven't sat down at nights and had a crack. You're going away for a month, not forever; but no; she seemed to be on the verge of breaking down and he did not want that to happen. And there was tomorrow morning to get over, and the parting at the station.

The parting at the station was harrowing. Moira stood outside the open reserved-carriage door, marked plainly by red stickers on the side windows. The main luggage was in the guard's van, the baskets and boxes of food were on the racks, and as she looked along towards where the guard was talking to the engine driver, she longed for him to signal with his green flag that they were about to go, because any minute now she was going to release the tears that were already in her eyes.

She was saved from speaking to Daniel by the chattering of the children.

"I'll write to you, Daniel," Margaret was saying now as she clung on to his arm, "and tell you all about everything. Oh, I wish you were coming with us."

"I will, next year, you'll see."

"The little boat can be sailed along the stream for a hundred yards, it said in Mama's letter."

"That'll be fine, Patrick. You'll learn how to row."

"I hope Annabella won't be sick on the boat," said Catherine, hugging a long-legged clouty doll tight in her arms, while the others laughed at her.

"Come on!" Moira cried at them. "Say goodbye to Daniel." And as they did so she hoisted them one after the other up the steep step and into the carriage...that is, until she came to Sean. He was standing in front of Daniel and when he raised his arms Daniel lifted him up and, their faces close, they looked hard at each other; then Daniel kissed Sean, and he kissed Daniel and said, "Will you come and see me sometime?"

"What did he say?" said Moira now as she helped Sean up into the carriage. Then she glanced for a moment from the back of her son to Daniel before, at the sound of carriage doors being banged, she cried,

"We're ready for the off."

She was standing in front of Daniel and for a second she looked straight into his face, before her arms were about him, holding him tightly as he held her. Then she kissed him, and her voice was a whisper as she said, "Thank you, dear. Thank you for all you've given me." And now swinging about, she pulled herself up into the carriage before his hands could assist her. But when he closed the door there was the mass of faces smiling at him and all talking at once; but Moira was standing behind them, her hand across her mouth, her eyes streaming. And the thought went through his mind, Why is she so upset? You would think she was going away for ever...Like Sean.

The whistle blew, the train shuddered, and the platform was enveloped in steam, and now with a gentle "choo-choo-choo", they were moving away. Daniel walked by the side of the door until he was forced to trot, hearing the unintelligible words the children were shouting at him. And when he came to the slope at the end of the platform, he stopped and, his hand raised, he returned their waves.

He didn't move from the spot until all he could see was the end of the train disappearing into the distance, when he turned about, walked slowly up the platform, over the bridge, out into the main station and then into the street. And there he stood gazing about him for a moment as if he had been dropped into a strange town and didn't know which way to turn.

He had brought them all into Newcastle on the cart, and now he made his way to the farrier's and, after retrieving Prue and the farm cart, he set out for home.

Once clear of the city, and then Gateshead, he sat

on the box, the reins slack in his hands, and left it to the horse, for the drive through Low Fell was straight and it knew its way from Fellburn market to its own stable in the farmyard.

Arthur Beaney greeted him with, "Well, Mr Daniel, you've got them off your hands for a month. What are you goin' to do with yourself?" And to this he replied, "Oh, that's easily answered, Arthur. What time I have in the house I shall be busy looking after myself. But there's so much food stacked up for me, I doubt if that'll take much time."

"You'll miss them, the children?"

"Doubtless. And a good thing in one way; I'll be able to have a little peace at night... Everything all right?" he added.

"Yes, there hasn't been much change since you left early this morning. But give us some fine weather, dry that is. Well, I don't mean very dry, because we had enough of that last year, didn't we? By God! that'll take some getting over all round the country. Another year like that and we'd all be finished. What d'you say?"

"I say, with you, Arthur, we'd all be finished."

With this he left the farmyard and made for the house, and after unlocking the front door, he stood for a moment in the hall and looked about him. Everything looked bright, cleaner and brighter than he had seen it for years. The floorboards surrounding the carpets were shining—yesterday Moira had had Patrick on his knees polishing them.

He was about to go upstairs to change his clothes when he stopped, telling himself there'd be plenty of time for that. So he went into the kitchen. Here, everything was in order. There was even a place set for a meal and a note on the table, which read, "There's a hotpot simmering in the bottom of the oven; it should do you for two days. You know where the pies are, and the bread is all wrapped up." And at the bottom of the note were the words, "I'm missing you already."

Dear Moira—he took up the piece of paper and read it again—so thoughtful, so caring. He seemed to have lost his mother again; yet, she was more than a mother.

He put the piece of paper back on the table, went out of the room, through the hall and into the drawing-room. Here, a fire that had been banked down was glowing red. His chair was set at an angle within leg reach of the ornamental brass fender on which he could place his feet. A pair of his slippers lay at the end of the fender. He wasn't in the habit of changing his boots in this room but there they were. He stood with his back to the fire and looked round the room. It was a really beautiful room. The velvet upholstery on the chairs was faded as much as the curtain drapes; the chintz cover on the couch was clean and showed up patches that hadn't been so evident before; the hearthrug he was standing on was the remains of a thick Indian carpet. He looked down at it and for a moment he saw a picture of himself and Pattie lying on it. Pattie with her legs stretched out, her back supported by a chair, a book in her hand, he lying on his stomach stroking a large tabby cat. He hadn't thought of the cat for years. Tiddles, they had called it. He had found her bloated and dead one day under the bushes. She had been poisoned. He recalled that he had screamed so much that his father had sworn that it was the last animal they would have in the house, as the farmyard was the place for cats and dogs. And he never had a pet after that.

As he stood there he realised that perhaps this was the first occasion the house had had one person living in it, and that for a time this morning it had been quite empty. Perhaps it was because of this that the memories of the past came flooding back. And it could have been he was looking back over eighty years, not twenty, for his mind became flooded with scenes, snatches of conversation, angry voices, and laughter. Oh yes, there had been a lot of laughter, especially since the Irish women came on the scene. He could recall laughter: Moira's laughter, Maggie Ann's laughter. But of course, they had both been hiding something behind their laughter. And there was the children's laughter, the laughter that was the product of glee. They had all been gleeful, with the exception of Sean. Poor Sean. When he had clung to him at the station it was as if he were saying a final farewell. And it would be if he entered a seminary.

The question that now sprang to his mind was, how would Moira react when the boy told her that he wasn't going to return home with her? Oh, dear, there'd be trouble. Yet, she was a Catholic at heart and perhaps she might understand. Anyway, their priests were persuasive enough; they would certainly help her to understand, if not actually make her.

"Anyone at home?"

He leapt from the rug and ran to the drawing-room door, and when he pulled it open and saw Janie divesting herself of her hat and coat, his face spread into a broad smile, and there was so much sincerity in his voice that she couldn't help but believe him when he said, "Oh, hello, Janie. Am I glad to see you!" He was taking her coat from her as he added, "I never thought it would be like this. It's like a morgue, an unusually clean and bright morgue. I've never seen the house so shining. But it's dead. Oh, I'm going to miss them."

"I thought you would."

"Is that why you popped over?"

"One of the reasons. One thing I didn't do was bring you any food, because I knew that Moira would leave you enough to last for days. Are we going to stand here until I leave or am I allowed to go into the drawing-room?"

He laughed outright now, saying, "Well, your presence is like a visitation from above. Come on, come on." He actually put out his hand and caught her arm. And when they entered the drawing-room, she said, "My goodness! yes, it is different; everything's so tidy. Well, of course, the absence of seven children was bound to have an effect."

"And of course," he nodded now, "Moira was never one for making them mind their p's and q's and clearing away their debris after them. I used to be at them most of the time. But you know, I hardly recognised this room when I came into it, so I can understand your surprise."

"It's a lovely room. I've always liked it." Her voice was soft.

"Sit down," he said, and he pulled a chair on the opposite side of the hearth closer to the fire. As she sat down, she said, "Have you had anything to eat?"

"Not yet. But there was a note on the kitchen table telling me where to find the food, and that there was a hotpot in the bottom of the oven. But look, can I get you a drink; tea or something?"

"Yes, I would love a cup of tea, but I'll make it."

"You'll do nothing of the sort. From now on—" he struck a pose, then repeated, "From now on, I am mistress in my own house, and I know how to treat visitors."

Her head went back and she laughed. But then she added, "I thought I had passed the visitor stage and was called a friend of the family."

He had taken several steps down the room when he stopped and, looking back at her, he said, "Definitely a friend of the family, Janie. A dear friend of the family."

From where she sat she could see him crossing the hall and she repeated to herself, Yes, definitely a friend of the family, Janie. A very dear friend of the family. That's what they said about women who died old maids, women who sat furthest away from the fire in someone else's house, sewing, sewing, sewing, mending this, mending that, or reading aloud to the mistress, who might be her sister or her sister-in-law, or even her mother. Oh, be quiet! she warned herself. Be quiet! Leave such talk for discussion with Pattie. Accept what is being offered and be thankful.

No! No! The refusal in her mind brought her upright in the chair. Oh no! She had decided last night what she was going to do. She'd give it to the end of the month or until Moira returned, by which time she should know for sure. It was a long shot, but nevertheless she was determined on it. No sitting back and waiting for crumbs. Her mother had said that to her last night. "Your father's worried," she had said, "because you seem prepared to waste your life following a shadow." And her mother had been so kind, so understanding. She had grasped her hands and said, "Although I say it myself, you've inherited my nature, and I'm glad of that. But you have your father's mind, and a wonderful personality." And at this she had cried, "Where does that get me?" And her mother had said, "It will get you a fine man some time. You must come with Father and me at the end of the month; he might even leave before then. But whatever, you must get away, for your own good and your own happiness; because there is happiness ahead of you, dear. I know how you feel about Daniel, and we like him, but as you know yourself, right from when he was a boy he had shown where his affection lay. Misplaced, oh yes, because quite candidly I could never tolerate Frances Talbot's company for more than a short time, because she was flippant and brainless."

"Oh, no. No, Mother," she had said, "she may be flippant but she's not brainless. Frances has a very calculating mind, one that makes her wily and devious. She's the kind of person who gets her own way in the end."

"Yes, I suppose she is," her mother had said, "because she has no moral fibre. There she is, marrying someone she doesn't really care for, I'm sure of that. But he's got money, or his people have. She takes after her father in that way, because I'm sure Lilian would have been glad to see her married to Daniel." And then she had added softly, "And I've got to say this, although it's like pressing it home, dear, but there's Pieter Van der Meer in Holland. When you and your father went over the time before last, he took you all about; then last time your father said he kept asking after you, and Father promised that you would accompany him on the next trip. He's a very nice man, older, I know, by fifteen years; but then your father is almost ten years older than me, and you know what our life together has been like. We couldn't be happier. We are all concerned for you, dear...the boys, too.''

It was at this point that she had said, "Mother, I'll tell you something. I'm concerned for myself, really I am. I'll tell you something else; I'm going to give myself until Moira returns. This I've finally decided upon. You get my meaning?" And her mother had looked up at her with that kindly smile and said, "Yes, dear, I get your meaning and I'm so glad to hear about your decision.''

And here she was in this house, in this strangely empty house, and the man who was constantly in her thoughts had promoted her from being a visitor to a friend of the family.

Well, she felt she had been a friend of the family for long enough...

After Daniel had brought in the tray of tea and placed it on the table between them, he pulled his chair further up to the table and exclaimed, "Isn't this nice;" then added, "I'll let you pour out because I'm going to take my boots off and get into those slippers, at least for an hour or two. I've never before changed my boots in this room, but Moira must have left those slippers there on purpose."

Slippers on, he stretched out and put his feet on the fender, and when she handed him the cup of tea, laughing, he said, "Thank you, ma'am." And she, picking up his mood, said, "You're very welcome, sir. And I'm so glad you were able to visit us today. As you will gather, the family is not at home; they've slipped over to Ireland for a month."

At this he put his cup of tea back on to the table

because it was rattling in the saucer, and he said, "Drawing-room farce."

"What did you say?"

He laughed at her now, saying, "It's like a drawing-room farce: if you had rehearsed that, you couldn't have acted it better."

"Oh, well, I'll have to think about that. When I'm looking for a job I might consider the stage."

"You're not going back to teaching, then?"

"No. As I think I told you, Father is going to Holland sometime early next month and I promised to go with him, conditionally, that is."

"Well, what are the conditions?"

"Oh, they're private."

"Oh, I'm sorry; I didn't mean to pry."

"Oh, you're not prying. I have a friend...I mean, we all have friends there."

"Someone like Pattie?"

"No, no—" her voice was stiff now—"not someone like Pattie. It happens to be a man."

"Oh." There was a pause and again he said, "Oh. I...I didn't know."

She remained silent. Why had she said that? But it was true. Pieter was her friend and wanted to be more than her friend. She liked him, and he was a gentleman and, like her father, he was in the jewellery business. But there was another side to it. He was good-looking, very bright and very entertaining, and as she had said to her mother, she couldn't imagine him being without a mistress but she felt able to compete with one. She recalled that her mother had been shocked and had said, "Oh! Janie, Janie," and she had replied on a laugh, "Oh! Mother, Mother."

Daniel too was left with his thoughts. So that was

why her father always wanted her to accompany him. It was likely already arranged with the Dutchman. That would mean she would live in Holland. He asked himself how long had he known Janie? Well, as long as he had known Frances. And he asked himself another question: why hadn't he been able to talk to her and enjoy her company years ago as he did now? and received an almost angry answer. That was a damned silly question to ask when he'd had eyes for only one girl. And yet what had he and Frances talked about? Nothing. He couldn't remember them having one serious conversation. Yet it wasn't conversation that either of them had needed in those days. What had spoken to them both loud and clear were the demands of their bodies, and they hadn't been answered.

He was surprised when he heard himself, in quite an ordinary voice, ask, "Are you going to marry this...Dutchman?"

"Marry Pieter? Huh! Chance would be a fine thing, so they say. As yet in my life, I have never had a proposal of marriage. I don't happen to be the type that men flock around, dropping on one knee and begging me to be their partner in life. I happen to be the kind of girl who's always asked to be a bridesmaid. Once, when I was fifteen, I asked the question, why? because by then I had twice been a bridesmaid, and my brother Hal, who was then twelve, with brotherly brutal honesty replied, 'They pick you because you show up the bride by contrast.'"

"*What?*" The word came sharp from Daniel. "Surely he would never say a thing like that."

"Oh, yes, he did; and it was quite true; it still is. I have no delusions about myself, Daniel. I am plain: I have what has been called a homely face. My other protrusions are right and adequate both at the back and at the front.'' She was smiling widely now as she went on, ''And I carry myself erect and walk well, because I look after my feet; I wear sensible shoes, not the narrow, attractive ones. But all this does nothing for me because, you see, I am tall; and my hair doesn't help me because it's too thick and bushy. But my great defect is that I not only talk but I argue. In fact, when I get going I'm much worse than Pattie. Oh, Daniel''—she pulled herself up in the seat—''don't look like that. This is meant to be funny!''

''I see nothing funny about it, Janie, and I cannot believe that is how you see yourself, because you *are* an attractive woman. You call yourself plain, but only you would think so. When you start to speak your voice is beautiful and your character is so kindly.''

''Daniel.''

''Yes, Janie?''

''Do you know you are making things worse? Any woman who looks like me would swap all my so-called assets''—she almost said, to have a face like Frances, but changed it quickly to, ''to be called pretty. And the thing today, you know, the height of attraction in a female is to lisp. I'm sure you've never sat in a room, Daniel, and heard a lady lisp.'' She now lisped, ''Oh, they are tho pretty and tho dainty, the 'lithpers', and the men dote on them.''

''Don't be silly. What's come over you? Men don't dote on women who lisp!''

''You know nothing about it, Mr Stewart. You haven't sat through drawing-room teas as I have when accompanying Mother on her rounds.''

''But where are all the new females that you and Pattie say are swarming the country now? women who are demanding fresh laws, women's rights, the dignity of womanhood, freedom for all women, so on and so on.''

"Oh, there are quite a number of us. But compared to the 'lispers' of this world, we can't be counted as yet. But wait till the end of the century or until Edward comes on to the throne, then we'll see changes.''

"Are you for him''—he was smiling at her now—"*him*, with his fancy women?''

"Well, he has one outstanding point in my estimation: his main friend is a woman who has made a career for herself, and she's a thinker, and she's accepted as such. Anyway, how did we get on to this conversation? And my tea's gone cold.''

"Would you like another?''

"I would.''

"Well, I'll go and fill up the pot, madam. And while I'm gone, think of some more surprises for me.''

Left alone, she sat on the edge of the chair and stared into the fire. What had she done by introducing Pieter's name? Was it to make him think? No, nothing could make him think otherwise than he did. She'd like to make a bet that if Frances was brave enough to leave Ray tomorrow and walk in that door, he'd be all over her. No, the real reason she had mentioned Pieter was that she wanted to leave this long one-sided love affair with some dignity. She wanted to show him, she supposed, that if he couldn't see anything in her, another man could. Yet, as she had stated, she had not yet had any proposal of marriage; although at the same time, she knew she could have, and she would have if she went to Holland with her father next month. One thing Moira's brood had taught her was that she wanted children; even more so than she wanted the love of a man, she wanted to carry a child, and bear it; and not one, but a number. And if she couldn't have them by Daniel Stewart then she would have them through Pieter Van der Meer; and perhaps through time she would come to love him, too. But in the meantime, she would laugh with Daniel, because he, like Moira, enjoyed laughter.

So be it. The next four weeks would set the seal on her future life.

6

The first week seemed long; or, at least, the nights did. After cooking himself a meal he would rekindle the fire that he had damped down in the drawing-room, then stretch out in the chair with a book, intending to read. But somehow he could never get very far with it: the book would fall into his lap and he would start wondering, What were they doing over there? How had they found the place? Would it be up to Moira's expectations? Well, if he had just to go by the photograph, it must be.

He was surprised, when he came to the end of the first week, that he hadn't seen Janie again. As she wasn't teaching he had expected her to pop over; but then there *was* the weather to contend with.

On the Saturday, he had taken into Fellburn half a dozen hens, a few ducks, and the carcasses of three suckling pigs, besides a few dozen eggs, the small number due to the hens moulting; even so, he knew that the sum total would bring in very little money.

His business over, he went through the market and along the main street, then asked himself why he was wasting time? Who did he expect to see? There were plenty of nodding acquaintances but no-one with whom he could stop and talk. So, within an hour of entering the town, he left and made for home.

In the farmyard Barney said to him, "How're you faring, Mr Daniel...I mean, up at the house?" And he answered, "Oh, not too bad at all, Barney, though I must admit it's like a graveyard at night. I miss the children."

"Bound to. Bound to. I'm sorry the missis can't make it to the house, but she can hardly crawl round the kitchen now."

"Oh, don't worry about that. Anyway, there's only another three weeks to go before they'll be back; and then I bet I'll wish they weren't."

"Oh, I doubt it, Mr Daniel, I doubt it."

And he doubted it himself.

He went in by the back door and although he wouldn't have been surprised at all to see Janie in the kitchen, when he saw her coming through from the passage, almost staggering under the weight of a full bucket of ashes, he was amazed and cried at her, "What d'you think you're doing?"

"I'm doing, I think, what you should have done some days ago. The ashes were almost reaching the rug, and some of them were still warm. You could have had the place on fire."

"I meant to clear them out today. And these are hot. My goodness! Give them here!" And he almost pushed her to one side as he took the bucket from her.

After dropping it in the yard, he remonstrated with her: "You would pick a bucket, wouldn't you?"

"Well, what else could I have put them in?"

He laughed now, and she said, "You can laugh, but it might have been past a laughing matter. The fire was blazing and I tell you that that ash was hot; it really could have set the rug on fire.''

"It couldn't have got past the fender, Miss Farringdon. Have you noticed there's a fender there?''

"Yes, I have, Mr Stewart, but it has a filigree front and the ashes had reached up to some of the holes.''

Quietly now, he said, "It never struck me. I'm sorry. I see what you mean. I won't let it happen again.''

"Did you have any dinner in town?''

"Dinner in town? No, of course not.''

"Well, it would have been a sensible thing to do, because as far as I can see now, there's only cold ham, bread and pickles left.''

"Well, that'll suit me. Will it suit you?''

"Oh, yes, it'll suit me; but you can't live on just that.''

"Well, tomorrow's Sunday; then I'll do some cooking for myself.''

He had taken off his coat and cap and hung them on the back of the kitchen door; and now he said, "Let me get these leggings and boots off, then I'll go into the drawing-room and see how you've messed up the hearth.''

"You'll do no such thing. I've got to sweep it up yet. But what you *can* do is get that ham, and bread, and pickles out and let us have something to eat.''

"As you say, Miss Farringdon, as you say.''

As she left the kitchen with a dustpan and a small brush in her hand, he set about cutting slices of ham off a leg that was only half consumed. Then he piled the bread, pickles and butter on to the tray, together with some crockery, and left the kitchen, to meet Janie crossing the hall with a dustpan full of ashes in one hand and the brush in the other and, as he passed her, he said, "If you intend to remain in my service, miss, in future you had better wear an apron."

He did not hear the answer she gave him because he was chuckling to himself. He felt strangely happy; in fact, merry.

Having laid the tray on the couch, he cleared a sofa table of knick-knacks, pulled it up in front of the couch, and on it he spread the crockery and the victuals. When Janie came back into the room she was rolling down the sleeves of her brown dress, and as she took her place on the couch, she said, "What you should have in the kitchen is one of these iron stoves with a boiler to the side, then you'd always have hot water."

He paused as he was forking some slices of ham on to her plate; then he said, "Yes, ma'am, I'll see to that. Come Monday I'll have that fireplace out and a new one put in. Yes, I will; indeed I will."

She laughed now at his attempted Irish brogue, but said, "I'm not joking, I mean that. And Moira would appreciate it—oh yes, how she would—to have some hot water on hand instead of having to fill kettles and pans."

"There's the boiler outside in the wash-house. She often keeps that on for the hot water for washing them all."

"That's all very well, but it isn't in the kitchen; and these new stoves have a boiler with a tap, which you just turn and there you are."

"All this because you've had to wash your hands in cold water?"

"Yes, it was like ice."

"What pickles would you like, onions or cabbage?"

"Onions smell on the breath and pickled cabbage always gives me tummy ache."

"Well, you can't eat that ham on its own."

"Well, if it's the same as I've had before in this house, I can eat it and enjoy it with bread and butter."

He smiled at her now as he said, "You are contrary, aren't you?"

"It's the only privilege left to me."

After a few minutes she said, "I notice there's a lot of bottled fruit in the larder. Will we have that for the pudding?"

"Take your choice," he said; "but I'm not fond of cold fruit. I like hot puddings."

"That's a pity, because I can't see you getting any for the next few weeks. I like cold fruit, so if I may I'll go and open a bottle."

"Whatever you like, miss. And you can make a pot of tea when you're out there."

As she rose from the couch his tone changed and he said, "I'm sorry, Janie, but I have nothing to offer in the way of drink besides tea; unless you'd like whisky."

"That doesn't worry me, Daniel." Her voice was as changed as his now. "Tea's my drink at any time of the day."

He experienced a most strange feeling as he watched her go out of the room: the house no longer seemed empty but just right. He looked at the hearth. She was right, the ash could have set the mat on fire and the whole place with it. Last night, he had thought he should take those ashes out. But he had come in so tired and weary and wet through. And then this morning he was up and out at half-past five. But in future he would see to those ashes. My goodness! Yes. Fancy, if the place had gone up in flames.

She was some time in coming back; and now she was carrying a tray of tea things; also on the tray was a jar of plums and an empty fruit dish with another jug beside it.

Immediately getting to his feet, he said, "Good gracious! Why didn't you give me a shout? Have you brought the kitchen in with you?"

"Yes, just about..."

After she had poured him another cup of tea she spooned some of the fruit into a bowl, then poured cream on it from the small jug. And Daniel, bending forward, said, "Cream? Where did you get that? I never brought any up."

"I skimmed it from the churn in the larder."

"Oh, you did. Well, it looks nice enough to eat; I think I could try some of that myself."

"Well, there're plenty of bowls in the kitchen."

"That means I've got to go and get one?"

"Yes, or do without."

His voice full of mock sternness, he said, "This would never have happened in Moira's time."

"No." Janie's voice was cool. "But Moira doesn't happen to be here at present and it's happening now."

He began to chuckle. He pushed his cup and saucer to one side, put his elbow on the table and rested his head on his hand; then, as the china began to move on the shining surface of the sofa table, her voice still cool, she said, "If you don't want these things on the floor, you'd better control yourself."

At this he was convulsed with laughter. It was loud, even raucous, and he lay back against the side of the couch and laughed until the tears rolled down his face, the while she sat smiling at him. Suddenly his hand came out and caught hers and he hitched himself towards her, saying, "Oh! Janie, I've not laughed like that, I don't think, in years. You do me good. You're a blessing in disguise. Oh! Janie." And he finished by saying, "If Maggie Ann were here she would say you're as good as a dose of jollop."

Her eyes widened, her lips fell together, then her head nodded, before she said, "Well, I have never received many compliments, but I think that's the most edifying one I have had." And now she, too, was laughing, and she lay back against her corner of the couch.

And there they sat for a moment, their hands still joined until, somewhat selfconsciously, he released hers, and said, "Quite candidly, Janie, I've had a rotten week. It takes some getting used to, you know, living in an empty house after it's been full for years."

"I can understand that, but time will fly now and they'll soon be back."

"Well, the sooner the better."

She did not endorse this in her mind but, looking towards the fire, she wondered how often she could come during the next three weeks without making it too obvious that she was finding it impossible to stay away.

Janie paid Daniel six visits during the next two weeks, when they ate together and they laughed together and sometimes they talked seriously about world affairs, as she was wont to do with Pattie and John. But more often they talked about Moira and the children and the two letters he had received since their leaving.

The house in Ireland, apparently, was a wonderful place. It had everything one would wish for. And on Janie's last visit Daniel had said, "Have you noticed one thing missing in Moira's letters? She has never once said she is dying to come back."

Then, on what should have been the last Sunday before Moira returned, Janie came to the house and into a different situation...

Daniel had, as usual, gone out early that morning and when he returned to make himself breakfast he found the postman had left four letters.

Three of them were bills, the fourth postmarked Ireland.

He sat at the kitchen table when he read it and he could scarcely believe his eyes. The letter began:

My dear, dear, Daniel,
What you are about to read will, I know, come as a shock. I should have told you earlier but I couldn't bring myself to do so. I shall first of all state the facts plainly. My daughter and her husband did not buy this place with the intention of making it their holiday home, but of giving it to me and the children; in fact, last week she handed me the deeds. They are in my name. In one way it is like a miracle straight from heaven: I have a house of my own and in my own land and the children are in their seventh heaven. And I am going to stay here. But oh, Daniel, the pain in my heart at having to leave you, and in that place alone! But there is another side to the fact that I have accepted this miracle: I am thinking of you yourself. You would never have married as long as I was there with the children; or at least you

might have, but it would have been an impossible situation to have two women aiming to run one house. It would never have worked. And unfortunately this has already been pointed out to you.

There's a big ache in my heart, Daniel; the only solace I have is that you will soon come over and see us. When I told the children of the new arrangement, the joy went out of them for a moment, for they all said, "What about Daniel? We'll not see Daniel." That is, all except Sean. I'm having some trouble with Sean. He's got the idea into his head he wants to be a priest. I think Father Lowe had been at him, and I knew nothing about this. Yet he seems happier here than he was at home—you know, Daniel, I'll still think of that house, in a way, as home, because you are there.

Now please, my dear Daniel, I beg you to arrange your life so as you won't be alone. You know what I mean. I cannot bear to think of you going on as you are now and have been for some long time. You won't have to look far around you to find a partner. Forget the past and open your heart to the future. I send you my love, as you've always had it and always will.

Moira.

He laid the letter on the table; then, as if in a daze, he smoothed out the corners of it and all his mind was saying at the moment was, She's not coming back. None of them is coming back. What am I to do? They are not coming back.

When there was a knock on the back door he started, then called, "Come in!" And when he saw

Alex Towney there he said, "What is it? What's wrong?"

"Oh, nothing very much, Mr Daniel, nothing that a blacksmith won't put right. It's...it's Daisy. She's shot a shoe and Barney thought I had better tell you I'll be taking her in to the village, and so he won't be able to get on with the ploughing. And as you weren't goin' into the market this mornin' I didn't know whether you'd be comin' over again, so I thought I'd better tell you what was happenin', because you expected the dry field to be done, didn't you?"

"Yes. Yes, but that's all right."

Alex now walked slowly towards the table and bent slightly towards Daniel, saying, "Anything wrong? I mean, bad news or somethin'?"

Daniel looked down at the letter that was still lying on the table and sighed as he said, "They're not coming back, Alex."

"Who? You don't mean...?"

Daniel turned towards him, nodding his head vigorously, "I do mean...yes, the lot of them."

"No, never! Mr Daniel, never! Leaving you here on your own? Never!"

"Well, it appears that the missis's daughter has bought the place for her mother and they're all settled in and that's that."

It seemed quite natural that he should talk to Alex like this. He had been brought up with Alex and Barney; they seemed to be part of the family. And in any case they would soon have heard of it when, at the end of next week, the tribe didn't come scrambling through the farm, in and out of the byres, the barns, the tack room, yelling their excitement at the events that they had experienced in Ireland and also of being back home.

But that wouldn't happen now, so the men would have known sooner or later.

"What you goin' to do? I mean, how you goin' to manage?"

Daniel seemed to have to make an effort to pull himself to his feet. He hadn't asked himself that question yet. But now he answered it by saying, "Oh, I'll get someone in to see to the house and do a bit of cooking. Anyway, I've managed well enough during the last few weeks."

"I would never have believed it. The mistress...I thought she loved this place."

"It wasn't her home country, Alex. At bottom she's always longed to be back there."

"Anyway," Alex smiled now, "it'll give you an excuse to go over to Ireland for a holiday and see them. You've never had a holiday, not to my knowledge."

"No; nor to my knowledge either, Alex. It's a good idea, and it's something to look forward to."

"Aye; aye, it is; it will be. Well, I must away and get that one down to the smithy's. I've never known an animal go through so many shoes as that one. Barney says it's vanity, but he would, wouldn't he?" Alex went out on a laugh and left Daniel standing by the table folding up the letter.

Slowly, he walked out of the kitchen and up the stairs to what had been Maggie Ann's room. He opened the door and looked in. There was no feeling of her presence left. Then, one after the other he looked into each of the other rooms.

When he opened the study door the problems held

between the pages of the ledger and the letters on the desk seemed to fly at him. And he closed the door with a bang.

When he entered the drawing-room he did not look about but went to the fire and, taking up the bellows, he blew the small ring of cinders into a flame. Suddenly, he sat down on the couch and, placing his elbows on his knees, brought his head down to rest in his hands; now he had the strongest desire to cry. And he did cry. The tears welled in his eyes and, although he wiped them quickly away, they were there again rolling on to his cheeks. And this time he let them come. After a while they ceased and he lay against the back of the couch feeling as he had done years ago, when he used to cry in bed over the loss of his mother, or more so for that which she had withheld from him during her lifetime. But Moira's arrival had compensated for that, and his burgeoning love for Frances seemed to completely cure his earlier loneliness. But now, with the loss of both, his life ahead did appear as a desert. Even Janie, his friend, his only real friend, she, too, would be going to Holland next week with her father. Her mind seemed to be made up.

This thought brought him to his feet. He was going to miss Janie. Oh, yes, he would miss Janie. She was the only one he seemed to be able to talk to these days. Their friendship and their chaffing of each other had blossomed into a kind of intimacy. He spoke to her in a way he could never had done to Moira, because, strangely, Moira would never have understood such backchat. And now, once Janie was in Holland, she would likely marry that fellow.

God! Everyone seemed to be flying off at tangents.

It was as if his life had suddenly exploded and there were the fragments of it, scattering far and wide.

Well, what was to stop *him* from travelling to a different country. He could sell up and move to Ireland and be with the family again, or he could go... But why go to Holland? Janie would be married and settled there.

He went quickly from the room and upstairs and to his bedroom. The wash-hand basin still held the scummed water he had used yesterday, and the slop pail was almost three quarters full. Early this morning he had washed and shaved downstairs in the kitchen. With an impatient movement he emptied the dirty water into the pail, then carried it downstairs.

There was now a growing anger inside him and it was mainly directed at Moira. Plan his life, she had said. Run a farm from five in the morning till last light and later, seven days a week; and see to a house like this, cook his own food, clean the place... She shouldn't have done it; it was unfair of her.

He could get someone in, he had said. Well, he'd have to, wouldn't he? And a strange woman, one from the village who would tittle-tattle, and while he was out of the house, most of the day as he was, she'd help herself here and there. Oh, he knew what would happen. Even Rosie hadn't been above that: cutlery had disappeared from the dining-room, and the children had got the blame for taking it outside for picnics.

He went into the scullery and pumped the sink full of water and sluiced not only his face but his head too, as if that might cool and clear his brain.

Following on this he went back to the farm, but stayed only a couple of hours before he was back in the kitchen cooking a meal, the while telling himself that, at least for once, Janie would have a decent meal when she called. He even rubbed some pig's fat into flour as he had seen Moira do, made it into a dough and put it into a dish ready to go into the oven about half an hour before the pork would be cooked. Then he went into the drawing-room and, using the sofa table again, he covered it with a white cloth and set two places for a meal.

Finally, he poured himself out a larger than usual glass of whisky and sat before the fire sipping it and waiting.

At half past twelve the dinner was ready and he served it up on plates which he then kept hot in the lower oven. But when, by half past one, Janie had not put in an appearance he took out one of the plates and, sitting at the corner of the kitchen table, he ate his meal, chewing almost viciously on each bite.

When three o'clock came and there was no longer any chance of her appearing, for she wouldn't drive back in the dark, he again took to wandering about the house, until, thoroughly exasperated, he clashed the kitchen door behind him and made for the farm, telling himself he had to talk to somebody, even if it was only the animals, or he would do something stupid, silly, like breaking something.

Janie arrived about half past eleven on the Sunday morning. He was returning from the farm and walking into the house yard when he saw the trap approaching. And as she drew it to a standstill she smiled at him, saying, ''Isn't it a lovely day? There's a promise of spring in the air and it's not March yet.''

He forced himself to say politely, ''There's been snow in March before now.''

"Yes. Yes, I suppose so." She had got down from the trap and, turning the pony, she led it into the open barn, saying, "I won't take him out of the shafts, because I can't stay long."

"Oh well, nice seeing you. Goodbye."

She turned a quick glance on him, then said, "Oh, well, if you feel like that I could make it goodbye now."

His head dropped and he bit on his lip before apologising, saying, "I'm...I'm sorry, Janie, it's how I'm feeling at the moment. And...and I thought you might have called in yesterday."

"Oh, I was in Newcastle most of the day, shopping. You know we're off a week tomorrow—"

"It's all settled then?"

"Oh, yes, yes." She was in the kitchen now. "I told you."

"You indicated, but you didn't seem to be sure."

"Oh, well, I'm sure now." She half-smiled at him; then her eyes narrowing, she said, "What is it? Has something happened?"

"Yes, you could say that something has happened. I'll tell you about it in a minute. But first I must say that there is nothing in the cupboard to eat today."

"Oh, well, that isn't surprising. I've never come here since Moira's been away and found much to eat."

"Well, there *was* something yesterday."

"Yes?"

"Yes. Roast pork, vegetables, and a suet pudding, and as much bottled fruit as you could have eaten." There was a slight smile on his face now. But hers was quite unsmiling as she said, "Oh, Daniel, I'm sorry. I really am. And you went to all that trouble. Oh, no wonder you're vexed."

"Oh, I'm not vexed about that," he lied gallantly; then he said, "I got a shock yesterday morning. Oh, well, come on in. I suppose you can stay for half an hour to hear my news."

"Well, I can give you twice as long as that, because if I am to judge by your face and your manner it will take an hour or so."

She walked before him out of the kitchen and into the drawing-room and there, laughingly she said, "I see you've taken the ashes out. That's something. You're learning."

"It's just as well, as things are."

"What do you mean, as things are?" She had seated herself on the couch.

"Well, I won't try to explain it, so just hang on a minute and I'll go and get the written word."

She watched him hurry out, and then looked about her. There was a smear of dust everywhere and an air of untidiness. Nothing seemed to be in its right place. That the cushions on the couch hadn't been plumped up for some time was evident, because she found she was sitting in a hollow.

He was soon back and holding out a sheet of paper with writing on both sides. Taking it from him, she began to read. But she hadn't got very far when she looked up at him, saying, "Oh no. Oh no." And as she turned the page, her head was still shaking. Then when she had finished she let the letter drop to her knees and, looking up at him where he was standing with his back to the fire, she said, "Oh, Daniel; it must have come as a terrible shock. Oh, I could never imagine her doing that."

"You know something, Janie? Looking back, I think it must have been in her mind before she left, because I've found she took all her little trinkets with her. I went through her dressing-table yesterday. And all the children's clothes; the chests in their rooms were empty. I had wondered why there were so many boxes. But then, of course, I thought, there were seven of them.''

"Oh, I'm so sorry, Daniel, really so sorry. What are you going to do? I mean about running the house?''

"Oh, I'll have to get someone in, I suppose. But the thought did cross my mind that I would sell up, and since everybody else is going to strange lands, I'd pick one for myself; she's gone to Ireland, you're going to Holland; there's a world left for me to choose from.''

"Yes, I suppose so. But I always imagined that, in spite of all the setbacks you've had, you love this house and this farm too much to leave it. And given a chance and some decent weather, it could be successful again.''

"For what?''

"What do you mean, for what?''

"Just what I say. Successful again, for what? For whom?''

"Well, that will be up to you, won't it?'' Her voice was flat, unemotional.

And he looked at her as he said, "Yes. Yes, you're right; but to tell you the truth, at the moment I don't know which end of me is up. I've really gone through the gamut of emotions since that letter came yesterday morning. For a time I hated her. Oh, and what I said about you when I had to dump that lovely dinner, and it was a lovely dinner''—he was smiling faintly now—"and, as I say who shouldn't, I made a good hand at it.''

"Did you eat my share too?"

"No, it went in the pig bucket." And he almost added, Where I wanted to put you at the time, because you had disappointed me, let me down, as it were.

He now sat down at the far end of the couch and, staring towards the fire, he said, "It's odd, you know, that when one person decides to make a change in their lifestyle it can affect so many. Mine, for instance, has been turned topsy-turvy, for I don't know what line I'm going to take from here."

Her voice was quiet as she said, "Give yourself a few days to get used to the idea that they are not coming back, and likely things will fall into place. Anyway, as I see it, and I think I am seeing it in the same way as Moira says in her letter, it's leaving you free to run your own life. You'll no longer be saddled with her or the children. No matter how dear they were to you, they would have remained a tie. I think she has taken all this into consideration."

"Yes, perhaps you're right. But there are some ties that one doesn't want to loosen." He swivelled round on the couch now and asked abruptly, "All your arrangements are made, then?"

"Yes, Father is very good at making arrangements—I suppose he's had plenty of practice—and weeks beforehand the tickets are bought, the seats are booked, the hotel reservation is made, and he even plans out the places of interest to be visited." She pulled a slight face here, saying, "I think Mother gets a little weary of the tourist arrangements, because her idea of a holiday is lying in a deck chair on a warm beach, not traipsing round picture galleries and museums and such like. So very often she does just that, which is why I've got to take her place."

"You like touring round galleries and such?"

"In moderation, but this time I think the pattern will be a little different for, some of the time, we'll be out of the Hague district and on Pieter's estate. He has a place about thirty miles out. Mother will enjoy it because she finds it very restful there."

"Oh, yes, yes... Would you like a cup of tea?"

"Yes, I wouldn't mind. But who's making it, me or you?"

"Oh, I'll do it, as it will likely be for the last time I'll have the privilege of serving my friend with tea. I can imagine you have a very busy week ahead of you."

"Likely. Likely."

He waited as if he expected her to say, Oh, I'll be over during the week sometime, but when she didn't speak, he went out of the room; and looking towards the far window, she repeated to herself, The last time I'll likely have the privilege of serving my friend with tea. Why did she suffer it? It had been evident for so long. There was hardly a time she came in this house but he called her his dear friend. It was as if he was emphasising "friend" and no further. And she understood. Then why did she insist on piling on the agony? For that's what she did with every visit here. If she was strong enough this could be the last time she would look on him.

She now sprang up from the couch. She couldn't stand any more of this. She would have to go. It was ridiculous, humiliating. Mother had said to her before she left, "It pains me, dear, it pains me. Why must you go over there again?" And she had answered, "Well, it doesn't pain me; I know where I stand."

And in answer to this her mother had said pityingly, "Oh, my dear. My dear."

Well, she was not going to pity herself.

She surprised him by coming into the kitchen and saying, "I've just remembered that Elizabeth, Robert's fiancée is visiting this afternoon. I'll have to get back."

"I've just mashed the tea."

"I'm sorry; I should have remembered."

He followed her out of the kitchen and into the yard, and as she backed the pony and trap from the barn he looked at her in some surprise, saying, "What is it? Have I annoyed you?"

"Oh, no, not at all. It's just that…well, I'm not very fond of Elizabeth and I was really trying to avoid the meeting, although I know that was very bad of me. So do excuse me."

When she was seated in the trap, the reins in her hand, he put out his hand and caught her arm, saying, "But I'll see you again, surely?"

"Well, if I can manage it. I don't know."

"Janie; what is it? I can't let you go like this. Look, I've been hit from all sides these last couple of days. Please don't go. I mean, like this."

She swallowed deeply. The lump in her throat was about to burst and her voice was cracked as she said, "I'll try to make it, but I won't promise." Then, "Gee up! there, Paddy." And the horse trotted out of the yard, leaving him standing gazing after her, his mind in a whirl with questions seeming to be stotting off his brain like bouncing balls. Why, when she had been so kind, so thoughtful. It couldn't be that…?

No, no. She was all set to marry this fellow in Holland. She had said as much. Then what was wrong with her?

He turned now and looked towards the house. He was looking at the side that formed part of the court-yard, but he was seeing beyond it into the big empti-ness of it. He didn't think he could stand much more. He would sell up. Yes, that's what he'd do, he'd sell up.

7

~~~ooo~~~

During the following week, what time he didn't spend on the farm, and the short time it took to eat cold victuals washed down with strong tea, he spent in the study working out what a decent harvest would bring in—even with the prices as low as they were for corn, there was a good return for root crops—and further, what the farm and the house and the furniture would be likely to bring at the present market price; and finally, the amount that would be left after he had cleared the mortgage, which wasn't all that much now.

And so it was Saturday again, and Janie had not put in an appearance. It was with the hope that she might still come that he sent Alex into the market with the cart and the odds and ends of produce that were available. And while he spent the morning tidying up the kitchen and the drawing-room, and even flicking the dust from the furniture in the hall, he asked himself, if she did come, then would it be her last visit?

He did not attempt to cook a meal but made a pan of broth, and at twelve o'clock he drank a bowl of it, ate a shive of cold pork and bread, then went upstairs and changed into his best suit. And standing before the mirror brushing his hair back, he heard his own voice say aloud, "What difference is it going to make?" only to swing about quickly as a voice came from the hall, calling, "Anyone at home?"

When he reached the head of the stairs he saw her standing in the hall. She was dressed in a long fawn coat with a fur collar that had tails hanging from it over her shoulders, and on her head she had a soft brown velour hat. It had a large brim and was trimmed with a pale pink ribbon. He had never seen her in this attire; she had seemed always to favour tweeds. She looked taller, rather elegant. When he reached the foot of the stairs it was she who spoke again, saying, "Oh, you were going out?"

"No, no. I just thought I had to get changed. I never knew housework messed one up so much."

She smiled now, saying, "You've been cleaning up?"

"Attempting. I'm going to advertise for help and I didn't want them to be frightened away by the muck. Come on." He made a gesture towards the drawing-room, adding, "The ashes are out."

"I bet you left those to the last."

"No, I didn't, it was the first job I tackled."

It was like old times the way they were talking, not as if it was to be a parting.

Once in the drawing-room she stood and looked about her as she exclaimed, "My! my! you *have* been busy."

"Well, I told you, I've just taken my apron off." He laughed gently. And then he said, "It's no use asking if you've eaten; I'm sure you have."

"Yes. Yes, we had dinner in town."

"And you're all ready for the road then?"

"Yes, you could say that, all packed and ready."
She took her seat on the couch, noticing that the cushions had been puffed up.

"Monday, is it?"

"Yes, at eight o'clock in the morning. Father is nothing if not an early riser, and Mother's complaining all the time. She doesn't really want to go. You see, there's Robert's wedding arrangements; but as Father said, that's up to the bride's mother; the groom's people are just lookers on, although you wouldn't think so, with the invitations that are being sent out to cousins and nephews and nieces."

"It's to be a big affair, then?"

"Yes. Oh, yes. Not that Robert wants it, but Elizabeth and her mother are definitely out for a big do."

"How long are you likely to be away?"

"Oh, a month or six weeks, I'm not sure. It all depends."

She did not go on to say on what it all depended, and there was a short silence between them until she said, "Have you heard anything more from Moira?"

"No."

"Have you written to her?"

"No."

"You haven't?"

"That's what I said, no. No, I haven't."

"Well, I should. She'll be worrying; I mean, about how you are taking her news."

"Oh, I think she'll have a pretty good idea of how I'm taking it, and the hole she's left me in. If things had gone as I imagined, they would have all been back today. Do you realise that?"

"Yes. Yes, I do, and that's why I popped over."

"You mean you wouldn't have otherwise come over to say goodbye?"

"Well"—she shrugged her shoulders—"I really didn't see the necessity. Whatever happens in Holland, I'll be coming back in a few weeks' time. It isn't as if I was leaving the country for ever."

"No, no, there's that in it." And following another short silence he said, "Would you like a cup of tea?"

She turned and faced him now, and then she smiled, "Yes," she said, "Yes, I would, but I'll make it. For the last time, I'll make it."

"What! In that rig-out?"

"Oh, I can take my coat and hat off and leave them in the hall."

"You really want to do that?"

"Yes. Yes, I'd like to, for it will be the last time, because the next time I come here you will likely have a maid or two. And I used to enjoy making the tea when Moira was here. Yes, I'd like to do that."

As she rose from the couch he rose, too, and followed her to the door, and watched her take the pin out of her hat, then divest herself of her coat and lay them on a hall chair. He noticed that she was wearing a blue woollen dress, drawn tight in the waist by a broad scarlet belt, accentuating the full skirt. She looked different today somehow. He wondered why he had always considered her so plain. She was walking on towards the kitchen when the doorbell rang. Then he heard a voice say, "You?" and the sound of it seemed to fling open a door in his chest.

Janie looked at Frances Talbot and she answered, "Yes, me. Yes, me, Frances. Have you called to see someone?"

"Don't be sarcastic with me, Janie Farringdon."

Frances was now standing in the hall and she hadn't as yet looked towards the drawing-room doorway. But Janie, addressing Daniel, said, "Someone to see you, Daniel."

As Janie swung about, Daniel called, "Hello! Hello, Frances... Well, come in." And Frances walked towards the drawing-room.

Janie had stopped at the kitchen door and stood for a minute or two as if waiting to hear raised voices. But what she heard was laughter, Daniel's laughter.

It wasn't loud laughter, but it was enough to make her dash for her coat and hat and then quickly make for the kitchen and out the back way. She had been given the inevitable answer she had known would come.

Back in the drawing-room, Daniel was standing facing the woman who had once been a girl, the girl who had torn his feelings to shreds, and through her desertion had turned days into agonising nightmares. He couldn't recall a time when he hadn't loved her, and longed for her, yet had been willing to wait for her, for years if necessary. And here she was, standing before him offering herself wholeheartedly to him. She had just heard, she said, that the Irish family, as she called them, were no longer coming back. She had said she knew she was to be married next month, but that didn't matter: Ray meant nothing to her; all she wanted was him, now that the house was clear.

He stopped laughing; and now she was speaking again: "Don't...don't laugh at me, Daniel. I...I mean it. I...I couldn't stay away, and I know you love me still as I love you."

He cut in on her now, saying, "How would your father take your change of heart?"

"Oh, he'd get over it. And he knows that, since your father died, you're making a go of this place."

"And what about Ray? How would you tell him?"

"Oh, Daniel"—she took a step towards him—"I'll just tell him…I'll just tell him I can't go through with it. There's only you, and it's only ever been you. Anyway, he drinks too much and his people aren't all that they are cracked up to be; and before me they had someone else mapped out for him, but he got round them. Oh, Daniel." When she thrust her arms out towards him he suddenly took his forearm and brought it down across them with such force that she screamed.

As she staggered back he cried at her, "You know what you are, Frances Talbot, you're a slut! Yes, I loved you; at one time I would have killed for you; but I was a boy and took a long time to mature. Now I'm no longer a boy, so listen to what I'm saying: believe me, I wouldn't touch you now, Frances, if you happened to be the last woman on God's earth. I'll tell you something else. If you had come and offered yourself as you're doing now when Moira and the children were here, I'd have fallen on my knees before you, and, metaphorically speaking, I would have remained there all my life. And yet my feelings for you haven't changed just in this minute: over the past months I've been comparing you with others. Your brother once called you a silly bitch of a girl, and at the time I felt like hitting him. Nevertheless, his description was not far off the mark because, added to that, you're a mean, nasty individual. Whatever Ray is, he's too good for you. You hooked on to him because you thought he could offer you a big house and money and the life of a lady. But that's what you will never be, Frances, a lady."

"You'll...you'll be sorry for this, and I don't believe a word you've said because I know you still want me. You're not likely to have stopped loving me, not after the way you went on."

"Believe what you like, Frances, if it comforts you any, because you're going to have a very lonely life, a life, though, that you deserve. As you led me on, so you led Ray, I'm sure of that, because if you had left him alone he would have married Janie."

"Huh!" Her laugh was high. "Him marry Janie? or Janie marry him? Janie could never see anybody but you. And there she is out there still seeing you, still hoping. You once told me you pitied her for being so plain, and she hasn't improved with the years. Ray marry Janie...indeed!"

When there was a thumping on the front door, intermingled with the bell ringing, he stared at her for a moment, because the light her words had shone into his mind was suddenly blinding him. Then he hurried from the room and when he opened the front door a fuddled voice yelled at him, "She's here, isn't she?"

"Yes, Ray; she's here."

"Her father said she would be here; as soon as she heard the news, she would be here. She's a bitch."

He pushed past Daniel now, then turned and faced him, saying, "She is, Dan, isn't she? She's here?"

"Yes; as I said, Ray. She's in the drawing-room waiting for you."

As Ray Melton marched erratically towards the drawing-room door, Frances appeared, and when he reached her it was to grab her by the arm and pull her forward, as he yelled, "You're not going to play any of those games with me, madam! You're not leaving me in the lurch as you did him. Oh no. If anybody's going to walk out it's going to be me. Do you hear?''

Daniel stood aside as he saw his one-time school friend, now a drunken, enraged man, shake the woman whom he had once loved passionately; and he made no effort to stay him. And then he also watched the same woman send Ray staggering back as she cried at him, ''You take your hands off me, and you shake me again like that and you'll see if I'll walk out on you or not.''

Turning to Daniel, Ray Melton now laughed as he said, ''We were to be married in a fortnight, having brought the wedding forward. Do you know why? You know why, Dan? I'll give you a guess. She couldn't wait. As I told her, she'd make a good living in Bog's End.''

''You beast, you! That's what you are, you are a beast!''

''Yes, my dear Frances, I'm a beast because I'm tight; but when I'm sober and I remember what you've done this day, throwing yourself at Dan here, and your belly swelling, I just might decide to take a quick trip abroad. My dad suggested it and I just might do it.''

With this he now flung his arm out in mock courtesy towards her, saying, ''I'll give you one minute to get into the trap, my dear, and I will drop you off at your parents' estab...estab...lishment, and then we will take it from there, because as I said, who knows what will happen when I sober up.''

At this he staggered out of the door and down the steps, and she, making to follow him, paused for a moment and threw a look at Daniel that was so vicious as to contort the beauty that was still in her face into an almost evil mask. And she hissed at him, ''I once loved you; but it's nothing compared to the hate I feel for you now. I hope you rot with that Irish crop that spoiled my life.''

As she turned from him to run to the door, he followed her and watched her run to where Ray Melton was turning the horse and trap preparatory to leaving without her. And as he saw her gripping the back rails of the trap and having to pull herself on to the already moving vehicle, then fling herself on to the seat, he felt for a moment a wave of pity pass over him; but then it was gone when he recalled Ray's words as to what she was carrying in her belly. My God! If he had relented, she would have tricked him into that!

He closed the door and for a moment lay with his back against it and his eyes closed. Then he looked towards the chair where Janie's coat and hat had lain. Swiftly now, he went into the kitchen. It was empty. And when he reached the barn it too was empty. With his fist he beat his forehead: if ever there was an idiot in this world it was he, a thoughtlessly blind one. He had for years been worshipping that empty-headed slut, the while failing to recognise the worth of such a girl...a woman as Janie.

8

How long he sat in the drawing-room, his body bent forward as he stared into the fire, he didn't know, but his mind was going over and over the scene that had been enacted in this room a short while earlier and what it had revealed to him. And what he was dwelling on, much more than Frances's duplicity, was the fact that it had taken her bitter tongue to open the door and reveal fully something that he had only probed at in the recesses of his mind. And the truth was that it wasn't just friendship he felt for Janie, but love; yet not the kind of love he had wasted his youth on, the kind of love that had made him older than his years. It hadn't been so much the weight of the farm, nor the responsibility of the family, but the tearing madness that a beautiful face had created in him, and which had so fascinated him that he couldn't see the true character that lay beyond the beauty. And all the time there had been Janie standing aside, watching, and waiting in vain, as she must have felt right up till this very day...right up to an hour ago, when she must have visualised his being seduced by Frances's charm.

What an idiot! He rose to his feet. Talk about a

village bumpkin who couldn't see further than his nose! He was that and more. And just think that if the recent scene had taken place next Monday, say, when Janie was in Holland…well, that would have been that, because once she had given her word to another man she wouldn't have broken it, not for him or for anyone else.

Why was he standing here talking to himself? Get the trap out, man!

He dashed from the room, but as he was crossing the hall he paused, ran to the front door, shot the bolts; then he was actually in the kitchen when he realised he wasn't wearing a hat, so he dashed back and up the stairs, grabbed his best hat from the cupboard and also an overcoat. Then, rushing through the back doorway he stopped again to take the big key from the inside and to lock the door from the outside; then to ask himself why he was bothering with such trifles; hat, coat, locks and bolts.

Minutes later, seated in the trap, he gazed about him. He was surrounded by fine, sturdy stone buildings, by stables, tack and workshops. The yard itself was dry today, the mud ridges flattened by the animals' feet and the wheels of the carts. And his thoughts escaped for a moment from the emotion that was filling his mind, and he thought, It could be slabbed and the drains run into the middle. Then as he was about to say, "Gee up! there," another thought hit him, an immediate one this time: he likely wouldn't be back until it was dark; he'd better put the lamps on the front of the trap.

Down again he jumped, dashed into the tack room, brought out two long shanked lamps, stuck them in the sockets each side of the trap, jumped up again, then shouted, "Gee up! there," and the horse broke into a sharp trot.

Janie's home lay to the west side of Fellburn, about half a mile from the town itself, but a good five miles from where he was at the moment. It would take him forty minutes at least. What if she was out? What if she hadn't gone straight home? What if she wouldn't see him?

Well, he would demand to see her. Yes, he would. And Mr and Mrs Farringdon were a nice couple; they would persuade her, they would...

For God's sake! man, stop yapping at yourself!

But she had seen Frances, and she could have heard him laugh.

Well, on seeing him, wouldn't she realise that Frances was no more? Oh, he didn't know. And she had a pride about her. Yet...yet she had humbled herself for years. God! when he thought about it now. Well, he'd have plenty of time to think about it in the future if for some reason or other she said she'd had enough. The women were queer cattle, as old Barney had said many a time. He'd said he took his pattern from the cows: one that he had milked for years kicked him in the backside one morning and sent him flying and wouldn't have him near her. He said she had gone wrong in the head, like women did at a critical time in their lives.

What on earth was he on about? "Gee up! there. Gee up!"

He arrived at the Farringdon residence later than he had hoped, and as he drove into the yard he saw Robert and Hal. They were making towards the stable, and they stopped. And when, to his cheery, "Hello, there!" they made no response, he got down from the trap and rather tentatively now he asked, "Is…is Janie in?"

"I'd like to have a word with you, Daniel." It was Robert speaking. "Tie him up there," he said, indicating the iron post. Slightly disturbed now, Daniel did as he was directed, then followed them into the harness room. There they both faced him, and Robert said, "I might ask you the reason for this visit."

"I…I've come to see Janie."

"Yes? And what do you want to see her about?"

Daniel now reared slightly against Robert's hostile manner and the antagonism emanating from the two brothers, and he said stiffly, "I think that's my business."

"It's ours an' all," Hal rapped out the words. "You've played hot and cold with her for long enough. You've used her as a comforter, and now likely you've come to tell her that your dear Frances, that empty-headed little bitch, has come back into your fold. Well, let me tell you something…" he said, digging his forefinger into Daniel's shoulder, only for Daniel, instinctively, to thrust him backwards, so causing him to fall against the wall. And at this Robert cried, "Now look here! Don't start any of that."

"Don't start!" said Daniel now, his temper flaring. "Who started this? You…you two, by not minding your own bloody business!"

"She is our business. And I can tell you for nothing," said Robert, "I've wanted to knock your bloody head off long before this. You've had her trailing across there in all weathers, stripping her of her pride; and at bottom she's a proud girl. And what's more, let me tell you, she could have been married two years ago. There's a fellow in Holland just waiting for her word, and she's going over on Monday and she'll give it. So, if you've come to say that you know she'll be happy that you're getting back with that little trollop, you can forget about it, because you're not going to see her.''

''I damn well am going to see her! And you're not going to stop me, nor is anybody else. Now keep your distance, for I'll not only knock your heads together, I'll lay you out. I don't want to do that, for it'll be a bad start, but you lay your hands on me, either of you, and I will. Now, I'm warning you.''

As he stepped back towards the door it was pushed open and a voice said, ''Oh! there you are. Oh, hello, Daniel. Have you just arrived?''

Robert and Hal Farringdon looked at their father, and Daniel, too, looked at Mr Farringdon, and Daniel was the first to recover. ''Yes, sir,'' he said; ''I've just popped over to see Janie.''

''Oh...'' It was rather a long-drawn-out word, and Mr Farringdon looked from one to the other of his sons; then, turning to Daniel, he said, ''Well, you won't find her in the tack room. And by the way, boys''—he turned again to his sons—''Mother's awaiting tea. You know what time it is; where were you off to?''

''Oh, well...er, we...we were really going over to see Daniel but...then he just popped in.''

Again Mr Farringdon let out a long-drawn ''O...h'' then added briskly, ''Well, he's saved you a journey. Come on, all of you. Janie's upstairs but Mother's in the drawing-room.''

Daniel cast a backward glance at the two young men before he turned and followed their father; and then they followed him.

In the hall, a maid was passing and Mr Farringdon said, "Go upstairs, Phyllis, and tell Miss Janie that she has a visitor, and that he's in the small sitting-room. Oh, and by the way, take another cup into your mistress; there'll be an extra one for tea."

"Yes, sir."

"And you two"—he turned to his sons—"go and repeat that message to your mother. She'll be very pleased; she always likes a tea party. And...and Daniel, will you come this way?"

Daniel followed Mr Farringdon across the hall and down a short corridor and into a small room, where the older man, pointing to an easy chair, said, "Make yourself comfortable, Daniel, until she comes down." And then, his voice changing, he said, "In a way, I'm very pleased to see you today, but I hope you haven't come to hurt my daughter further. I've always had a great respect for you, but if I was to speak the truth, I think that you have been blind with regard to her, besides being a little callous. Now, she'll be here presently, but if you have anything to say that might distress her further, I would rather you tell me, and leave now. I am very, very fond of my daughter. I like my sons and I respect them, but I love my daughter and never in her life have I seen her cry as she did a short while ago."

Daniel's head was bowed and his voice was thick as he said, "I'm sorry, sir, to the heart of me. I've been a blind fool, an idiot. I...I somehow couldn't have explained my feelings for her until today, when Frances came and, I...I might as well tell you, offered herself to me again. It was then I knew that the feeling I had for Frances had been an adolescent craving, one which the man in me now recognises as merely that.

But the feeling I have for Janie is love. But when I went to tell her so, she was gone."

"Well, I'm glad to hear this, Daniel, very, very glad, for I've never seen that girl in such a state. All I could get out of her was, 'They were laughing.'"

"What?"

"Well, that's all she kept saying, 'They were laughing.'"

"Not Frances, sir, no. She was in a rage. It was me. I was laughing. I was laughing at her offer. I know it was an awful thing to do because...because she was degrading herself, but I was seeing her as she really was, and...and, oh, dear, dear, what a mess! I'm so sorry. But I can promise you one thing, Mr Farringdon: that I'll not live long enough to make it up to Janie for my seeming stupidity."

A relieved smile showed on Mr Farringdon's face, and he laid a hand on Daniel's shoulder as he said, "Well, there's one thing sure, you'll be welcomed into this family." Then his smile broadening, he added, "I'm glad you didn't go for my sons, because I think they may have got the worse of it. Now make yourself comfortable; she won't be long." And on this, Mr Farringdon left the room.

Daniel decided not to sit down. He was tense from his toes to the roots of his hair. When he had set out from home it had all seemed so straightforward. He would tell her what a fool he had been and that he loved her. He had not realised he'd have her family to contend with. Oh yes, they were right. Putting himself in her brothers' place, he would have done the same, he supposed.

It was a comfortable room. After standing still for some time, he began to pace up and down. He looked at the clock on the mantelpiece. It was three minutes since Mr Farringdon had left the room. When five minutes had gone, he sat down. When seven minutes had passed, he stood up again. After ten minutes he began to pace the floor again; then the door opened and there she was.

She didn't speak but walked slowly towards him, stopping within an arm's length of him.

And gazing at her he saw that her eyes were red-rimmed and that her face was straight, no anticipation showing for what he might have to say. And at this moment he could find no words to say; all he wanted to do was to put his arms about her and draw her close. But her expression forbade that.

She was looking him straight in the eyes, and when she spoke her voice was even, as if she was asking an ordinary question. "Are you sure, Daniel?"

"Oh, Janie. Janie. I must have been sure in my mind for such a long time but I didn't realise it. She…she had to come to open my eyes and get through my stupid thick head. Yet, all the signs were there long before that, as for weeks, for months now, the feeling of warmth when I saw you, the feeling of loss when you left the house, lying awake at nights worrying about you going to Holland: they were all there. All the signs were there, telling me what I hadn't the sense to open my eyes to see, that…that it wasn't just friendship, it was love. I love you, Janie. And I now realise that I have loved you for a long time. When she had gone, when they had gone, because Ray came for her, I went looking for you. You'll never know the emptiness of that kitchen and that yard when I saw you had gone; and the terror that rose in me when I realised that I may have lost you for good! I love you, Janie, and want you so much; but other than that love, I have very little to offer, except hard work for years ahead.''

He watched her lids close and the tears press from beneath them, and he beseeched her, ''Oh, don't, don't, Janie, don't cry. For God's sake, don't cry.''

''Daniel. Daniel.'' Slowly her body fell against his, and when his arms went about her, they were gentle, just holding her as if she were fragile and could easily break. And when her head lifted to his and he laid his mouth on hers, the kiss was soft and tender, just as were her lips. Then her head was resting on his shoulder as if from exhaustion; and after a moment, he said, ''We must be married soon, Janie, soon.'' And when he felt her nod, he asked, ''How soon?''

When she now lifted her face to his she was smiling, the old warm smile, and she answered him, ''Tomorrow.'' And at this, his arms hugged her tightly to him and they laughed quietly together, and she was the old Janie again; yet at the same time not the old Janie but a new Janie, his Janie. And characteristically now, she said, ''On one condition...''

Their faces were close again, and her voice was low as she said, ''I want the choice of where we should spend our...our honeymoon.''

The statement surprised him a little, and he said, ''Yes...well, anywhere.''

''Ireland, in Moira Stewart's house.''

He stared at her, his face straight now, and there was a slight tremble to his lips as he said, ''As you say, my dearest Janie, as you say...in Moira Stewart's house.''

New York Times bestselling author
Debbie Macomber welcomes you
to Buffalo Valley, a town that
you'll never forget…

MIRA

Dakota
BORN

Buffalo Valley, North Dakota, is like many small
towns—it's dying. But despite it all, there's a spirit
of hope here, a defiance. And the few people left
are fighting for their town.

Lindsay Snyder is a newcomer who decides to
stay…and discovers in this broken little town the
love and purpose she's been seeking.

"One of the few true
originals in women's fiction."
—Anne Stuart

DEBBIE
MACOMBER

On sale mid-April 2000 wherever paperbacks are sold!

Visit us at www.mirabooks.com   MDM576

**A daughter who's run away from home.
A mother who's run away from herself.**

RACHEL LEE

Snow in September

The tragedy of her husband's death has taken its toll on
both Meg Williams and her teenage daughter, Allie.
Now Allie has run away.

Sheriff Earl Sanders feels a responsibility to look after
Meg and Allie. Though he's determined not to let his love
and desire for his best friend's widow make her life even
harder, he's doing all he can to find her daughter. And as
days and nights pass, some startling secrets come to light.
Truths too painful to accept have stretched a family to
the breaking point, until a woman who nearly lost
everything discovers what matters most.

"A magnificent presence in romantic fiction.
Rachel Lee is an author to treasure forever."
—Romantic Times Magazine

On sale mid-April 2000 wherever paperbacks are sold!

MIRA

Visit us at www.mirabooks.com   MRL554

MIRABooks.com

We've got the lowdown on your favorite author!

☆ Read an excerpt of your favorite author's newest book

☆ Check out her bio and read our famous "20 questions" interview

☆ Talk to her in our Discussion Forums

☆ Get the latest information on her touring schedule

☆ Find her current besteller, and even her backlist titles

All this and more available at

www.MiraBooks.com
on Women.com Networks

MEAUT1

One small spark ignites the entire city
of Chicago, but amid the chaos, a chance
encounter leads to an unexpected new love....

THE
HOSTAGE

As Deborah Sinclair confronts her powerful
father, determined to refuse the society
marriage he has arranged for her, a stranger
with vengeance on his mind suddenly appears
and takes the fragile, sheltered heiress hostage.

Swept off to Isle Royale, Deborah finds herself
the pawn in Tom Silver's dangerous game of
revenge. Soon she begins to understand the
injustice that fuels his anger, an injustice
wrought by her own family. And as winter
imprisons the isolated land, she finds
herself a hostage of her own heart....

SUSAN WIGGS

MIRA

"...draws readers in with delightful characters,
engaging dialogue, humor, emotion
and sizzling sensuality."
—*Costa Mesa Sunday Times* on *The Charm School*

On sale mid-April 2000 wherever paperbacks are sold!

Visit us at www.mirabooks.com   MSW592

BARBARA

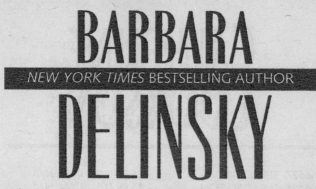

NEW YORK TIMES BESTSELLING AUTHOR

DELINSKY

When Leah Gates arrives at a remote cabin in the woods, all she is seeking is refuge from a vicious storm. But instead she finds Garrick Rodenheiser, a man wary of strangers and hiding from his past. He can't refuse Leah shelter, but he's determined to protect his isolated life. But somehow Leah and Garrick can't seem to resist each other. Because sometimes love finds you, no matter how well you hide....

Twelve Across

"Ms. Delinsky is a joy to read."
—*Romantic Times Magazine*

Available mid-April 2000 wherever paperbacks are sold!

Visit us at www.mirabooks.com   MBD579

CATHERINE COOKSON

66527 THE UPSTART _____ $5.99 U.S. CAN. N/A
66454 THE OBSESSION _____ $5.99 U.S. CAN. N/A

(limited quantities available)

TOTAL AMOUNT $_____
POSTAGE & HANDLING $_____
($1.00 for one book; 50¢ for each additional)
APPLICABLE TAXES* $_____
TOTAL PAYABLE $_____
(check or money order—please do not send cash)

To order, complete this form and send it, along with a check
or money order for the total above, payable to MIRA Books®,
to: **In the U.S.:** 3010 Walden Avenue, P.O. Box 9077, Buffalo,
NY 14269-9077.

Name:_____
Address:_____ City:_____
State/Prov.:_____ Zip/Postal Code:_____
Account Number (if applicable):_____
075 CSAS

   *New York residents remit applicable sales taxes.

MIRA